Love will grow…

DIAMONDS
are Forever

Three sensational, emotional novels from
Rebecca Winters, Carole Mortimer
and Lucy Gordon

Diamonds are a Girl's Best Friend!

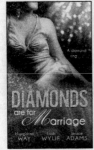

DIAMONDS
are for *Marriage*

Margaret WAY · Trish WYLIE · Jennie ADAMS

January 2013

DIAMONDS
are for *Surrender*

Fronwyn JAMESON · Tessa RADLEY · Maxine SULLIVAN

February 2013

DIAMONDS
are for *Lovers*

Jan COLLEY · Rosie ROE · Yvonne LINDSAY

March 2013

DIAMONDS
are for *Sharing*

Raye MORGAN · Nina HARRINGTON · Shirley JUMP

April 2013

DIAMONDS
are for *Deception*

Lee WILKINSON · Teresa HILL · Julia JAMES

May 2013

DIAMONDS
are for *Forever*

Rebecca WINTERS · Carole MORTIMER · Lucy GORDON

June 2013

DIAMONDS
are Forever

Rebecca
WINTERS

Carole
MORTIMER

Lucy
GORDON

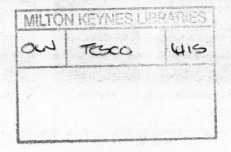

MILLS & BOON

Mills & Boon, an imprint of Harlequin (UK) Limited, Eton House, 18-24 Paradise Road, Richmond, Surrey TW9 1SR

DIAMONDS ARE FOREVER
© Harlequin Enterprises II B.V./S.à.r.l 2013

The Royal Marriage Arrangement © Rebecca Winters 2008
The Diamond Bride © Carole Mortimer 1997
The Diamond Dad © Lucy Gordon 1998

ISBN: 978 0 263 90290 7

025-0613

Harlequin (UK) policy is to use papers that are natural, renewable and recyclable products and made from wood grown in sustainable forests. The logging and manufacturing processes conform to the legal environmental regulations of the country of origin.

Printed and bound in Spain
by Blackprint CPI, Barcelona

THE ROYAL MARRIAGE ARRANGEMENT

REBECCA WINTERS

Rebecca Winters, whose family of four children has now swelled to include three beautiful grandchildren, lives in Salt Lake City, Utah, in the land of the Rocky Mountains. With canyons and high alpine meadows full of wildflowers, she never runs out of places to explore. They, plus her favourite vacation spots in Europe, often end up as backgrounds for her Mills & Boon® romance novels, because writing is her passion, along with her family and church. Rebecca loves to hear from her readers. If you wish to e-mail her, please visit her website at: www.cleanromances.com.

CHAPTER ONE

"How much is still owing to satisfy the creditors, Mr. Watkins?"

The aging attorney raised his shaggy gray eyebrows. "Twelve million dollars."

Alex's heart plunged to her feet. That much? She felt the worst about Manny Horowitz. Her mother's agent was a good man who'd done everything to further her mother's career all these years. He was still owed close to two million dollars. How could her mother not have paid him?

"I've auctioned everything except my mother's diamonds. They've got to cover it!"

Jewelry was the only thing remaining for Alex to sell from her mother's Beverly Hills estate. If she couldn't meet the sum, then the tabloids would hear of it and trash her mother's blighted reputation even more than they'd already done by exploiting her drug-related death. Some whispered that after her last divorce from Sheik Mustafah Tahar, Kathryn Carlisle had committed suicide, but nothing had been proved conclusively. Alex didn't know what to believe.

"I'm sorry it's come to this, Alexandra. A child shouldn't have to be burdened this way."

"Thank you, Mr. Watkins, but I haven't been a child for

a long time." In fact, she'd been through so much already as the unwanted offspring of the world's most beautiful woman that Alex felt ancient, but she supposed twenty-five still sounded young to him.

Since her mother's death on Christmas morning five months ago, Mr. Watkins had bent over backward to help her find ways to pay off her mother's debts. Furthermore he'd never once said a bad thing about her narcissistic parent who'd been married and divorced six times. As Kathryn's attorney from the beginning of her career, he'd had more right than anyone to castigate the willful, infamous Hollywood phenomenon of the film world who'd disregarded his advice and had run through money like she did alcohol.

At only forty-five years of age Kathryn Carlisle had come to a shockingly ugly end with nothing to show for it but a history of disastrous marriages, explosive divorces, unpaid bills despite her millions and a criminally neglected child from her first failed union. "Where would you suggest I go to get the best price for her jewelry?"

"The House of Savoy on Fifth Avenue in New York."

"My father gave her a diamond bracelet from there on their wedding night."

It was the only thing Alex remembered her mother telling her about her father. As Alex had matured she had learned for herself that her father, Oleg Grigory, had owned one of the biggest casinos in Las Vegas. When she'd grown old enough to understand, she'd heard rumors that he had ties to the Russian mafia, but no one knew for sure. His early death in an airplane crash was purported to be the work of a rivaling mob family.

Mr. Watkins nodded. "Without question they're the world's expert on diamonds."

Alex frowned because it meant paying for an airline ticket to the East Coast. She would have to juggle her bills to come up with the money, but Alex's mother had claimed she possessed a king's ransom in diamonds from her various husbands. If that were true, maybe all her debts would be satisfied. Only then could Alex bury the past and try to get on with her life.

"I'll call you as soon as I've booked my flight."

"Good. Considering we're talking about your mother's collection, I feel they're the one company that will be totally honest in their dealings with you. And…discreet."

Ah, yes. Discreet. For this last, financial transaction, maybe it would be best to get away from Hollywood and the scandalmongers.

Oh, Mother… Why couldn't you have been a mother *instead of Kathryn Carlisle?*

Mr. Watkins eyed her with compassion. "Once you know your flight, I'll make the appointment for you with the head jeweler. Drop by the bank on your way to the airport, and I'll arrange for them to hand over the jewel case from her strongbox."

With a nod she left his office and headed for her job as a makeup artist on a studio lot. She would have to talk to her boss, Michelle, about getting some time off. The older woman who headed the department had always been good to her and would certainly let Alex take the time she needed, but this was the last favor she intended to ask of her.

A few days later Alex stepped out of a New York taxi into unseasonable June heat and humidity. She checked her watch. It was 10:20 a.m. That gave her ten more minutes.

Alex imagined the temperature would soar by the afternoon and congratulated Mr. Watkins for getting her an early appointment at the House of Savoy.

After gripping her purse and the small overnight bag carrying the jewel case and one change of clothes, she started across the intersection toward the exclusive store. To her surprise there was a long line of people that went from its entrance and down the street to disappear around the next corner. Security was everywhere. She approached one of the women standing there reading a book.

"Excuse me?" The other woman looked up, not particularly happy to be bothered. "What's going on here? Why is there such a long line?"

"The Ligurian diamond is on display today," she answered in her heavy Bronx accent before going back to her reading as if that explained everything.

Ligurian?

"I see. Thank you."

Alex had never heard of the Ligurian diamond. She had heard of the Hope diamond and she'd seen pictures of the British crown jewels, but that was about the extent of her knowledge of the world's most famous diamonds. As far as she was concerned, diamonds were synonymous with tragedy. The diamonds from six husbands hadn't brought her mother any happiness. To Alex's mind they represented the ashes of the mother-and-daughter relationship that had never happened.

She approached one of the security men at the door. When she explained that she had an appointment with the head jeweler, Mr. Defore, the guard made a quick phone call. A minute later he allowed her inside, where another guard escorted her through an installed metal detector.

When the beep went off, she was asked to open her purse and overnight bag.

Once he was satisfied with the search, she was free to continue with the other guard. As they moved to the elevator past yet some other guards keeping a close eye on the orderly crowd, she glimpsed a dark, teardrop-shaped diamond on display in the center of the elegant foyer. The dazzling stone had been placed on a brilliantly lit pedestal within a closed glass casing, but she was too far away to determine its color. No doubt a diamond of such a large size would easily pay her mother's debt.

The guard joined her inside the elevator. "Mr. Defore's office is on the second floor," he explained, drawing her attention back to the business at hand. When the doors opened again, he guided her to a suite on the right of the bank of elevators. A secretary in the reception area told her to sit down. Five minutes later Alex was shown in to Mr. Defore's private office.

"Come in, Ms. Grigory. You're right on time. I hope you had a pleasant flight from Los Angeles."

"I did. Thank you, Mr. Defore."

"Sit down over here." The short, pleasant-faced jeweler held out a chair for her, then went around the desk to his swivel chair to face her. "Coffee? Tea? A soft drink?"

"No, nothing, thank you. When Mr. Watkins made this appointment for me, we didn't realize you would have a diamond exhibit going on."

He smiled. "Once a year the Principality of Castelmare allows it to be on loan here for a day."

Castelmare, ruled by King Vittorio, had replaced Monaco as the favorite vacation destination on the Riviera for the world's most rich and famous. The former city-state was located on the Mediterranean where her mother had spent part of her sixth honeymoon.

"Do you know if the diamond will be on display in California?" Alex's boss would definitely want to see it.

Mr. Defore cocked his head. "It won't. Except for a yearly one-day showing in New York, London, Rio, Sydney, Hong Kong and Dubai, it stays in Castelmare."

Alex reflected that Rodeo Drive in L.A. was supposed to have some of the most exclusive shops in North America, but apparently not exclusive enough. "The House of Savoy is very fortunate to have been chosen to display it."

His brows lifted. "I don't think you understand, Ms. Grigory. The present day king of Castelmare is the latest Italian sovereign of the ancient House of Savoy. This store is the monarchy's property."

She blinked. "I had no idea."

No wonder her mother had been so ecstatic over the diamond bracelet her father had purchased here. Alex was indebted to Mr. Watkins for directing her to this store, where she would almost certainly get the highest price for the stones to pay off her mother's horrendous debts.

"Shall I take a look at your mother's collection now?"

His question jerked Alex from her torturous thoughts. "Of course." She opened the overnight bag and placed the jewel case on his desk, positioning it for Mr. Defore to open it himself. Mr. Defore nodded and got to work. Alex had never seen all her mother's jewelry before, only heard about it. She'd put the inventory from the bank in her purse. It listed seven diamond rings, four pairs of diamond earrings, one diamond bracelet, three diamond necklaces and two diamond ankle bracelets.

When he finally lifted the lid, the sight of the diamonds

would have impressed anyone except Alex, who simply mourned the life she'd never had with her mother. Money had been her mother's God, and Alex wondered how one person could have been so devoid of motherly instinct and could have demonstrated so much bad judgment in everything she did?

Mr. Defore said nothing as he began his examination. Because the House of Savoy dealt regularly with the world's wealthiest people, Alex realized her mother's possessions would cause no great stir. Certainly this jeweler had little interest in Kathryn Carlisle and simply got to work studying each piece with his loupe.

He finally lifted his head. Wearing a distinct frown he said, "Who told you these were diamonds?"

Caught off guard by the stunning question, Alex took a moment before she could recover enough to say, "Mr. Watkins, my mother's attorney."

The man shook his head. "These are imitations."

What?

Alex reeled, causing her to clutch the edge of the desk for support. "But that's impossible!"

"Perhaps she kept the real jewels in another case?"

She swallowed hard. There was no other case. "This was the only one in the bank vault," she whispered.

"I'm very sorry, Ms. Grigory. We deal with mined diamonds, not fabrications. I'm sure there are shops in Los Angeles that would pay twenty, maybe twenty-five hundred dollars for this assortment of costume jewelry."

"Surely you're joking!" During the flight she'd begun to get excited about being able to pay off the last of the huge debt whose weight felt like a stone sitting in the pit of her stomach.

"I assure you I'm not. Scientists have synthesized and created diamond alternatives meant to trick the naked eye. However, when you view them through the loupe, they haven't the fire or brilliance."

She shot out of the chair, too shaken to sit still. "Is there someone else I could speak to about this?"

A dull red entered his cheeks. "I'm the head jeweler here."

His rigid attitude prompted her to reach in the case and lift out a piece. "My father, Oleg Grigory, my mother's first husband, bought this diamond bracelet *here* twenty-six years ago. He was the owner of one of the largest casinos in Las Vegas. Surely you have a record of it somewhere, if only so I can verify it."

"One moment," he said quietly. "I'll research it on the computer."

She was shaking so hard from shock, she could hardly sit still while she waited.

"Yes. He did make such a purchase." His gaze switched to hers. "But I'm afraid it was not *that* bracelet. Perhaps your mother sold her jewels without telling anyone and had these replicas made to wear?"

Is that what you did, Mother? Did you sell your diamonds along with your soul? The possibility pierced her like a fiery metal shaft.

Taking a deep breath, she said, "I'd still like another opinion. Who's the manager of the House of Savoy?"

"Mr. Bernard Hudson. I'm afraid he's occupied with the showing of the Ligurian diamond."

"Will you tell him these are Kathryn Carlisle's jewels? When he learns of this situation, I know he'll want to talk to me." By now Alex was desperate enough to use her mother's name for leverage.

"You don't understand. He won't be available until tomorrow. I'll ask my secretary to make you an appointment with him."

"Surely he can spare five minutes? I'll wait."

"Impossible. Now I'm very sorry, Ms. Grigory, but I'm afraid you'll have to leave my office because I have other clients to see." He shut the case, leaving her holding the bracelet.

Her body tautened. "Look, Mr. Defore…I flew all the way from Los Angeles for this appointment. My return flight is booked for tonight." Her hand tightened around the bracelet, which according to him was nothing more than paste. "By tomorrow I'll be back on the West Coast. I have to talk to him!"

She fought not to lose her temper in front of this composed jeweler, who was probably paid an indecent sum of money not to lose his.

"At the risk of repeating myself, Ms. Grigory, there's nothing more I can do for you at present."

"Your manager has to eat lunch sometime today. Since he's on the premises, I can't believe he wouldn't take out a moment to see me."

"I'm sorry." The jeweler was implacable.

"What kind of a man are you?" she cried out in torment. "You can at least call him on the phone. Tell him who I am. Inform him this is a matter of life and death!" Without hesitation she grabbed the phone on his desk and held the receiver in front of him.

Maybe it was the fact that her five-foot-nine height gave her the advantage over him, or possibly it was the narrowing of her eyelids with their slightly tilted shape. Whatever the explanation, he finally took the receiver from her, but then hung it up.

Out of the corner of her eye she saw his hand move to press a button on his console. He was probably summoning security. So be it. Alex had come to New York on a mission.

Alex's mother had once accused her of being incredibly stubborn like her father. She'd been born Alexandra Carlisle Grigory. The one picture she had of her father showed him to be a tall man who'd died when Alex was just nine months old. Like her mother's death, the police still hadn't determined if his was accidental or staged to look like one.

The few people who knew she was Kathryn Carlisle's only offspring remarked that she must have inherited her father's genes. Michelle had once told her, "Your father gave you great bones, and your eyes are exactly the same gray as Greta Garbo's—you could be her double!" Nevertheless, Alex and her mother had been as different as apples and bananas.

Kathryn had been of medium height, and curvy. On or off the set, the platinum-blond bombshell had been the ultimate drama queen.

Alex on the other hand had unruly dark blond hair with nothing remarkable about her looks, even though Manny, like Michelle, had also insisted there was a similarity between her and Garbo. Alex had laughed off both their comments. They might think she looked like a film star, but Alex preferred to work behind the scenes where she transformed other people who acted in front of the camera.

Selfishly neglected by her mother and tragically deprived of the father she never knew, Alex had learned to function on her own from an early age. She had no extended family, but did have a few close friends that she could rely on. However, no one understood the extent of her grief, or her shame....

The pitiful legacy from both her parents had left a burning stain on Alex's soul. Now the questions surrounding her mother's death had left new scars on Alex, whose conception, according to her mother, had been a mistake from the beginning.

Kathryn Carlisle had been a film-star idol. She had been like a brilliant comet who had swept in and out of her daughter's existence once every millennium for only brief moments without an atom of motherly love. Alex had been raised by a trail of nannies from the age of three weeks old, and there'd been no anchor in her life except for Betty, the nanny who had taken a liking to her and who had introduced her to Michelle, head of the makeup department at one of the film studios.

When Alex had been set adrift physically and financially by her mother when she turned eighteen, Betty had been instrumental in getting her her first job in the makeup department. Alex had started off just helping out at first, but then over the years she had continued to work there while she attended college and after.

Michelle had said she was a fast learner with a natural talent. In time she paid a salary that allowed Alex to get a modest apartment and take care of herself. After her apprenticeship, Michelle had asked Alex to stay on. Lately she had hinted that she planned to give Alex more responsibility and a raise.

Alex was grateful, of course, and she'd never want to hurt Michelle's feelings, but she'd always had a dream of doing something else. Tragically it seemed out of reach now that she was saddled with her mother's debts and needed to find a fast way to pay for them.

Surely Mr. Defore had made a mistake, or the bank hadn't realized there were two jewel cases in the vault. One way or another Alex would straighten things out. It would be too excruciatingly painful to go home without the money.

She simply couldn't do it.

While the thirty-four-year-old crown prince of Castelmare sat in the security room of the House of Savoy chatting quietly with Carlo, one of his bodyguards, other local security guards manned the monitors of the twenty-four-hour surveillance cameras. They'd been strategically placed around the store to watch for anything out of the ordinary.

This stop in New York represented the last leg of a long trip that had taken Lucca around the world on business for his country. Unfortunately, he had no more excuses to stay away from Castelmare. The dreaded reunion with his parents was coming and inevitable. When he returned home this time, there'd be no escape from certain matters that would change his life forever.

Suddenly his attention was caught by the American woman he could see in the monitor. She was obviously upset, and he found himself listening intently. It seemed there was a situation developing in Defore's office.

Lucca's ears picked up the word Grigory, a name associated with the old Russian aristocracy. Curious, he turned to one of the computers and logged into several Web sites including the store's archives.

When he found what he wanted to know, he moved closer to the monitor with its black-and-white screen. That's when he heard another exchange that gave him pause. The woman battling with the head jeweler was Kathryn Carlisle's daughter?

He was stunned because he didn't know the Hollywood film idol even had children—he could see no physical resemblance.

Like all hot-blooded Italian males, Lucca appreciated a beautiful woman. He'd seen one of the star's films several years ago during a flight to Asia. The tempestuous actress, whose life had come to a tragic end like all too many American A-list celebrities, *did* have exceptional looks with her come-hither blue eyes and champagne-blond hair. Yet it appeared the only thing she'd passed on to her off-spring was her legendary, impossible temperament. Like mother, like daughter.

Defore didn't make mistakes. For that exact reason Lucca had appointed him to be head jeweler three years ago. Naturally he couldn't help but be fascinated by the woman's refusal to take Defore at his word. Evidently she was as spoiled as her mother and even more naive.

How could her daughter not have known the troubled star with her uncontrollable hunger for money would have run through her own finances a long time ago and had hocked her jewels as a last resort?

When the security alarm sounded, one of the guards said he'd take care of the problem and started for the door, but Lucca moved his six-foot-three frame out of the chair and reached it ahead of him.

"I'll deal with it." As he left the room with Carlo, he nodded to his other bodyguard standing outside the door. The three of them walked down the hall to Defore's office.

"Wait for me and don't let anyone else in," he told them both before opening the door. Once inside, he told the wide-eyed secretary she could take a long lunch, then he entered Defore's office.

The jeweler took one look at Lucca and was so shocked to see him rather than one of the security guards, he was struck dumb. Lucca had never had reason to interfere with Defore while he was working with a client, but then, he'd never been this intrigued before.

"I'll take over," he murmured, freeing a worried-looking Defore so he could leave. Lucca gave a barely perceptible shake of his head, warning the jeweler not to give him away.

"Yes, yes. Of course."

Lucca shut the door behind him before turning to face the flushed woman whose tall, willowy figure hadn't been noticeable from watching the screen. "Signorina Grigory?" He extended his hand.

After a slight hesitation she held on in a firm grip before releasing it. "I'm embarrassed Mr. Defore had to call in security, but all I wanted was to speak to Mr. Hudson for a minute," sounded a tearful voice she didn't try to hide.

He in turn didn't bother to correct her faulty assumption that he was part of the security team. In fact, he was glad of it, since it didn't happen very often that he wasn't recognized. The photos and lies perpetuated in the tabloids about Castelmare's playboy prince made anonymity virtually impossible no matter the continent where he traveled to do business for the crown.

Right now he was fascinated by her slightly windblown, dark blond hair and her lack of self-awareness. To his surprise there was nothing fake about her. Somehow he hadn't expected Kathryn Carlisle's daughter to be her total opposite in every way.

She was dressed in a draped, smoky-blue blouse tucked

into pleated beige pants, putting him in mind of a 1940s style. Only a woman of grace with long elegant legs, soft curves and square shoulders could get away with it.

This close he could see shadows beneath her pewter-gray eyes with their sweeping dark lashes. Lines caused by suffering bracketed her wide, voluptuous mouth, one of the few physical traits she'd inherited from her infamous mother.

The other familiar trait was less definable. She had a certain breathlessness bequeathed to her by her mother who'd exhibited that same quality on the screen. In person it created an air of urgency Lucca found exceptionally distracting.

"You said this was a matter of life and death?"

She tossed her head back nervously. "Yes," she blurted, "b-but I didn't realize our whole conversation had been captured on camera," she stammered. "Evidently you heard every word of it."

He shrugged. "A necessary precaution in this business." She eventually nodded. "Why don't we both sit down."

"Thank you." She returned to the chair opposite the desk. "I didn't mean to take you away from your duties when you have the responsibility of helping keep an eye on the Ligurian diamond display."

Lucca hadn't expected her to be this polite. Now that she was in control he found her low, husky voice incredibly attractive.

"It's under heavy guard. I'm not worried." He noticed she was still torturing the bracelet in her hand. "May I see it, please? Everyone hired by the House of Savoy is trained to recognize a mined diamond from a fake." Which was true.

As she handed it to him, their fingers brushed. Strange that he would be so aware of her he could still feel the sensation while he examined the stones beneath the loupe.

After a moment he said, "I'm afraid Mr. Defore was right. This bracelet is pure imitation. Dare I say not even a good one?"

The second he saw her face lose color, he moved to the corner of the room where he switched off the camera and the audio so they would have complete privacy.

"But my fath—"

"Your father *did* purchase a bracelet exactly like this years ago. I checked the records. It was valued at $500,000.00 back then and would probably be worth several million today."

Her expressive face crumpled. Alex knew that her mother had always kept certain secrets from her daughter. Yet this one had been quite a secret, since the whole collection would have brought her a nice sum of money if the stones had been genuine diamonds.

"I'm sorry, *signorina*." After the sensational headlines built up in the tabloids concerning her mother's lifestyle, he suspected the star hadn't been in control of her spending and had been forced to sell off her diamonds upon running into dire straits. It was a story that came out of Hollywood and circulated throughout Europe all too often.

He heard a despairing cry before a shadow crossed over her features. Then she buried her face in her hands. The sound of it found its way to his gut.

"Do you know if jewelry was ever insured?"

A minute passed. Eventually she regained her composure and lifted her head. Her creamy complexion had gone splotchy again. "If it was, her attorney didn't know about it."

"I realize this news has come as a blow."

"A blow?" Her cry resonated in the room. "You have no idea— I *must* find a way to pay off her debts. I'd planned on this money. It was my last resort," her voice throbbed.

"Do you have a husband who would help out?"

"No." She looked away. "After my mother's track record, I have no interest in marriage," came the bitter response.

"I see." One could hardly blame her. "What about a lover?"

Her hands gripped the arms of the chair in what looked like a death grip. "Even if I did have one and he had the funds, I would never ask that of him."

Unaccountably moved by her vehement declaration he said, "Do you have any siblings?"

Her eyes closed for a second. "No. I'm her only child."

An only child so well hidden Lucca hadn't known of it. "Did she leave the diamonds to you in her will?" If Signorina Grigory had relied on this jewelry as her only hope of money after her mother's death, it would explain her shock.

"No," came the wooden reply. "She didn't make a will."

Lucca rubbed the back of his neck absently. Kathryn Carlisle with all her doomed marriages to wealthy men hadn't had the foresight to provide for her daughter? He wasn't able to comprehend it. "Why?"

"Why?" she repeated, staring at him through dull eyes. "That's like asking why she didn't abort when she found out she was pregnant with me. I came into her world unplanned and unwanted. She never publicly acknowledged me. Most of the time she forgot I was alive. It's all right. I learned life's lessons early, but I must admit I'm devastated about this."

She held up the bracelet he'd given back to her. "The money from her diamonds was supposed to pay what was left owing to salvage her reputation. I wanted the slate wiped clean so the creditors would go away once and for all. It's bad enough having to live with the terrible things people say about her, however true.

"I guess I hoped that if her bills got paid, it would be the one thing the world couldn't castigate her for. Her agent has every right to be paid what's owing him. I'm sick about it, that's all."

He inhaled heavily. "How much did she leave owing?"

"Twelve million dollars."

Not exactly small change. "What about your father? I realize they've been divorced for a long time, but would he consider covering part of it, if only for your sake?" The Grigory family would still have hidden resources.

"No," she answered without hesitation.

"Does he know about your situation?"

One graceful eyebrow lifted sardonically. "If he does, it's too late. He died before I was a year old. In fact, three of her husbands are dead. I have no idea what's happened to the other three."

Hearing the bald facts about the six-times-divorced actress made him wish he hadn't brought up the subject.

"Have you no extended family? Grandparents on your mother's side perhaps?" Lucca's world was filled with both.

"No. Mother was an orphan."

He rubbed his lower lip with his thumb. "Is there no property left to sell?"

She smiled, but it didn't reach her expressive eyes. "None. Except for the footage of her films, which I don't own, there's nothing left to prove she ever inhabited this world. The police lieutenant who investigated her death still hasn't ruled out suicide.

"No matter how estranged my mother and I were from day one, I didn't want to believe she was capable of taking her own life." After a silence she whispered, "Now I'm certain she did."

The break in her voice found a spot in Lucca's psyche that haunted him.

In the next instant she put the bracelet inside the jewelry case and shut it. "Will you please ask Mr. Defore to dispose of this and everything in it? I don't want to see it again and know I can rely on him for his discretion."

Before he could countenance it, she shoved it toward him. "Thank you for being so decent about this. You could've had me arrested. Please tell Mr. Defore I'm sorry for having a breakdown in front of him. He was very civilized and should be given a raise for his composure."

"I'll convey the message."

"I appreciate it. Though I hate to admit it, the dark side of the Carlisle in me comes out from time to time. The truth is, for good or evil I *am* part Carlisle. No matter how much I'd like to, I can't run away from my destiny."

Her words shook Lucca to the foundations. He felt like someone had just walked over his grave.

Tears dripped down her cheeks, but she didn't seem to be aware of it. "Do you know I've been sitting here calculating how long it will take me to pay back her debt so that I can restore some good to the Carlisle name?" She made a little sound of despair. "I don't know what the House of Savoy pays its security guards, but if I can eke out $500.00 a month—which is all I can afford on my present salary, it will only take me 2,000 years to wipe out the debt."

Her pain-filled laugh bordered on hysteria, but considering her fierce disappointment, he could well understand the display of raw emotion.

She jumped up from the chair and closed her overnight bag. "I'm the world's biggest fool not to know these jewels were as fake as the life she led. Forgive me for venting in front of you like this—I've probably said too much already." Before he could countenance it, her regal-like strides had taken her halfway across the room, leaving a trail of peach scent behind.

"Come back and sit down, Signorina Grigory. I'm not through with you." He knew his voice had sounded peremptory just now, but it was an acquired trait he couldn't seem to help any more than he could stop breathing.

She whirled around white-faced. "So, you *are* going to have me charged with unruly conduct. My mistake."

Lucca stared at her for a long moment. "Nothing could be further from the truth," his voice grated. The sadness she'd encountered in her life made him want to shield her from any more. "You haven't done anything wrong. What I would like to do is talk to you further about your situation."

Even from the distance separating them he could see her body tauten. "Why? It's no one else's business but mine. If you were hoping for an autographed photo of my mother, I'm afraid I don't have one and never did."

How tragic her first assumption was all tangled up with Kathryn Carlisle's effect on men. He got to his feet. "What I have on my mind has nothing to do with your mother. Since I was willing to listen to you, I would hope you would grant me the same courtesy."

There was a fight going on inside of her. He'd appealed to her sense of fair play while he waited for her capitulation. "I have a solution to your problem," he said to add weight.

She let out an incredulous laugh. "*You* have a solution. Does that mean you can arrange for me to win the lottery?"

"In a manner of speaking," he came back. His response managed to erase the mocking expression from her features. "However, I'd prefer it if we were seated to discuss it. Shall we start over again?"

Caught on the horns of a dilemma, she didn't advance or retreat. She needed help. He intended to give it to her.

"Before we go any further, let me introduce myself. My name is Lucca Umberto Schiaparelli Vittorio V."

CHAPTER TWO

ALEX studied the black-haired male who'd been interrogating her all this time. The second he'd walked in to Mr. Defore's office wearing a light gray, hand-tailored silk suit that molded his powerful frame to perfection, he'd no more looked, talked or acted like a security guard than fly!

He was too well bred, too sophisticated. His faintly accented English had polish. Combined with his aristocratic bearing, she hadn't been able to put him in any kind of a slot. There was much more to him than the fact that he was a tall, darkly handsome, olive-skinned Italian—in truth, the most attractive man she'd ever met in her life.

Now that she knew who he was, she realized she'd seen pictures of him flashed across the screen. She'd never paid much attention for the very fact that her mother had always gone for the larger-than-life types, just like Lucca. Anyone the media had hyped Alex chose to ignore.

In the flesh, the crown prince of Castelmare defied the normal adjectives one would apply to a good-looking man. There weren't enough in the English language to do justice to his charisma.

With the Ligurian diamond on display, it was no coincidence he was here in New York. Undoubtedly he'd brought the famous stone to the States via the monarchy's private plane.

This was her unlucky day. No man or woman had ever seen her this vulnerable before.

"You lied to me," she accused him hotly.

"If you mean I didn't correct your assumption that I was a security guard, then I have to plead guilty."

"Does the royal Riviera playboy make it a regular practice to impersonate the hired help?" His dark eyes with their jet-black lashes suddenly took on a strange glitter that lent heat to her growing anger. "Or was it on a whim you decided to amuse yourself by toying with Kathryn Carlisle's daughter while she poured out her guts? Either way, congratulations. You've made my humiliation doubly complete."

Burning with rage, she turned on her heel and fled to the next room, but she was stopped at the outer door by an unsmiling, robust, Italian secret-service type planted there.

Naturally the prince wouldn't make a move without all his bets being covered. She shut the door in the bodyguard's face and wheeled around. Her nemesis lounged against the doorjamb of Mr. Defore's office with his strong arms folded, insolently at ease.

More infuriated than ever, she said, "Am I to assume *you're* the lottery, as long as I provide certain services? Would it give you some kind of perverted rush to claim you slept with Kathryn Carlisle's daughter?" An angry laugh escaped as she shook her head. "You *must* be hard up for new thrills to consider handing over twelve million dollars to me, but unlike my mother, my body's not for sale at any price!"

Undaunted he said, "I'm glad to hear it. Lovely as your body is, I'm not asking for it. However, I *am* in need of something else you could give me that would solve the most serious problem of my life…and yours. Come back in and sit down while we talk about it. This could take a while."

"I can't imagine being able to offer anything that would solve your problem…whatever it is."

"You'd be surprised," came the cryptic comment. "Give me half an hour of your time."

She shook her head. "I'm sorry. I have to be at the airport later today and don't have time to spare."

He gazed at her intently. "Not even if the result of our meeting might mean clearing your mother's debts once and for all? When I heard you cry out earlier that this was a matter of life and death, it sounded like you meant it."

Alex studied him without averting her eyes. "I did."

She heard his deep intake of breath. "What if I told you I have a situation that's a matter of life and death for me, too. Would that make a difference to you?"

What was she supposed to say to such a question? Something in his tone led her to believe he might be telling the truth. Incredible how he'd turned things around so she felt guilty if she didn't at least listen to what he had to say.

"I'll give you five minutes."

"Thank you. Come back inside the other room."

Against her better judgment she did his bidding and retraced her steps. As she sat down, he spoke in Italian to someone on the phone before he took his place across from her. Then he typed something on the computer and printed it out.

Handing it to her, he said, "Your mother was married to royalty, did you know that?"

"Mother was married to four men with supposed titles,

but in time those claims turned out to be false. Everything about her life was a sham."

He eyed her narrowly. "Except that your father was the real thing."

"You mean, a Las Vegas racketeer."

"Rumors have a lot to answer for, particularly when they're founded in jealousy and greed. Read what's on the paper. You should find the information of the greatest interest."

Alex looked down:

After the October Revolution of 1917 all classes of the Russian nobility were legally abolished. Many members of the Russian nobility who fled Russia after the Bolshevik Revolution played a significant role in the white emigré communities that settled in Europe, in North America and in other parts of the world.

In the 1920s and 1930s, several Russian nobility associations were established outside Russia, including groups in France, Belgium and the United States. By 1938, the Russian Nobility Association in New York was founded. Since the collapse of the Soviet Union, there has been a growing interest among Russians in the role the Russian nobility played in their historical and cultural development.

Membership is exclusively reserved to persons who are listed in the nobility archives. Those titled members are recorded below with their former titles, genealogies and photos available.

Alex scanned the list until her gaze fell on the name Grigory. She gasped softly when she saw the last name on the Grigory royal family tree. It read "Prince Oleg

Rostokof Grigory, son of Prince Nicholas Grigory and Princess Vladmila Rostokof, born in New York, 1958, now living in Las Vegas, Nevada."

Her heart clapped like thunder as she looked at a picture of her handsome, dark blond father, who couldn't be more than eighteen in this picture. The strong physical resemblance between daughter and father at that age was uncanny.

As her head flew back, a security guard entered and brought them two sodas. After he left, the prince pushed one toward her and took a lengthy swallow from the other. When he put it down again, he said, "Where did you get the idea that your father was part of the underworld?"

"One of my nannies mentioned that she'd heard my father was involved with the Russian mafia. As I grew older and realized what that meant, I was ashamed and frightened by the possibility. I hid away in case one of them tried to find me and hurt me. My repulsion over my mother's ghastly lack of judgment in marrying him was so severe I didn't want to know anything more about him.

"By the time she'd gone through her sixth divorce, so many preposterous tales were circulating about her and her past husbands, I couldn't handle it and tried to shut it out. To my horror the police came to my work and told me she'd died of what looked like too much alcohol mixed with drugs. At that point it was too late to ever ask her what the truth was. I'm not sure she would have told me anyway." Her voice shook.

He finished the rest of his soda. "You've been through a great deal of pain in your life. Nothing can wipe that away, but the sooner her bills are paid, the sooner you can start to concentrate on other things."

A fresh spurt of anger filled her system. She looked back

at her father's picture. "Are you saying I should do something as crass and ignoble as turn to my father's family for the money? Is *that* what you're suggesting? A modern-day Anastasia story with an ugly twist?" she said. Her shrill voice reverberated in the room's confines.

"Not at all," came his bland reply, exasperating her even more. "But it might be of some comfort to you to get acquainted with the extended family you've never met or known. Your grandparents are no longer alive, but your great-uncle Yuri Grigory, is still living and has an apartment here in New York. I met him a year ago at an embassy function. I can arrange for you two to get acquainted."

Alex was so stunned by what he'd just told her she didn't know what to say. Realizing she needed to get hold of herself, she drank half of her soda without taking a breath.

The news about her father's lineage had come as a total shock. Mafia or not, it appeared he did descend from a royal background, otherwise the crown prince of Castelmare wouldn't have been able to produce the evidence she held in her hand.

Puzzled and confused by this whole experience, she eyed him warily. "If you hoped this information would help give me a sense of identity, I...I appreciate it." Her voice faltered. "However, I still fail to understand where this conversation is headed. What does any of this have to do with you?"

He sat forward, impaling her with his midnight-brown eyes. She'd thought at first they were black. "My life has been the opposite of yours. I was raised in a happy home with loving parents, a loving sister, a large extended family on all sides and good friends. Everything has been ideal except for one glaring obstacle that has driven a wedge between my father and me."

"You mean, he wants you to give up your wicked, worldly bachelor ways and marry the princess he's had picked out for you from birth."

After a pause, "I can see you've heard this story before."

"One of my nannies read *Cinderella* to me. I didn't like it."

He cocked his dark head. "Why not?"

"When Cinderella's mother died, she had to be raised by a cruel stepmother. I thought it was an awful story, probably because I felt like my mother had died. In fact, it was much worse because I knew she was alive, but she never wanted to be with me."

The glimmer of compassion in his eyes forced her to look away. Once more she was embarrassed to have been caught baring her soul to this man who was a perfect stranger to her. The prince of Castelmare no less. "I always hated fairy tales after that."

"Then you and I have something in common," he muttered in his deep-toned voice. "When my mother read *Cinderella* to my sister and me, I hated it, too, because I wasn't a normal little boy who could grow up to do what I wanted. I was a prince, and my father was the king. Because I loved him, I knew that one day I'd have to do what he wanted and marry a princess who was ugly and mean and whom I'd despise."

Once the words sank in, Alex burst into laughter. She couldn't help it. What had started out as a strange, surreal conversation between the two of them had taken on something that went beneath the surface and resonated.

After her amusement faded there was an awkward silence before she said, "I've seen some of the princesses you've been with in the news and know for a fact they're beautiful. Whether they're mean or not, I have no idea, but none of the photos would convince me you despised them. Far from it," she added pointedly.

He sat back in the swivel chair. "You're right, of course. Several of my parents' royal favorites are charming, lovely and I think genuinely kind. However, I have a little problem because I've never been attracted to them."

"Just to the nonroyals."

For a moment a bleakness entered his eyes tugging at her emotions, then it vanished as if it had never been. "What was it your George Washington said? I cannot tell a lie." The prince had too much charm for his own good. "Have you ever had that problem with a man?" he asked, studying her features rather intently. "He has all the right qualities, but he doesn't speak to your soul?"

All the time, Alex muttered inwardly. "Errol Flynn was the only man who became my fantasy. When I saw him in *Robinhood,* I asked my nanny to take me again and again. We saw it twenty-five times."

It was his turn to laugh, the full-bodied male kind she felt to her toes. "I understand he still has a habit of speaking to every woman's soul, even from beyond the grave."

She nodded. "Some men are like that. Bigger than life." Alex realized she was looking at one of them.

"Bigger than life," his voice trailed. "A sort of chemistry of the body and spirit, wouldn't you say?"

"Yes," she whispered. This was no shallow prince, let alone man.

"That's what I'd hoped to find before now in the royal pickings, but it hasn't happened."

Alex had never given much thought to a problem like his until this minute. She was glad she wasn't in his royal shoes because she knew herself too well and could never marry anyone for the sake of duty. Perish the thought of being tied to someone you didn't love with your whole heart and soul.

Obviously, her mother hadn't had the capacity to truly love anything or anyone except herself. Sometimes it frightened Alex to think that because she was her daughter, she might have inherited that same inability to be devoted to one man.

There'd been boyfriends, but Alex hadn't yet suffered that grand passion her mother had managed to portray on the screen instead of real life. Maybe Alex never would. Aware something was expected of her, she said, "That could change in time. Some royal princess could come into your life you've overlooked. How old are you?"

"Thirty-four."

Nine years older than herself.

"That's still relatively young."

"From my point of view I agree, but my parents had hoped I'd be married by twenty-five and a father by twenty-six. To quote my mother, 'For you to be thirty-four and still single is positively indecent, Lucca. The whole country is waiting.'"

The way he imitated his parent made Alex chuckle. "At least your mother cares about you and loves you."

"She does, but there's more to it than that. My father's not well and needs to step down. It's within my power to lengthen his days by becoming king, thus relieving him of all responsibilities, but I can't become his successor without first taking a wife. Those are the rules.

"As a way of playing on my guilt, my mother and sister continually remind me I'm the only son and the only one who can perform this duty to save the day."

And Alex had thought *she'd* lived with a burden all these years.

She smoothed an errant curl away from her forehead. "What's wrong with your father?"

"He's had lung cancer."

"I'm sorry. How cruel to him and hard for all of you."

"It has been," the prince conceded, causing her to feel an empathy for him she didn't want to feel. "Part of his right lung was removed, leaving him in a weakened condition. Though he's in remission, the doctor says this disease is tenacious and it's only a matter of time before it comes back. The best medicine for him would be to give up the throne and relax."

Alex cleared her throat. "Since you love him so much, it seems you don't have a choice. Is there someone from the royal pickings you believe cares for you enough that you could see yourself married to her?"

"I can't answer that question since I haven't given them much of a chance to get to know me. The thought of marriage to any of them is something I can't abide."

Well, Alex. Ask a foolish question…

There was one princess Lucca had known for several years. Neither he nor Sofia were romantically involved, but they'd become good friends. Both sets of parents expected them to marry, but she wanted to abdicate her title and serve a humanitarian cause, thus allowing her younger sister to be the next in line. Sofia was waiting for Lucca to marry before she made the secret known to her family.

Out of loyalty to her and her wishes, he'd remained silent. Suddenly restless, he got up from the chair. "I need to choose someone who understands the situation for exactly what it is. No lies. No self-deception or pretense."

"You mean, someone who has no expectation of love. Is there such a woman?"

"Among my parents' short list? No." Except for Sofia. Sofia who devoted her life to charity work in Africa and had a missionary zeal to help people.

He came to sit on the corner of the desk so his legs brushed hers. "But an extraordinary thing happened to me today. I've met someone who would be the perfect consort to come to my rescue in this emergency situation. At the same time I could help her in ways no one else can. She's of royal blood yet is under no illusions about life or me. Better yet, she's single and uninvolved with a man at present."

As the portent of his words sank in, Alex's eyes widened in disbelief. What he'd just intimated was so outrageous, an odd sound escaped her lips. She slid out of the chair to put distance between them.

"You *are* out of your mind and can't possibly mean what you're saying."

He rose to his intimidating height. "I never say what I don't mean," came the words of steel. "When you get to know me better, you'll realize I've never been more serious about anything in my life."

She shook her head. "So you'll pay my mother's debts if I agree to marry you. Then you'll become king and two strangers will live unhappily ever after in a loveless marriage with no hope of producing an heir and both of us sneaking behind the scenes looking for fulfillment elsewhere."

He gave a careless shrug of his elegant shoulders. "If that's what you want."

Alex hugged her arms to her waist. "What I want doesn't come into it. This conversation is utterly absurd!

Don't you know that old movie script has been done and redone ad nauseum?"

One dark brow quirked. "But not to the tune of twelve million dollars. That will be my wedding present to you. In return, you'll play the loving wife in front of other people, be it my family or the public."

"I will not!"

"I've spent time with your great-uncle," he continued talking, unfazed by her outburst. "Do you know you have the same regal bearing? I noticed it immediately. The perfect plum from the royal Grigory tree."

She let out a strangled cry that was probably heard by everyone inside the House of Savoy.

"I meant that as a compliment, Alexandra."

The way he said her name just now with his slight Italian accent made her body tremble. That angered her further.

"However tarnished the sordid legacy from my mother, I'm not a piece of fruit to be plucked!"

His expression grew solemn. "No. Like a gift from the gods you've fallen into my hands at the providential moment to save us both from a hideous fate."

Hideous was the word, all right. The thought of going back to Los Angeles to face her mother's creditors, to face poor Manny, let alone live with the smear tactics the media would always use against her caused bile to rise in her throat.

"I'm not asking that this arrangement last forever," he added in a velvety tone.

"Of course not. Just a lifetime," she blurted on a note of sarcasm.

One dark eyebrow dipped. "Who knows? Neither of us can see that far ahead into the future."

She bit her lip. "How inconvenient for you."

"You have no idea," his voice grated, conveying some deep-seated emotion that caught her on the raw.

"When is your wedding supposed to take place?"

"Preferably yesterday."

"Obviously." She tried to hide her smile but lost the struggle.

"To answer your question, my parents have planned it for a month from today. The wedding ceremony will follow my coronation in the cathedral."

Only four weeks? "I'm sure a royal wedding takes a great deal more time than that to organize."

"You don't know my parents. Everything's been arranged. It's only a matter of adding one detail…the name of the woman I've chosen. They've been living for this day."

"That's nice. I can't say the same thing about mine. Now I'm afraid I have to go. My job is waiting for me back in Los Angeles and I have a plane to catch." She started for the outer door once more.

"Is it your chosen career?"

When she reached it, she looked over her shoulder at him. "What? Putting makeup on movie stars? No. The job chose me and has kept me alive."

He moved closer. Her heart did a funny kick. "What job would you choose if you could?"

That gave her pause. "You mean, in my wildest dreams?"

It was his turn to chuckle. "Is it that out of the ordinary?"

"For me, yes."

"You want to be an astronaut?"

"No." Her mouth curved upward once more. "This is something very down-to-earth."

"What would that be?"

"It's as improbable as my meeting a real prince today."

"Why?"

"In the first place, I have to find a job where I can earn a lot of money in order to pay off mother's debts before I do anything else."

"And in the second place?" he queried.

"I don't know if I could make the grade."

"Doing what? Humor me," he prodded.

"Plastic surgery."

His intelligent gaze grew thoughtful. "Why that particular profession?"

"My mother was labeled the most beautiful woman in the world. Her love affair with herself was obscene. There are people out there born with facial problems who'd give everything they possessed to be able to look in the mirror and not cringe or grieve at the sight.

"If I could change one person's looks enough to make life more bearable for them, I'd give anything to do it."

A marked stillness pervaded the atmosphere before he spread his hands in a typical Italian gesture. "A noble aspiration. If that's your raison d'être, then make it a reality once we're married."

Maybe she was hallucinating.

"Why not?" He read her mind. "Castelmare University in Capriccio has a medical school linked with the University of Genoa."

The man was starting to get to her and that was frightening.

"Look—I was talking about my wildest dreams. The point is, not even *I* would want to be married to me. And lest you forget, one has to speak Italian to go to your university. For your information, I can only say one word in your language. It's *ciao*."

She opened the door to leave, but it was blocked by the same person as before. Another bodybuilder type was standing behind him. In the next breath she shut it again and turned on the man whose charisma was positively lethal. "Will you please tell Salvatore and his brother out there to let me pass?"

He let out a hearty laugh at her reference to the famous Italian bodyguard Salvatore Bartolotta, who lost his life trying to protect an antimafia prosecutor during the 1930s. While admiring his quick mind, Alex tried hard not to react to his full-bodied response. It made him appear younger and even more appealing. She hadn't thought it was possible.

"Carlo will be flattered when I tell him. You're obsessed by the mafia. Why is that, Alexandra? More than likely it was the mob that targeted your father because of his title and financial affluence. When he wouldn't cooperate, they rubbed him out. I believe that's the American term."

The prince knew it was. He was too intelligent by far.

"Wherever the truth lies, anyone linked to the mafia eventually dies like the father I never knew." She looked down. "I don't know why we're having this conversation. You've picked the wrong woman to help you out of your nightmare. I need to go home and face mine."

"I'm not prepared to let you go yet," he whispered silkily. "A little while ago you accused me of being hard up. That's putting it mildly. My back's up against the proverbial wall and my time has run out. I can't fly home and face my parents without producing the name of my intended bride. As I've told you, I've been overdue in that department for the past ten years."

She couldn't believe she was still standing here listening to him instead of banging on the door to demand her freedom.

"And you honestly believe they'll be overjoyed you've chosen the most unsuitable female on the planet to parade before your kingdom? Marriage to Kathryn Carlisle's daughter will make you the laughingstock of the civilized world."

"Let me worry about it."

"I'll do better than that. You won't have to be concerned about anything because my answer is no! Can you imagine what the media would make of it?

"In a shocking palace exclusive today, the bachelor crown prince of Castelmare has bypassed many a royal swan to choose the ugly duckling of the deceased, washed-up American film goddess Kathryn Carlisle for his bride.

"Rumors at court say the prince hasn't been himself since a golf ball hit him in the temple in Pebble Beach, California, where he was on hand for the U.S. Open with international supermodel Germaine."

His grin disarmed her. "You, of all people, should know better than to believe the tabloids. That ball hit one of my bodyguards in the knee. Any photo of a model was super-imposed for effect."

Her jaw hardened. "Where my mother was concerned, I *do* believe them. Don't forget they wrote the truth about her. Marrying you will give them enough fodder to start a whole new feeding frenzy.

"The headlines will read, 'With the promise of a twelve-million-dollar wedding present, it appears the daughter is following in the footsteps of the mother. Time will tell if this is the first of her many marriages destined to fail. Bets in the Las Vegas underworld are already running high that the marriage will fall apart within months.'"

Something flickered in the dark recesses of his eyes. "Then prove them wrong, Alexandra."

There he went again saying her name in that unusual way, making her nerve endings tingle. While blood surged into her cheeks, her hands formed fists. "Enough is enough! I could never take your money."

Lucca liked tangling with her. He'd finally met a woman who set off exhilarating sparks when they were together. He couldn't remember the last time this had happened.

"Fine. Then become a surgeon and pay back the debt with your hard-earned money. A few operations for those who can afford it and you'll have wiped your mother's slate clean as you indicated earlier."

Her chin lifted. "Even if by some miracle I did get in medical school, I wouldn't be able to start practicing for another eight years!"

"I'll pay for your medical school for as long as it takes. Once you do your residency, you'll receive a salary and can start paying me back like you would a school loan. It's a good bargain. I guarantee you couldn't do better with anyone else."

She stared at him through glazed eyes. "Attending medical school isn't one of the duties of a king's consort."

"My consort will do what she wants because I won't be a normal sort of king." He flashed her a self-satisfied smile. "Your only royal duties will be to accompany me on certain occasions that will come up from time to time."

"I see."

"I'll arrange for you to start Italian lessons tomorrow after we arrive at the palace. By the time we've returned from our honeymoon six weeks from now, the fall semester will be starting. With the help of a tutor, you'll be able to keep up with your fellow medical students."

"Perhaps you didn't hear me. I'm terrible at languages and I'm not going anywhere with you." Least of all on a honeymoon.

"When I explain your predicament with the American press, my parents will insist you live at the palace for the next month. Being sequestered with the family will protect you from the worst of the media for a while."

She felt like stomping both feet. "Aside from the fact that you're speaking pure nonsense, I can't just quit my job and leave my apartment!"

"We'll talk about that later." He checked his watch. "Right now we're going to meet your great-uncle. He's the deputy consul at the Russian Federation here in New York. When he finds out you're his brother's granddaughter, he'll be overjoyed and insist we meet to get acquainted."

The prince moved past her and opened the door where both his bodyguards were still standing on alert. With a hand cupping her elbow he said, "While you visit the ladies' room on your right, I'll make the arrangements.

"Don't take too long. There's a lot to accomplish before we board my private jet this evening. And one more thing. My name is Lucca. I'd like you to use it."

CHAPTER THREE

"YURI Pavlovich Grigory? May I present your grand-niece, Princess Alexandra Carlisle Grigory."

"Alexandra, my child." The tall, eighty-year-old widower with his strong Russian accent kissed her on both cheeks. "Welcome to the family."

"I can't believe I have living family," Alex whispered shakily, touched by his unexpected warmth. She was still incredulous any of this was happening. If it weren't for Lucca, she would never have been united with her father's family, let alone known of their existence.

Though she was indebted to him, she was also terrified because this reunion had come about at a price. There was only one way Lucca wanted repayment, but she couldn't do what he asked.

"There are quite a few of us Grigorys so you'll *have* to believe it." He chuckled. "Call me Uncle Yuri."

She blinked back the tears. "If you don't mind."

"Mind?" He shook his gray head. "I'd be hurt if you called me anything else. This is a great day. Do you know you're the living image of my nephew, except you're much prettier?" He squeezed her hand. "That's because of your mother. She and Oleg created a beautiful daughter." His eyes misted over. "If only your father and grandfather could see you."

"Thank you, Uncle Yuri. I'd give anything to have known them."

"Well—" He wiped his eyes. "I'll do my best to tell you all about them. Come into the conference room and we'll talk over lunch."

Lucca escorted her through the double doors to the other room where a meal was waiting for them. Over the next few hours her Uncle Yuri told her so many wonderful stories, the time flew by and she never wanted the afternoon to end. Between the pictures and anecdotes, she felt as if she really did belong to a great family.

Yuri's kindness about her mother made it easy for Alex to love him. So far he'd said nothing disparaging about her parent. It was like a balm to her scarred heart.

"First Vladmila, then Nicholas got pneumonia and died. Oleg left New York to figure out what he wanted to do with his life. Once he reached Las Vegas, I'm afraid he didn't keep in touch. We didn't hear until after the fact that he'd died in a plane crash. Such a young age to lose his life. I wish I'd known he had a daughter. To think you grew up in Los Angeles without him."

While she fought to control her tears, his moist gray eyes swerved in Lucca's direction. "My children and grandchildren will be surprised and thrilled to learn of Alexandra's existence. I have you to thank for uniting us, Lucca."

The prince sat there at ease, the quintessential picture of royal sophistication. "It was my pleasure, believe me."

"Whatever I can do to repay you, name it."

Alex felt Lucca's dark eyes on her and shivered, wondering what he was thinking. She didn't have to wait long to find out.

"I'm glad you said that because I've asked Alexandra to marry me." She gasped. "We hope to gain your blessing and would request that you do us the honor of giving her away at our wedding next month."

"Is this true?" Yuri cried. He looked delighted.

Her breath caught. "I...I haven't said yes yet, Uncle," she stumbled over the words.

"Why ever not?"

Alex wanted to blurt that they'd only met six hours ago, but she was too embarrassed to tell him the truth. Instead she said, "We haven't known each other very long."

Her great-uncle stared into her eyes. "That's what marriage is for, to get to know each other, my child. You'll have years of togetherness while you learn more and more how to make each other happy."

She moistened her lips nervously. "You don't understand, Uncle Yuri. My mother was married six times." Not to mention that before today Alex and Lucca had been total strangers. Marriages like this simply didn't happen.

"I can understand why you're frightened. But think about this." He lifted his forefinger as if he was giving a speech. "Maybe part of it's because she lost Oleg, and maybe the other part is because she didn't have parents to teach her what a good marriage is all about. Hmm?"

"Maybe," she answered in a tiny voice. He'd confounded her thoughts with his reasoning, and it didn't help that Lucca sat there looking pleased and impossibly confident.

"Don't forget you've got *me* now. My marriage to your great-aunt Natasha lasted sixty years. There's no reason yours won't last that long or longer!"

He was very sweet. She squeezed his hand back. Already a bond had developed, but he didn't have the faintest clue what was going on here. Alex felt as though she'd been caught up in a tornado and had no idea where it was carrying her.

"If Lucca has the good sense to choose a Grigory when there are other eligible royals who've had their eye on him for years, then I can guarantee a happy union. Our family stays faithful to each other."

Lucca sat forward, capturing her gaze. "For my part I intend to do everything to make you happy."

"There," her uncle cried out. "You see?"

Yes…she saw. What her uncle didn't know was that the most vital ingredient in their marriage would be missing, but she held back in deference to her newly found relative who was beaming. Too agitated to sit still, she reached for her coffee and drank it.

"Alexandra?" he said excitedly. "You're the loveliest of all the Grigory women. I noticed it when you walked in with Lucca. You two make a splendid match."

"I thought the same thing the first time I laid eyes on her," Lucca concurred with an unmistakable tone of sensuality.

Alex choked on the hot liquid and put the cup back on the saucer. He'd gauged it just right to convince her great-uncle he was in love. The crown prince of Castelmare was a sensational actor.

While she wiped the corner of her mouth with her napkin, Lucca got to his feet and went around to her chair. "I dislike cutting this meeting short, Yuri, but Alexandra and I have to leave for the airport."

This was Alex's cue to get up from the table. As she stood, their arms brushed. The contact sent a shockwave through her body. She hurried ahead while her great-uncle, who was as tall as Lucca, followed suit. He moved to the outer door of his office like a person ten years younger and kissed her on both cheeks.

"Lucca has my number. Let me know you've arrived safely in Castelmare. Now that we've met, I want the two of you to be part of my life, Alexandra."

Tears smarted her eyes. "I want that, too!" She gave him a big hug. "You'll never know what this day has meant to me."

"I think I do." He sniffed before handing her a manila envelope full of family pictures. His gaze shifted to Lucca. "Take good care of her. She's very precious to me."

To her shock Lucca put his arm around her shoulders. Dazzling her with his white smile, he said, "I intend to." It sounded more like a fierce avowal. "When the time comes, I'll send the jet for you and your family."

"That won't be necessary."

"I insist," Lucca stated in a tone of finality.

"Then we'll be waiting most impatiently." Yuri gave her a grandfatherly kiss on the forehead before Lucca whisked her through the door.

Paolo and Carlo, the bodyguards he'd introduced to her earlier were waiting to escort them out a rear exit. In the back alley three bullet-proofed limousines with smoked glass were parked. She had no idea who was inside the first one. Carlo followed them into the middle one. Paolo rode in the limo behind. Lucca sat next to her. Whether on purpose or not, his body rested against hers.

"You should never have said anything to my uncle. I haven't agreed to marry you. I don't even have a passport."

"I can let anyone I want into the country."

She gripped the armrest. With Lucca this close to her,

she couldn't think clearly. "Uncle Yuri thought you were serious about your marital intentions."

"I am. I wish I could convince you this is a good way out for both of us." An almost mournful quality had crept into his voice. "You gave me the impression you would do whatever it takes to pay the debt, even if it requires eight years at medical school to accomplish, but it appears I was wrong."

Alex edged against the door. "Everyone will say I'm just like my mother, running after a prince for his money."

"You're a princess in your own right and don't need anyone's money, but it doesn't matter what other people think," he came back suavely. "We're the only two people who know the truth or need to know."

She kneaded her hands. "We'd never be able to fool your parents," her voice throbbed.

"We don't have to. They're painfully aware I'll be struggling to do my duty, but it's expected."

Her thoughts reeled. "So there is a woman."

After a slight pause she heard him murmur yes.

Alex shouldn't have been surprised by his last-minute confession. He loved a woman with whom he could never share his life openly or marry. He couldn't have children with her, couldn't grow old with her. From the moment he was born, he'd been robbed of his free agency. How dreadful.

"No one else has knowledge of our situation, Alexandra, not even my sister, and she's my closest confidante. You're the only person who knows the truth."

She lowered her head. "I can't imagine your pain. I'm so sorry."

"I'm sorry your mother's debts have placed such an un-bearable burden on you. We could help each other out, but if you can't bring yourself to do it, then I won't pressure you further."

Alex clasped her hands together, not having expected this kind of honesty from him. He was in love with someone. What could be more natural, except that he couldn't marry a commoner. When it got right down to it, how many men were honorable enough to sacrifice their personal happiness to this degree?

Earlier he'd indicated that his interest in women lay with nonroyals, but not until this second did she realize what exactly he was being forced to give up for the sake of his father's health and the kingdom.

No matter how hard Alex fought it, she felt a wrench in her heart for him. For the first time all day it didn't seem quite so ridiculous that he'd chosen Kathryn Carlisle's daughter of all people to carry off this charade. Through the backhand of fate she had enough Grigory royal blood in her veins to satisfy his parents. Lucca knew her darkest secrets. There would be no pretense between them in private, no surprises. She'd already told him she never planned to marry. There'd be no expectations of love on either side.

From her point of view she'd be getting the best of the bargain by being able to pursue her education toward a career. If she became a doctor, she would eventually pay him back. If she couldn't get into medical school, she'd find another career and pay him back. When that became a reality, she'd start paying off the twelve million dollars.

What would he get besides a titular wife?

Not much…unless she helped him find a way to be with the woman he loved. Now that would be worth something no one else could give him.

Alex could do that! She *wanted* to. It would even things up and they'd both get what they wanted.

"We're approaching the lane for the airport," he said, breaking in on her chaotic thoughts. "Tell me the terminal where your flight will be taking off so I can alert the driver."

Her pulse throbbed against her temples. By the timbre of his voice you'd never guess the turmoil going on inside of him, but she knew.

"What princess will you choose?"

"I have no idea. If we had more time I'd let you pick her for me. Somewhere over the Atlantic I'll have to make my choice. We're almost there. Where shall we drop you?"

She closed her eyes tightly. "You really want to go through with this?" It was a stupid question of course.

In the quiet that followed, his hand slid over her wrist. "Let's put it this way. I would never have come into Defore's office otherwise." While she digested that revelation he added, "If you're saying what I think you're saying, be very sure, Alexandra. There's no going back."

Her breath caught. "I know."

In the next instant he lifted her hand and kissed the palm. It set off a charge that ignited every atom of her body.

Lucca felt her quiver. She was frightened, but not too frightened to have agreed to his proposal. He'd counted on her desire to pay back her mother's debts being greater than any other consideration and she hadn't disappointed him. Later he would deal with his guilt over allowing her to think he was in love with Sofia. Right now his overriding emotion was one of exquisite relief bordering on triumph.

They drove the rest of the way in an electrifying silence he felt no compunction to break. She could change her mind at any moment. He wouldn't be able to relax until she was safely on board the jet and they'd attained cruising speed.

When Lucca was on business for the monarchy, he traveled with a staff of twelve, not including the pilot, copilot, steward or his bodyguards. By the time they reached the plane, everyone in his entourage had assembled ahead of him. At seven in the evening there was still plenty of light.

As Alexandra climbed out of the limousine, the sun gilded the white-gold strands of her hair swirled among the darker blond shades. She reminded him of an aviatrix who'd just jumped down from her biplane and pulled off her cap to reveal a riot of jaw-length curls. There was nothing artificial about her. She wore no lipstick, but with her wide, seductive mouth it wasn't necessary.

His first impression of her hadn't changed. She was totally unaware of herself. He found himself studying her naturally arched brows. They framed large, sad, luminous gray eyes set in a classically shaped face. Sometimes they were inscrutable. Other times when she talked about the debt she couldn't pay, he was shaken to the gut by their emotional intensity.

The woman he'd chosen for his bride had an innate glamour that couldn't be manufactured or purchased. He saw shocked wonder in the eyes of his pilot and staff as he introduced her. Not only was he flying back to Castelmare with his intended, but they'd just learned that Princess Alexandra Grigory was Kathryn Carlisle's daughter.

He could hear their minds making comparisons between the screen idol and her flesh-and-blood offspring. Alexandra's impenetrable gaze added a certain mystery to her demeanor that set her apart from her mother.

After a word to his pilot, Lucca joined her. Once up the steps he ushered her through the body of the plane to his study. "As soon as we're in the air, the steward will show you to your cabin where you can freshen up."

"Thank you," she whispered, not looking at him as she found a place to sit. In case she was getting cold feet, it was too late to renege on their arrangement now.

Per his instructions the pilot started the engines. Lucca noted with satisfaction that the Fasten Seat Belts sign had flashed on. The sound of her strapping herself in was music to his ears. For the first time all day he was able to let go of the tension gripping him. He fastened his.

Soon they were taxiing out to the runway. He glanced at her striking profile. She had a proud nose. He liked that. He liked everything about her. "Once we've reached altitude, I'll ask dinner to be served."

"I'm afraid I'm still full from lunch."

"Even so, you might change your mind later."

In a few minutes the engines screamed and they were moving faster. Soon the wheels left the tarmac and the jet was airborne.

Lucca felt a sense of excitement he hadn't experienced since he was a young boy taking his first ride in his father's plane, but this time it had nothing to do with power and everything to do with his passenger.

All his life he'd known the day would come when he would have to marry someone royal like himself. But to reach his midthirties and still not feel as much as a spark for one of them had thrust him into a living nightmare from which he hadn't awakened until this morning.

Who could have imagined a scenario as unlikely as the one he'd commandeered in Defore's office? Meeting Alexandra had constituted nothing short of a miracle. Their marriage would solve Sofia's problem, as well.

"Veni, vidi, vici," Lucca found himself muttering aloud. He felt like the great Roman emperor Julius Caesar who after one of his victories said, "I came, I saw, I conquered."

She glanced over at him with those hypnotic eyes. "Were you talking to me?"

It was better she didn't know what was going on in his mind. "I was telling you the seat-belt light has gone off. We've reached cruising speed. I'll ring for the steward."

By the time she'd unfastened hers, the other man appeared and requested she follow him. The second she was out the door Lucca rang one of his bodyguards and gave him a flurry of instructions he wanted followed immediately. While he waited for his bodyguard to appear, he phoned the galley and advised them to prepare some sandwiches and fruit.

In a few minutes Paolo the bodyguard entered the study, carrying a square eight-by-eight inch metallic box by the handle. Lucca took it from him and placed it on the conference table where he ate his meals.

They walked to the door and he thanked him before getting on the phone to his secretary working in the rear compartment of the jet. Bringing home a bride-to-be at the midnight hour meant dictating a ton of new instructions. When Alexandra reentered the cabin, his breath caught to realize he hadn't been hallucinating after all. She really was on the plane with him. He rang off to give her his full attention.

"Come and sit at the table. There's something I want to show you."

Her gaze fastened on the box, then swerved to his with an expression that held traces of pain. "If that's what I think it is, I don't need to see it. If I never lay eyes on another diamond again, it will be too soon."

He grimaced. "Nevertheless, you need to look at this. Every wife should know how her husband makes a living. Sit down and close your eyes."

She complied, wondering exactly what he meant. He opened the box and removed the smaller black jewel case, then lifted the lid. "You can look now."

Alex couldn't stop the gasp that escaped her throat. Nestled against silver velvet lay the teardrop-shaped diamond almost the size of an American half dollar. It was a shade of green, darker than peridot but lighter than emerald.

"The true color of nature," he spoke her thoughts.

"I didn't know a diamond could be green. The hue of the stone is utterly incredible."

He nodded his dark head. "Its color was caused by the crystals in a volcanic pipe coming into contact with a radioactive source at some point during its lifetime. The phenomenon is so rare in a diamond this size, the Ligurian is rated among the top five diamonds in the world."

"Why do you call it that?"

"Castelmare is situated on the Ligurian coast we share with Italy."

"I'm ashamed I don't know my geography better."

"Don't be. The majority of people haven't heard of it, either. In 1906 my great-grandfather started buying diamonds from the owner of a mine in South Africa, and they established a business relationship.

"As a result, he created a diamond-cutting industry in Castelmare to augment the kingdom's prosperity. Today it's a thriving concern. People from all over the world flock there to buy diamonds, which brings us a good percentage of our wealth."

"I had no idea," her voice trailed. "Forgive my temper. That's twice today." Already she was aware her soon-to-be husband soon-to-be king was a hardworking man, as well as a monarch.

With jewelry stores in New York and around the globe, this little lesson about the Ligurian diamond was just the beginning of many others. One of the most daunting would be to learn Italian. Help!

"I've already forgotten." He was a much kinder person than she was. Her Carlisle temperament had a nasty habit of coming out at precarious moments.

By agreeing to their unique marriage arrangement, she was entering a brand-new world. Only now did she realize how much she would have to learn, starting with this rare gemstone.

"It's the most exquisite thing I've ever seen."

"It's flawless from the inside out. You have no idea how rare that it is."

There was a reverence in his voice. She wondered if he was thinking about something else. Someone else…

"How many karats is it?"

A pause ensued before he said, "It is 44.16. Go ahead and hold it up so you can view the facets' reflections."

"You're not afraid I'll run off with it?"

His lips formed a half smile. "Where would you go?" he teased dryly.

The next thing she knew he reached for her right hand and placed the famous diamond in her palm much the same way he'd kissed it in the limousine. Her body had turned to jelly then, too. This had to stop! Every time he came near or touched her, she reacted the same way.

Alex couldn't believe any of today had really happened,

let alone that she was holding something this precious in her hand. When she raised it to the light, she let out another cry. "The sight's so dazzling, it hurts your eyes."

"My thoughts exactly when I saw it in its uncut state for the first time," he whispered, but he was looking down at her as he said it. She got this fluttery feeling in her chest and put the diamond back in the case.

"When was that?"

"I was on a buying trip at nineteen when the mine owner showed me what they'd just discovered. After I purchased it, I kept it hidden. A few years later I got the best diamond cutters in the business together. Between us we decided a teardrop shape would show it off to the best advantage."

"Do you keep it on display year round?"

"Except for the six weeks while I take it on a world tour doing business." He placed it in the carrying case and shut the lid. "The rest of the time it stays in a museum on the palace grounds. Several hours each day it's open to the public, where tourists can view the family jewels and various items dating from the Middle Ages."

"I can't imagine having a family history you can trace back that far."

"Have you forgotten your uncle Yuri is going to bring you your family's genealogy? He said it goes back much further."

So he did. There'd been too much information to process today. "What other kinds of business do you do?" Her curiosity had gotten the better of her.

"Banking, investments, tourism, space-age technologies."

She wanted to hear more, but the steward came in with a tray of food and drinks, interrupting them. The two men conversed in such rapid Italian that Alex despaired of ever being able to catch on, let alone speak it with any degree of fluency.

Once the steward had left them alone again, nervousness drove her to bite into one of the ham-and-cheese sandwiches. Lucca sat down opposite her. What intangible force had possessed her to agree to his insane marriage proposal?

Because you felt sorry for him, a little voice inside nagged.

For once in her life she'd met someone who had an even worse problem than she did and she was in a position to help him.

Keep telling yourself that, Alex.

But what if I make a mistake? she cried inwardly, her emotions containing a hint of hysteria.

"I think you're exhausted," he commiserated, without her having said anything. It was frightening how easily he read her thoughts and moods.

She drank part of her soda. "I think I am, too. What about you?"

He'd already consumed two sandwiches and some grapes. "I still have work to do and I've never been more energized. Feel free to use my phone to call whomever you like—your boss maybe? If you'll give me the numbers, I'll make the necessary arrangements for your apartment and belongings."

"That's all right. I'll take care of everything tomorrow afternoon when I know I can reach people at the best time for them."

"Then why don't you go to bed. Tomorrow morning we'll be landing at seven-thirty and have breakfast on board first. Once we're ready to leave, it's a fifteen-mile hop by helicopter to the palace in Capriccio. In case you're wondering, our part of the Mediterranean is too hilly for an airport so we use our French neighbor's to the west."

"I see." Alex bit her lower lip. "Are your parents expecting you tomorrow?"

Over the rim of his coffee, he gave her an intense regard. *"Si."*

"Do they know about me?"

"Not yet."

She stirred restlessly. "I can't meet them looking like this."

He put the cup down. This time his brown eyes were shuttered as if his thoughts were far away. "I don't see anything wrong with the way you look."

"When I left Los Angeles I only brought one change of clothes with me. I'm afraid a casual top and trousers is hardly the kind of attire they'd expect of a future daughter-in-law."

His brows unexpectedly furrowed, giving him an almost formidable appearance. She didn't know he could look like that, and her heart skipped a beat.

"Maybe I didn't make myself clear. Ours is an unorthodox relationship."

"Oh, I'm well aware of that!" she said in a torrent of words.

"Bene," he drawled, "because nothing's going to change between you and me. What we both see is what we get. Your wardrobe from California will arrive soon enough. If you feel you need to add to it before time, then go shopping. Understood?"

Nothing could be clearer than that! Maybe one dress and some shoes to match. Beyond those items she had no more money and wouldn't ask for any.

"For the honor of the House of Savoy going back many generations, I'm doing my duty by marrying a royal," he informed her. "However, beyond the business of running the kingdom, no one, not even my parents will have the right to question either of us or dictate how we conduct our personal lives."

His final words had been delivered in code, but she'd

already deciphered it without problem: "No one, not even you, Alexandra, will have the right to question me on the way I spend my free time or how much of it will be given to the woman I love."

That was Alex's part of the pact. Naturally she intended to keep it. One of these days soon she would tell him what she was prepared to do for him and the woman he loved.

Lucca's part was to help her achieve a career that only this morning had seemed beyond the realm of possibility.

She knew he wouldn't let her down, so it defied logic why she would suddenly have this hollow feeling, almost as if she'd lost something precious even though it had never been hers in the first place.

"Thank you for the meal. I'm going to take your advice and say good-night."

He got up and followed her out the door to her cabin located midway down the lighted corridor.

She walked inside while he lingered in the doorway. Lucca was a powerful-looking male and totally gorgeous standing there in his elegant summer suit and tie. A vital, living presence even though he must have been up with the birds. Alex knew she wasn't in a dream, but it felt like it.

"Are you comfortable in here?"

His deep voice permeated to her insides. Why on earth was she feeling shy? "The steward has seen to everything. Thank you."

"Is there anything else you need *I* can do for you?"

She rubbed her upper arms with her hands for want of something to do with them. "After uniting me with my great-uncle and making it possible for me to go to medical school—that is, if I make it in—I'd be an ungrateful wretch to ask you for anything else."

"Ungrateful wretch?" He did an exaggerated imitation, making her laugh once more. "Your language has its colorful moments. Life with you is going to be…fascinating." Maybe it was a trick of light, but she thought he looked pleased. "Now I'll teach you your second word in Italian. *Buonanotte,* Alexandra."

"*Buonanotte.*"

"Lucca," came the reminder.

"Lucca."

He gave a nod of approbation. "You have an excellent ear. The best kind of omen for the future." So saying, he quietly closed the door.

Alex's feet stayed rooted in place.

The Prince of Castelmare was happy——possibly happier than he'd ever been in his life because he'd solved his problem.

Of course he was still wide-awake! Now that Alex had gone to bed he could phone his lover and tell her a miracle had happened. He'd found his way out of the abyss that had been burying him alive all these years.

Yet just imagining the other woman's joy sent a surprising stab of pain through Alex's heart, causing her to stagger for a moment.

CHAPTER FOUR

"Lucca?" His sister's anxious cry almost broke his eardrum.

It was the middle of the night, yet she sounded as if she hadn't been to bed yet. Not so the members of the palace staff he could trust. They'd already received a rude awakening from his nocturnal phone calls. At the moment they were busy carrying out his orders.

"*Ciao*, Regina."

"Please don't tell me you're not coming home. It's been close to two months. I've run all the interference with the parents I can."

"No man ever had a better friend. Only one more favor."

"Lucca—"

"*Scusimi, cara.* Don't talk, just listen. This is important." He heard a groan.

"It's four-thirty palace time. In three hours the helicopter will be waiting to fly you to the airport in Nice. We need privacy, so we'll meet for breakfast on board the jet."

"But—"

"No questions now. I've been working half the night and need a few hours' sleep before the plane lands. All will be answered when we see each other. *Ciao*."

Lucca clicked off. Now that everything had been set in motion, he could pass out. After putting his phone on the bedside table, he turned on his stomach and buried his face in the pillow for what was left of the night.

"Your Highness?"

Through waves of torpor he heard the steward's voice and let out a moan.

"*Sì*. What is it?"

"You asked me to waken you at seven."

Lucca frowned before glancing at his watch. He'd been asleep three hours already? How was that possible?

"Is Princess Alexandra up yet?"

"If she is, she hasn't left her cabin."

The thought of seeing her this morning produced an adrenaline rush, bringing him fully awake. "Before we're ready to land, ask her to join me in the study."

He nodded and left the cabin.

Once Lucca had showered and shaved, he opened his closet doors. After a quick perusal, "The tan suit I think with the brown silk shirt. No tie," he muttered to himself.

Five minutes later he entered the study to discover she was seated near the window drinking coffee. Filled with relief that yesterday's earthshaking events hadn't been a figment of his imagination, his muscles relaxed.

"*Buongiorno, Alexandra.*"

"*Buongiorno, Lucca. Come va?*"

She must have asked the steward for help. It pleased him she was already trying to communicate in his native tongue. One day she would be fluent.

"*Va bene. Grazie.*" His gaze took in her plum-colored silk mandarin-collar shirt and gray denims. She had superb dress sense. Most Italian women of his personal acquaintance weren't as tall. None had her artless sophistication. When he realized he was staring, he poured himself coffee from the tray placed on the table. Then he sat down opposite her. "How did you sleep?"

She smoothed some hair away from her temple in an unconsciously feminine gesture. "Probably as well as you did."

He chuckled before swallowing the hot liquid. "If we're always this honest with each other, we'll have no problems."

"Lucca—" She put her mug in the drink holder. "This is all new territory for both of us and we'll have to make it up as we go along, but there are a few things we need to discuss before I meet your parents." Her breathlessness was more pronounced this morning, a sign her composure was only surface deep.

"You took the words out of my mouth. As soon as we land, I'll do my best to prepare you so you'll feel at ease."

In reaction to his comment she rolled those fabulous eyes of hers. The unexpected gesture made him smile. Along with everything else about her, Alexandra had a healthy sense of humor. Living with her was going to be fun.

With perfect timing the seat-belt light flashed on. "Have you been to Europe before?"

"No."

They both buckled up.

"I envy you seeing everything for the first time."

Her knuckles looked white where she gripped the armrests. "If there is a first time."

Lucca's laughter resounded in the cabin. He'd done this hundreds of times before, but had forgotten the steep descent wasn't to everyone's taste. While she took in the view of one of the world's most famous coastlines, he preferred to concentrate on the view seated across from him. She was all soft shoulders and long legs.

Mio dio, her mouth…

* * *

No sooner had they taxied to a stop than Lucca was at his desk, talking to someone on the phone. Alex sensed a hum of activity both in and outside the plane.

Cocooned as she was in the body of the jet, she felt a certain comfort in being relatively isolated from the world, but her heart did a double clutch to realize that before long she'd be stepping into his world. The gravity of what she'd done was starting to seep in.

Footsteps in the corridor drew her attention away from the window where she could see men and maintenance vehicles clustering around to service the plane. Her ear picked up a woman's voice.

Alex felt her stomach muscles bunch in apprehension. Lucca had virtually promised her they'd talk before she met his parents. Surprised she might not be able to trust him after all, she turned to him. However, no words escaped because the steward had just wheeled in a cart of food. Behind him came a woman who couldn't possibly be his mother.

"Lucca—" cried the adorable-looking female who launched herself at him. She was maybe five-four with a cap of glossy black curls and a figure to rival that of Gina Lollobrigida.

Alex's boss, Michelle, had worked around movie stars for years and thought the curvaceous Italian film idol of the fifties was the essence of feminine beauty. Apparently, Lucca thought the same thing. Was this the woman he loved? His dark eyes flashed with emotion as he rushed around to crush her in his arms.

"Regina," he murmured.

The sight of him rocking her curvy body dressed in a trendy-looking, ribbed top in navy with white cargo pants drew a groan from Alex. Though she'd made a promise to herself to help the two of them all she could, she hadn't expected to be thrown in at the deep end this fast.

Obviously, something very private was going on. The other woman was crying gut-wrenching tears. They seemed to pour from her soul, and why not? After all, the separation must be brutal for both of them. Even Alex with only ten Italian words in her vocabulary at the moment could tell he was crooning endearments to her. Suddenly she knew a terrible envy to be loved like that.

The steward continued to lay out breakfast, seemingly oblivious to their uninhibited reunion. Alex wished she could remain as unaffected. Shocked by another strange jolt of pain and embarrassed for anyone to notice, she turned her head away and ended up looking blindly out the window again.

"Regina? I want you to meet someone." Lucca had switched to English. That was Alex's cue to give them her attention. With pounding heart, she pivoted around, then came to an abrupt stop because the lovely face and moist eyes staring at her was the feminine version of Lucca's.

She was his sister!

A wave of intense relief washed over Alex, catching her by surprise. She clung to the back of the seat.

"May I present Princess Alexandra Carlisle Grigory of Beverly Hills, California. Alexandra? I would like you to meet my one and only sibling, Princess Regina Schiaparelli Vittorio."

"How do you do?" both women said at once and shook hands. The puzzled, curious look in his sister's expression couldn't hope to match Alex's dazed condition. In trying to recover, she made the mistake of glancing at Lucca.

His eyes were so alive Alex knew he had to be thinking about the freedom he now had. It wouldn't be long now before he could go to his lover and tell her there was a way they could be together. "Regina, I wanted you to be the first to know that Alexandra has consented to be my wife."

Following that revelation a gasp broke from his sister. Her eyes, a burgundy brown, stared at Alex in shock before darting to Lucca. "I-is this the truth?" she stammered, as if she were afraid to believe it.

"As God is my witness," came his solemn response.

Alex wasn't prepared for the way Regina's eyes lit up or her strong hug that came close to knocking Alex down. It was a good thing she was taller and could take the impact.

Once again Lucca's sister was sobbing, but these seemed to be happy sobs for her brother who appeared to have picked the bride he wanted. All these years Regina had to have been aware of Lucca's pain. Now she was misinterpreting the situation, but it didn't matter. In witnessing the degree of love Regina felt for her brother, Alex was more determined than ever to facilitate matters for the two lovers.

Already Alex loved Regina for being so devoted to him. This was the way family should be, all for one and one for all. Lucca's happiness was the goal that would bind her friendship with his sister.

Over Regina's heaving shoulder, Alex met Lucca's gaze. His dark orbs were thanking her. She smiled slowly at him, letting him know he could trust her to be his friend. He smiled back. The moment was so piercingly sweet she closed her eyes to savor it.

In the next instant Regina moved out of his arms. "Forgive me," she said, wiping her eyes. "What a beginning!"

"Being an only child I've always wondered what it would be like to have a sister," Alex confided. "I'm no longer nervous."

Regina laughed gently, but was still shaking her head, bewildered. "How did it happen? Where did you two meet? When? Mama and Papa know nothing! This has to be the best-kept secret of the century."

Better stick to the truth as much as possible. "In a round-about way through my mother."

"That's right. On business," Lucca added. "Let's eat while we talk, shall we?" By tacit agreement the three of them sat down at the table.

Breakfast for a king, that's what had been ordered. Alex was starving. She filled her plate with a little bit of everything and ate her fill. Lucca's healthy appetite told its own story this morning, but Regina was too excited to eat more than a peach.

"Men are never good with the details, so I want to hear the whole thing from you, Alexandra."

Alex flashed Lucca a signal of distress but he was no help and bit into another roll with those beautiful white teeth of his. Apparently he and his sister had few secrets…except the biggest one.

"My mother died a little more than five months ago leaving a large debt. Her attorney advised me to sell her diamonds and suggested the House of Savoy in New York. I flew out and—"

"And that's how we met," Lucca took over. "The attraction between us caught us both by surprise. It will interest you to know that Alexandra's mother was Kathryn Carlisle, the film star. Her first husband was Alexandra's father, Prince Oleg Grigory."

Regina cocked her head and studied Alex for a full minute. "With those Russian roots, I think you're even more beautiful than your mother and that's saying a lot considering I've seen several of her pictures. Trust my brother to find the cream over in America."

She breathed deeply. "Thank you, Regina. I feel the same way about him. We complement each other in the ways that are most important." What else could she say? Theirs wasn't a love match or anything close to it, but Lucca expected her to reciprocate his affection in front of the public and his family. That's what he'd said.

"With many discoveries still to be made," Lucca imparted unexpectedly. His hand closed over hers across the table. "Isn't that right, *bellissima?*"

A glorious word to hear from a man *if* he truly loved you.

Alex crinkled her nose. "That's what has me worried, Regina. I sing off-key, I'm messy and I don't know if I snore. There, Lucca." She squeezed his hand before letting it go. Hers was on fire. "That's my confession for today. Tomorrow, three more."

Lucca threw his head back and laughed. Regina joined him. When it subsided she said, "I could tell you a lot of things about my brother."

"But you won't," he clipped out. "Let Alexandra discover them one at a time so I don't scare her off."

"Is there a reason why she's not wearing the betrothal ring yet?"

"*Si, piccina.* All the reason in the world. I didn't happen to be carrying it around with me when I left on business weeks ago."

"Besides, Lucca knows I don't like rings," Alex inserted before he could say anything else. "In between working toward my degree, I've been a makeup artist at a movie studio for the past eight years. Rings and bracelets just get in the way."

"Even so," he supplied, "we've decided on a simple gold wedding band at the ceremony. That's all two people need to symbolize their true feelings."

"I agree," Regina murmured as if she had something else on her mind. "What did you major in?"

"Biology."

"You've led an amazing life."

Alex's gaze collided with Lucca's before she looked away. "I was rather thinking the same thing about you, Regina. My father died before I was a year old, and I was raised by nannies. I didn't grow up in a palace like Castelmare with two doting parents and grandparents and a loving brother like Lucca."

"Which brings us to the subject at hand," he stated in a way Alex was coming to recognize as his monarch voice. He'd used it at the store when she'd tried to get away from him. "Alexandra will be living at the palace from now on. Until the ceremony I've arranged for her to sleep in the blue suite next to yours, Regina."

"I hoped you'd suggest it. I'd love it if Alexandra were close to me. It's lonely down that hall."

"I thought you might like the idea." Lucca grinned. "She's eager to learn Italian, and I can't think of a better way for her to pick it up than to spend time with you after her lessons."

"I'll ring Professor Emilio. He'll be the best teacher for her, Lucca. Between sightseeing and shopping, it won't be long before she's rattling off Italian with me."

"*Bene.* I knew I could count on you." He sounded inordinately pleased with his sister's ideas.

Alex smiled at her, reassured by her warmth and generous nature. "You and Lucca speak impeccable English. I'm very impressed."

"Thank you. We had excellent teachers and spent time in England."

"It shows. How many languages do you speak?"

"Five."

"Now *that's* incredible."

"Not really. Papa speaks a dozen." Regina's expression suddenly grew sober. "Has Lucca told you how sick he's been?"

"Yes. I'm so sorry."

"When he hears the news about you two, he'll be overjoyed. Mama and I are convinced it will add years to his life."

"Knowing Lucca is going to take over will come as a major release for him, I'm certain of it," Alex assured her.

On that note her husband-to-be got up from the table and came around to place his hands on her shoulders, massaging them gently. "What do you say we fly on to the palace. I'm anxious to get you installed and comfortable. This evening will be soon enough to present you to our parents."

Her relief was so great that he was going to give her the rest of the day to get her bearings that she wasn't prepared when he leaned over without warning and kissed the side of her neck. Regina was getting the totally wrong impression of the way things really were, but that was the whole idea.

The feel of his mouth against her hot skin was positively erotic. Liquid fire ran its course through her body. She wasn't sure she could leave the cabin on her own power. Her weakness increased when Lucca put his hand behind her neck and guided her out of the jet into a lovely warm June midmorning.

They walked a short distance to the waiting helicopter.

Regina and her own bodyguards had gone ahead of them. Lucca's bodyguards stayed close. Paolo was the last one inside the ten-passenger interior before they lifted off.

Alex didn't know why, but all of a sudden the upward movement seemed to break the trance she'd been in for the past twenty-four hours. The people surrounding her were strangers, all speaking a language she didn't understand.

The sight of the gleaming white jet with its royal coat of arms receding from view was as unfamiliar as the curved coastline bordering the plain of Nice. She was being whisked away to the home of the future king of Castelmare. In four weeks, she would be his wife.

Like a leaf tossed in the wind, she was rootless, being swept along over high-perched villages and blue-green water by some unseen force so much greater than she could comprehend, she started to shiver and couldn't stop.

A hard-muscled arm slid around her shoulders. Lucca pulled her into his side as close as the straps would allow. "It'll be all right," he whispered into her hair. "You should have told me you don't like helicopters. We could have driven the short distance instead. Just cling to me. We'll be landing on the north grounds of the palace in two minutes. I swear it."

"I'm fine," she croaked, too shaken by events to correct his erroneous assumption. He smelled divinely male and felt so solid she rested against him, needing his strength. She was probably creasing the expensive-looking tan suit adorning his striking male physique, but he didn't seem to mind.

By the time they landed on the helipad, her tremors had subsided. To her chagrin other sensations had taken over she didn't want to feel or acknowledge. Fearing he could sense her emotional turmoil, she undid her seat belt and stood up, forcing him to relinquish his hold on her. At the same time she noticed the speculative glance Regina had given her and Lucca.

One day Regina would observe too closely and learn the truth, that she and Lucca were only playacting. Though her brother was in love with another woman, he had to walk a fine line in order to convince everyone his marriage to Alex was built on solid ground. For the moment she had to respond like a woman in love, yet already she was worn-out with the strain of it and longed to be alone to think.

When it came her turn to climb out of the helicopter with Lucca's assistance, she noticed a swarm of staff from the palace descending on them. The crown prince and favorite son had come home at last.

No sooner did that thought fill her mind than Regina put a hand on Alex's arm. "Now that we've arrived, my brother's life won't be his own. Come on. I'll show you to your suite. After a transatlantic flight I'm always exhausted, even if I've slept." Regina understood a great deal.

Lucca stood behind her and gave her waist a surreptitious squeeze, melting her insides. "Go with my sister," he whispered before kissing her temple. "I'll ring you later in the day when you've had a chance to rest." It was clear there'd be no introductions to anyone until she'd been presented to his parents.

Alex nodded without looking at him and followed Regina's lead, but with each stride that took her away from him, she felt the keen loss of his presence.

Better get used to it, Alex. Lucca is only a figurehead in your life. Concentrate on obtaining your goals, then you won't be a pathetic creature who listens for his every footstep and hangs like a heavy millstone around his neck. Focus on your surroundings.

Her surroundings…

She paused midway to the north portico at the rear of the sprawling Renaissance palace. It was perched on the lower part of a steep hillside. In the late-morning sun the ornate, three-story structure gleamed like a dazzling white jewel against a backdrop of an impossibly blue sea and sky.

Her gaze lifted to the stunning flag with a white cross on a red field designating the House of Savoy. Below it was a flag with a crown and shield of the reigning Vittorio family coat-of-arms. She'd seen the same insignia emblazoned on the jet's exterior.

Everywhere her eyes traveled she discovered fruit and palm trees. Flower gardens with too many varieties to name dotted the fluid carpet of velvety green. The marvelous scent of roses mixed with lemon and orange filled her lungs.

Southern California had its share of fabulous estates, but nothing she'd ever seen came close to this. Regina walked back to her. "It's breathtaking to me, too, and I've lived here all my life."

"No ordinary gardener created this paradise. It's been done by a master planner. I'm staggered by so much beauty."

Regina's heart-shaped mouth curved into a smile that lit her warm brown eyes. "I'll tell Dizo what you said."

"Who's that?"

"His real name is Dinozzo. He's the oldest son of Guido Fornese, the head gardener, but between you and me Dizo is the genius. I'd never say that to anyone else because I wouldn't want to hurt Guido's feelings."

"I'll never tell," Alex assured her.

The younger woman stared at her. "You're nice."

"So are you, Regina." She had a sweetness in her. Though they were only a year apart in age, their life's experience had been so different Alex felt much older.

"Wait till you see the view of the front from your bedroom balcony."

Alex put a hand to her breast. "Do you think my heart can take it?" she teased to cover her emotions spilling all over the place.

In that lovely face raised to her she saw traces of the charismatic man who'd cast a spell over her. Otherwise why would she be standing in this Garden of Eden instead of a cubicle on the studio lot in Culver City building a nose for Cyrano de Bergerac.

Gentle laughter broke from Regina. "I'm still alive if that means anything."

"It means a lot."

"There's another reason why Lucca wants you in the blue suite."

"What is that?" Alex asked quietly.

"I'd better not tell. You'll find out soon enough." The comment made her feel giddy with curiosity. "Come on, before he gets after me for not taking the proper care of you."

The palace had a staff of a small army of people, two of whom opened the doors for her and Regina. Alex stepped onto a checkerboard floor of deep rose and white marble. Across the grand foyer rose an exquisitely carved marble staircase. The walls and niches were filled with statuary and gold-framed paintings of immense size.

When Regina noticed Alex's interest in everything, she said, "The core of the present palazzo dates from 1467 and was originally the town residence of an ambitious Capriccio banker. The ruling family of the House of Savoy liked the location and bought it in 1498. The families that came after began to build on to it, filling it with great treasures until it looks the way it does today."

"You're surrounded by history," Alex marveled. "The palace is absolutely beautiful inside and out."

"I think so, too. Some of the most precious items have been moved to the museum so visitors can see them." They started up the stairs to the second floor.

"Lucca told me the family jewels are kept there."

"Yes, including the Ligurian diamond. Did you happen to see it on display in New York?"

"Only a glimpse, but during the flight here he let me hold it up to the light so I could see into its heart," she explained as they curved around to the next story.

Regina paused on the top step to study her for a moment. Alex had no way of deciphering the other woman's thoughts before following her down the spacious corridor. Everywhere she looked the ceilings and walls were a masterpiece of frescoes and gilt cornices forming frames around them.

When Regina opened the double doors halfway down the east wing, Alex let out a cry of delight. The large apartment with its ornate white woodwork was a vision of blue and white stripes against a smaller blue-and-white pattern on the walls.

Through one set of double doors was a den with a computer and every possible accoutrement for her comfort.

"Lucca will have ordered a lunch tray for you. He wants you to relax and enjoy yourself."

"Thank you for everything, Regina."

"You're welcome. If you need anything, pick up the phone and dial 1 for housekeeping. Dial 2 for Lucca, 3 for me and 0 for an outside line. Talk to you later."

Dial 2 for Lucca…

Regina shut the doors behind her, leaving Alex, who was charmed by her new world. A fabulous blue-and-white Persian rug covered the gleaming white, marble floors of the sitting room. She walked across it to the bedroom. Alex saw that her suitcase had already been placed at the end of the king-size bed. At the opposite end of the room was a fireplace framed by hand-painted blue-and-white tiles. Exquisite.

Tall French doors had been opened to reveal Capriccio's curved bay with its myriad of yachts. Drawn to the balcony, she looked down on the terraced grounds where she saw a long, blue rectangular pool graced by ornamental flowering trees and statuary. Exotic plants delineated the borders of each terrace. Steps led down to the private beach. Between the view and the warm, sweetly scented air, the whole ambience was out of a dream and left her speechless.

"After your fright on the helicopter, I didn't think you'd make it any further than the bed."

Lucca's deep male voice jarred her out of her trance. She turned around but couldn't see him.

"Look up."

Surprised, she lifted her head and discovered him staring down at her from a balcony on the third floor, one suite over.

"I put you in there so I could keep an eye on you without an audience."

She assumed he meant the bodyguards. Minus his suit jacket, he was leaning on his forearms, giving her the impression he'd been out there for several minutes and was happy to be home after being away so long. Knowing there were no secrets between the two of them had to make this the supreme moment of his life.

Alex wished she could feel happier about it. "I thought you'd be with your parents."

"I spoke to them from the plane. They're expecting me at five this evening after Papa's nap."

"So they still don't know about me?"

"No. I'll come for you at ten to five. We'll make our entrance together. In the meantime I have business I must attend to. Enjoy your meal. It happens to be one of my favorites."

Alex couldn't fault him for anything.

As he turned away, she glimpsed the play of muscle in those masculine shoulders covered by his silk shirt. His well-honed physique was proof he kept fit. Not wanting to think where his personal business might take him this afternoon, she went back inside the apartment to eat. One of the maids had set the tray on the oval table in the sitting room.

Though the scallops and pasta were delicious, she ate with little enthusiasm, leaving most of it to start making phone calls home. Michelle was her first priority. Alex glanced at her watch. Her boss would be up and getting ready for work by now. Once she arrived on the lot, pure chaos reigned. Now would be the best time to catch her.

Alex hadn't been looking forward to telling her she wouldn't be coming back to work. For the moment all she would say was that while she was in New York, she realized she needed a complete break from her life in California. For the time being she was looking into attending medical school and would get in touch with her when her plans solidified.

As for her apartment, she would phone her landlord and arrange through him to get her belongings packed and shipped to Castelmare. Her used car could be dealt with through the car dealership where she'd purchased it.

Her last call would be to Mr. Watkins who'd be shocked about the faux diamonds. For the moment, all he needed to know was that she wouldn't be returning to California for a while.

Later on she would tell him the truth. He alone would understand why she was ready to do anything to pay off her mother's debt, even to being a stand-in consort for an equally desperate prince. But kind as Mr. Watkins was, he wouldn't fail to remind her that two wrongs still made a wrong.

Deep in her psyche Alex knew what she was doing was wrong, but it was far too late to back out now. She was more her mother's daughter than she wanted to admit.

CHAPTER FIVE

AT QUARTER to five Alex stood in front of the bathroom mirror wearing the newly cleaned and pressed outfit she'd worn to the jewelry store yesterday. The maid who'd taken her lunch tray away had seen to it. Naturally it had to have been on Lucca's suggestion since he knew Alex only had two outfits with her.

She brushed her freshly washed hair into some semblance of order. It would cooperate for all of five minutes, then the natural curl would take on a life of its own and become unruly once more. In deference to meeting his parents, she applied a soft pink lipstick.

Since talking with her boss and Mr. Watkins, both of whom had been surprisingly understanding and supportive of her plans, she'd tried to sleep, but it never came. No matter how much she rationalized it, her conscience wouldn't allow her to forget she and Lucca were about to perpetrate a great fraud on his family.

When she heard a knock on the door of the suite, she jumped. Her nerves were frayed to the point she wanted to hide.

"Alexandra? I'm coming in." The next thing she knew

Lucca was striding over the threshold, his hard-muscled legs covered in casual stone-colored trousers.

Her stunned gaze lifted to the navy cotton crew-neck pullover stretched across his powerful frame with the sleeves pushed up to the elbows. With his black wavy hair and striking aquiline features, his looks transcended every known superlative in her vocabulary.

He'd purposely worn an outfit that would make her comfortable in hers. Everything he did was for her welfare, causing her to care a little more for him when she didn't want to.

They met halfway across the sitting room. To her dismay she was out of breath. His dark eyes searched hers with an intensity that made it impossible to look away. "Only one thing is missing. Stand still while I pin this on you."

He reached in his trouser pocket and pulled something out. She assumed it was a family heirloom of some kind, but almost fainted when she glimpsed the unmistakable Ligurian diamond suspended beneath a small gold crown. In one deft move he'd attached it to the draped part of her blouse covering her right shoulder.

How could he have had the jewel fashioned into a pin this fast?

She pressed her hand against it, as shaken by the brush of his fingers against her skin through the thin material as anything else. "What have you done?" she cried in panic. "I can't wear *this!*"

"Why not?" came his mellow query. "It's mine to give and was meant to be worn by a woman of your height and looks. No one else could carry it off."

Heat scorched her cheeks. "I'm not my mother!"

"That's true. You're your own self with a little of her thrown in."

"You know what I meant. This is a mockery."

"Only in your mind."

She tried to remove it, but Lucca prevented it, shaking his dark head with a determination that sent shivers down her spine. "This is my signature. The sight of it will convince my father I'm happy with my choice of bride and am ready at last to relieve him of his burdens."

He had an answer for everything. It stopped her every time. "You should have given this to the woman you love." Her voice trembled. "She alone has the right."

Lucca gave an unconscious shrug of his broad shoulders. "You're going to be my wife. It's expected that you wear a family jewel. Nothing in the museum would suit you better than this. Are you ready?"

No, she wanted to scream, but she didn't dare. On the ride to the airport a century ago she'd agreed to marry him and she had no right to question what he felt was necessary to make his parents happy.

After reaching for her purse, she followed him to the door of her suite. As she moved past him their bodies touched. She might as well have come in contact with a current of electricity and rushed into the hall ahead of him.

Carlo stood a short distance away. He probably saw her reaction. Great. Lucca never went anywhere without him. His permanent shadow. The bodyguard probably pitied Alex who was going to be nothing more than a token wife. Alex didn't want his pity. The thought sickened her.

"Is everything all right?" Lucca asked with concern. "My parents are waiting for me in the sitting room of their apartment, but if you need more time…"

Me, he'd said. Not *us.* She shuddered.

She flashed him a little smile. "Not time, just courage."

"I promise you they're wonderful people."

"They would have to be in order to raise a man like you…and Regina," she added as an afterthought so he wouldn't get the wrong idea. Already she was letting things slip he could misinterpret.

"She likes you, Alexandra, not simply for my sake." When Alex shook her head he said, "Believe it or not, that's what she told me a little while ago. My sister's a good judge of character. I'm glad you're going to get along."

If he was glad, she was, too. He dictated their pace down the hall toward the west end. He had to know she'd never been this nervous in her life. Though he pointed out various murals from his family history in an effort to put her at ease, she wasn't in a mood to appreciate his anecdotes, amusing as they were.

They could have been out for a leisurely stroll on the palace grounds instead of inside its walls walking the plank. That's what it felt like to Alex.

When they neared the double doors where more palace personnel were on guard, Lucca reached for her hand. His hooded eyes flicked to hers. "Your presence is going to add a year, maybe even several to my father's life. For that you have my undying gratitude." With another disturbing kiss to her palm, he opened both doors.

By tacit agreement they moved inside the sumptuously decorated room, yet it showed signs of modernization with several comfortable-looking couches and chairs with ottomans. Lucca left her side long enough to kiss his parents, who were casually dressed in pants and shirts. Both sat in front of a television set.

While they conversed in Italian, she hung back where she could study his attractive mother. She was small-framed with stylishly short dark hair, an older version of Regina both in coloring and features. Alex sobered, however, at the sight of his thin father, who shut off the TV with the remote. It sounded as if they'd been watching a golf match.

No doubt the recent loss of weight and hair was due to his chemo treatments, but she could tell he'd been a very handsome man when he'd been healthy, just like his son. An oxygen tank with tubes rested against the side of his chair. This was a sight the public would never be allowed to see. The significance of it weighed on her.

Lucca stood up and turned to her, motioning her forward. In English he said, "Mama? Papa? I brought someone home from America with me. Please speak in English until she learns our language."

"Don't get up," Alex begged when they both started to rise.

His mother's brown eyes caught sight of the diamond pin, and she let out a surprised cry. "Look, Rudy!"

"I see it, Betta," her husband's voice shook. He sounded shocked and upset. "What does this mean, *figlio mio?*"

In a lightning move Lucca reached for Alex and put his arm around her waist, drawing her breathtakingly close to his side. "It means there's going to be a wedding." He smiled down at her, kissing the side of her cheek. "Who knew my gorgeous bride-to-be has been waiting in the States all this time for me to find her. If I'd known about her sooner, we would have been married ages ago and would probably have had a child or two by now."

Oh, please don't make the lie any worse than it is, Lucca.

"May I introduce you to your future daughter-in-law, Princess Alexandra Carlisle Grigory."

"Grigory?" His father's hazel eyes rounded. By now he'd gotten to his feet with some difficulty. Now she knew where Lucca's height had come from. His wife joined him. Both were nonplussed.

"Alexandra, these are my parents Rudolfo and Isabetta."

"It's wonderful to meet you at last," Alex whispered shakily. Lucca held on to her and hugged her tighter. "Her mother was the American film star Kathryn Carlisle, who tragically passed away this last Christmas Day. Her father, Prince Oleg, died when she was only nine months old. She never knew her grandfather, Prince Nicholas. However, her great-uncle Yuri is still alive and will be giving her away.

"The three of us spent a very enjoyable afternoon together at the Russian Federation in New York while he helped Alexandra become better acquainted with her Grigory heritage. He'll be sending you and Mama formal greetings right away."

His mother's brown eyes brimmed with tears before she hurried around the low table to clap her hands on Lucca's cheeks. "You've made me the happiest mother in the world," she said in English before switching to Italian. The muttered endearments needed no translation. After hugging him hard, she turned to embrace Alex.

"Welcome to the family, Alexandra. Except for when the children were born, this is the most joyful day of our married lives."

"It certainly is," Lucca's father concurred, and leaned closer to kiss Alex on both cheeks. She could detect his shallow breathing. "However, I know half a dozen young women who'll want to scratch your eyes out, as my little Regina would say."

"Rudy," his wife scolded him with mock feeling. "Lucca's made his choice. Let that be the end of it."

Lucca caught Alex from behind and pulled her against his chest where she could feel the strong solid beat of his heart. "The truth is, from the moment she and I met in New York, it was love at first sight for both of us."

Alex swallowed a groan. How gallantly he played the part when he knew his parents were aware he'd chosen her out of duty. But being nobles themselves, they would pretend this was a love match and treat her accordingly. Only one person would be able to intervene for Lucca's personal happiness. That would be his arranged wife, Alex.

His father's eyes flicked from the diamond to his son's face. He nodded solemnly. "I can tell. There's a light in your eyes that was never there before."

The king's playacting was beyond comprehension.

"I see it, too, Rudy. Have you told your sister?"

"*Si, Mama.*"

All three of them should be given the Oscar that had always eluded Alex's mother.

Lucca let go of Alex long enough to help his father be seated once more, then he pulled Alex down next to him on the opposite couch and grasped her hand in a gesture of ownership his parents couldn't fail to notice. "They met this morning after the plane landed in Nice. Alexandra will be staying in the blue suite next to Regina's until our wedding."

"That's as it should be," his mother emoted. "Now we'll all have time to get acquainted before the ceremony."

"Regina's wonderful," Alex interjected, knowing something was expected of her. In this case she'd told the truth. Lucca's sister had the same charisma as her brother. Already Alex liked them all too much.

Lucca's thumb started making lazy circles against her palm, sending sensations like shooting stars through her veins. "Alexandra is everything I could ever want. With her at my side, I look forward to taking over from you, Papa. In fact, I wish the wedding could be moved up a week. Not only for your sake, but for mine," his voice ended on a husky inflection. The next thing Alex knew he'd brushed his lips against hers.

Ohh.

His father cleared his throat. "What do you think, Betta?"

"You're still the king. It's for you to say. Why not?"

He slapped his hand against his knee. "Then so be it. A little Russian blood in our grandchildren will be an exciting addition." Help! "You want children?" His father eyed Alex frankly.

Since she knew it wouldn't happen, she said, "Of course. Having been an only child I'd love three or four."

The king's face lit up. "That settles it. We'll have a wedding here in three weeks." His wife nodded in obvious delight.

"Grazie, Papa." Lucca stated as his hand slid up Alex's back and around her shoulders. "Because we can't wait any longer."

"He always was in a hurry," his father confided to Alex. "If I'm going to hold one of them on my lap before the end, that's probably a good thing."

"You'll hold more than one, Papa!" his son vowed, forgetting that theirs was a marriage in name only, but Alex understood that he'd blurted the declaration out of fear over his father's fragile state of health.

"Yuri gave Alexandra an envelope with Grigory family memorabilia. I've been working with my secretary on it since we arrived. He's already delivered a list to yours so the invitations can be finished and sent out immediately."

If that was true, then Lucca hadn't had an opportunity to see his lover yet.

To Alex's surprise he rose to his feet and drew her with him. As they started to leave, his father called out, "Wait…we've barely visited yet. Where are you going?" The longing in his voice was a beautiful thing to witness. Lucca had a father's love. Alex envied him that.

"Out," Lucca said in that commanding voice. "After this news you need to rest while Mama and Regina get the ball rolling."

"He's right, Rudy," his mother said, patting her husband's arm.

"There are things I want to show my bride-to-be, but we'll be back," Lucca said from the double doors. "I'm home to stay, Papa. Every day until the wedding you and I will spend a little time going over your affairs. I'll never be able to fill your shoes, but when the time comes, I promise to be ready to take on your cares."

Alex felt his avowal to the depths of her soul. Before he shut the doors behind them, she saw his father weep against his wife's shoulder.

Outside in the hall Lucca turned to her, grasping both her hands. His dark eyes traveled over her features with such intensity she was witless. "How do I thank you for what you did in there? They love you already." He kissed her fingertips.

She'd said too much, but she'd had no choice. "I was never given the opportunity to do anything for my parents, but I felt your parents' happiness, Lucca. This is the next best thing." Alex cleared her throat. "Besides, I haven't forgotten the pact we made. With your help I'm going after a career that will pay off all my debts including the one to you. So you don't need to thank me for anything."

His chest rose and fell with visible emotion. Not wanting to prolong the moment, for fear he could see into the deepest corners of her psyche, she said, "And now if you don't mind, I'd like to take a walk around Capriccio before dark by myself. I'm in the mood to explore. Is that permitted?"

Though his facial expression didn't change, she felt a stillness steal through him. Slowly he released her hands. "Of course. You've been assigned bodyguards, but they'll be unobtrusive. Always come and go through the north doors of the palace. Follow the road out to the west gate."

"I'll remember."

After another sweep of his eyes he said, "Do you have enough money in case you need to buy something?"

"Yes."

The fact that he didn't put up an argument or insist that they be together on their first night in Castelmare underlined the depth of his eagerness to be somewhere else, with someone else. She wasn't about to deny him that joy. The sooner she and Lucca began leading their separate lives the way it had been decided on the plane, the better. To accept the status quo with grace would be her motto starting now.

He stayed with her until they reached the grand staircase. "Have a pleasant evening, Alexandra."

Suddenly there was an aloofness emanating from him. It was a feeling foreign to her. "Thank you, Your Highness. I'd better get used to saying it."

Lines marred his arresting features. "You've never called me that before. Please never do it again."

She blinked. "I'm sorry. I meant n—"

"My name is Lucca," he broke in on a terse note. "Except for our wedding day where you'll have to address me as Your Majesty when you pledge your loyalty to your sovereign king and husband, I never want to hear anything else. *Capisci?*"

Her heart slammed against her ribs. She understood that word well enough. Alex had angered him. *"Capisci."*

"Lucca," he corrected her.

Alex repeated the words aloud, then continued on to her bedroom. With every step she felt his piercing gaze on her retreating back. He really disliked being reminded he was royalty. In retrospect she realized it came from years of knowing he would have to put his personal happiness aside to follow in his father's footsteps.

But now that had all changed for him. By getting engaged to Alex, he'd become a free man. Ironically it now appeared *she* was the one in bondage. Her hand moved instinctively to the diamond pin. Before she went anywhere else, she needed to take it off.

The loss of her mother's real diamonds hadn't been Alex's fault, but heaven help her if something happened to Lucca's prized possession. On the plane she'd sensed it had a significance for him beyond its monetary value.

Once she'd removed it she felt better. After putting it away she reached for her purse and left the suite. She was glad she didn't bump into Regina. His sister would ask questions. Alex dreaded having to explain why she and Lucca weren't together on his first night home.

At the outer gate where the palace grounds met the coastal road she could tell her bodyguards had formed a network around her. You wouldn't know them for the

Castelmarians walking up and down the street. Until she and Lucca divorced and went their separate ways, they would always be with her. It was another thing she had to get used to.

She soon discovered that the palace and grounds bordering the Mediterranean were positioned like the center jewel in Capriccio's crown. The capitol city itself was sprawled on either side and above. The steep roads zigzagged to dizzying heights where she saw the crowns of several small villages that went to make up the rest of the principality.

With every twist and turn of the road the charming clusters of flower-covered Italian villas and greenery enchanted Alex, who wasn't used to this kind of exercise to get about. What she'd gleaned from Lucca told her the country derived most of its income from tourism. She could see why. Between its beauty and the perfumed air, this had to be the most glorious place on earth.

Alex paused for a moment to take in the spectacular scenery. No wonder her mother had spent part of her honeymoon here. Who would ever have imagined Alex ending up being engaged to the prince of its ruling family?

It's all because of you, Mother.

And her father. She couldn't forget him.

The name "Grigory" had transformed Alex from a commoner to someone Lucca could present to his parents. In her case "a rose by any other name" would *not* smell as sweet. An accident of birth had made all the difference. Without it Lucca would never have decided to break in on her meeting with Mr. Defore.

Without her mother's diamonds being facsimiles of the real thing, Alex wouldn't have created the disturbance that had caught Lucca's attention in the first place.

Two desperate people from two unrelated worlds colliding in the cosmos at the critical moment in time, for both of them. One minute earlier or later and there wouldn't have been impact. They would have hurtled on by without the slightest knowledge of the other one.

She swallowed hard. Already it was impossible to contemplate a world without Lucca in it. The realization terrified her, and she started walking faster. Before long she reached the inner district of the prosperous city bursting with boutiques, sidewalk cafés, art galleries, restaurants, souvenir shops and jewelry boutiques. The display of diamonds attracted droves of people milling about from every country in the world.

Alex entered one of the crowded souvenir shops. By the time it came her turn to check out with one of her traveler's cheques, she'd loaded up with a map of the Principality of Castelmare, a tiny Italian-English phrase book and a picture book on Castelmare's House of Savoy from past to present printed in Italian. There were photos of Lucca and his family. She couldn't wait to study them.

Two doors up she spied a restaurant. The delicious smells coming from inside made her realize she was hungry. When she checked her watch, she was surprised to discover it was quarter to eight. With the sun setting later, she'd been deceived into thinking it was much earlier.

Better eat now. No way would she go back to the palace and ask for a meal, but this place was packed. She stood around with her packages waiting for someone to leave.

"Mademoiselle? Signorina? Miss?" a male voice called to her.

For a while she ignored the guy sitting in one of the crowded booths, but he persisted in trying to get her attention. Finally she looked over at him. He was with a bunch of college-aged guys and girls talking and laughing.

The student singling her out could be one of any number of dark-haired Mediterranean types. Obviously there was room for one more in the booth. He stood up and made an extravagant gesture for her to sit down. Soon everyone was beckoning her over.

Why not? She was hungry and tired.

"Thank you," she said as he took her sack from her and put it under the table by her legs. He had an inviting smile and was just her height.

"Hello," everyone said with their heavy Italian accents. The friendly crowd proceeded to introduce themselves.

"My name is Fabbio."

"I'm Alex."

He frowned. "You have man's name?"

"It's short for Alexandra."

"Ah…very classy." Alex chuckled. "My English is not good?"

"It's very good. My Italian's terrible. Have you eaten here before?"

"*Si.*"

"What's that called?" She stared at his meal.

"Pasta."

She could see that.

"You like?"

"Yes."

"I get it for you." He called to the waiter, and before long a plate of hot pasta with potatoes and beans was placed in front of her. While they all conversed in spates of Italian, then English, she ate her dinner. Her first mouthful was so delicious she consumed everything in short order. The five of them shared a bottle of wine. He poured her a glass. "Drink."

"Thank you very much."

The fruity flavored rosé served for her dessert. She hadn't had a glass of wine in years. This was the perfect setting for it.

He pulled a flier out of his pocket. "You want to come?" She took a look at it. Some kind of concert was being held in the city. Before she could turn him down she heard footsteps coming closer, then a deep male voice said, "*Bellissima*—I'm sorry I'm late."

The whole restaurant went silent.

Her head whipped around in time to see Lucca standing there in the same clothes he'd had on earlier, but he was wearing sunglasses. A gasp escaped her throat. He was supposed to be with someone else. At least, that was why she'd left the palace in the first place, so he could go to her.

Alex was so shocked to see him here, her mouth went dry. She couldn't get any words out. Neither could the clientele who had recognized the crown prince and were obviously stunned to see him walk in here of all places.

Before she could credit it, Lucca lowered his mouth to hers in what could only be construed as a possessive kiss, urgently coaxing her lips apart. Caught off guard she welcomed the electrifying invasion of that incredibly male mouth. Her body reeled in response.

Scarcely aware of what was happening, she realized he'd pulled some Euros from his wallet and put them on the table. Still speaking English he said to the others, "Enjoy the concert."

In a lightning move he retrieved her sack from beneath

the table. Her body couldn't stop weaving from the excitement of his kiss as he helped her to her feet. She smiled at Fabbio. "Thank you for being so nice to a stranger."

He nodded, still tongue-tied.

Lucca escorted her from the restaurant. A black limo stood parked outside. The net of bodyguards had increased. She thought Carlo gave her a frown before Lucca climbed in the back next to her and shut the door behind him.

Halfway to the palace she couldn't stand the silence any longer. "Obviously, I don't know all the rules yet, but was it absolutely necessary for you to do what you did just now?"

"I'm afraid so," he muttered in an oblique tone. "In three weeks the world will know you're my wife, but those students will remember that you went into the restaurant unaccompanied and responded to an invitation to sit with them. I'm aware you accepted because there was no other place available, but from their point of view you looked and acted like you welcomed his attention.

"I wouldn't want the incident, no matter how inconsequential it might have seemed in your eyes, to reach my parents' ears."

"Of course not." She felt sick inside. "I honestly didn't think. Forgive me, Lucca. I promise it won't ever happen again."

He extended his legs and crossed his arms. "It'll happen again and again because you're the kind of woman a man can't forget. From now on, all you have to do when you're out by yourself for any reason is to remember that you're already taken. Let the interested party know where he stands before he weaves fantasies about being alone with you."

"No man has ever had dreams about me."

"That's not what one of your bodyguards reported.

Apparently the young boy and his friends had a bet to see how long it would take him to bed the goddess standing inside the doorway."

Her cheeks went crimson. "Then the bodyguard made it up!"

"A lie to me could cost him his job and worse."

Alex shivered. "It was all a big mistake. I shopped too long and then I got hungry."

"You could have eaten at the palace. That's your home now."

"But I didn't want to bother anyone this late."

Instead of commenting, he asked a question. "How did you like your *trenette?*"

"*Trenette?*"

"It's what you had for dinner. Pasta Ligurian style."

"Oh…I loved it!"

"*Bene.*"

She darted him a furtive glance. "Your parents will probably hear about my big faux pas and consider me unfit to be your wife. They'd be right!"

"I'll tell them about it as soon as we get back to the palace, then it won't matter when they hear it distorted on the news."

Alex let out a small cry. She was a fool, just like her mother whose antics were made into the news every night of the week.

"Like parasites, the paparazzi live on their hosts. Over the years I've learned the best defense is offense," he explained.

She stared at her hands. "How will you explain about my being in town without you?"

"The truth always helps. I'll tell them I had a lot of business and you didn't want to bother me on my first day home. You went exploring in town and stopped for something to eat, unaware some man had his sights set on you. Tomorrow Papa will remind you that you're not in America now. Mama will laugh and accuse me of being jealous. The whole incident will be forgotten."

Maybe, but Alex knew Lucca could never be jealous. He would have to be in love with Alex for that to happen.

"Let's hope."

He reached for her sack. "I wonder what you bought."

She was afraid he would laugh. "Touristy things. Didn't my bodyguards tell you?"

His expression remained impassive. "They'll only report if you're in danger." A sobering thought. "May I see?"

Since he appeared so determined, she didn't try to stop him. "Go ahead."

The book came out first. "This isn't the best history," he pointed out seconds later, "but it's not the worst, either."

"I wouldn't know, since I can't read Italian yet. I bought it for the pictures."

He suddenly lifted his head and gave her a long, unsmiling look. "After the coronation and our marriage, a plethora of new books will appear in the shops. You'll be in every one of them and every account will say that Princess Alexandra is the most beautiful of all the brides of the House of Savoy."

Lucca could tell superb lies. She rolled her eyes. "If you insist."

His laughter helped dissipate her worry that he was upset with her for the second time since their arrival in his country.

He pulled out the next item and thumbed through it. "I approve of your pocket phrase book. It's how I began to learn English."

For some reason his comment reassured her.

After scanning the map, he said, "This needs a little help. I'll fix it when we get back to the palace." He returned everything to the sack. "I noticed you're not wearing my pin."

"No. It's too precious to flaunt."

He grasped her hand, entwining their fingers. "You're my fiancée now. After what you told Regina, I couldn't very well give you an engagement ring. Wear the pin for me?"

"You mean, all the time?"

"Yes, all the time."

She sucked in her breath. "If you wish."

"Is it such a burden?" he whispered.

"Lucca—surely you understand the worry I have about losing it. The stone is irreplaceable."

"What good is it if it's never worn?"

"You really feel strongly about this, don't you?"

"Yes."

"All right," her voice trembled.

"Grazie."

The limo pulled to a stop beneath the north portico of the palace. Lucca cupped her elbow and ushered her inside. They parted company at the second floor.

"Buonanotte, Alexandra." After pressing a light, un-expected kiss to her parted lips, he strode swiftly toward his parents' suite. She knew he was on his way to put out a fire the media would have started.

Little did he know the damage he'd done to her at the restaurant. That deeply searching kiss for the crowd's bene-fit had fanned the flames of a conflagration growing inside her with no power to contain it.

CHAPTER SIX

LUCCA checked his watch. Five to twelve. Alexandra's first day of learning Italian with Professor Emilio ought to be over by now. He was retired from the university, but according to Regina, the older man still did tutoring.

He left his palace office on the main floor and hurried up the steps to the third floor where the schoolroom was located, but his excitement dissipated when he opened the door and heard Alex laughing quietly with a man who couldn't be much older than Lucca.

The sight of the two of them enjoying each other's company in this intimate atmosphere shook him to the roots, something that hadn't happened to him before where a woman was concerned.

One look at the tutor's face and body language and Lucca knew Alexandra had him enchanted just as she'd done that idiot college kid at the restaurant last night. It didn't take a two-hour lesson for her to work her magic. Lucca ought to know because to his great surprise, it was beginning to work on him.

She was dressed in the familiar plum silk shirt and gray pants he'd admired before. After lunch he had plans to do something about her bare-bones wardrobe, but at the mo-

ment the only thing Lucca was feeling was irrationally ter-
ritorial.

He moved inside.

The other man saw him before Alexandra did. He slid
off the corner of the desk and stood up. The fact that he
was lean and almost as tall as Lucca irritated him further.

"Your Highness."

Alexandra turned in her chair. "Lucca—"

He couldn't tell if she was pleased to see him or not, but
she was wearing his pin. That was something at least and
should have appeased him. It didn't.

She got to her feet, very much in command of the situation. "Lucca? This is Professor Morelli. Professor Emilio
is ill so he sent Tomaso in his place."

Lucca gave Tomaso a brief nod. "I'm sorry to hear that.
How long will it take him to recover?"

"He has influenza. His doctor says two weeks, maybe
a little longer."

That was too long.

"How is my wife-to-be doing?" *Besides giving you a
heart attack.* Lucca ground his teeth together. Wife-to-be
sounded more permanent than fiancée. He wanted that
made clear to Tomaso at the outset.

"Signorina Grigory is an excellent student. By the time
of your wedding she'll be speaking a little Italian and understanding some of it."

She smiled. "One lives in hope, Tomaso. Thank you for
taking me on."

"It's an honor for me."

*And a rush you won't be able to do a thing in hell
about, professor.*

"I'll see you tomorrow."

Alexandra nodded. *"Si. Domani. Ore due. Ciao, Tomaso."*

"Ciao, Alex."

The hackles stood on the back of his neck. *Alex?* She'd given him permission to call her that?

His gaze slid to Lucca. "Your Highness," he said in passing.

"Why two o'clock?" Lucca asked after the other man had left the room.

She picked up the book and notebook he hadn't seen before. "Tomaso teaches classes all morning, but he can come after lunch. If I'd had a teacher like him for Spanish in high school, I might have learned how to conjugate verbs."

Intrigued in spite of his foul mood he asked, "What was wrong with your Spanish teacher?"

"He taught by immersion, and no one ever understood anything. He gave everyone an A for trying. It was ridiculous."

Laughter burst out of him. "What verb did Professor Morelli teach you to conjugate today?"

"To be. *Essere. Io sono, tu sei, lui e, noi siamo, voi siete, loro sono."*

"I'm impressed." He was more than impressed. Her little conversation a moment ago sounded as if she'd been studying a lot longer than two hours.

"He said I have good pronunciation. Do you think he was just saying that to make me feel better?" Lucca realized she wasn't fishing for compliments. She really wanted to know. It dawned on him she really was a good woman, someone he would be proud to call his wife.

"I told you the other day you have an excellent ear. Why do you doubt it?"

She averted her eyes. "I don't know."

Lucca knew. Alexandra's mother had never given her confidence. Considering her father had died in her infancy, it was a miracle she had any at all. Fate had made her strong, courageous. Lucca had plans to fill in the rest. The thought of it taking a lifetime lightened his spirits.

"Come on. I'm taking you to lunch at a favorite restaurant of mine."

"Oh, good!" Her seductive mouth smiled as they left the room, giving him his reward. "Tomaso taught me some phrases to practice when I order. We went over the names of the basic foods."

Diavolo!

She turned to him. "Did you say something?"

"Nothing worth repeating."

Her eyes played over his features. "You sound a bit like snappy turtle today."

"Snappy turtle?" he barked with barely suppressed amusement.

"You know. A little cross. With all you're taking on, I don't blame you. How can I help?"

He drew in a deep breath. "Just be with me today."

"Your wish is my command, Your Highness."

"I asked you not to say that."

A pained expression crossed over her face. "I'm sorry. It came out before I realized it. I really wasn't thinking of you in that sense. I believe you're emotionally exhausted, Lucca."

Without conscious thought he put his arms around her and pulled her close. Burying his face in her sweet smelling hair he whispered, "I think you know me better than I know myself."

"That's what arranged wives are for." *And this one-to-be knows exactly what is ailing you.*

Again Alex had spoken freely, not weighing her words beforehand. When he held her like this, she forgot the reason she was here at all. The desire to kiss his sensual mouth and go on kissing it the way she'd wanted to at the restaurant was turning into a driving need, blinding her to common sense.

The only reason he didn't feel the same urge was because someone else was in his thoughts, someone he couldn't wait to be with on a permanent basis. In a curious way he needed Alex. Almost overnight they'd become friends. She understood that and didn't read into the moment that it was emotional for him.

"I have an idea." Though it was the last thing she wanted to do, she slowly eased out of his arms. "After we eat lunch, why don't you give yourself permission to take time off and do what you really want to do until tomorrow."

He studied her through veiled eyes. "That's excellent advice. Shall we go?"

Apparently, she'd said the magic words. He was planning to act on her suggestion. Another shaft of pain splintered her heart. *Get used to it, Alex.*

When they reached the second floor, he turned to her. "Meet me at the north portico in five minutes."

"I'll be there." She hurried down the hall to her suite, tossing her Italian book and notebook on the bed. Once she'd washed her face and brushed her hair, she grabbed her purse and flew out the door.

"Ciao, Alexandra." Lucca's sister was just coming out of her room.

She drew to a halt. *"Ciao, Regina."*

She smiled. "How did the Italian lesson go?"

"I loved it."

"Good. Where are you off to in such a hurry now?"

"Lucca and I are going out for lunch."

Her brown eyes smiled. "I was about to ask if you'd like to have a meal in town with me, but I can see you have a much more pressing engagement."

Alex liked Regina and wanted to include her, even though she was looking forward to being alone with Lucca. "Why don't we all go together?"

Regina shook her head. "If my brother had wanted me along, he would have asked me. Go and enjoy yourselves."

"You're sure? Come with me and we'll ask him."

"His favorite car only fits two."

"Maybe we're going in the limo."

"I doubt it."

"Then you can squeeze in with us."

After a gentle laugh she put a hand on Alex's arm. "I believe you *would* make room for me, but under the circumstances I'm going to check on my parents. Have a lovely outing."

"*Grazie, Regina.*" She'd practiced it with Tomaso. It was one of the Italian words she loved to say.

"*Prego, Alexandra.*"

They walked together, then parted company at the stairway. Alex felt like flying down it, but since it would look as if she couldn't wait to be with Lucca, she controlled herself and descended as gracefully as she knew how.

It would be good practice for their wedding day, when she had to walk up and down the front steps of the cathedral she'd passed in town last evening. What would she do if she fell flat on her face?

Lucca was waiting for her at the entrance, but his expression darkened as she drew closer. "Tell me what's put that worried look in your eyes. Something's happened."

The man's radar didn't miss anything. "No." She shook her head. "I was thinking how awful it would be to trip on the steps of the cathedral in my wedding dress."

His taut body relaxed. "Should that occur, everyone would feel better for knowing you're human, too. If anything, you would endear yourself to the crowd."

She stared at him. "Were you born a diplomat or did you learn it from your parents through osmosis?"

His lips twitched as he put a hand behind her waist and ushered her out the doors to a black Ferrari. Once inside his sensational car, he helped her fasten the seat belt. Too much bodily contact within the elegant leather confines set her trembling.

"My parents will tell you I was born a hellion and will probably go out of this world the same way." As they sped away from the palace, she acknowledged he drove like one.

Every woman loved a bad boy. Wasn't that the collective opinion?

Alex had to admit, it was Lucca's wild side that made him the bigger-than-life, exciting male who'd overcome every obstacle to get her on that plane. No ordinary man could have managed it.

She still couldn't comprehend how it had happened. All she knew for a certainty was that in a little over two days she'd fallen hopelessly in love with him.

"I met Regina in the hall and asked her to come with us, but she declined."

"Smart girl," he quipped.

Alex smiled to herself. "She's such a natural person. I like her very much."

"So do I."

They wound up the hillside behind Capriccio and on through a town called Savono. With every kilometer the traffic thinned until they came to a tiny hamlet nestled beneath a mountaintop. It looked ancient, almost untouched by time. Forgotten even.

Lucca pulled to a stop in front of a stone church in partial ruin. No one was about. His bodyguards were doing an amazing job of keeping the paparazzi at bay.

"This is Dirupo. The word means crag, the northernmost boundary of Castelmare. Historians say it came into being in the twelfth century. There's one grocery store with a bank and post office inside. The inn only has twelve rooms."

"This place has a lonely feel, doesn't it, yet that's the reason for its charm," Alex murmured. She got out of the car to look around. There was a plaque on one of the church's stones with an explanation in four languages. She read the English version with interest. He joined her.

"I thought the same thing when I first explored up here as a boy. Right now it's on a long list of things to be discussed at the cabinet meeting tomorrow. Several of the ministers want to allow hotels and restaurants to be built up here to bring in more tourism. Because of the mountain streams they're talking of creating a spa. Yet others argue it will destroy the watershed."

She drew in a deep breath. "The view of the Mediterranean is unmatched, Lucca. Tourists would kill to vacation in a spot like this. You could charge a fortune for a one-night stay."

Alex continued to look out at the spectacular view. Being with him filled her with feelings of euphoria. "On the other hand it could be overrun and lose the bit of history that makes it so unique. There aren't many untouched places like this left in the world…."

Lucca's gaze wandered over her features. "I knew if I brought you up here, I'd be able to resolve it in my mind."

For no good reason her heart rate sped up. "What have you concluded?"

"I'm going to suggest we put a moratorium on any building, but we'll restore the church and any existing structures needing repair work."

She smiled at him. "Two hundred years from now your country will praise you for your vision."

He cocked his head. "You think I want praise?"

"In the best sense, yes. If I were a monarch, I would like to think I'd left a legacy that preserved a vital slice of the country's origins. Otherwise what would people in the future have to look forward to?"

Lucca seemed to ponder her comment before he said, "You've just helped me write the essence of my coronation speech. For that gift I'm going to take you inside the inn and buy you a lunch of fresh brook trout that will melt in your mouth."

By now she was famished. "How do you say trout?"

"Trota di fiume."

"Do you mind if I order for us?"

He reached for her hand and they started walking toward the entrance. "I'm planning on it."

"I promised Tomaso I would take advantage of every opportunity."

His hand seemed to tighten around her fingers before he let it go long enough to open the door for her. "After we eat, we'll stop by the cathedral to visit with the archbishop.

The banns have to go out for our marriage. Then we'll buy you some clothes for tomorrow."

She gulped. "Why? I thought we were going to wait until my belongings arrived."

"There's no time. My father has already put things in motion. In the morning before the cabinet meeting at ten, the journalists from the major American and European television networks will come to the palace to broadcast the official news of the upcoming coronation and our marriage. I'll be at your side the entire time and field any difficult questions."

Her jaw hardened. "You mean, about me following in my mother's footsteps."

He lifted a wayward curl off her forehead. "Love is no respecter of persons past or present. Everyone has an equal right to it with whomever and wherever they find it."

Except for a prince who must do his duty.

Two hours later his words were still revolving in her head as they entered an exclusive boutique in Capriccio where, Lucca told her, his mother and sister often shopped.

The clerk who waited on them recognized him, of course. When Lucca explained what they wanted, she told him she had the perfect outfit for Alex, who was still replete from their delicious meal.

Within seconds the woman produced a knee-length dress of woven lightweight silk in a heavenly shade of oyster. The diamond pin would look fabulous against it. As soon as Alex slipped it on, she had to admit the jewel neckline and tiered short sleeves suited her tall, softly rounded figure.

Lucca said as much when she left the fitting room and

modeled it for him. His searching gaze started at her feet and made a slow, intimate perusal of her body. By the time it reached her face, her cheeks were on fire.

"The color of the material matches your eyes." His gaze flicked to the clerk. "We'll take it and some other outfits for day and evening. She'll need shoes and lingerie." On that note he refocused his attention on Alex. "Take your time, *bellissima*. We're in no hurry."

When Alex was a child, she used to pretend she'd been let loose in a store and could have anything she wanted. It felt like that now. After agreeing to marry him she couldn't keep going around in the same two outfits. The clothes being shipped might not arrive for weeks and probably wouldn't be appropriate for many future occasions, anyway. Naturally he wanted to be proud of her.

For once she decided to take him at his word. Unfortunately, she had so much fun they didn't get out of there until it was close to 6:00 p.m. The clerk told her the packages would be delivered to the palace by eight. It was embarrassingly late already and Lucca had been sitting there for hours!

So much for letting him have time alone with his lover this afternoon. Red-faced, she apologized. "I'm sorry I took so long."

"I'm not. This has helped me get my mind off affairs of state. I don't remember the last time I felt this relaxed." He got to his feet. "You're good for me, Alexandra."

She sobered. "Thank you for being so generous. I promise to pa—" but nothing else came out because he silenced her with his lips.

"No talk of repaying me now or ever," he whispered.

Alex had said the wrong thing again, but she had to

remember that when they were out in public, his actions were always orchestrated to convince their audience he was in love. "I promise," she whispered back, but she did intend to repay him one day. She just wouldn't talk about it.

They left the boutique through the back door, where he'd parked his car. His security people had set up a barricade on the tiny street to give them space, but people pressed against it, eager for a glimpse of the prince.

Lucca had grown up learning how to handle the public. No matter where they went or what they did, he didn't seem to give them any thought. Alex wondered how long it would take her not to feel like she was a goldfish on display.

The crowded streets made it impossible for Lucca to zip back to the palace at warp speed, but she gave him credit for trying. "Home at last and in one piece," he drawled after shutting off the powerful engine.

"At last?" she teased. "A fighter jet couldn't have arrived here any sooner."

Suddenly he looked repentant. "Alexandra— I forgot about the helicopter. I should have requested it—"

"Don't apologize," she cut him off. "It was the events of the day that knocked me off balance, not the lack of a helicopter. The truth is, I found out in New York you only function at high speed. I like speed, too. If I owned a car like this, I'd be banned from driving it after the first time I went around the block."

His hand slid from the gearshift to her lower thigh, sending out one heatwave after another. "Next week I'll take you to a track in Monaco where you can let it rip to your heart's content."

"You'd let me drive this?"

His gaze sobered. "Of course. I don't think you understand yet. Everything I have is yours." After squeezing her leg gently he levered himself from the driver's seat and came around to help her. She was glad she was wearing pants. With her long limbs it would be impossible to keep them modestly covered while trying to climb out under his all-seeing eye.

"How much time do you need to freshen up?" he asked once they'd reached the second floor.

Surely he wanted to get away on his own, but being the dutiful prince, he felt he owed her his time in order to look like the attentive fiancé. Today he'd done more than any engaged woman could ask for. Now it was up to her to return the favor.

"Since I'm going to have to face my first press conference in the morning, I'd prefer to have an early night, but in case you need me in an official capacity, I can be ready whenever you want."

A remote expression crossed over his masculine features. There was a pause. "What I had in mind can wait."

Of course it could. His thoughts were on his lover. They'd been apart long enough.

"Then if you don't mind, I'll ask the kitchen to send up a sandwich while I get started on my writing exercises for Tomaso."

On impulse she kissed his hard-boned jaw where she could feel the beginnings of his beard. Another enticement she mustn't dwell on. "Thank you for a wonderful day. I'll always remember it. *Buonanotte*, Lucca."

"I'll come by your room at quarter past nine in the morning. *Sogni d'oro*, Alexandra."

Tomorrow she would have to ask Tomaso what it meant.

* * *

Lucca spent a restless night tossing and turning. Her last words to him before running off sounded like a goodbye speech, and they weren't even married yet. She was more excited about her next Italian lesson than being with him.

He couldn't fault her for anything where their agreement was concerned. Her performance so far was nothing short of miraculous. Unfortunately, he found himself wanting more from her. Because his feelings for her were growing, it was probably just as well he'd been forced to come back to his room and take a cold shower.

She was right about him. He didn't know how to take things slow, but it appeared that for once in his life he was going to have to learn that lesson. In the past few days he'd come to realize his whole life's happiness depended on it.

At eight the next morning, he and Regina ate breakfast in his parents' suite. By nine o'clock he'd showered and shaved. At 9:10 a.m. he left his suite wearing a dark gray business suit and tie. Aware his need to see Alexandra was over the top, he had to tamp down his excitement, but he couldn't prevent the explosion of his senses when she opened the door to him, the embodiment of feminine allure.

Her silver high heels added two inches, making it easier for him to capture that supple mouth wearing a light pink frost. He almost acted on his desire to taste her, but remembering who was waiting for them downstairs, he caught himself in time.

If his eyes didn't deceive him, her heart was pounding faster than normal. The diamond seemed to be in constant motion, pulsating with bursts of green light. Each beat matched the rhythm of his own heart, increasing in speed like his Ferrari.

She raised those solemn gray eyes to his. "Do I look all

right? I wouldn't want to embarrass you." Her freshly washed hair smelled of peaches, a scent he would always associate with her.

The thing about Alexandra was that she didn't have one selfish, self-absorbed, narcissistic atom in her body.

"You'll do," was all he could manage to say. In an automatic gesture he grasped her hand, twining his fingers around hers as they started down the hall.

"Where are we going?"

"To the conference room of my office on the main floor."

She flashed him an anxious glance. "You don't show it, but are you scared? Just a little bit?"

He took a steadying breath. "I was a lot scared until you opened your door just now." If she hadn't been there... If she'd run away because she couldn't go through with it after all...

"You always say and do the right thing, Lucca. Thank you for sending the manicurist and hair dresser. My nails needed help, but I'm afraid my hair is hopeless."

"I like your hair exactly the way it is. As for your nails, I've never noticed. Mama saw to those details this morning."

"Then I'll have to thank her later. Has your father forgiven me for the other night?"

"Since I'm not exactly the poster boy of perfection, either, he said your escapade convinced him we're made for each other."

"That's not very reassuring."

Lucca chuckled before giving in to the urge to kiss her neck. "All in all, we're off to a better start than I would have imagined." Just getting her to Castelmare had been a feat.

Once they reached the main floor, he caught hold of her upper arms. "You'll see a lot of government officials in there.

Don't let it bother you. Their presence will help keep the news conference civilized. Remember you're half Carlisle, half Grigory, a unique combination unlike any other."

She gave a meek nod.

He cupped her chin and raised it a trifle. "One more thing. Keep your eyes on me."

"I already planned on doing that," came her quiet response.

Their mouths were only centimeters apart. Unable to help himself, he gave a quick kiss to those pliant lips, uncaring that some of her lipstick stayed on his...a little part of her he could savor until the day came when he would taste all of her.

Carlo cleared his throat behind them. "Everyone's waiting."

"Ready?" Lucca asked her. They stared into each other's eyes for a moment. Hers were guarded. Then she surprised him by lifting her hand to wipe the lipstick off his mouth with her fingers.

"Now I am."

It reminded him of the things his mother did for his father before an important dinner or conference so he would look his best. Alexandra could have no idea how the small gesture moved him.

Binding her hand to his once more, he drew her toward the west end of the palace where the double doors of the conference room were opened wide. The buzz of voices filtered down the hall.

The president of the cabinet was officiating today. He stood at the lectern placed on a raised platform in the center of the room. Everyone was seated below him. Regina sat to the side of the lectern representing Lucca's immediate family. As soon as the statesman saw Lucca, he struck a staff to the floor several times.

"Ladies and gentlemen of the press, members of the cabinet, His Royal Highness, the Crown Prince Lucca Umberto Schiaparelli Vittorio the Fifth of Castelmare and the Princess Alexandra Carlisle Grigory."

Everyone rose to their feet and began clapping. Amidst the cheers came the inevitable shower of flashbulbs going off.

For Lucca it was a source of intense personal pride that Alexandra handled it as though she'd been born to it. All his life he'd dreaded this day coming, but that was before Alex....

CHAPTER SEVEN

KEEP your eyes on Lucca. Like a mantra Alex repeated his advice.

The huge room, as ornate and splendid as the rest of the palace, had to be filled with several hundred people if you included all the security assembled. Regina, looking beautiful in a dusky-rose suit, gloves and a broad-brimmed hat with a cluster of real roses at the side of the crown, sent her a private smile.

Alex reciprocated before ascending the platform with Lucca. A dozen microphones had been set up to carry the broadcast. It was the middle of the night in Los Angeles. By morning Alex's friends would see all this on TV at work and go into shock. Before the end of the day she would have to make phone calls of explanation to them and Mr. Watkins.

Unfortunately, she couldn't tell anyone the truth in case it ended up hurting Lucca. All she could say was that Lucca was responsible for helping her unite with her family and in the process he'd swept her off her feet.

Any woman seeing Lucca would understand how that could happen. Anyone catching sight of the green diamond fastened to her dress would agree that Alex was as greedy as her mother.

Yet strangely enough, none of it stung, because she had Lucca on her side. They'd entered into a pact to help each other. With him championing her, she had nothing to fear except an inability to get into medical school. But she wouldn't think in defeatist terms. Right now her only job was to play Lucca's adoring fiancée in front of the camcorders, a role she found came as naturally to her as breathing.

After the head of the cabinet sat down, Lucca moved to the lectern taking Alex with him. Together they faced the sea of faces.

"Ladies and gentlemen of the press, translators, members of the cabinet and their assistants," he began in English, "I've called this news conference to announce my ascendancy to the throne on the twenty-eighth of this month. My father's health demands that he step down." Lucca's voice broke, revealing the depth of his concern for his parent. In the stillness following his news, Alex slid her hand into his. He gripped it so hard, he had no idea of his strength.

"As all of you can see, I picked up something precious while I was in New York. Alexandra has consented to become my wife. Regretfully, her father, Prince Oleg Grigory, and her mother, Kathryn Carlisle, are both deceased. But it's most fortunate that her great-uncle Yuri Grigory is still alive and will walk her down the aisle.

"My parents have declared the twenty-eighth of this month a state holiday in honor of the coronation and my wedding to this wonderful woman." He lifted her hand and kissed the back of it. The barrage of flashes almost blinded her.

"Before the cabinet meeting starts, Alexandra and I will entertain a few questions now."

Too many voices called out at once. "One at a time please," Lucca said with enviable calm.

"Princess Alexandra, how does it feel to be wearing the Ligurian teardrop diamond?"

Lucca darted her an amused glance, obviously curious to know what she was going to say.

"Like I'm carrying a monument around." Her comment set off an explosion of laughter in the room that included Lucca's own deep, attractive brand. It took a minute for the noise to subside.

"Princess Alexandra?" came another voice. "How did you manage to keep your involvement with the prince a secret all this time?"

"I have my ways." Taking a risk she added, "My mother was always in the news. I learned certain tricks to remain invisible."

"Over here, Princess Alexandra—" This from a burly journalist in the corner. "Rumor has it your father had ties to the mafia in Las Vegas. Can you confirm that?"

Lucca stiffened. She could tell he was ready to intervene but she preempted him.

"Yes," she spoke clearly. "It was rumor. My father was an excellent businessman who used his own money to be successful. Sadly, his life was cut short in an airplane crash. I would give anything if he were still alive." Her voice shook.

A strong arm slipped around her waist, pulling her closer, then Lucca said, "One last question."

"Princess Alexandra?" This from an older woman journalist. "It's obvious that like your mother you could have your choice of many men, be they sheiks, royals or film stars." That was news to Alex. "What was it about Prince Lucca you couldn't resist?"

Alex needed to put on a convincing act, but it wasn't hard. She slowly smiled at him. "We met while I was in a shop. At first I mistook him for a security guard. I was in a very anxious state at the time and I'm afraid I unfairly took it out on one of the employees.

"When Lucca intervened, I assumed he'd been watching and had decided to take charge. We exchanged words. Actually I flung insults at him and demanded to know if he was going to have me arrested. In his maddeningly reasonable way he assured me nothing could be further from the truth and suggested I sit down. Now when I look back on the incident, I realize he'd used his monarch voice on me."

Laughter burst from the audience. Lucca eyed her with a devilish gleam.

"The man had so much charm that before long I discovered I was having the time of my life. When he finally admitted who he was, I'm afraid I was hooked." At this point she fought to keep her voice steady.

"I say afraid because I didn't want him to be a prince, but once the heart feels that pull, you have no choice in the matter. He more or less took me away, but not to prison, thank heaven. Of course, the fact that he was easily the most attractive man I'd ever met didn't hurt the situation any."

Everyone jumped to their feet cheering and clapping their approval, but not Lucca. He studied her out of dark, veiled eyes, his expression suddenly indecipherable. Had she said too much? Was he worried what his lover would make of it?

Honesty was usually the best policy, but maybe not in this case. Her off-the-cuff speech would be circling the world before long. It was too late to recall it.

Lucca let go of her hand and put both of his on the lectern. "As you have deduced," he began in his deep voice, "our marriage is going to be a lively, twenty-first-century version of thrills."

The crowd gave them a standing ovation. He waited for the din to subside before he said, "I want to thank those members of the media for coming. Because of the cabinet's urgent business now that my father is stepping down, we would appreciate it if you cleared the conference room so our meeting can begin."

On cue the cameramen and reporters started to exit the room. While the president of the cabinet engaged Lucca in conversation, Regina came running up to Alex. "You were wonderful," she whispered, catching hold of her arm.

Alex hadn't seen her leave her seat. "Thanks, Regina, but I'm afraid I said too much."

"No. It was perfect!" she argued. "I've been dying to learn how you met, but you know my close-mouthed brother. I saw everyone's reaction, Alexandra. They love you. *I* love you for loving my brother so much. He badly needs to be loved by a woman like you."

Lucca was already badly loved by a woman, but Regina didn't know that. However, the sincerity of her words made Alex realize she'd pulled off her part of the agreement with Lucca. If Regina could accept they were a love match, then she wasn't worried about other people.

"Come on," Regina urged. "Papa and Mama asked me to bring you to their suite after the news conference. Lucca will be tied up all day."

That's what Alex feared. The hours dragged when she wasn't with him. "All right."

"Lucca?" she called to her brother who was busy talking to several men by now. He turned his head in their direction. "We're going upstairs."

"I'll join you later." His glance swerved to Alex. She saw a nerve throbbing at the corner of his jaw. "You had them eating out of your hand, Alexandra."

Then why aren't you happy about it? Alex didn't understand his unexpected change of mood, but she couldn't ask him about it. At this juncture the press of dignitaries surrounding him had grown.

Averting her eyes, she turned her attention back to Regina. They left through a private door at the rear of the room. "After we've checked in with my parents, I thought you might like a tour of the grounds."

"I'd love it, but I have another Italian lesson at two with Professor Morelli."

"There'll be time for both." She gave Alex a sideways glance. "I saw him on the stairs after he left the schoolroom yesterday. Apparently Professor Emilio is ill."

"That's what I understand."

"He's very nice looking."

Alex smiled. "I agree. He's a terrific teacher, too."

One of Regina's brows lifted. "Does Lucca know about the change?"

"Yes."

"Ah, that explains it."

"Explains what?" Alex prodded.

"Lucca's mood at breakfast after Mama asked if you'd begun your Italian lessons. He didn't seem to want to talk about it."

"You know he did seem a little offish after I introduced him to Tomaso. I assumed he was disappointed Professor Emilio couldn't make it."

A knowing smile broke out on Regina's face. "My brother's jealous."

"Don't be silly, Regina. I've done nothing to make him feel that way."

"You don't have to. It's an emotion completely new to him. I love seeing him out of control for once."

Alex couldn't afford to protest too much. "I think you're wrong."

"Better not refer to Professor Morelli as Tomaso in front of him," she said.

"Does that mean I'm breaking some kind of royal protocol to address him by his first name?"

"Of course not, but you don't know my brother like I do. At least not yet. He has a possessive streak about certain things he considers his."

"I *am* his," she blurted. Sort of. Come to think of it, he was pretty obsessed over her wearing his pin all the time.

"You and I both know that. However, to be safe I implore you to be formal with Tomaso in front of Lucca and whatever you do, don't praise your teacher. Lucca would never be able to handle it."

Alex broke into laughter. She couldn't help it, but Regina remained serious. "Laugh if you want, but don't say I didn't warn you."

At quarter to three that afternoon Alex was reminded of their conversation when Lucca came striding into the schoolroom unannounced. He was still dressed in the stunning gray suit he'd worn for the press conference. Her breath caught at the magnificent sight of him.

She'd been working on the next chapter in her Italian book while she waited for Tomaso. Evidently he'd been held up at the university and was running late.

"Hi," was all she could get out.

"Hi, yourself." He removed his elegant suit jacket and

flung it over a chair. Then he removed his tie and rolled up the sleeves of his immaculate white shirt to the elbow, revealing bronzed arms.

"P-Professor Morelli's late," she tripped over the word because she almost said Tomaso. "So I've just been studying."

Lucca sat down at the desk facing her. He flashed her a look of male admiration. She'd changed clothes and was wearing a soft orange linen wraparound dress he'd admired on her at the boutique. Her only adornment was the pin. "He won't be coming anymore. I'll instruct you every day until Professor Emilio is well enough to do it."

Joy.

Remembering Regina's warning, she said, "I'm glad because I'd rather be taught by you." Her comment seemed to smooth the waters a little. She took advantage of the silence. "How did the cabinet meeting go?"

"Fine," he answered, but she could tell his mind wasn't on government affairs. "Every man in the room envied me today."

"They can envy you all they want, but could any of them make as good a king?"

"You know damn well I wasn't referring to the title," his voice rasped.

Adrenaline gushed through her veins. "How do you say damn in Italian? I think I should learn some curse words. In the States all the foreigners can swear in English before they say anything else."

A quick smile transformed his chiseled features. "Like English, Italian has many subtleties," he said in a more relaxed tone. "You can say *managgia*. The slang for it is *accidenti*. A politer version is *diavolo*."

Her head flew back. "I heard you say that word the other day."

"So I did." He suddenly shoved himself away from the desk and stood up. "Let's get out of here. You can work on those words while we take a drive."

She rolled her eyes. "Something tells me they're going to come in handy."

He let out a bark of laughter before reaching for his coat and tie. "Have you ever ridden on the back of a motorcycle before?"

A thrill of excitement ran through her body. "No."

"You said you liked speed. I'm going to take you at your word."

Almost jumping out of her skin in anticipation, she hurried over to the door ahead of him. "I'll need to change first."

"Meet me in the north portico in ten minutes. Wear those blue jeans you bought yesterday. On our way out of town, we'll pick up the rest of the items you'll need."

"All right."

She reached her room breathless over their plans, but when she discovered all the phone messages waiting for her from the States, they brought her back to the grim reality that every gesture on Lucca's part was meant for show.

Outwardly he was carrying on his role as the ardent fiancé but she'd be a much greater fool than her mother if she allowed herself to stay in denial about his deepest feelings. There *was* another woman. He'd told her in the car on the way to airport.

In order not to displease his parents, Alex was beginning to think he intended to stay away from his lover until the honeymoon was over. When Lucca had talked about his work schedule, he'd told Alex that after he performed his royal duties each day, he would indulge his other interests. She'd known what he'd meant, but it was getting harder and harder to accept.

Deflated by the unpalatable truth about her deepest feelings, she checked each message. All of them could wait except the one from Manny. *SOS, Alex. Must talk to you immediately! Call me no matter what time it is! This could settle all your mother's debts and then some!*

Her heart thudded in her chest. How was that possible?

She quickly returned the call. He picked up on the second ring. "You're a good girl for calling me back so fast, Alex. How would you like to be a very, very rich one in no time at all?"

"Were mother's real diamonds found?" she cried.

"No, no, honey. Those are long gone."

Her brief elation dissipated. She sank down on the side of the bed. "Then I don't understand."

"Listen to me and don't interrupt. Can you do that?"

If she didn't get downstairs soon, Lucca would come looking for her. "Yes—if you make it quick. I'm on my way out the door."

"I've got the part of the century for you!"

She frowned. "What are you talking about, Manny?"

"Oh, honey, after seeing your beautiful face splashed all over the news and the Internet this morning, you're the only one who can play it."

"Play what?"

"*Garbo!* I've got the script in my hand. Every actress in Hollywood wants the part. None of them can do it. They don't have what it takes. You do! Come home, Alex. I've already got the audition arranged for you."

She shot to her feet. "Manny, I'm not an actress!"

"Ah, honey…you've been around it all your life."

It was hard to breathe. "If you saw me on TV, then you'd know I'm getting married."

"You can work around that. The point is, you can carry off the role so people will believe you're Garbo. I just talked to Michelle. She agrees with that me you've got those great bones—everything it takes including her sad eyes.

"Between your portrayal, plus the fact that you're Kathryn's daughter and the consort of Prince Vittorio of Castelmare, the box-office take will be *in the millions.* One film of the definitive Garbo, honey. Just one and you'll be on easy street for the rest of your life!"

And you'll get paid what mother owed you within the year instead of ten or twelve years from now.

For the first time in all these years, she was beginning to realize the kind of pressure her mother had lived under. Manny said and did all the right things. He was a master manipulator.

Alex's mind went back to the conversation with her Uncle Yuri:

"My mother was married six times," she'd said.

"I can understand why you're frightened. But think about this. Maybe part of it's because she lost Oleg, and maybe the other part is because she didn't have parents to teach her what a good marriage is all about. Hmm?" Yuri had told her.

There was a familiar rap on the door. "Alexandra?"

"I'll be right there, Lucca," she called out, then put the phone back to her ear. "Listen, Manny. I have to go."

"No way. Whatever else you have to do can wait."

She took a deep breath. "I'm afraid it can't, Manny. I'll have to call you later."

"When? This thing is big, honey. An opportunity like this only comes knocking once in a lifetime."

Manny never gave up!

Oh, Mother, he must have had you bound up so tightly, is it any wonder you tried to find escape with other men?

Her hand gripped the phone tighter. She could hardly concentrate for the knocking on the outer door, which was growing louder. "I realize that. Give me some time to think about it." She didn't want to hurt Manny, after all he was still waiting for his money. On the other hand she had to consider Lucca and the agreement she'd entered into with him. "I have to hang up now."

She dropped the phone on the receiver and ran through the suite. "Lucca? I need two more minutes."

"Are you all right?" he demanded.

"Y-yes."

"You don't sound it. Do you need help?"

"No...I'll be right there."

Alex half hopped out of her dress as she hurried to the dresser for the jeans and top she planned to wear. She'd barely slipped on her separates when Lucca entered her bedroom wearing jeans, a blue T-shirt beneath a black bomber-type leather jacket and riding boots. He looked fantastic.

"I'm not going to apologize for invading your privacy," he said worriedly, breathing hard. "You're as pale as parchment. After what you had to face this morning, it wouldn't surprise me if you're sick to your stomach. There's no way I'm taking you out on my motorcycle when you're ill."

Brushing a lock of hair off her forehead, she brazened out his intimate scrutiny. "I...I had a personal phone call I couldn't ignore," her voice faltered.

He folded his strong arms. His eyes glittered ominously. "Personal? From whom?"

"It was Manny, but it doesn't concern you. Like I said, it was personal."

"And might I ask who this Manny is who demands your attention but who is of no concern to me? Is he perhaps a former lover who saw you on the early-morning news in Los Angeles?"

"What?"

"Come on, Alexandra. You don't have to continue to lie to me. Clearly there is someone important in your life back home...a love interest—"

"I told you before there is no one. Thank you for having so much faith in me." She let the sarcasm fly.

He stared her down. "Today we told the whole world we're going to be married. I have a right to know who the man is who could change your entire countenance in an instant."

"Why is it you have to know *his* name when you haven't felt inclined to divulge *your* lover's name to me? I thought you trusted me, or isn't our marriage going to be on an equal footing after all? Wasn't it you who said no secrets?"

When his gaze slid away from hers, Alex knew she had him, but it gave her no joy. She sat down in the nearest upholstered chair. "I thought we could be friends, Lucca. The last thing I want to do is fight with you."

The tension between them was combustible. "How long have you known him?"

"A long time, but it's not what you think." She didn't want to tell him about this. Not today of all days.

"It never is," he ground out.

She shook her head in bewilderment. "For the sake of

argument, isn't that what you wanted? To present a united front in public, but live private lives behind the scenes?"

He raked a bronzed hand through his black hair. "That was your invention, not mine."

"Invention—" Too shaken to talk, she got to her feet. "I...I think you'd better leave and we'll talk later when we've both had a chance to cool down."

"If you think that's going to happen, then you haven't got a clue about me."

She had every intention of going to her bedroom, but he blocked the way. "We'll sort this out now." He'd closed in on her.

"Lucca—" Alex had this suffocating feeling in her chest.

He reached for her. "I love the way you say my name in that husky voice," he murmured against her lips. Then his mouth closed over hers with a hunger she would never have imagined. This wasn't like the other times. Not anything like the other times.

He clamped her hard against him, eliminating any air between them. The feel of his powerful legs against hers was so erotic they almost buckled. She clung helplessly to him.

"Kiss me back, Alexandra. I need to taste your mouth. It was agony to have to walk away from you this morning and face a crowd when it was the last thing I wanted to do."

His confession was a revelation that broke down her defenses. She found herself melting against him, giving him a response not even she was prepared for. Their kisses turned molten. Like rivers of fire they merged in an explosion of flame, consuming everything in their path. She lost track of time and surroundings.

When he finally allowed her to breathe, she was delirious with yearnings he'd brought to life, exposing her to herself. She'd never slept with a man, but she was precariously close to begging Lucca to make love to her. Once that happened she would despise herself for the same weakness that had driven her mother into so many men's arms.

"Tell me something my sweet, vulnerable Alexandra—" he nibbled her neck and throat, deepening her desire "—is your relationship with Manny this passionate? Do you give yourself so completely to him, too, when he reaches for you?"

His questions penetrated her consciousness.

Lucca was jealous!

Despite Regina's insistence, Alex hadn't believed he was capable of that emotion. Yet the way he was acting now made her wonder.

Lucca was a man and could separate his emotions. Italian men particularly were noted for having a wife who bore their children and a lover who fulfilled their fantasies. Being his fiancée, she didn't fit in either category yet, and he was sexually frustrated. As Regina had told her, Lucca was a possessive man. After he learned the truth about Manny, his ardor would cool.

Her hands slid from the back of his neck. "Lucca, Manny Horowitz is in his fifties. He's probably the most sought-after agent in Hollywood and one of the nicest.

"When my mother was eighteen, he discovered her singing in a nightclub. After pulling her out of obscurity, he built her career and stuck with her until the very end. She repaid him by still owing him two million dollars when she died. He's never asked me for one dime of it."

Lucca kneaded her shoulders while he stared into her eyes. "Until today. Is that what made you ill? Was he hoping you would ask me for the money and you were afraid to approach me? I'll send it to him right now."

No. Her head moved from side to side in a drugged-like state.

"You know I'd give it to you in an instant."

Tears stung her eyelids. "I know, but his request had nothing to do with you."

"After the news conference, you expect me to believe that?"

"Yes," she answered soberly.

"Why are you so reluctant to tell me what his phone call was all about?"

Moisture bathed her cheeks. "Because I'm tempted to do what he wants, but it would mean asking something of you that wouldn't be fair."

"Is it illegal or immoral?" He was being perfectly serious.

"Worse. Do you remember saying that ours wouldn't be an orthodox marriage?"

Lucca kissed her moist eyelids for his answer.

She couldn't handle his tenderness and moved out of his arms. "I'll be right back."

Once Alex reached the bathroom, she washed her face and freshened up. When she returned to the bedroom, she found him out on the balcony with his back toward her. After the brief rapture they'd shared where she'd all but given herself away, she approached him with trepidation.

"What if I told you there was a way for me to pay back the twelve million dollars within the year?"

He turned around, resting his hip against the railing in a totally masculine stance. Those dark, intelligent eyes looked their fill. "I take it Manny wants to turn you into an even greater film star than your mother." His gravelly voice sounded like it had escaped from a hidden grotto.

"One movie. The revenue would solve all my financial problems."

Lucca shifted his weight. "I still don't understand your dilemma."

She took a second breath. "Don't you?"

His face lost expression. "You want out of our arrangement?"

"I would never do that to you."

"You want my permission to make the movie?"

"I'm not asking for that either," she cried in anguish, "but when you compare three or four months of work to maybe ten to twelve years if not much longer for the same kind of money... Manny says the revenue will surpass anything in recent history. Just think—I could pay him and the creditors right away."

Lines marred his features. "What's the movie about?"

Alex rubbed her arms nervously. "The life of Greta Garbo."

He pursed his lips. "I can't imagine anyone more perfect than you to impersonate her, but the answer is no, Alexandra. I need a *wife,* not an actress!"

"You don't have to sound so angry about it," she fired back, wounded. "I've tried to do everything you've asked of me. Why are you being so unfair?"

His eyes narrowed. "Whatever happened to your dreams of becoming a plastic surgeon?"

"That hasn't changed. I wish—"

"You wish we hadn't met?" he finished for her. "It's too late for that." The bleakness of his tone devastated her.

"Those are your thoughts, Lucca, not mine."

"Then what are you saying?"

"I'm saying that whatever I do, it's not right for you."

"Suppose you let me be the judge of my needs."

"When you say that, it makes me feel like you're carrying the whole burden."

"You see our relationship as a burden?" came the frosty query.

"No," she cried. "Now you're twisting my words, but let's face it. I bring a lot of excess baggage to the wedding," she mumbled, fighting her chaotic emotions. "You heard that journalist ask about my father."

"You handled him beautifully."

"Only because you gave me confidence. You see, Lucca?" She eyed him directly. "You don't have *any* baggage." Except for the woman he loved. She would always have to remain unexposed.

Alex heard his sharp intake of breath. "Everyone has baggage, but I don't put your parents in that category any more than I do my own. Forget Manny's proposition and come with me."

She sniffed. "You mean, you're still in the mood?"

His sudden smile transformed him into a man five years younger. She could hardly keep up with his mercurial behavior. "When we're talking about my motorcycle, always."

Since he was making an effort, she would to. "I'd love it. Let's go."

Once they'd gone downstairs, he put her into the limo, then took off on a black-and-silver sport bike without any sign of the Vittorio royal crest. In his leathers and black helmet, no one would guess he was the prince.

Good luck to his bodyguards trying to keep up with him.

The chauffeur drove Alex to a motorcycle dealership where they outfitted her with her own helmet and boots.

While she was trying on a leather jacket, Lucca walked in, bigger than life. He checked to be sure it was the right size. After tossing her a pair of gloves, they left through the rear door.

Lucca got on the cycle first. "This is the best part, Alexandra. All day I've been waiting to feel those fabulous legs of yours tucked around mine." Heat filled her cheeks. "Climb on and hold me tight around the waist. We're going for a ride to Eze."

"Eze?"

"When we get there, you won't need an explanation."

He told her how to get on and made certain she was comfortable.

"Ready?"

She gave the thumb's-up signal.

Down went his face mask. He revved the motor and wound his way through a couple of back streets to the main road. Progress was slow. She feared he was driving this way on purpose not to frighten her. But that's what she got for thinking, because the second they reached the coast highway he opened her up and let it rip.

There ought to be a better word than *ecstasy,* but she couldn't think of one. All she could do was cling to his leather-clad torso and let him do all the work. He drove like a pro racer, weaving in and out of traffic with precision. She had a legitimate excuse to press against his strong back and relished the sensation.

They whizzed by a sign for Ventimiglia. Soon the signs were written in French. They passed through Menton and came to Monaco. Then they began the climb up the Moyenne Corniche road. Alex had seen films portraying this area between Monte Carlo and Nice, but nothing took the place of being here in person, clutching Lucca as if her life depended on it. The realization came to Alex he *was* her whole life.

She saw the sign for Eze before they reached it. The medieval village sat perched like an eagle's nest on a rocky peak overlooking the Mediterranean. But unlike the tiny hamlet of "crag," this spot was offset by a multitude of souvenir shops and streets full of tourists.

Lucca pulled to the side of the road across the road from a shop and shut off the motor. She jumped down first and removed her helmet. He followed suit, his eyes never straying from her face. "What do you think?"

Alex studied him briefly. With his hair disheveled from the helmet, she thought him the most exciting man in existence. "I think riding with you is going to become my addiction."

Something flickered in the darkest recesses of his eyes. "I'm pleased to hear it. What about the view?"

What view? Being with Lucca blotted out everything else from her consciousness.

CHAPTER EIGHT

LUCCA was still trying to recover from that moment of ecstasy in her arms and the period of agony that followed.

"Well, what do you think?" he queried again just to say something to break the silence.

"It's stupendous, but then, so is the one from Dirupo where civilization hasn't encroached. Did I pronounce *Dirupo* right?" Alex answered breathlessly.

"Perfettamente."

"I'm serious."

"So am I. There was no trace of an American accent just then."

"Thank you. With only one word to pronounce, there shouldn't be." She rolled her eyes, an unconscious trait he never tired of watching. "Wait until I try to string a sentence together. But I'll keep working on it, Lucca, for you."

"You sound charming."

"Americans don't sound charming. Ours isn't a charming language."

A smile lifted the corner of his mouth. "Who told you that?"

"No one. You can simply tell. The way you speak Italian, Lucca, it sounds beautiful, like melted butter dripping all over the place. Americans speak English like they're spewing meat through a grinder, plopping big globs everywhere."

Lucca thought he'd heard everything, but that wasn't the case because he never knew what was going to come out of that succulent mouth. Earlier it had given him a heart attack. Right now he couldn't stop laughing.

"You see?" She grinned. "I was right."

He held up his hands. "As they say in your country, I plead the Fifth."

"Always the diplomat, and brilliant besides," she muttered.

Once his shoulders stopped shaking he said, "Are you hungry?"

"Yes! You didn't know your grocery bill was going to go up when you took me on."

He chuckled once more. "It's worth the price for the pleasure of your entertaining company. Let's go inside the *epicerie* across the road. You choose the items for our picnic."

"And what will you do?"

"Hold the basket for you."

After he took both their helmets and locked them on his bike, he slid his hand up her back to her tender neck and guided her toward the store. In the open doorway was an inviting display of fruits and vegetables.

All the little signs were in French, but she'd learned her first Italian lesson on foods well enough to impress him. "We'll have *pane, mela, formaggio* and *suco d'uva*." She dropped the items in the basket. Darting him an impish glance she said, "Can we afford dessert?"

"What do you have your eye on?"

"Anything. You choose."

"Done." He took two napoleons from the plate and put

them in the basket. They moved to the counter so he could pay. It had been too long since Lucca had enjoyed this kind of fun with a woman.

As he was putting his wallet back in his jeans his cell phone rang. It was Carlo. *"Si?"*

"Someone broke through the blockade and rammed into your cycle!"

"Accidenti!"

Alexandra knew that word well enough and shot him an anxious glance. He turned away from her.

"We don't know if it was intentional. Leave through the back door where the limo's waiting to drive you to the helicopter."

"Capisco." He hung up.

"Lucca?"

"No time for explanations now. Come with me."

Paolo was there to help hustle her through the back of the shop to the alley. A dozen of Lucca's people hovered around three limos. Now that he had Alexandra to worry about, he was thankful for the added security.

"What's wrong?" she begged after they drove away.

"Some crazy ran into the motorcycle."

"Oh, no—"

"It might have been accidental. Whatever the explanation, I'm not taking any chances with you."

Another minute and they arrived at the helipad where he helped her into the helicopter. Within seconds it lifted off and he could relax.

"Sorry about our picnic, *bellissima.* Another time."

"Do you think I care?" she cried softly. "What if someone was intentionally trying to hurt you?"

"It's happened before."

She shuddered. "I'll never complain about Carlo and Paolo again." Her eyes searched his. "This will be all over the news. What will you father say when he finds out? It could set him back."

"By now he's already been told you and I escaped any injury," Lucca muttered morosely. "Until the coronation, we'll maintain a low profile. That'll keep both him and my mother happy."

"Lucca?" He could hear her mind working. "Do you always plan exactly where you're going to be at any given moment?"

He clasped the hand closest to him. "Pretty much."

"That kind of kills any spontaneity on your part."

"*Si.*"

"It must be hard on your security people, too."

"I'm afraid there'll be times when it'll be much harder on you."

"Forget me."

Then he might as well quit breathing. "We're almost home. I'm afraid I'm going to be tied up for a while with the debriefing. Do me a favor and relax. I'll have dinner sent up to your room. Feel free to explore any part of the palace you like. If it's possible, I'll join you later."

"That won't be necessary. I'm going to work on my next lesson and impress you."

If she did any more to impress him, he was seriously thinking of a honeymoon before the ceremony.

Besides today's incident, which brought home as nothing else could the fact that Alexandra's life had been in danger, he needed to get his security people to do a thorough background check on Manny Horowitz. Lucca wanted to know chapter and verse about the man preying on Alex. The phone call from her mother's agent was the one contingency he hadn't conceived of when contemplating the many obstacles to their marriage.

He didn't really believe she had a romantic interest in Manny, but he didn't want her going near the man no matter the reason. The desire to pay off her mother's debts had driven her to fall in with Lucca's plans, but even he could see how Manny's offer held great appeal. A love of acting could be in her blood and she just didn't know it yet. Alexandra was a Carlisle after all, still young and damnably vulnerable.

The woman journalist had been right. Alexandra could have any man she wanted. Some idiot actor could get to her. There'd be physical intimacy on the set with the men playing opposite her. She could be enticed to do another picture and another. It would be an escape from the prison she'd walked into by agreeing to marry him. One day she'd want her freedom and reach for it without looking back.

That wasn't the way Lucca intended for things to happen. That wasn't acceptable. *"Maledizzione!"*

He felt a light touch on his arm. "Lucca? Does that mean damn or hell?"

Alexandra, Alexandra.

Regina rushed down the steps to embrace them. She cried something in Italian to Lucca before remembering to speak English.

"Are you all right?" she asked Alex, her eyes full of concern.

Before Alex could answer, Lucca pressed a hard kiss to her mouth. "I'll see you later," he whispered. After tweaking Regina's cheek he took the steps two at a time to the second floor.

His physical demonstrations of love for the benefit of the family were getting more difficult for Alex to handle when she knew the real reason behind them. Trying to ward off the latest assault on her senses, she linked her arm through Regina's and they finished climbing the stairs to the second floor. Both of them watched his swift progress down the hall toward their parents' suite.

"Thank God nothing happened to you." Regina sounded shaken. Slowly they moved in the direction of their own bedrooms.

"I had no idea anything was going on. We were in a small grocery store and suddenly Lucca told me we had to leave."

"Then you don't know?" his sister cried.

"About the motorcycle, yes."

"No." She shook her head. "The police uncovered a plot to assassinate Lucca. It won't have been the first time. He had a close call in Rio a year ago while he was there doing business."

"How close?"

"He was shot."

Alex gasped.

"Carlo was able to deflect the bullet. It lodged in Lucca's shoulder instead of his heart."

She squeezed her eyes together. For a moment Alex felt sick to her stomach. Lucca had been so clever in playing down the trouble today, she had no clue of the magnitude of the situation.

"He's all right, Alexandra. So far four men have been arrested, one of them a plant at the motorcycle dealership Lucca patronizes."

"We were just there," her voice trailed shakily.

Regina nodded. "Intelligence says two more men are

involved but have left the country. It's because they don't want Lucca on the throne. Since Papa's illness last year, Lucca has virtually run the government. His rigid policy for closed immigration borders and strict banking laws has frustrated certain elements as you can imagine."

"Do you agree with him?"

"Absolutely. Papa has stopped short of allowing electronic eavesdropping for surveillance to go on, but once Lucca is king, all that is going to change and the enemy knows it."

Alex shuddered. "He'll never be safe, will he?"

"No, but his first duty is to keep the rest of us safe."

Regina sounded like a queen herself.

"That explains why there was so much extra security at the House of Savoy in New York."

Her dark head whipped around. "So that was the shop you referred to at the press conference? I've been dying to know where your great love affair began."

Alex moaned inwardly. "He was in the security room with his bodyguards and saw me on one of the monitors getting upset with the head jeweler."

"My brother can't make a move without a small army protecting him."

The reason Lucca hadn't been to see his lover was no longer a mystery. It looked like it was time for Regina to know everything. Until his sister was armed with the whole truth about the reason for their engagement, Alex wouldn't be able to help him.

"Regina? Will you have dinner with me in my room?"

"I was going to suggest we eat together. Mama and Papa want to be alone with Lucca."

"I'm sure he wants that, too, if only to reassure them he won't be planning any more crazy outings with me."

"They're not crazy." His sister sounded mournful. "He just wants to live a normal life like other men."

Alex opened the door to her suite. "There's something else he wants, Regina."

"What do you mean?"

The way she asked that question in all naiveté led Alex to believe Lucca's sister really didn't know about his secret love.

He was a private man who gave so little away, you had to have radar to catch the slips. Alex had a private nature, too. Maybe that was why she'd been able to pick up on them.

"Come inside and let's talk."

Once they'd ordered a sandwich, Alex took off her new leather jacket and boots and curled up on one end of the couch. Regina slipped out of her sandals and tucked her legs beneath her on the chair facing Alex.

"Regina…what I'm going to tell you has to stay between us."

She crossed herself. "I swear it."

Alex sat forward. "You're going to fight me on it."

Lucca's sister looked utterly bewildered. After a long pause she said, "I promise I won't."

"Grazie." Both women smiled at each other with a perfect understanding.

"Your brother's in love."

"I know. He's so madly in love with you, I'm euphoric. So are my parents. None of us thought it would or could happen. When he asked me to meet him at the plane, I knew he'd reached the darkest point in his life and needed me. I'm afraid that's why I fell apart the moment I saw him. I was so upset for him, I didn't realize you were standing nearby."

"He's a better actor than my mother ever was."

Alex waited for those words to sink in before she continued.

"There's a commoner he's been in love with for a long time. I don't know her name. We don't discuss her. I have no idea if she's Castelmarian, French, Italian, British, Australian or American, or from somewhere else entirely for that matter. I'm presuming they spend their time together whenever he leaves the country to go on those six-week business trips."

Regina stayed true to her word. She didn't make a sound, but suddenly her lovely face was all brown eyes.

"If she *is* one of your countrywomen, then the heightened security would explain why he hasn't tried to be with her since our arrival. However, I'm digressing from the main point which is this—your brother and I are getting married to solve two problems that appeared insoluble to us both until we met. Love doesn't come into it and never did."

Alex waited for lightning to strike her dead. When it didn't, she unloaded on poor Regina who sat there for the next five minutes looking shell-shocked. "So now you understand everything."

The words had scarcely left her mouth when the maid knocked and brought in a tray. After thanking her and seeing her to the door, Alex walked back to Regina.

"What I need you to do is go to him in private and tell him that you know the truth. Convince him I want to help him so he can be with her before the wedding. She needs an explanation.

"He'll be furious with me, but I don't care. His happiness and safety are more important to me than anything else in this world." Her voice trembled. "I know you feel the same way. On the plane I witnessed that love."

Regina's eyes filled, but she continued to remain silent.

"I have a plan." One that had been burning up Alex's mind during the motorcycle ride to Eze. The scare after they'd been shopping for a picnic had set the seal on it. "Tell Lucca it will enable him to be with her right away without worrying about anyone's safety.

"When he asks why I didn't talk to him about this myself, tell him I didn't think he would take me seriously. But I knew he'd listen to you because he loves and trusts you, Regina. We both need your support if this is going to work."

Alex took another fortifying breath. "You, above all people, know how much he's suffered over the years knowing he would have to marry someone he didn't love. It shouldn't have to happen to anyone. My mother went in and out of six marriages. None of them worked, and her life was a ruin.

"I don't want that for Lucca. He's the most unselfish, wonderful man in the world and deserves every happiness. With your backing we can help make his life bearable. Will you do it?" she implored.

Regina's solemn eyes stared at her for the longest time. "How could I not? What's your plan?"

Lucca bade the head of security good-night. It was close to midnight. Much as he wanted to talk to Alexandra, he would have to wait until tomorrow. She'd be asleep by now. Though he was exhausted, it was the emotional kind. He was positive he wouldn't be able to sleep yet and opted to go for a swim in the pool in front of the palace.

He slipped out the south entrance into the warm night air and ambled down the steps. After leaving his T-shirt and jeans in a pile, he removed his socks and boots. For the sake of propriety because he was never solely alone, he kept on his boxers and dove into the tepid water.

On his tenth lap he heard a splash. Was it Alexandra?

His heart practically leaped out of his chest until he realized it was his sister doing the breaststroke toward him, leaving him fiercely disappointed.

Lucca's sister was a champion swimmer. Still, he couldn't help but wonder what had brought her out here this time of night.

"*Ao, piccina.*"

"*Ciao, fratello mio.* I've been waiting to talk to you. This is the perfect spot." They both treaded water.

"You sound serious tonight."

"I am."

Some nuance in her voice convinced him. "Did the parents send you?"

"No."

"I give up. What's on your mind?"

"Alexandra has told me everything."

"Everything covers a lot of territory," he teased, not liking the direction this conversation had taken.

"Please let me talk until I'm finished. This time I won't let you put me off because you're uncomfortable."

He tossed his head back to stop the water from dripping in his eyes. "Is that what I do?"

"When it gets too personal, yes, it's exactly what you do. Like you're doing right now."

"Consider me suitably chastened."

"Lucca…I know the real reason why Alexandra is going to marry you. While you fund her tuition for medical school, she'll play the loving fiancée to get you off the hook. She told me all about the fake diamonds and her mother's debts. I understand she plans to pay them off by earning the money. It does her great credit."

"I agree."

"What I don't understand is why you told her you were in love with someone else when we both know it's not true?"

"That's my business."

"Not any longer, but I'm beginning to understand why she asked for my help. You can be forbidding over the things you hold most dear. Did you know she has an elaborate plan to help you and your supposed lover spend some time together before the wedding without putting you at risk? I think it's the most selfless thing I ever heard of."

"Go on." He couldn't wait to hear the rest. Alexandra's mind fascinated him.

"She has to fly to Los Angeles to finish closing up her apartment."

A tight band constricted his breathing. "How is that supposed to aid me?" It seemed his fiancée had conveniently left Manny out of the conversation with his sister.

No way was Lucca going to let her go near him, not since his security people had found out the agent had a lot more to do with her mother's bankruptcy than anyone had let on. He'd been taking huge cuts out of her income for years and figured he could do the same with Alexandra. Lucca would protect her from that barracuda at all costs.

"She'll be coming right back, Lucca. When she returns to Castelmare, she intends to bring a friend with her for the upcoming wedding. That friend will be your fictional lover."

"For once I have to confess I'm speechless."

"You haven't heard anything yet! Alexandra's done makeup for years and says that if you're worried about anyone recognizing your girlfriend, she can change her looks enough so that no one could identify her. I'd say it was a master plan. She even thinks they'll stay in the blue suite together where you can have access to her."

Santo Cielo!

Only Alexandra could have concocted anything so diabolically clever and insane at the same time. Today's assassination attempt had brought out that deep well of compassion inside her. In the process she'd inveigled his tender-hearted sister, who'd worried over his secret sadness for too many years.

He moved to the edge of the pool and levered himself up onto the deck. Regina climbed out behind him. "You can't let this lie go on any longer. She deserves the truth. Why have you allowed her to go on believing something so outrageous?"

"I have my reasons." Lucca was still waiting for Sofia to return his call and release him from the promise he'd made to keep her plans a secret. The newscast announcing his forthcoming marriage to Alexandra had already devastated Sofia's parents. There'd been phone calls to his parents. The sooner Sofia explained everything to her parents, the sooner the pain, for everyone, could end.

"Don't take too long to be honest with her. She wants to leave for Los Angeles right away."

He pulled on his jeans. After he'd gathered his other clothes, they returned to the palace. When they reached the second floor, he said, "I'll talk to her tomorrow afternoon."

"Why don't you tell her first thing in the morning?"

"Because Papa has to go into the hospital for blood work and Mama wants me there. I'll be back in time to give Alexandra another Italian lesson."

"What do you mean another?"

"Until Professor Emilio returns, I've decided to take a break from my work schedule to give her some of my time each afternoon."

In the privacy of the schoolroom he would tell her about Manny, who'd used her mother mercilessly. Lucca would do anything to protect her. He hoped this new information would help her develop a more-positive view of her parent.

Regina eyed him speculatively. "Are you sure you want to do that?"

"You don't approve?"

"Of course, but cut her a little slack. Not everyone is the scary perfectionist you are. I ought to know. *Buonanotte.*"

Alex left for the schoolroom in a nervous state. She thought by now she would have heard from Lucca. A phone call. Anything. But he'd been out of touch. So had Regina, who, Alex had found out the day before, volunteered at an animal shelter run by her family.

The local news channel had been showing repeated clips of the smashed motorcycle followed by photos of the men arrested. She could follow bits and pieces of the Italian coverage because she'd been part of the story.

Though there were no clips of her and Lucca on his sport bike, they replayed segments from the broadcast showing him kissing the back of her hand. The television audience could be forgiven for thinking the crown prince was truly in love.

Had his lover seen the coverage? How could she stand to know he might have been killed yesterday? How could she bear to see him with Alex?

"Buon pomeriggio, Alexandra."

Her heart did a kick. *"Buon pomeriggio, Lucca."*

She didn't quite know what to expect this afternoon. If Regina had found an opportunity to talk to him already, then there was no telling how angry he was that his sister had learned the truth behind their engagement. Even if he adored Regina, he would consider that Alex had broken a sacred trust.

Right now she couldn't gauge his frame of mind. Being a royal he'd learned how to present a facade that gave nothing away.

Today he'd dispensed with a suit in favor of chinos and a dark green pullover. He always smelled wonderful. Afraid to be caught staring, she quickly averted her eyes and opened up her notebook to the exercises she'd written out.

He walked by her desk and reached for it. His arm brushed against her shoulder, reminding her of the way he'd made her feel when he'd crushed her against his hard body yesterday. She was a fool to expect a repeat performance, but the sensual part of her nature ached to experience those sensations again.

Until Lucca had aroused her passion, she'd thought she was one of those women who couldn't get worked up over a man, probably because of her mother's pattern of going from one unsatisfying relationship to another. Yet all he'd had to do was pluck her from the Grigory royal tree—yes, plucked—and after he'd taken one bite, she'd practically begged to be devoured whole.

"No mistakes," he muttered. "*Molto bene.* Now let's see how you do with your second verb. The most important one after 'to be,'" he added in a tone as smooth as satin.

"To eat?" she quipped, knowing full well he'd meant something else.

"*Mangiare* comes third." He sat on the corner of the

teacher's desk, way too close to her. "Repeat after me." His dark eyes impaled her. *"Io amo."*

Alex struggled to maintain her composure. *"Io amo."* I love you, her heart whispered. Could he hear it?

"Again."

She looked down at her book, unable to sustain his glance. *"Io amo."*

"Perfetto," he declared. *"Tu ami."*

The lesson continued until she'd gone through all the conjugations of *amare*.

"Eccellente. You've mastered the present tense of the three verbs necessary for happiness."

"Only three?"

He crossed his powerful legs at the ankles. "To be alive, to love, to eat— What else is required?"

Maybe this was his way of letting her know Regina had talked to him. Alex had to risk finding out.

"For everyone else, nothing more. For the king, an added subtlety—to be able to love the woman he wants?" she challenged, meeting his gaze head-on.

His expression remained inscrutable. "So you think we need to add a fourth verb to the list of life's necessities?" The air thickened with tension.

"Where the king is concerned, yes."

A lengthy silence ensued. "As long as you felt compelled to tell Regina the truth, why didn't you reveal all of it?"

The question he shot at her was one she wasn't prepared for. Her gentle frown gave her a piquant look. "What do you mean?"

Lucca stood up. "What about Manny and his film offer? I told you before I didn't want you to do it, but I'm afraid now it's out of the question. I had him investigated. He not only exploited your mother, he milked her out of millions of dollars and should be brought up on criminal charges."

She lowered her head. "I think I already figured that out. My mother must have been the perfect pawn. This morning I phoned him and told him I wasn't interested in his offer."

Lucca's solid body froze in place. "And he accepted it, just like that?"

"He had no choice. I told him I'm getting married and want as far away from Hollywood as possible for the rest of my life."

Grazie a Dio.

She chewed on her lower lip. "I hope you don't mind that I won't be able to pay you back for my schooling for a long time."

He moved closer to her. "We've already had that discussion. Let me pay the twelve million dollars and be done with it."

"No, Lucca. We made a pact."

He hadn't meant to put more pressure on her. "So we did. What I want to know is why you told Regina you were flying to Los Angeles. We've already dealt with your apartment and personal things."

Her gaze collided with his. "Didn't she tell you about my plan to get you and your lover together?"

His hands gripped her shoulders. For a minute Lucca *had* forgotten. The knowledge that she'd turned Manny down flat had driven everything else from his mind.

"As my sister said, it was a selfless thought on your part, Alexandra, but it would never have worked."

"You're right," she muttered. "I should have realized it would never have worked. I've been thinking what I could do to help the two of you, but sneaking her into the palace under false pretenses is pretty absurd.

"The thing is, yesterday it hit me hard that you're a prisoner in so many dreadful ways. How can you possibly be with her when your every move is under surveillance? I…I thought I could help," she stammered.

Lucca needed to be released from his promise to Sofia ASAP. He relinquished his hold on her before he lost complete control. "You'll never know what your concern means to me, Alexandra. Give me a little more time and I'll tell you all about her."

She nodded. "Please forgive me for involving Regina. The poor thing. I was terrible to her," she admitted.

He eyed her speculatively. "In what way?"

"I asked her to listen to me and not interrupt because I knew she would fight me. Regina loves you so much, she did exactly as I said. I've never met a sweeter person. She knew it was futile to go to you, but she did it for me."

"My sister cares a great deal for you."

She moistened her lips anxiously. "But you're angry with me for telling her."

"You're wrong, Alexandra. I've taken you away from everything familiar. When I swore you to secrecy, I hadn't considered how much you would need a friend to confide in."

She peeked at him from beneath her lashes. "Who is it you confide in?"

Before Alexandra had come into his life, he and Sofia had used each other to commiserate, but those days were over. "I have *you* now."

"That places a grave responsibility on me," she whispered.

He studied her for a moment. "When I asked you to

marry me, you didn't realize what you were getting into. I'm afraid I didn't play fair."

Alex brushed an errant curl from her forehead. "You've been more than fair. Thank you for finding out about Manny. I've been naive about so many things, but I'm learning."

"Aren't we all," he whispered. "Can I hope you don't hate me too much?"

"That question doesn't deserve an answer." Alex let out a tormented sigh. "I haven't even asked about your parents. How's your father? When I watched the news this morning, all I could think of was his reaction."

He rubbed the back of his bronzed neck absently. "Now that I've promised him there'll be no unnecessary trips outside the palace until the honeymoon, he was in surprisingly good spirits after his blood test this morning and hasn't had to rely on his oxygen today."

"I'm glad he's doing that well." She hugged her arms to her chest. "I guess we have to take a honeymoon."

He nodded. "Where would you like to go, and I'll get my security people working on it."

Her pulse quickened. "I haven't traveled much, so anything would sound exciting. Is there some place you've never been you'd like to visit?"

"Dozens of them."

Every once in a while she heard that yearning in his voice to disappear to the other side of the planet and be accountable to no one.

"What would be the easiest as far as security's concerned?"

"The yacht."

"I've never been on one."

"It's ideal if you're looking for relaxation."

She cast him a worried glance. "Would that appeal to you?"

"I have to admit it would be for the best. As long as we're somewhere on the Mediterranean, it's not too far away should Papa take a turn for the worse."

"Then it's settled. I'll have hours every day to practice my Italian. What will you do?"

"Besides teach you?" A ghost of a smile hovered around his mouth. "Probably get back to my research."

"What kind?"

"I'm a geophysicist."

"You are?" Alex was stunned. She blinked. "So if you didn't have to be king—"

"I would go on doing fieldwork around the globe looking for new diamond finds to shore up more resources for Castelmare."

Her hand automatically crept to the pin attached to her cotton knit top. His gaze settled on it. "The Ligurian diamond is the reason I became interested in the subject. To understand how they're formed and where to look for them captivated me from the outset."

"I knew there was something more significant about this stone than the obvious."

His eyes lifted to hers. "It has been my lucky piece in more ways than one."

"How so?" she whispered. His nearness made her feel giddy.

"It brought me to New York at the precise moment Kathryn Carlisle's daughter walked through the doors. Call it destiny… Kismet…our meeting lifted me out of the black void of my existence. For agreeing to marry me, you have my eternal devotion."

Devotion, not love, so don't kill me with your earthshaking brand of kindness, Lucca.

Her plea came too late as he cupped her face in his hands and lowered his mouth to hers. It wasn't like yesterday after his escape from harm when he'd taken out his desires on her because he was missing his beloved. This time he kissed her as if she were his most cherished possession.

But it couldn't go on. She wouldn't allow it, because Alex had very recently discovered she wasn't a half-a-loaf girl.

Slowly he put her from him. It wasn't a moment too soon, because in another second she would have given in to the needs engulfing her.

His gaze found hers. "We'll finish your Italian lesson tomorrow. Right now the dressmaker is with Mama. They want to go over the design for your wedding gown. Afterward we'll have dinner with the family and Regina will join us. Later my father's personal assistant will walk us through the wedding day so we won't be apprehensive."

"What do you mean 'we'?"

She heard him inhale deeply. "In case you've forgotten, I've never been married before, either. *I* could trip on the steps outside the cathedral."

"Lucca—"

He kissed the corner of her mouth. Alex felt it long after they'd left the schoolroom.

CHAPTER NINE

FOR the next two weeks a routine was established. Mostly Alex saw Lucca when he came upstairs to help her with her Italian. Afterward they usually had dinner with his parents. When she wasn't studying, she often swam with Regina in the indoor pool and worked out in the palace gym.

Three days before the wedding, Professor Emilio made his appearance in the schoolroom. She put on a happy face, but inside she was wretchedly disappointed that her formal lessons with Lucca had come to an end.

The professor was a fine teacher and complimented her on her progress so far. She had no complaints. It was just that those two hours alone with Lucca had become the focal point of her daily existence.

Now that he was sequestered in his office dealing with government business and finishing his coronation speech, she hardly saw him. If this was setting a precedent for the future, then she needed to stop feeling sorry for herself and get on with plans that didn't include Lucca.

After breakfast she phoned Regina and asked if she'd go to the university with her. It was time for her to look into taking the exam that would allow her to go to medical school. She could study for it on her honeymoon. Regina fell in with her plans at once. They decided to make a full day of it, with lunch and shopping thrown in.

At five that afternoon Alex heard a man call to her. She and Regina were about to leave the university's student test center. She turned to her left.

"Tomaso! Come va?"

He seemed to have materialized out of nowhere. His dark blue eyes were alive with obvious pleasure. *"In questo momento sono di ottimo umore. E tu?"*

That was one of the greetings she'd practiced with Lucca. Tomaso had just said he was in a good mood now. It was exciting to be able to understand basic phrases.

"Molto bene."

She felt Regina nudge her arm. *"Buon pomeriggio, Professore Morelli."*

His gaze swerved to Regina. He looked taken back to see her standing there. Remembering his manners, he gave a slight bow. *"Principessa.* I'm finished for the day. May I take you ladies across the piazza for some *gelato?"*

"We'd enjoy that," Regina spoke up before Alex had the chance to turn him down. At first she didn't understand Lucca's sister until it dawned on her Regina might be attracted to the Italian professor. He *was* attractive, and intelligent.

The crowded street made their progress slow but they finally arrived at one of the little sidewalk cafés. Tomaso challenged Alex to order in Italian, then complimented her on not making one mistake. While she basked in his praise, the waiter brought them ice cream. Tomaso insisted on paying.

She'd almost finished hers when a black limo from the palace pulled up in front of the café. Regina gave Alex the eye, signaling it was time to go.

Alex ate the last spoonful before thanking Tomaso.

"Next time it will be our treat," Regina assured him.

"I'll remember." He walked them to the car. *"A presto,"* he said after they were settled.

When the door closed, Regina smiled at her. "I think you're in trouble."

"Why?"

"I didn't arrange for this limo. It means one of your bodyguards phoned Lucca."

"We didn't do anything wrong."

"That doesn't matter. My brother won't care that I was the one who accepted Professor Morelli's invitation."

"Lucca told me my bodyguards would never say anything unless I was in danger."

Her brows lifted. "There's danger, and then there's danger. You know what I mean?"

"But that's ridiculous."

"Tomaso is clearly infatuated with you," Regina declared.

There was little point in arguing with her, because Alex had to admit he'd acted a little too happy to see her.

"Why did you accept his invitation, Regina?"

"Because my brother dismissed him too fast for something that wasn't his fault. I wanted to let him know it wasn't anything personal."

"I think that was wonderful of you." She smiled. "If Lucca says anything, I'll defend you to the death."

"Let's hope it doesn't come to that."

"Regina—"

She opened her smoke tinted window a crack. "Don't look now, but there he is."

"Who?"

"Lucca. I can tell from here he's in battle mode."

Alex's husband-to-be made a frightening adversary

when provoked, but this time she had right on her side and would stand up to him. However, when he opened the rear door, her heartbeat tripled at the breathtaking sight of him, knocking her off balance. He was dressed in cream trousers and a black silk shirt, exuding a male potency to die for. Before she could recover, he leaned inside.

"Welcome home, *amata*," he murmured against her lips. "Umm. You taste of strawberry gelato. That was very nice of Professor Morelli." His gaze made an intimate appraisal, taking in her light blue two-piece suit, another outfit he'd asked her to try on at the shop.

"About him, Lucca, he—"

"We'll talk about it later," he broke in. "Your uncle Yuri arrived an hour ago and is eager to see you."

The palace had been filling up with Lucca's closest relatives, all of whom were gracious, but none of them were her family. Warmth filled her system to realize her own great-uncle had come. "I can't wait to see him."

Compassion shone from Lucca's eyes as he helped her from the limo. "He brought more of your father's family with him. Right now he's with Papa. I'll take you up there."

Alex saw no sign of Regina, who'd disappeared without her realizing it. She must have taken their things with her, including a brochure and several handouts from the university.

They started up the stairs with his hand in its usual place at the back of her neck. While he asked her how soon she could take the test, she felt his fingers rub her skin with disturbing insistence.

"When e-ever I feel ready." The answer came out jerkily. "They'll let me do it in English, but after that—" It was impossible to concentrate with him touching her. Lucca had no idea at all how impossible it was to be around him anymore and pretend she wasn't affected by the little things he did.

He was a sensual man. To her shock she'd discovered that she was a sensual creature, too. Every move he made, whether it was the way he sometimes made furrows in his hair without realizing it, or slipped off his jacket to get comfortable before they started a lesson. Whatever he did was guaranteed to draw her attention, filling her mind with forbidden thoughts that caused her to blush.

She wanted to run her hands through his hair. She dreamed of removing his jacket and tie and shirt so she could really touch him. She desired so many things she couldn't have. When Lucca had once asked her to join him swimming, she'd purposely avoided it. He'd never pressed her, but it was a pleasure she knew he enjoyed.

If she gave in to the temptation, he would know she wasn't in control. Then it would all come out that she was a fraud, that she'd clearly and simply fallen in love with him in Mr. Defore's office and would have followed him to the ends of the earth if he'd asked it of her.

"That's quite a conversation you're having with yourself," he whispered against her cheek. They'd reached the entrance to his parents' suite and she hadn't even noticed.

"I just wanted you to know that it was by chance Regina and I met Professor Morelli."

Maybe he didn't realize it, but he'd backed her up against one of the doors with his arms loosely holding her. "I'm quite aware he did all the running. As I told you before, it'll happen over and over again in your life because you're a beautiful woman who's totally unaware of her appeal. That's what makes you a magnet for men who are free to look but know they can't touch."

Lucca might not want her, but she was about to become his legal consort and that made her his possession. She wore his diamond for everyone to see. How appropriate that he'd had it cut in the shape of a teardrop. A presentiment of things to come even at the young age of nineteen, because he knew he'd never find fulfillment in marriage? Certainly her heart was bleeding all over the place, too. A fine wedding couple they made.

Maybe now was the time to give him something she'd bought him today. He might not be her possession, but being his wife she would have certain claims on him. As king he would wear the monarch seal on his right hand. As husband, he could wear her gift on his left for everyone to see, but it wouldn't prevent the woman he loved from touching him.

"Close your eyes for a minute, Lucca."

His black brows furrowed. Whatever he'd expected her to say, that wasn't it. "Why?"

"Because I have something for you. I hope you're going to like it. I'd planned to put it on you before you left for your coronation, but I've changed my mind."

Surprise registered in his eyes before he closed them. It meant her bodyguards hadn't blabbed all to him. She would remember to thank them later.

Compared to the worth of the Ligurian diamond, the $150 she'd paid for it was negligible. She'd put the tiny box in her suit jacket pocket to wrap later.

"Remember the day you took me to Dirupo? There was a little plaque outside the church in memory of St. Anthony of Padua and his companion Lucca Belludi, a nobleman who'd traveled with him to that spot. I did a little research and learned that after St. Anthony's death, Lucca took his place, becoming the guardian and miracle worker.

"That's how I think of you, taking your father's place, becoming the guardian of the kingdom and working miracles for Castelmare."

She took the gold ring from the box and slid it on his ring finger. Regina had helped her gauge the size. It looked like a perfect fit. The face of the ring was square shaped. An outline of the head of Lucca Belludi stood out in gold against a brilliant red background of pyrope. She loved the color. It reminded her of the red in the flag of the House of Savoy.

"You can open your eyes now."

His heart nearly failed him when he looked down at the ring. While he'd been thinking up ways to pulverize Tomaso and incarcerate Manny, she'd been buying him a wedding ring unlike any other.

Lucca would never forget that day at Dirupo. There'd been so much he'd wanted to share with her he hadn't known where to start first. In the process he hadn't realized she'd paid that much attention. What she'd just told him astounded him.

This gift held a significance beyond price, but shame consumed him because he hadn't told her about Sofia yet.

How ironic that throughout his adult life he'd grieved for the kind of love he would never know, yet now that Alexandra had colored his world, he would go on grieving because it seemed the only love she felt for him translated into lofty tributes.

She'd put him on a pedestal where he didn't belong, not realizing he wanted to be in her bed, in her arms. He wanted to fill every centimeter of her heart, share every part of her soul.

So help him, if it took the rest of his life, he'd find a way. But he would have to be clever. The old tale about the sun and the wind came to mind:

The sun and the wind made a wager to see who could get the man below them to take off his coat. The wind boasted he would blow it off him, but it only resulted in the man wrapping it tighter around him. The sun smiled and kept shining until it grew so hot the man finally removed it.

That would be his technique. Just keep pouring on a little more heat until she opened up to him because she couldn't help herself.

He reached for her hands, kissing the inside of her wrists. "You've paid me a supreme compliment. I'm not worthy of it, but I'll make you a promise never to remove it. This ring will be a constant reminder of your faith in me and my great fortune in taking you for my bride. I'm the luckiest of men."

"No, you're not," she whispered in a mournful tone. "It should be the woman you love giving you the wedding gift from her heart."

Lucca couldn't take much more. "I'd rather talk about your happiness."

She avoided his eyes. "I'm very happy. To be able to go to medical school and help people one day is more than I could ask for."

"But will it be enough?"

"Like you said, we don't know what the future has in store."

Pain shot through him as real as the bullet that could have killed him last year if it had hit the intended organ. Thanks to Carlo's heroics, Lucca only had a scar near the top of his left shoulder to remind him of his mortality.

With reluctance, he let go of her. "Alexandra, something vital came up earlier I must take care of. Do you mind if I don't go in with you?"

"Of course not."

"Your uncle and I had a good chat earlier, but I'll meet up with you both later."

"Don't worry. You're about to take on a new mantle. I understand that."

It wasn't the answer he wanted, but when she never made a fuss over his comings and goings, he had no right to complain.

"Enjoy your evening with him."

She nodded before going inside.

While she looked forward to a happy reunion with one of her only living relatives, Lucca headed for Regina's suite. He rapped on her door. They had their own signal. After doing it one more time to make certain she heard it, he walked in.

She was curled up in a chair in the sitting room, brushing her hair while she watched TV. "*Ciao, caro*. I've been expecting you."

His expression grim, he turned it off. "We have to talk."

"You stole my line."

"This is serious, *piccina*."

"I agree. You still haven't told Alexandra the truth." She put the brush down. "I happen to know you're so in love with her your behavior is off the wall. What's going on with you?"

"It's about Sofia." In the next breath he told her everything.

"All this time I thought Sofia was hurting for you," Regina murmured. "Surely you can tell Alexandra the truth now."

"I will, but——"

"Oh, Lucca," she cried out, "you're terrified she won't forgive you! I never thought I'd live to see the day my brother was frightened of anything."

Her comment brought him to a standstill.

"Do you honestly believe you could have talked a total stranger into marrying you unless she'd wanted it with the same passion?"

"She was desperate for financial help, Regina. When she wouldn't let me give her the money, I had to come up with another plan."

His sister eyed him shrewdly. "Knowing her tragic background, you do realize Alexandra would be the last woman on earth to repeat the mistakes of her mother and go near a king or be tempted by all the trappings unless she couldn't help herself. By the way, I know all about her turning down the chance to make that film."

Lucca's head reared. "When did she tell you that?"

"Today during the flight from Nice."

"What flight?" he thundered.

"The one she insisted we take to Padua, Italy, to find you that ring you're wearing."

"No one informed me!"

"They didn't dare after I threatened them with being fired. Isn't it interesting she couldn't even wait until the ceremony to give it to you. But to get back to my other point, she said she couldn't go to Hollywood because you might need her. In case you're still blind, deaf and dumb, it's code for she couldn't bear to be away from you."

Dio mio.

"I'm the one who accepted Professor Morelli's invitation for ice cream today. Alexandra wasn't the slightest bit interested and tried to stop me, but I thought it was the least I could do after your fit of jealousy drove you to get rid of him. That was totally unlike you. However, I do understand.

"Lucca—" she sighed "—there's only one answer for

her willingness to throw herself on the pyre of public scrutiny and risk the ridicule that followed her mother around in order to be your wife."

"She's never once taken the initiative to be with me."

Regina shook her head in exasperation. "Because you told her you were in love with someone else!"

He punched his fist into his palm. "Don't you think I want to believe what you're saying?"

"For someone so brilliant, there are times when you can be positively obtuse. You would never have approached Alexandra in New York if you hadn't been halfway falling in love with her already. She had to have felt the same way. You're a scientist. Show me proof that it can only happen once on a planet and that it only happened to you."

Lucca tried to find fault with her logic. Regina got out of the chair and hugged him. "I knew you couldn't." His emotions in chaos, he hugged her back harder. It was time to confess all to Alexandra.

After kissing the top of her head, he let her go. "Do I dare ask one more favor of you?"

"That all depends."

"Tonight when Alexandra comes back to her suite, use the excuse of some wedding detail to talk to her. I need the diamond pin, but I don't want her to know why. Do whatever it takes and bring it to me without alarming her."

He could hear her brain plotting. "I've got the perfect idea."

"Thank you. Did I ever tell you you're my favorite person?"

"I used to be," she muttered, but she smiled as she said it.

Needing to be by himself, he left her room and went downstairs to his office to call Sofia. Thankfully she answered. After telling her everything, Sofia felt terrible she'd held him to their secret for so long and released him from it. They wished each other the very best and promised to keep in touch. When he hung up, he felt an enormous weight had been lifted.

Now he could get down to some business he'd left off doing after learning about Alexandra's chance meeting with Professor Morelli. Regina was right. Lucca had behaved like an ass and needed to do something about it. Maybe an invitation to the wedding.

He lounged back in his swivel chair. The more he thought about it, the more he liked the idea that Tomaso would see his beautiful student pledge her life and love to her liege. Without hesitation he rang his secretary and told him to take care of it, then he got to work.

Two hours later Regina walked in his office and put the little jewel case on his desk. "Mission accomplished."

He reached for it. "What did you tell her?"

"That the people making the wedding dress needed to arrange everything ahead of time so there'd be no fuss the morning she left for the cathedral. Naturally I explained that you had authorized it."

"*Perfetto.* How did she respond?"

"She loves it more than anything, but I think she's relieved not to have the responsibility of it for a few days. I noticed she kept touching it today as if to make sure it was still there. Every woman should have such a fear."

"Is she in her room now?"

"Yes." Regina came around his desk and pecked him on the cheek. "See you tomorrow at breakfast. It'll be our last one before you're a married man."

Lucca detected a distinct wobble in her voice. "I'm not going anywhere."

"Yes, you are. You're going to a new place to start a new life with the woman you adore. That's the way it should be."

She dashed out of his office. He would have gone after her, but he knew she wouldn't want to be caught. Up until three weeks ago he'd been where she was tonight and every night before that. Grief needed no onlookers.

He rubbed his temples, then phoned the palace jeweler. "I have the item we talked about. It'll be in your hands shortly."

Once he'd buzzed his secretary and everything was taken care of, he realized he couldn't put off talking to Alexandra any longer. He rang her room. When she answered he said, "I'm coming up now." Afraid she'd find some excuse why he shouldn't, he hung up and left his office for his bedroom. He needed to change first.

Alex gripped the phone a little tighter before she put it back on the hook. Something was wrong. He'd sounded terse. She checked her watch. It was after eleven. Normally he would wait until tomorrow to talk to her.

Somewhat anxious, she went into the bathroom to freshen up, but he was at her door before she could run the brush through her hair. Sensing his impatience, she hurried to the entry and opened it. He was dressed in black bathing trunks and a dark T-shirt, the epitome of male beauty.

She felt the full battery of those brown eyes examining her. "I need to talk to you, but not here. Put on your suit and come swimming with me."

Her pulse sped up. "You mean, the indoor pool?"

"No. The one in front of the palace."

"But I thought it was only ornamental."

"During the day it is. At night when the grounds are locked up and no one can see me, I do laps to work out. Tonight I prefer being in the open. We'll slip out through the south entrance."

Just the way he talked caused her insides to melt. Being alone with him tonight wouldn't be a good idea. She'd left her terrace doors open. The air felt as if they were in the tropics.

She put a hand to her throat. "Would you mind if we do it tomorrow night instead? I'm afraid I'm still full from dinner with Uncle Yuri."

His face closed up. "You don't have to swim if you don't want to."

Without spelling it out, he was insisting she join him. Somehow she knew she wasn't going to like what he had to say.

"Give me a minute to change."

He moved inside the sitting room while she ran in the bathroom. After donning her cherry-red bikini, she put on a cotton wrap that hit her midthigh. She exchanged her heels for sandals, then met up with him at the entry.

Beneath his black-fringed lids his gaze swept over her, missing nothing. They walked down the hallway not quite touching. Her heart pounded in her throat with alternating waves of excitement and fear.

The palace grounds were a fairyland. Combined with the lights from the yachts in the bay, it was like something out of an enchanted dream complete with her own tall, dark prince. But she'd never seen him this brooding or remote. She ached to find some semblance of the man who'd worked his magic over her for the past three weeks.

Where had the man gone she'd given the ring to earlier?

He'd acted pleased, even touched by her gift, but maybe it had been a mistake. A turnoff because he didn't want any tokens from her. It wasn't part of their pact and she'd overstepped the bounds. Was that it?

They reached the edge of the pool, but Lucca hadn't said a word yet. That, more than anything, made her feel as though someone had just knocked the wind out of her. She stepped out of her sandals. Needing to channel her pain with something physical, she whipped off her wrap and dived in.

Alex didn't care if the excuse that she was too full made a liar out of her. This silence between them was something new. She couldn't deal with it. At the end of her first lap he caught up to her. Her intention to do a second was impeded by his hand. He caught her wrist in his strong grasp. "Stay here."

As she lifted her dripping head she saw a flash of pain in his eyes. What in heaven's name was wrong? She could be forgiven for thinking someone close to him had died.

The quiet stretched between them, causing her mind to imagine other unpalatable possibilities. Tomorrow was his last day of freedom. In thirty-six hours they'd be married. Had it suddenly caught up with him that he couldn't go through with this? Was that what he needed to tell her?

She was supposed to be the one who'd decided that this was all too much. Any other woman with a modicum of pride would have fled a bogus engagement long before now. But not Alex Carlisle Grigory who'd willingly been swept off her feet into an arranged marriage.

It wasn't his fault he'd grown on her second by second from the moment they'd met until she couldn't draw another breath without him.

Alex slowly eased her arm out of his grasp. Any other

time his touch would have turned her insides to mush. Not tonight. He was in the throes of unutterable pain and her body sensed it. She had the sick feeling that at this moment the very sight of her repulsed him.

His hardened features had taken on a sculpted appearance, as if he'd been cast in bronze.

"Obviously, you're in hell, Lucca. Say whatever it is you have to say."

CHAPTER TEN

"When I do, there might not be a wedding."

Alex clutched the rim of the pool. She had never fought so hard to remain in control. "From your demeanor I assumed as much." She swallowed hard. "Under normal circumstances engagements are made to be broken. That's what they're for, to see if both parties are ready for the big commitment. But there's nothing normal about your life, which has been in crisis for a very long time."

His rigid body seemed to tauten more, if that was possible.

"The ring I gave you didn't help. It reminded you of your duty and made everything all too real. Don't you know I understand?" she cried softly.

He breathed heavily. "That's the point. You don't." His voice was gruff.

She edged away from him a few inches. "Maybe not completely, but give me credit for realizing what this news will do to your father and mother. I'd do anything for you, Lucca, but I'm afraid in this case I don't know how to help you. This is a situation that needs the wisdom of Solomon to sort out."

"His wisdom would tell us a marriage based on a lie is no marriage."

Alex treaded water for a moment while she gathered her thoughts. "I agree, but I don't know what you're talking about. We were totally honest with each other. Regina knows everything. You said your parents are aware of the relationship with your lover, so what you just said doesn't make sense."

"Take my word for it, it does." His eyes closed tightly. "There's something I didn't tell you when I asked you to marry me."

"Lucca—if you're afraid to admit you have a child with this woman, don't be. The possibility did cross my mind. Is she afraid I'll keep you from recognizing it or some such crazy thing? I'd never do that to anyone. After growing up without my parents, I'd do everything in my power to help you make sure your son or daughter was welcomed and loved."

She heard a strange sound come from his throat before he smoothed his black hair off his forehead. "What if I told you there isn't another woman?"

Alex was pretty sure her face had gone a paste color, but she refused to fall apart now. "Do you mean you and Carlo? Sometimes I've felt he didn't like me, and I wondered if it was jealousy on his part."

"*Santa Vergine!* I'm almost afraid to hear what's going to come out of your mouth next. Obviously, that database in your mind has run through every possible conclusion except for the one answer not programmed. There were two reasons I lied to you.

"The first was because I owed my loyalty to Princess Sofia."

"Of San Marino?"

"So you know of her."

"Yes." Alex's love for Lucca had caused her to learn everything she could from Regina about the women in his life. She wasn't proud of her jealousy, which had driven her to look up their pictures on the Internet.

"We've been friends for many years and our parents wanted us to marry, but neither of us were inclined. Recently she confided that as soon as I got married she would forsake her title and live her life in Africa doing missionary work, but we've had to keep everything a secret for obvious reasons. Until she told me it was all right, I couldn't tell you."

Alexandra's chin lifted. "Instead you let me think she was a love interest. Why bother?"

She heard him draw in a labored breath as if this was the last thing he wanted to confess. "I didn't want you to think there was anything more to my proposal than a business transaction that would be beneficial to both of us."

Everything went dead inside Alex. "And that's what has caused all this needless suffering?" She laughed at him before getting out of the pool. Within seconds she'd slipped into her wrap and sandals.

"Don't you realize I know I'm the last woman any man would want unless he needs a consort within six hours? I thought you understood that, when we made our pact on the way to the airport. You didn't need to pretend Princess Sofia was your lover on my account.

"When I think of all the needless hours I've spent trying to figure out ways to help you…" Her eyes glittered like silver shards. "Well, now that you've gotten that off your chest, relax! Enjoy your swim! As for me, I'm going to bed and spend tomorrow with my family. If you're smart, you'll enjoy the bachelor party Regina told me your friends have planned for you."

She gave him the benefit of her full-bodied smile. "The next time we see each other will be in church. Hopefully we'll both stay upright throughout the ordeal. You're going to make a splendid king. *Ciao*, Lucca."

As soon as she reached her suite, she turned white-faced to her bodyguards trailing after her. "Would you two mind staying in here tonight as a special favor to me? One of you can lie on the lounger on the terrace, and the other on the couch in the sitting room. If anyone tries to come in either way, and I mean *anyone*, don't let them. Especially Lucca. It's bad luck for him to see me before the wedding."

She was thankful they'd be around till morning. Their presence would ensure she didn't sob her heart out all night. It would take her until the day after tomorrow to recover enough to get through the ceremony. Once she and Lucca went off on their honeymoon, he would learn the true meaning of a business transaction.

"You look so beautiful I can't believe it. That dress… The eggshell silk is perfect with your eyes, and the simplicity of it is pure genius on your figure."

Lucca's sister had come into her room at the last minute to walk downstairs with her. Alex had to admit the dressmaker had outdone herself. The cap sleeves and rounded neck were the right style for her.

"You're tall enough to wear something that flows and flows. At times like this I wish I could grow about four more inches."

"You're ravishing the way you are, Regina." Today she was in a filmy gown of the softest shade of lavender.

"I still don't understand why the dressmaker didn't fasten your diamond pin on it."

Alex could have told her why. Lucca had taken it back. No more pretense. "I'm not worried. I'm sure there's a perfectly logical explanation."

Regina frowned. "I hope so. My brother was in such a bad way this morning, everyone ran clear of him."

"It's called the bachelor blues. After his party he's feeling trapped."

"No, Alexandra. Something terrible was bothering him. He wouldn't talk to anybody."

"Well, he has to give a speech today. I don't suppose he's looking forward to it."

"He gives speeches all the time. That's not what's wrong. You really haven't seen him since night before last?"

"No. We went swimming and then we said good-night."

If Lucca had tried to come to her room in the last thirty-six hours, she didn't know about it. She'd purposely turned off the phones so there'd be no chance for communication. Her bodyguards had done everything for her. They were great.

"You look a vision, Alexandra!" Lucca's mother exclaimed. She swept into the room in a full-length gown of pale blue. In her arms she carried Alex's alençon lace veil. Behind her came the hairdresser holding a case.

"What's inside?"

His mother smiled. "Your own tiara. Lucca had it specially made for you to wear when you entertain and go to official functions."

He hadn't said anything about entertaining when he'd asked her to marry him.

"It's lightweight so your head won't ache. I think what he's had done with the diamond is stunning, don't you?"

The diamond?

Alex watched as the hairdresser lifted it from the velvet lining. The entire piece was so delicate and lacy it looked like a fairy crown strung with golden spider webs. There was only one jewel. The green teardrop dominated the center. Alex gasped, because the tiara was the perfect setting for it.

Once it was placed on her head, everyone helped drape the veil while the hairdresser secured it.

Lucca's mother kissed Alex's forehead. "You're a blessing to this family. We love you, my dear."

"I love you, too," Alex said with heartfelt emotion. Both of them wiped their tears away before Regina announced it was time.

"You're right." Her mother nodded. "My son went ahead half an hour ago. If I know him, and I do, he's waiting most impatiently for the first sight of his bride."

His very arranged bride.

The moment was bittersweet for so many reasons, not the least of them being the absence of both her parents. Yet no one could have been welcomed into a more wonderful family than the Vittorios.

Lucca's father would attend the ceremony, but arrangements had been made for him to leave if he felt too weak. This was such a huge day for father and son, Alex hoped Rudy would be able to see all of it.

It took an army of people to help Alex down the palace steps to the limo where her uncle was waiting. There was a stream of limos lined up on the north drive to take everyone to the fifteenth-century cathedral in the upper part of the city.

"What a glorious sight you make, Alexandra. I'm proud to be your great-uncle."

"Thank you, Uncle Yuri. You don't know what it means to me to have my family here."

"Lucca's a lucky man, but he already knows that."

Alex smiled but didn't respond.

"Are you all right?"

"Yes."

"Why do I get the feeling there's something wrong? You can tell me."

"I'm a little nervous."

"Today you're going to become Lucca's wife. His queen. You look like one. When we reach the cathedral, act like one. Lift your head high so that when everyone goes to bed tonight, they'll feel good knowing their new king is in the very best of hands."

Her uncle had a way of looking at life that was touching and oddly enough stiffened her backbone. She did have a role to play, albeit a much less important one. But she would do it and show Lucca she wasn't a person to be pitied. She leaned forward and caught his hand to squeeze it.

The city, lined with the royal flags, swarmed with people craning their necks to get a look as the limousine climbed the winding streets. It looked like the whole world had turned out for the coronation. After they stopped in front of the cathedral, everything became a blur.

Once Alex was helped out of the backseat, someone handed her a bouquet of white roses. Her uncle lowered the front of the veil over her face. Then he held her arm and they ascended the steps while dozens of photographers recorded their progress. She could hear organ music. People called to her and shouted, "Alexandra!"

Until they entered the cathedral, Alex smiled and turned her head to oblige them. Down the long aisle they walked, flanked by hundreds of beautifully dressed guests who filled the nave. The archbishop manned the pulpit. On his right stood Lucca, as straight as a lance and heartbreakingly resplendent in his white coronation suit and crown. He wore the wide blue ribbon from shoulder to waist that proclaimed him the crown prince.

Alex could see him through her veil, but she kept her eyes on his chest. He stepped forward to take her hand from Yuri and seat her next to him. Next to them sat his mother and father in full ceremonial dress. Her uncle sat down by Regina.

The whole time the archbishop led them in prayer, Lucca kept hold of her right hand in a firm grip while she balanced the roses with her left. When it ended, Lucca had perforce to let go of her and take his place in the centuries-old chair reserved for former sovereigns.

Wasting no time, the archbishop performed the rites. First the blue band was replaced with a red one, then Lucca's crown was exchanged for the larger crown that proclaimed him king. Following that process he gave his coronation speech in Italian. She only understood bits and pieces here and there. No matter how he'd hurt Alex, a feeling of such fierce pride and love for him swept over her she was afraid she couldn't contain it.

When his crown was removed, that was the signal for Regina to take the roses so Alex could stand by Lucca. At this point the archbishop led them in the wedding ceremony. Lucca did his part in Italian. Alex had been coached by Rudy's assistant so she knew when it came time to do her part in English. Despite Lucca's lack of affection for her, the vow she was about to make poured straight from her heart.

"I, Alexandra Carlisle Grigory, promise before the Church and Heaven to give my love, loyalty and devotion to my sovereign majesty and husband, His Royal Highness Lucca Umberto Schiaparelli Vittorio the Fifth, King of Castelmare, so help me God."

Lucca turned and lifted the veil with both hands. She kept her eyes level with his compelling mouth as he leaned closer. Inside the privacy of the lace hiding both their faces he whispered, "Why else would I have kidnapped you from the House of Savoy if I hadn't been totally and irrevocably in love with you?"

Alex came close to fainting from shock.

"But you wouldn't have believed love could happen that fast if I'd told you the truth. I used Sofia shamelessly to make you feel sorry for me because I wasn't about to return to Castelmare without you. I'd have said or done anything to have you, so be kind to me, *amore mio.*"

The kiss he gave her was a husband's kiss, hot with desire, bringing her to pulsating life so fast she started to weave and had to cling to the arms still holding up her veil. Outside the waves of ecstasy enveloping her body she heard the archbishop clear his throat.

"Lucca," she gasped quietly.

"You're my very heart. Tell me what I need to hear," he begged, "or I swear, my life means nothing."

"You *know* I love you. Now please—"

"Your word is my command, *bellissima.*"

He arranged the veil behind the tiara. She knew her face was scarlet, but as Lucca took hold of her hand, she remembered her uncle's advice and held her head high. The organ began to play and everyone got to their feet.

Lucca's thumb made provocative circles against her palm as they walked down the aisle. The moment they stepped outside the doors, she heard the cheers of the crowd.

"Viva il re! Viva Alexandra!"

The sound of church bells pealed sonorously over the city. But even louder were the fireworks shooting off inside her body as he kissed her again to the delight of their onlookers.

Together they descended the steps to the horse-drawn coach waiting at the bottom. As Lucca helped her inside, their eyes met. "We managed to stay upright, but don't plan on being in that position any longer than it takes for us to reach the yacht."

Alex wondered if her cheeks would ever go back to their normal color. "Have you no shame, Your Majesty?"

His white smile dazzled her. "None at all, Your Majesty." He climbed in next to her. A footman closed the door. "As breathtaking as you look," he murmured against her mouth, "there's one sight I haven't seen yet. I've been living for it.

"Now wave to the crowd. They came to look at you. Today you're making history, *mia moglie.*"

His wife. The most beautiful word in the world.

"Darling? Don't you think we should get up, if only to let your crew know we're alive?"

Lucca pulled her higher across his chest, trapping her with his powerful legs. "Every time the steward takes back another empty tray to the kitchen, he knows there are two people creating their own paradise."

She covered his impossibly handsome face with kisses, unable to get enough of him. "But it's been three days."

"Is my wife embarrassed because we haven't left the bedchamber in all that time?"

"No." She slid her arms around his neck. Looking into his slumberous black eyes she said, "I don't care if the whole world knows we've been this happy. Do you suppose Carlo has told your father?"

The smile she loved broke out on his face. "You mean, that we've been working on his grandchild day and night? There's no doubt about it. Did I tell you I've been having the time of my life in the process? Come closer, you gorgeous thing."

Alex needed no urging. Their mouths fused in passion. Once more the joy of making love with her husband surpassed all other experiences. There was no end to his giving or hers. At times the beauty of it brought her to tears.

"I don't ever want to do anything else," she admitted an hour later, temporarily sated by rapture. He looked down at her and his hands stilled in her hair. A look of profound seriousness had entered his eyes. "What is it?" she asked, so attuned to him already it was as if they were one.

"I never wanted to be king, but I've changed my mind."

Her breath caught. "Why is that?"

"These past three days have shown me a whole new life. I've discovered I want to spend as much of it as possible with you. We'll do everything together. Unlike most men who don't take their wives to work, it's expected that I involve you in the country's affairs.

"What's wonderful about the palace is that my home and my work place are under the same roof. We'll always be together, always travel together."

Alex couldn't believe what she was hearing. "My secret dream growing up was to find one man who would love only me and want to be with me all the time, but I didn't think it was possible."

"It's more than possible," he said before plundering her mouth once more. Time passed before she became cognizant of it again. They ended up lying on their sides holding each other.

"I want to make up for all your years of loneliness."

She cupped his handsome face in her hands. "You already have. I'm so happy it hurts, Lucca."

"Then you have some idea of how I feel. To think I found you on the very day I'd given up hope of ever knowing true fulfillment."

Alex ran a hand through his hair. "No one but a person like the Princess Sofia knows the kind of burden you've had to bear. Do you think Regina feels it the same way?"

"Yes," he whispered against her lips. "Papa ingrained it into her that she's second in line to the throne. No matter what, she'll always do her duty."

"Just like you. But what if she never meets a royal she loves the way we love each other?"

Lucca sighed into her neck. "I lie awake nights worrying about that. I'd give anything for my sister to know the kind of ecstasy you and I have found, but I refuse to worry about it right now. This time is for us, *squisita*."

"Oh, darling." She half sobbed with joy, unable to stop covering his face with kisses. *"Ti amo,"* she said against his eyes. *"Sono innamorata di te,"* she whispered against his jaw. *"Ti adoro,"* she mouthed the words against his lips.

"Someone's been teaching you besides me," he growled into her neck.

"I asked Professor Emilio to help me with some phrases for the honeymoon."

Lucca let go with full-bodied laughter. The happy sound reached right down inside her soul.

"Did I say them right?" Her beautiful gray eyes beseeched him.

He sobered. "*Perfetto.* I'm the luckiest man alive, Alexandra. We were meant to be together."

"I wanted to belong to you the moment you commanded me in your monarch voice, 'Come back and sit down, Signorina Grigory. I'm not through with you.'"

Lucca crushed her in his arms. "I was a monster. I don't know how you put up with me. Love me again so I know I'm not dreaming," he whispered urgently. "I've only begun to live."

THE DIAMOND BRIDE

CAROLE MORTIMER

Carole Mortimer was born in England, the youngest of three children. She began writing in 1978 and has now written over one hundred and fifty books for Mills & Boon. Carole has six sons, Matthew, Joshua, Timothy, Michael, David and Peter. She says, 'I'm happily married to Peter senior; we're best friends as well as lovers, which is probably the best recipe for a successful relationship. We live in a lovely part of England.'

CHAPTER ONE

'IF YOU'RE thinking of jumping, I should wait another couple of hours until the tide is back in!'

Annie turned with a start at the sound of that deeply masculine voice—a voice she didn't recognise!

A dark figure loomed in the fog. A tall, menacing figure.

'At the moment,' that deep voice continued, 'you'll most likely just find yourself buried up to your ankles in mud!'

She had been lost in thought as she stood on the end of this small jetty, troubled thoughts that went round and round in circles, their beginnings always meeting up with their ends, giving no answers.

She had been so lost in those thoughts she hadn't heard the man's approach, but she was conscious now of how alone she was, the thick, swirling afternoon fog meaning she couldn't be seen by anyone up at the house that stood so majestically on the clifftop above. This small, private beach was rarely used by any member of the Diamond family, and was certainly not going to be visited by any of them at this time of the day.

Alone now, with this stranger, she realised how foolish her choice had been.

'I also don't think the Diamond family would be too pleased at another suicide taking place on their estate,' the gravelly voice continued harshly.

Another suicide...? Had someone once killed themselves here? What—?

Another suicide! Surely this man didn't imagine that was what she intended doing down here? Although in truth, with the tide obviously out, and the fog making visibility negligible, it must seem strange for her to be standing out here on this waterless jetty. But suicide...!

She took an involuntary step backwards as the man moved towards her out of the mist, only to find herself pressed up against the railing with nowhere to go—except, as he'd said, down into the mud below.

Her eyes widened apprehensively as the fog seemed to part to allow the man to step out in front of her—a man, she was sure, who must be the epitome of every fictional hero.

She gasped even as the ridiculous thought jumped into her head. But at first sight he was the personification of that romantic hero Rochester: so tall, dark hair long and unruly, his face strong and powerful, eyes as dark as coal. He was Rochester come to life!

Annie shivered. Whether because of this overpowering stranger, or the dampness of the fog penetrating to her bones through the light jacket and denims she wore, she wasn't altogether sure.

'Cat got your tongue?' he challenged with a rise of one dark brow.

Up close—too close!—she could see that his eyes weren't black at all, but a very deep blue, the iris barely discernible from that dark cobalt, his features so hardly hewn they might have been carved from granite.

He tilted his head to one side, his expression speculative, black hair resting almost on his shoulders, seem-

ing immune himself to the dampness of the weather in
his dark jacket, blue casual shirt and faded blue denims.

'"Trespassers will be prosecuted"'. He dryly quoted
the sign that precluded access onto this secluded beach.

She swallowed hard, moistening her lips as she realised how dry her mouth had become. But the only way
off the jetty was past this man, and being slightly
built—only a little over five feet in height—she thought
her chances of making good her escape were probably
a little slim.

An avid reader, she tried to think what a fictional her-
oine would do in these circumstances. Humour him, that
was it. Then wait until he was off-guard—and make a
run for it. Once she had disappeared into the thick fog
he would have great trouble finding her again.

She attempted a slight, conciliatory smile. 'I'm sure
that if you leave now the Diamond family will never be
aware that you were ever here at all,' she suggested
lightly—desperately hoping that none of the panic she
felt was evident in her voice.

Dark eyes widened. 'If I leave…?' He frowned. 'My
dear girl, I have no intention of leaving.'

He didn't intend leaving…

Annie swallowed hard again, hands tightly clenched
in her jacket pockets. 'I really think that would be the
best thing for you to do.' She forced soothing calm into
her voice. 'Before—er—Mr Diamond comes down here
and finds you trespassing on his land.'

'Mr Diamond…?' he echoed questioningly.

'Anthony Diamond,' Annie supplied quickly, at last
feeling she might be making some progress in her effort
to get him to leave.

'He's here?' the man rasped, casting a look in the

direction of the house above on the cliff, now hidden by the fog.

'Oh, yes.' She nodded eagerly. 'All of the family are in residence.'

'Are they indeed?' he mused harshly, his brow clearing, his mouth twisting with contempt. 'Well, I can assure you there's no possibility of Anthony coming down here,' he dismissed derisively. 'He hates the sea and everything to do with it—more so since a boating accident several years ago. Unless, of course, the two of you have arranged to meet down here?' he added slowly.

Annie looked at him sharply, momentarily forgetting her fear. Exactly what did he mean by that remark? He couldn't possibly know anything about Anthony—or her, for that matter.

'Have you?' he prompted softly. 'It would be the one place Davina wouldn't think of looking for him; she knows of his aversion to moving water!' he mocked.

And this man, she realised, at the mention of Davina, Anthony's fiancée—whoever he was—knew far too much about the Diamond family!

The man looked at her consideringly now, seeming to take in everything about her appearance in that one sweeping glance: her short, curling red hair, which framed her gamine face, a face dominated by deep brown eyes; her small and snub nose, her wide and smiling mouth—usually, when she wasn't accosted by complete strangers!—a chin that was small and pointed, her figure boyish in her jacket, blue cropped top and fitted black denims.

'You don't look like Anthony's usual type,' the man finally drawled insultingly. 'But then, as he gets older, perhaps young and impressionable is easier to deal with!'

Easier to impress, his dismissive tone implied!

Well, at thirty-six, she didn't consider Anthony old, and she wasn't that young either; at twenty-two she could quite easily be married with small children.

She eyed the man coolly. 'Anthony Diamond, as you have already mentioned, already has a fiancée.' Some of her fear was fading now, to be replaced by anger; not only was this man trespassing on the Diamond estate, he was also insulting the family—well, one of them—as well now!

'Davina,' the man acknowledged. 'I'm sure their engagement is of mutual benefit to both of them,' he went on, 'but it hasn't stopped Anthony's roving eye. You must be new to the village,' he added tauntingly. 'Last I heard, Anthony had already gone through all the available females there. Unless, of course, you're one of the married ones?'

It had quickly become obvious to her that this man thought she was one of the girls from the local village two miles away. Which meant he must be new to the area himself, otherwise he would have known she was nanny to the youngest member of the Diamond family. Admittedly, she had only been working here for two months, but he seemed to know so much else about the Diamonds...

'I'm not married, but I'm not an "available female", either,' Annie told him tartly. 'And I would appreciate it if you didn't continue to insult members of the Diamond family!'

'But I'm only insulting Anthony,' he replied knowingly. 'And he makes it so easy to insult him,' he added scathingly, glancing at the plain gold watch on his wrist. 'It doesn't look as if he's coming now; I was watching you for at least ten minutes before I spoke to you,' he informed her softly.

She shrank back defensively, uncomfortable with the knowledge that she had been watched when she hadn't been aware of it. Her emotions had been in turmoil when she'd come down here, her thoughts troubled, and she was sure that must have been obvious from her expression when he'd first caught sight of her. Which was probably why he had made that assumption about suicide! Admittedly, her life did feel a bit complicated at the moment, but certainly not that desperate!

'Perhaps it's as well that he didn't. For your sake,' she snapped as he raised questioning brows. 'You're trespassing,' she pointed out irritably as he still looked unimpressed.

He shrugged unconcernedly. 'So are you. And although Anthony may not mind your being here, what about the rest of the family?' he challenged. 'Rufus, for example?'

'Rufus isn't here,' she told him impatiently, tired of this constant baiting.

Rufus Diamond, the male head of the family and her small charge's father, was away at the moment, and had been for the last three months. As an investigative reporter of some repute, he had been away in some war-torn country or other since before Annie had come to work with his daughter. His mother, Celia, the matriarch of the Diamond family, had been the one to employ her when the previous nanny had left without notice.

The man looked at her assessingly. 'I thought you said

all of the family were in residence?' He tauntingly echoed her words of earlier.

'They are.' She frowned at him. 'But Mr Diamond
senior—'

'You mean Rufus?' Amusement darkened his eyes
even more; his teeth were white and even as he gave a
wolfish grin. 'I've never heard him referred to as that
before; you make him sound ancient!'

'I have no idea how old Mr Diamond—Mr Rufus
Diamond—is,' Annie told him in a flustered voice. 'But
I do know he's older than Anthony.'

'By three years.' The man nodded. 'And, believe me,
I feel every one of them,' he added, watching her as he
waited for her reaction to his announcement.

And he wasn't disappointed, Annie felt sure!

This was Rufus Diamond? This man, with his shag-
gily long dark hair, piercing eyes, hard-hewn face, tall
and leanly powerful body? This was Rufus Diamond?

She didn't know what she had been expecting from
the brief mentions of him that had been made by the rest
of the family, or from the absolute adoration with which
Jessica spoke of her father, but it certainly hadn't been
this dangerously good-looking man with his assured air
of power!

Perhaps it was that he was such a complete contrast
to his brother; Anthony was tall and blond, extremely
handsome, with eyes as blue as the sky on a summer's
day, always immaculately dressed in his tailored, de-
signer clothes. The two men were complete opposites,
and she would never have guessed they were brothers.

She hadn't!

She drew in a controlling breath, doing her best to
gather her scattered wits back together. 'It's good to

meet you at last, Mr Diamond.' She held out her hand in formal greeting.

He didn't move, watching her through narrowed lids. 'Is it?' he returned guardedly.

She swallowed hard, her arm falling back to her side, her hands feeling slightly warm and damp, despite the cold clamminess of the fog that still surrounded them. 'I'm Jessica's new nanny, Mr Diamond—'

'Are you indeed?' he cut in grimly, all humour gone from those hard dark eyes now. 'What about Margaret?'

She moistened her dry lips once more, some of her earlier fear returning; this man was a power to be reckoned with when he was angry. As he was now. 'I believe she left—'

'I've already gathered that,' he rasped icily.

'Yes, well.' Annie looked confused. 'Mrs Diamond contacted the employment agency—'

'Why?' His grimness was increasing with each passing second.

Annie frowned. 'I just told you, Margaret left, and Jessica needed—'

'I meant, why did Margaret leave?' he bit out coldly.

'I have no idea.' She shook her head a little dazedly. 'You would have to ask Mrs Diamond that—'

'Don't worry, that's exactly what I'm here to do!' he replied harshly, turning on his heel and striding off down the jetty in the direction of the cliffs and the house. He paused before the fog swallowed him up completely, turning slightly. 'And I would advise you to get back to your young charge instead of mooning about down here waiting for my wastrel of a brother!' He disappeared into the swirling clouds, and everything suddenly became eerily quiet again.

As if he had never been there at all...

But Annie knew that he had, was still shaking from the encounter. She almost wished now that he had been a trespasser; that would have been far preferable to knowing he was actually her employer!

How quickly his mocking humour had vanished once he'd realised exactly who she was. He was obviously very angry at the departure of Jessica's previous nanny. And certainly not impressed with her replacement!

Rochester, indeed! She had read the classic story at a young, impressionable age, had found herself, probably because of her own parentless circumstances, relating to Jane Eyre, although her own time as an orphan in care had been a relatively happy one. But Rufus Diamond certainly wasn't Mr Rochester. Any more than she was Jane Eyre...!

Would she have behaved any differently if she had known who he was from the first? Probably, but only slightly, she conceded. After all, he had been the one, without knowing a thing about her, who'd been so insulting about her supposed relationship with his brother...

Her thoughts were even more troubled now than they had been when she'd come down onto the beach an hour ago! She had been so excited about the chance of this job on the east coast of England, had come here full of enthusiasm, glad to be out of London, the place she had lived all her life. And being out here, surrounded by rural countryside, had suited her perfectly. She loved the wide open spaces, the friendliness of the locals—she had certainly never been on a first-name basis with a milkman before! In London she hadn't even had a milkman; she had bought all her food supplies, including milk, from a convenience store around the corner from the flat she'd shared with three other girls.

Moving here had offered her a completely different way of life from the one she had always known. Her early years had been spent in care, and the college course to qualify as a children's nanny had seemed the obvious choice of career after years of helping look after younger children at the home where she had been placed. As had deciding to share a flat with three of the other girls from the children's home when the time had come to move out.

She had taken employment at a local kindergarten once she was qualified, but helping in the day-care of forty young children who went home to their own families at the end of each day hadn't given her any more roots than she had found at the children's home, and so she had signed on at an employment agency with the intention of working in a family environment. Jessica Diamond was her first individual charge. And Annie had quickly learnt to love her.

Aged eight, Jessica was a lovely child, tall for her age, with long, curling dark hair and eyes as blue as cornflowers, and a lively intelligence that Annie found enchanting. And with only Jessica's grandmother in residence most of the time, her uncle Anthony a regular visitor at weekends, it had been easy to become fond of the little girl who greeted her so eagerly at the end of each schoolday. Their weekends had been spent exploring the beach and horse-riding; even wet days had been fun as they'd played with the numerous toys Jessica had up in her bedroom.

But now Jessica's father had returned.

And he didn't seem at all happy about the fact that his daughter had a new nanny...

The future suddenly looked even bleaker than it had an hour ago. Even more so because once Rufus Diamond got up to the house he was going to discover that Jessica had fallen from her horse over the weekend and was resting in bed with a badly sprained ankle. So much for being in the care of her newly hired nanny!

Admittedly, there had been nothing Annie—a mere novice when it came to riding a horse—could have done to prevent Jessica's accident. But she very much doubted that Rufus Diamond would see it quite that way, especially as he already seemed so displeased at Jessica having a replacement nanny in the first place!

Annie felt the prick of tears in her eyes. She had loved Jessica on sight, their better acquaintance only deepening that emotion as she'd discovered just how hungry for affection Jessica was too. Perhaps she shouldn't have let Jessica become that fond of her, but when the young child was effectively as parentless as Annie had been herself, it was impossible to push the young girl aside.

As Jessica's mother had died when Jessica was still a very young child, she really had little memory of her. Celia Diamond, Jessica's paternal grandmother, was a tall, stately-looking woman, blonde and still beautiful despite her sixty-or-so years, but a woman who obviously found it difficult to show affection to a young child; a summons to her private sitting-room before bedtime was the most attention she paid her granddaughter.

But Jessica's father was back now, so perhaps things would change...

And one of those changes could be the dismissal of the new nanny!

Annie's feet dragged with reluctance as she made her way back up to the house. Nevertheless she took the path carefully—the weather seemed to be worse than when she had set out and she grabbed onto the handrail several times as she almost lost her footing on the rocky path, relieved when she saw the ominous shape of the house rising up in front of her.

Clifftop House was a magnificent building, almost gothic in proportions, and it had taken Annie a week to find her way around its many rooms. It had seemed incredible to her at the time of her arrival that one elderly lady and a small child should live in such a large house.

Although she had to admit that within several hours of Anthony's arrival at the weekend, with his fiancée, for a week's visit, the house hadn't seemed big enough for all of them!

She had a feeling it was going to seem even less so with Rufus Diamonds's impressive presence!

'Really, Rufus, I didn't see the point in contacting you,' Celia Diamond was protesting impatiently as Annie moved quietly past the sitting-room doorway. 'The doctor said it's a simple sprain, nothing to get in a panic about, and Annie has been taking very good care of her—'

'Who the hell is Annie?' that oh, so familiar voice rasped harshly.

'The new nanny you seem so angry about,' Celia responded coldly. 'You weren't here, Rufus—but then, you never are,' she added cuttingly. 'What else was I supposed to do when Margaret walked out so unexpectedly?'

Annie couldn't move, had become frozen to the spot the moment she heard her name mentioned…!

'I suppose it was too much to expect that you could look after Jessica yourself,' Rufus drawled scathingly. 'Although you still haven't given me an acceptable explanation as to exactly why Margaret walked out. And if this Annie is taking such good care of Jess, why is it that she's upstairs in bed at this moment with a leg injury?'

Annie gasped at the injustice of this last remark; there was simply no way, without completely smothering the child, that she could monitor every move of her young charge. And Jessica had been riding for years; in fact, this man had bought her the horse she had fallen from!

'Maybe I should just ask Annie that myself!' Even as Rufus spoke, the door to the sitting-room was wrenched completely open, exposing an embarrassed Annie eavesdropping in the hallway. 'Well?' Rufus Diamond barked at her. 'I presume you are Annie?'

She looked at him with widely startled eyes—and it wasn't all due to being caught out in this way. He knew damn well she was Annie; she had told him down at the jetty that she was his daughter's nanny.

'Really, Rufus,' Celia Diamond admonished haughtily. 'Sometimes I find it difficult to believe you could possibly be David's son; he was always such a gentleman, so aware of his position as head of this family,' she continued scathingly.

Rufus gave her a contemptuous glance. 'You mean you were always so aware of your position as wife of the head of this family!' he returned disgustedly. 'I'm sure my father only died at the relatively early age of sixty-five so that he could at last get away from you and your social-climbing!'

'Really, Rufus!' Celia's gasp was one of dismay now

as she clutched at the double string of pearls about her throat, her expression one of deep hurt. 'Your long absence hasn't made your tongue any kinder. And have you forgotten there are servants present?' She flicked a chilling look in Annie's direction.

She meant her, Annie realised after several stunned moments. A servant! Well…she supposed she was, in a way; she did work for these people, and was paid a wage for doing so. But even so…!

'I don't think Annie took too kindly to that last remark, Celia,' Rufus Diamond interjected.

Annie turned her gaze in his direction, only to find those dark eyes regarding her with amusement. He had obviously been watching her every expression—and deriving great enjoyment from doing so!

Her head went back proudly. 'Mrs Diamond is perfectly correct in her statement,' she said smoothly. 'This appears to be an extremely private family conversation. But I would be quite happy, Mr Diamond, to talk to you about Jessica's accident at a more convenient time.' She met his eyes challengingly, still slightly confused as to why he didn't seem to have told his mother that the two of them had already met earlier down on the beach.

Why hadn't he told Celia Diamond? Why hadn't she confessed? The answer to the last was easy; she shouldn't really have been down on the beach at all this afternoon. Celia Diamond had warned her when she'd first come to work here not to go down there when the weather was like it was today…

'Now is a convenient time for me,' Rufus Diamond invited her.

'It's Annie's afternoon off,' Celia told him quickly before Annie could make any sort of reply.

Rufus looked at her with narrowed eyes now. 'Is it indeed?' he finally drawled slowly.

Annie didn't need to be told that, with this new information, he was again adding up two and two and coming up with the answer of five! The speculation was clearly there in his mocking gaze.

'It is,' she confirmed briskly. 'But I'm not going anywhere, except upstairs to check on Jessica, so I'll be perfectly happy to talk to you once you've finished your conversation with your mother—' She broke off with a puzzled frown as her remark brought forth a harsh laugh from Rufus. 'Did I say something...funny?' she said haltingly—although for the life of her she couldn't imagine what it had been.

'To me, yes. To Celia, no,' Rufus replied, his grin wolfish again now, as it had been down on the beach. 'If you've been here two months someone really should have filled you in on the family history by now—'

'Rufus!' Celia admonished sharply, two spots of angry colour in her cheeks.

He gave her only a cursory glance. 'Something else the servants shouldn't know?' he taunted.

Celia gave him one of her chilling looks—a look that had no visible effect on him whatsoever!—before turning back to Annie. 'Perhaps if you wouldn't mind going and checking on Jessica now...?' she suggested smoothly—although it was more in the order of an instruction. 'I'm sure you and Rufus can catch up with each other later,' she dismissed.

Annie was beginning to wish she had never set eyes on the man!

There was no doubting that Celia Diamond could be slightly condescending in her manner, or that things had

become a little complicated since Anthony had arrived
with his fiancée for a visit, but for the main part Annie
had enjoyed her time here, found Jessica a delight to
work with. Admittedly, it hadn't all been peace and harmony, but she loved Jessica, and anything else was just
discomfort she had learnt to live with.

With the arrival of Rufus Diamond, she had a feeling
all that was about to change!

CHAPTER TWO

'ISN'T it wonderful?' Jessica's eyes glowed deeply blue. 'Daddy's home!' She clapped her hands together in pleasure.

Annie wished she could share the young girl's enthusiasm, but, having made her escape from the man downstairs only minutes ago, she was in no hurry to see Rufus Diamond again. Although it was obvious, from Jessica's excitement, that his daughter couldn't wait for him to come back up to her bedroom.

'It's a lovely surprise for you,' Annie acknowledged guardedly, straightening the pillows behind her charge. 'Does your father often return unexpectedly in this way?'

'Always!' Jessica nodded happily, dark curls bouncing. 'But he leaves just as suddenly too,' she added wistfully.

Annie realised he probably had to; as an investigative reporter he would just have to go where the story was, whenever it occurred. Which was pretty tough on his young daughter. Although, she had to admit, Jessica seemed a well-adjusted child to her; she certainly didn't qualify as neglected or psychologically disturbed!

Annie herself was still puzzled as to what she could have said earlier to so amuse Rufus Diamond. Neither he nor Celia had offered an explanation before she'd excused herself to come upstairs to Jessica. And she had no intention of asking the little girl; that would be most unfair.

'How are you feeling this afternoon?' She smiled down at her young charge.

Jessica grinned back at her—her grin, Annie now knew, was not unlike her father's! 'Well enough to go downstairs for dinner!' she announced cheerfully.

Annie felt her heart sink at the statement. If Jessica went down to the family dining-room for the meal, then it meant she had to join them too. And if the tension between Celia and Rufus was any indication of the man's effect on the rest of the family it boded ill for everyone's digestion—including her own!

'Are you sure?' she prompted lightly. 'You're still using the crutches to get about.' The accident had happened at the weekend, three days ago, and Jessica had been advised by the doctor to rest for several days before attempting to put any stress on her ankle.

The first day or so Jessica had enjoyed being waited on, having visitors come up to her bedroom, but after that the novelty had begun to pall. Consequently, this morning she had announced she would get up for a while, although after a couple of hours' activity she had been happy to spend the afternoon back in her bed resting. But not now, with the arrival of her father, it seemed!

'Daddy will carry me down,' Jessica assured her warmly, obviously liking this idea very much.

'The sooner you get up on your own two feet, the sooner you can go back to school,' Annie teased the little girl.

Jessica's face lit up at the thought. 'Can I go back tomorrow?'

Annie laughed indulgently, knowing that the week Jessica had been told to take as sick-leave from the private day school she attended twenty miles away had been an added incentive to Jessica when it came to the bed-rest. But even that had started to fade as Jessica had begun to miss her schoolfriends, especially her best friend, Lucy.

'I think that may be a little soon.' Annie shook her head regretfully. 'Besides, you can spend some time with your father now.' Her humour faded at that thought; hopefully she wouldn't have to spend time with him too! 'Speaking of which,' she added briskly, 'I had better go and shower and dress for dinner so that I can come back and help you later.'

'Is Daddy coming back up soon?' Jessica frowned at his non-appearance.

Very soon, if the abruptness of his conversation with Celia was anything to go by! 'I'm sure he is.' Annie squeezed the little girl's hand reassuringly. 'He was just saying hello to your grandmother when I came up.'

Jessica grimaced at this news. 'Oh.'

Obviously the tension that existed between her father and Celia wasn't a family secret, not even from someone as young as Jessica!

'Try and get some rest,' Annie encouraged. 'Then you won't feel sleepy over dinner.'

She wished, as she walked slowly down the hallway to her own bedroom, that she could sleep through dinner; it didn't promise, with Rufus Diamond's arrival, to be a very restful meal.

'Annie!'

She turned sharply at the sound of her name being called, colour warming her cheeks as she saw Anthony hurrying towards her, her heart giving its usual leap of excitement just at the sight of him, his blond good looks breathtaking to say the least. Annie had been bowled over by him the first time she'd looked at him.

'God, I'm sorry about earlier.' He spoke agitatedly as he reached her side, hair windswept, sky-blue eyes troubled as he looked down at her. 'Davina decided she just had to go into town, and I just had to drive her because the weather was so bad.' He mimicked a good impression of the slightly breathless way his fiancée spoke. 'I hope you didn't wait too long for me down on the jetty,' he said apologetically as he took one of her hands into his.

Annie was mesmerised once again by the deep blue of his eyes, her legs feeling suddenly weak, her hand trembling when it made contact with his.

How had Rufus Diamond guessed that she was waiting for his brother down on the jetty?

More important than that, how had he known she had become romantically entangled with his brother?

Because she had. Had been attracted to Anthony from the first moment she'd looked at him when he'd come to stay several weekends ago. Too late she had realised he was engaged to someone else. An engagement which was virtually impossible for him to get out of.

'Not very long,' she dismissed, though she had already waited almost an hour when Rufus Diamond had arrived. She sounded slightly breathless herself because of Anthony's close proximity.

'I'm really sorry.' Anthony squeezed her hand, smiling. 'I know that we need to talk, that there must be things you want to ask me.'

Annie felt that fluttering sensation in her chest again

as she thought of the possibility that some of their conversation might concern how he felt about her! She wondered if he would kiss her again, as he had on Sunday.

His mother and Davina had gone off that morning to visit neighbouring friends for a couple of hours, and Anthony had cried off because he had some notes to prepare for a case he was involved in when he got back to London the following week. He had told her later that he had also hoped for an opportunity to be alone with her...!

In one way it was lucky he had stayed behind on Sunday, because he'd been the one to help her after Jessica had come off her horse, driving them to the hospital so that Jessica could have her ankle X-rayed, carrying the little girl up to her bedroom once they'd returned, sitting with them both until Jessica had fallen asleep.

And that was when he had kissed her...!

Annie had been stunned. Elated. Ecstatic. Because the attraction she had felt towards him, for so many weeks, was returned.

And then she had felt devastated. Embarrassed. Because he was engaged to marry another woman.

Anthony had explained that he no longer loved Davina, but that it was almost impossible for him to tell her so at this time, since Davina's father was the senior partner in the law firm Anthony worked for.

Annie could sympathise with his dilemma, but she had no idea where that left her. 'It doesn't matter,' she excused him now abruptly, still uncomfortable with the fact that he was engaged to Davina. 'I—your brother is home,' she stated flatly, not sure that she would be able to see much more of Anthony anyway, still wondering if she would have a job after today.

It was as if she had given Anthony an electric shock. He stepped back abruptly, releasing her hand as he did so. 'Rufus is back?' he grated incredulously, blue eyes wide open now.

'He's downstairs with your mother.' Annie nodded, feeling totally miserable about the other man's return herself. In fact, the only one who seemed pleased to see him was Jessica! 'I'm surprised you didn't see him on your way up,' she added heavily. Or hear him, she added silently: Rufus Diamond hadn't exactly been quiet over his disapproval at Jessica having a replacement nanny.

Anthony still frowned. 'I came straight upstairs to look for you. Do you know how long he's staying?'

'He's only just arrived!' she responded ruefully.

'His last effort to be a father to Jess amounted to a full twenty-four hours, I believe,' Anthony scorned. 'Have you seen him? Spoken to him?' He looked at her searchingly. 'I can see by your expression that you have,' he said disgustedly. 'Throwing his weight about as usual, no doubt?'

She moistened dry lips. 'He didn't seem—too happy about Margaret's departure.'

Anthony raised dark blond brows. 'I wonder why? I mean, a nanny is just a nanny— Oh, not you, of course, my darling,' he quickly apologised as she looked taken aback. 'But Jess has had a succession of nannies; I'm just surprised Rufus could tell one from another!'

Well, he certainly seemed to know the difference this time! Although Annie was still stunned by Anthony's endearment; was she really his darling?

'Margaret was a blonde; Annie is a redhead,' drawled

a voice that was becoming all too recognisable. 'I think even I can tell the difference,' Rufus Diamond said sarcastically as he strode down the hallway.

Annie was once again struck by the lack of similarity between these two men: Rufus was at least a couple of inches taller than his brother as he stood beside the younger man, his hair long, dark and shaggy, while Anthony's was blond and kept expertly styled. Rufus was also the more powerfully built, and even the casual clothing they both wore was of a completely different style; the older man wore jeans, whereas Anthony's trousers were tailored. And, although both men were strikingly handsome, that was in a completely different way, too: Anthony's was a boyish handsomeness, while Rufus Diamond's face looked as if it had been hewn from the rocks along the seashore.

If Rufus had heard that remark about Jessica's nannies, had he also heard his brother call her his darling?

Cobalt-blue eyes were narrowed on the two of them in cool assessment before he turned to look at his brother. 'Davina seems to be wondering where you've got to,' he went on pointedly. 'I told her to look for the first pretty face and she was sure to find you there! And I was right,' he added softly, his speculative gaze encompassing Annie again as well now.

She felt the colour enter her cheeks, could feel its warmth. And it had nothing to do with being called pretty by this man. Why was Rufus so contemptuous of her? He didn't even know her! From the way he talked to her, and about her, she didn't think he was going to take the time to get to know her, either!

'I was merely asking Anthony if he knew whether or

not you were coming up to see Jessica again,' she told him tartly. 'She seemed to think you would be.'

'And she was right, because here I am,' he returned, amusement—at her expense!—darkening his eyes even more.

She met that look unblinkingly. 'I'm sure Jessica will be thrilled,' she said evenly.

To her surprise Rufus threw back his head and gave a shout of laughter, his expression warm now, that grin still curving his lips as he looked down at her. 'I was wondering if this unusual colour was real or from a bottle.' He reached out and lightly ruffled the deep red of her short, curling hair. 'Now I know it is red! I should watch yourself with this one, Anthony,' he told his brother. 'She may just turn round and bite!' And, with that last taunt left floating in the air between them, he strode off to Jessica's bedroom, quietly going inside. Jessica's squeals of delight were heard seconds later.

'What did he mean by that last remark?' Anthony asked sharply. 'Exactly what did the two of you talk about when you met earlier?'

Annie smoothed her mussed hair with irritated fingers. Really, Rufus Diamond treated her as if she were no older than Jessica! Although, from the implications he was making concerning herself and his brother, he didn't really believe that…!

'Annie!' Anthony snapped impatiently. 'I asked what you and Rufus talked about earlier,' he prompted at her puzzled look.

She thought back to that embarrassing conversation with him on the beach, when she had mistaken him for a trespasser—and knew she couldn't tell Anthony about that. She felt uncomfortable enough about the encounter already, without sharing it with anyone.

'Not a lot,' she responded vaguely. 'Although he did tell me to be careful on the beach; he said someone had once died there.' She looked up at Anthony, perplexed.

He pursed his lips thoughtfully. 'Did he, indeed?' he said slowly. 'Did he say who it was?'

'No.' She shrugged. 'We really weren't talking for that long.' Only long enough for Annie to make a complete fool of herself!

'Hmm.' Anthony was still attentive. 'It's interesting that he told you about that at all.'

Annie was intrigued now. 'Is it?'

'It isn't important,' Anthony dismissed carelessly. 'Although you do realise, with Rufus around, we're going to have to be even more careful about when and where the two of us meet?'

She had been debating this afternoon, as she'd stood on the jetty waiting for him—pointlessly, as it turned out—whether or not they should meet again. Oh, she was no less attracted to him, and she wanted to feel wanted by him, but he was engaged to another woman—no matter how much of a farce, on his part, the engagement now was.

This was the circle in which she had kept going round and round, and every time she'd come back to the fact that she was attracted to a man who was engaged to marry someone else. Even though the attraction seemed to be reciprocated, it was still wrong for her to feel this way about a man promised to another girl.

She drew in a controlling breath. 'Perhaps we shouldn't meet...'

'I was hoping you would say that!' Anthony gave her

a hug, smiling down at her when he released her. 'It won't be for long; as I've said, going by Rufus's last visit, this one may only be for a day or so. Then we can start to see each other without worrying about him.'

That hadn't been what she was about to say at all. Much as it pained her, the only conclusion she had come to concerning her relationship with Anthony—such as it was!—was that it would have to end. At least until Anthony had decided what he was going to do about his engagement. But Anthony seemed to have misunderstood her just now...

'You really are wonderful, Annie,' he told her huskily, blue eyes glowing. 'How could I have been so stupid as to think I could make a go of things with Davina?' He shook his head at his own lack of forethought. 'I'll sort things out, Annie, you'll see. In the meantime, I intend to stay as much out of Rufus's way as possible. I suggest you do the same.'

Easier said than done!

As Jessica had hoped, Daddy did come and carry her downstairs to dinner. Which meant he came up to Jessica's bedroom to collect her. And as Annie was there too, having helped the young girl to dress in her prettiest dress—red velvet edged with fine lace at the neck and cuffs—she encountered Rufus again not much more than an hour later.

As the Diamonds were a family that dressed for dinner, his black evening suit, snowy white shirt and black bow-tie came as nothing of a surprise to Annie. The fact that the formality of his clothing did little to disguise the leashed power within was also expected; Rufus Diamond was a man who exuded arrogant masculinity.

'Does our little mouse still have her roar this evening?' he teased. 'Or has Anthony managed to talk you down to a whimper?'

Jessica looked puzzled by his query. 'But we don't have any mice, Daddy.'

Annie didn't pretend not to know it was her he was referring to. Usually she was so calm and controlled—temper tantrums hadn't gone down too well at the children's homes! It was only this man who brought back echoes of the fiery side of her nature that over the years she had taken such care to quell.

As he did now! 'The younger Mr Diamond doesn't talk down to me at all,' she told him tartly.

The humour left Rufus's darkly mocking face as he frowned, giving him a slightly menacing appearance—and making Annie wonder if she was wise to talk back to him so sharply. He was her employer, after all...

'Don't backtrack, Annie,' he replied curtly—as if he was well able to read her inner uncertainty.

Maybe he could. She had never been any good at hiding her feelings. Another reason for ending this barely formed relationship with Anthony. It could only bring her grief, and possibly dismissal from working with the little girl she already adored. These sort of complications weren't something she had given any thought to when she had opted to work in a family environment!

'And I wasn't talking down to you, either,' Rufus continued firmly. 'Jessica did nothing but extol your virtues for the earlier part of this evening.' He ruffled his daughter's hair affectionately, receiving a pleased giggle in return. Rufus turned back to Annie with darkly piercing eyes. 'Children aren't easily deceived.'

That was true; she had easily been able to tell, when she was in care, which people were genuinely interested in her and who was just making a show of being kind. But she didn't see how anyone could be less than sincerely fond of a lovely child like Jessica.

'Daddy...' Jessica spoke carefully. 'What does "extol your virtues" mean?' She wrinkled her nose in confusion.

'It means, young lady—' Rufus easily swung his daughter up into his arms, grinning down at her '—that you think Annie is great!'

'But she is,' Jessica said without a shadow of doubt.

'I'm sure she is, poppet.' Rufus tickled his daughter as he carried her ceremoniously down the wide staircase.

Annie walked happily along behind them, pleased with the obvious closeness between father and daughter, despite Rufus's three-month absence. The two could have been together only yesterday, so naturally affectionate was their relationship.

'Mind you,' Rufus paused to whisper conspiratorially to Jessica, 'when I met Annie earlier, I didn't think she was much older than you!' This last, playful remark was accompanied by a glance back at a red-faced Annie. 'She looks—much older in that black dress,' he added lightly, blue gaze challenging.

'I helped her to choose it,' Jessica told him proudly.

And, in fact, she had. Having worked in a daytime kindergarten, where her evenings were her own, Annie hadn't had much call for the sort of formal clothes she would need for one of the Diamond dinners. After two evenings of coming down in serviceable skirts and blouses, of feeling exactly what she was—the hired help—she had decided to change that, taking Jessica into town with her shopping on their first available Saturday and buying three dresses that, when matched with differing accessories, could get her through an evening no matter what company happened to arrive. On the very evening she'd bought the dresses she had been presented with a bishop and a judge, so her purchases had been well worth the effort!

She had bought black, royal-blue and white dresses, and tonight, as Rufus Diamond had duly noted, she wore the black one, which while not accentuating her figure, didn't hide it either, the above-knee length revealing an expanse of shapely leg too. On a couple of other evenings she had worn a long floral scarf trailing from her throat, or a fitted jacket of powder-blue, but tonight she wore only a single silver broach fastened above her left breast; she hadn't wanted to wear anything this evening that would draw attention to her!

'And Annie is much older than me,' Jessica added in a scandalised voice. 'She's twenty-two. She told me she is.'

'Oh, that's much older!' Rufus agreed, only the twitch of his lips, as he turned briefly to Annie, telling of his repressed humour—again at her expense.

'Really, Daddy.' Jessica unwittingly sounded just like her grandmother at that moment. 'You can be so silly at times.' She gave an exasperated shake of her head—again, not unlike Celia would have done.

Annie doubted that the word 'silly' could be applied to Rufus—at any time. It certainly wasn't the impression he had given her since their first meeting this afternoon!

And while Annie, in her parentless state, might have little idea of what a family dinner should be like, she was sure that the following couple of hours spent at the Diamond dining table was not it!

It was the strangest meal Annie had ever been present

at—and she didn't mean food-wise; as usual Mrs Wilson, the cook, had provided an excellent meal; home-made pâté, followed by duck in a delicious orange sauce, with fresh fruit in port to finish. But for all the justice the Diamond family paid it, it might as well have been the beans on toast Annie had often enjoyed in the past as her own meal of the day!

The tension around the table was intolerable, felt by all, she was sure, except Jessica—a happy Jessica with her father seated at her side. And Rufus Diamond was the catalyst for everyone else's tension—although for all the notice he took of it he might have been as unaware of it as his daughter.

Or so Annie thought...

Jessica was seated between the two of them, and Rufus had to lean forward to speak to Annie. 'Enjoying yourself?' he asked, still with that repressed humour.

She had been wishing the meal over, at least her own and Jessica's part in it. The young girl usually retired to bed when the coffee and port stage was reached. Although that might be different tonight, as her father was here...

As for enjoying the meal...! Celia was at her most haughty, while Davina, a tall, elegant blonde, flirted shamelessly with Rufus at every opportunity, and Anthony—well, Anthony seemed lost in his own reverie, paying little attention to any of them. This Annie was relieved about; the last thing she wanted was to give Rufus any more ammunition to fire at herself and Anthony!

'Very much, thank you,' she returned primly.

He gave that wolfish grin at her politeness. 'Liar!' he rejoined quietly.

She met his gaze unflinchingly. 'I was referring to the food, of course.'

Once again she was taken aback when he threw back his head and gave a throaty laugh of pure enjoyment, those lines she had noticed earlier beside his eyes and mouth proving to be laughter lines—evidence that this man laughed a lot. And she didn't think it was always at other people; somehow she sensed that he had the ability to laugh at himself too. This man was an enigma, a chameleon, one moment distant and forbidding, the next full of humour. It could take a lifetime to know such a man—

Annie broke off her thoughts with a guilty glance in Anthony's direction, once again affected by his good looks, the way he smiled across at her conspiratorially, almost as if he had sensed her confusion—although not, thank goodness, the reason for it. She doubted he would smile at her in that way if he realised exactly what she had been thinking about his brother!

'Would you care to share the joke with us, Annie?' Celia Diamond's mildly arrogant voice broke in on her thoughts. 'I'm sure we could all do with some light amusement,' she added dryly—showing she was far from immune to the awkwardness of the evening.

But as she and the rest of the family, and the tension that existed between them with Rufus's presence, were the subject of that light amusement Annie somehow didn't think the other woman would be at all happy to share the joke!

Annie shot Rufus a look that clearly cried 'help'—although, even knowing Rufus's sense of humour as little as she did, she had a feeling he might just enjoy sitting back and watching her squirm!

'It was just a little anecdote about Jessica that Annie wished to share with me.' Thankfully, Rufus did come to her rescue. 'Speaking of which,' he added, with an affectionate wink at his daughter, 'I think it's time Jess went up to bed. No protests, young lady,' he added with gentle reproof as he sensed that was exactly what she was about to give him. 'You're going to need plenty of sleep if you're going to attempt to beat me at chess tomorrow.'

This was the first indication Annie had had that the child played chess; she seemed very young to have mastered such a complicated game. Nevertheless Annie had stood up to leave quickly enough herself at Rufus's first suggestion of it; this evening couldn't end quickly enough as far as she was concerned!

Although Rufus's next comment warned her that, for her at least, it was far from over…!

'Carry on and have coffee without me,' he told his family as he easily swung Jessica back up into his arms. 'Once we have Jessica settled for the night, I intend talking to Annie for a while.'

It wasn't the easy dismissal of her own coffee that bothered her, nor even Rufus's casual grouping of the two of them, but that innocuous-sounding mention of 'talking to Annie for a while'…

What did Rufus want to talk to her about? The fact that she was the new nanny to his daughter? Or something else…?

CHAPTER THREE

'THESE are excellent references.' Rufus put the two letters he had just read down on the desk in front of him,
his eyes narrowed thoughtfully. 'They must have been
sorry to lose you at the kindergarten.'

It was a statement, not a question, Annie knew
that—because Brenda Thompson, the person in charge
of the kindergarten, had clearly said so in her letter of
reference.

They were in Rufus Diamond's study, a spacious
room furnished with heavy mahogany furniture; it was
next to the library, and Annie hadn't even known it was
here, let alone entered it before. Not that this particularly
surprised her: Clifftop House was an enormous place,
with two completely self-contained wings at either end
of it. One housed the servants who lived in, the other
appeared to be unused, and there were dozens of rooms
that Annie had never been into.

Rufus had kissed his daughter goodnight once they
were upstairs, leaving Annie to prepare the little girl for
bed and informing her that he would see her downstairs
in his study as soon as she had finished what she was
doing. Annie had had to ask Jessica for directions to her
father's study.

As she sat across the desk from him now, it was as if
those moments of humour between them earlier had
never happened. She felt like one of the children at the
home, hauled before Mrs James for some misdemeanour

37

or other! Not that she ever had been. Keep your head down and stay out of trouble—that had been her motto. It had seemed to work quite well—

'Excellent references,' Rufus repeated slowly, the removal of his jacket and loosening of his bow-tie not making him look any more approachable. 'But they actually tell me very little about you. Who are you? Where are your family? Are you likely to leave at a moment's notice too?' he added grimly, obviously thinking of the absent Margaret. 'I think I have a right to ask these questions; after all, you are in charge of my daughter on a day-to-day basis.'

Annie agreed with him, knew she would be the same if her own daughter's welfare were at stake. And yet, from Rufus Diamond, these questions seemed an intrusion. It was totally illogical, but she found she didn't want to tell him any more about herself than she had to.

'I'm Annie Fletcher. And I'm your typical Orphan Annie,' she added self-derisively. 'I have no family that I'm aware of. And I wouldn't leave here, or Jessica, without giving you a good reason—and time enough to find a replacement!'

His mouth twisted. 'I believe Margaret told me the same thing.'

She shrugged. 'You'll have to take that up with Margaret; I never met her.' Jessica had been without a nanny for almost a week when Annie had arrived two months ago. 'All I can say is that I won't do the same thing.'

'Take it or leave it, hmm?' Rufus said shrewdly.

'I didn't mean that at all,' Annie defended quietly, hot colour in her cheeks. 'Of course you don't have to take it or leave it; you're my employer, and you're perfectly within your rights to want certain assurances. I seriously doubt I would ever choose to leave Jessica.' Her expression softened as she spoke of the child.

Dark eyes assessed her questioningly. 'You're fond of my daughter?'

'Very.' She didn't take offence at the question—not this one—although she felt sure there were plenty of others Rufus Diamond could and would ask that would be very offensive indeed!

'And just how fond of my brother are you?'

That was one of them! It wasn't altogether unexpected, though; she had known since the three of them met in the hallway earlier that Rufus would have to make some reference to it. She wasn't disappointed!

'I like all the family,' she said evasively.

Rufus's mouth thinned. 'Even Celia?' he queried.

The other woman could be extremely haughty, and Annie knew now she considered her a servant. But at least Celia was honest about it, made no pretence of it being otherwise, and for the main part she had treated Annie fairly, if not exactly warmly.

'Even Celia,' she confirmed firmly.

Rufus gave a humourless grin. 'Methinks the lady doth protest too much,' he said smoothly.

'Not at all,' Annie protested indignantly. 'Mrs Diamond has been very kind in her own way.' She regretted adding the last comment almost as soon as she had said it, knowing she had given Rufus an opening she hadn't meant to. She didn't have to wait long!

'"In her own way",' Rufus retorted. 'I've known Celia since I was two years old—and I've never seen her be kind to anyone. Not without a damn good reason!'

He added cynically, 'And nannies to my daughter do not come under that category.'

Annie wasn't particularly interested in his scathing comments concerning Celia, had no intention of getting into any sort of in-depth conversation concerning the other woman. What did interest her was Rufus's reference to knowing Celia since he was two years old... Of course, most children didn't begin to learn things about their parents until they were a few years old, but in this case she didn't think that was what was meant...

Rufus was watching her closely, well aware of her puzzlement, she was sure. The man seemed to miss nothing!

'You really don't know too much about this family, do you?' he said slowly.

She knew she loved Jessica, that Celia lived her role as lady of the manor to perfection—and that Anthony was trapped in an engagement he shouldn't be in! What else did she need to know?

'Perhaps I should get back to my original question.' Rufus spoke purposefully now, dark eyes watchful. 'How well do you know Anthony?'

Not well enough, obviously. Because until this last weekend she hadn't even realised he had a fiancée. He had been down for several weekend visits on his own, which was when Annie had found herself becoming attracted to his charm and good looks. It had been a shock—and a disappointment—when he had arrived on Saturday with Davina, to stay for a week. Then he had kissed her on Sunday... Now she was just confused about the whole thing.

'I don't,' she answered honestly. Did you have to know a person well to be attracted to them?

Rufus was still watching her with those shrewdly assessing eyes. 'In that case,' he finally said harshly, 'my advice to you is stay well away from him!'

She remained outwardly calm, but flinched inwardly at the force behind Rufus's words. It had been obvious from the first that there was little love lost between the two brothers, and that the dislike was mutual. But once more Rufus Diamond was talking to her as if she were no older than Jessica. Maybe falling for the charm of a man who had turned out to be engaged to marry another woman wasn't the most sensible thing she had ever done in her life, but, as Jessica had pointed out earlier, she was much older than her young charge—old enough to make her own mistakes, or otherwise!

'Fatherly advice, Mr Diamond?' she returned smartly.

His mouth tightened as her barb hit home. 'I was only joking with Jessica earlier when I made that remark about your age.' He easily guessed which comment of his she had taken exception to. 'I also take back what I said down on the beach, about your being young and impressionable,' he added at her bemused expression. 'Young you may be, but you're nobody's fool.'

Annie drew in a sharp breath; she wasn't so sure about that!

The fact remained that she hadn't known about Anthony's fiancée until Saturday, but even when she had found out she had still allowed him to kiss her. Wasn't that foolish in the extreme, even if she did feel so deeply attracted to him?

'Thank you,' she accepted huskily, not quite able to meet the deep blue of Rufus's gaze.

'And whether my advice just now was fatherly or not,' he continued briskly, 'you would do well to take it!'

She bristled indignantly. Rufus had arrived here only a few short hours ago, and yet he seemed to have done nothing in that time but issue orders and upset people—mostly her! And, while she accepted he had a right to tell her what he required of her as far as Jessica was concerned, she did not welcome his interference in what she considered to be her private life!

Nevertheless, she chose her next words carefully. 'You're very kind, Mr Diamond—'

'I'm no more kind than Celia,' he cut in scathingly. 'Anthony either, for that matter. In fact, we aren't a very kind family,' he concluded.

'In that case, I'm surprised you leave—' She broke off abruptly, warned by the sudden dark anger in his face that she would be overstepping the line with the observation she was about to make concerning Jessica. She looked up at him with wide, apprehensive eyes as he stood up forcefully, his size seeming to fill the room.

'Not young and impressionable at all,' he said with deliberation. 'And for God's sake take that scared-rabbit look off your face,' he told her disgustedly, moving around the desk to perch on it in front of her. 'I may not be kind, Annie, but by the same token I've never struck a woman in my life. And I don't intend to start with you. Even if you do say the damnedest things,' he added gratingly. 'I leave Jessica here because there is nowhere else for her to go. Her mother is dead.' It was a flat statement of fact, revealing none of his inner feelings concerning the loss. 'And I can hardly take her with me when I go on an assignment!'

Annie could see the sense of that; she also knew that Jessica fared so much better than she had herself. Her own mother had died shortly after giving birth to her, and she had never even known who her father was, only the circumstances of her birth. Whereas Jessica obviously adored her father, for all his long absences.

Annie moistened her lips. 'I'm sorry; I didn't mean to criticise—'

'Yes, you did,' he said without rancour. 'And I probably deserve it.' He reached out to put his hand beneath her chin and gently raise her face so that she had no choice but to look directly into his. He didn't look angry any more, his mouth curving into a smile. 'You'll do, Annie Fletcher,' he told her huskily. 'You love my daughter; that's all the reference you need.' He easily dismissed the two letters she had provided.

She was barely breathing, certainly not moving, very conscious of how very close they were, the deep cobalt-blue of his eyes so clear to her now—the only thing that was—as her gaze was held mesmerised by his, her face made immobile by the touch of his hand, his fingers warm against the softness of her throat.

She flicked her tongue over her lips again, colour warming her cheeks as she saw his eyes following the movement. She inwardly withdrew, then instantly moved back from the touch of his hand, gratefully drawing air into her lungs at the same time. What on earth was happening to her? She *wasn't* that young and impressionable—so how, feeling the way she did about Anthony, had she also felt the pull of this man's attraction?

She didn't know herself under these circumstances. But she was sure that, even if the Diamond men weren't kind, they were both possessed of an attractiveness she would be better off without!

'Can I go now?' she said abruptly, wishing he would move away from her—let her breathe a little!

Thankfully, he did, moving back behind the desk, although he didn't sit down again, merely looked at her from beneath lowered lids. 'No,' he finally replied forcefully. 'We haven't talked about Jessica's accident yet.'

Which was one of the things she was here to discuss; how could she have forgotten? This man, that was how; she was finding it difficult to keep up with his lightning changes of mood and conversation, knew she would look back on this time spent in his study with a feeling of exhaustion. She felt as if she had to constantly be on her guard, for one reason or another.

And the subject of Jessica's accident was no different. She didn't know how it had happened; one minute the little girl had been in the saddle, the next she had been on the ground. Annie was a novice rider herself; simply managing to stay seated in the saddle was a major feat! She had mastered just sitting on the back of the placid animal she had been given and letting the horse do all the work. She simply wasn't experienced enough to give any sort of judgement on Jessica's mishap.

That in itself would probably be a black mark against her in Rufus Diamond's book!

'Knowing how to ride a horse wasn't something that was discussed when I came here for an interview,' she told him defensively. 'But it's something Jessica loves to do, and as she can't possibly go out on her own—'

'You had to accompany her,' Rufus surmised, his eyes suddenly alight with humour, a slight twitch to those sculptured lips. 'Done much riding before, have you, Annie?' He raised innocently questioning brows.

Too innocently. He was laughing at her again, damn him!

'There wasn't much call for it in the inner London Children's home I was brought up in!' she told him sharply.

The stark contrast between her own childhood and Jessica's was apparent in that one blunt statement. There had never been too much spare cash at the home, certainly not enough to run to riding lessons. Even if she had wanted them. Which she hadn't.

And after Jessica's accident she wasn't sure she ever wanted to sit on a horse again! Jessica had been riding most of her life, it seemed, and still she had been thrown.

'So you meant it literally when you called yourself Orphan Annie?' Rufus said.

'Yes.' She was on the defensive, unsure of the turn of the conversation. Again!

Rufus took his time, sitting down in the chair behind the desk, his face softening as he looked across its width at her. 'In that case, I wouldn't take the Diamond family as a typical example of the species,' he drawled dryly. 'It had some sense of normality before my father died six years ago; since then it's deteriorated into anarchy,' he said matter-of-factly. 'A group of people who happen to share the same house but who can barely stand the sight of each other!'

'Surely not?' Annie gasped in dismay at the tragedy of such a thing. But hadn't she seen it herself this evening, in the barely maintained civility over dinner? And at the time she had thought Rufus to be the catalyst; she couldn't remember it having been quite as tense on other evenings when she and Jessica had joined in the evening meal.

'Surely, yes,' Rufus confirmed wryly. 'And as no one else seems to have filled you in on the family history perhaps I should do so,' he said wearily.

She wasn't sure she wanted to know, already felt uncomfortable enough with the little she did know. 'Is it relevant to Jessica that I know?' She frowned.

His mouth tightened. 'Before the weekend, I would have said no. Now I'm not so sure...' He grimaced darkly, then shook off that mood as he smiled across at her. 'Don't look so worried,' he chided, at her apprehensive expression. 'As far as I'm aware, there is no history of axe murderers or serial killers in the family. At least, none that Celia would ever allow to be discussed! Appearances are everything to my dear stepmama,' he told her wryly. 'Although she wasn't always so particular,' he amended harshly, eyes cold with anger once again.

'Stepmama'... Celia was his stepmother.

His earlier comments made complete sense now. Although it meant a bit of readjusting in Annie's own mind, she freely admitted. He and Anthony were half-brothers, which explained the stark contrast in their colouring, the fact that the two men shared so few characteristics. Oh, they were both handsome men, but in a completely different way. It also explained the lack of genuine affection between Rufus and Celia. Although Rufus could surely only have been a baby when Celia married his father...

Rufus was watching her with amusement. 'Your arithmetic is perfectly in order. I was barely two when my own mother died. And Celia, my father's secretary at the time, stepped in to help him over his loss. She did such a good job of it that Anthony was born exactly six months after their hurriedly arranged wedding!' he scorned. 'I'm not judging their morals, Annie,' he explained as she frowned a little more. 'Merely the lack of mourning accorded my own mother.'

She wasn't frowning because she thought he was being judgemental where his father and Celia's morals were concerned; it didn't seem to matter nowadays when so many children were born into relationships that didn't have a piece of paper to legalise them. No, she had been frowning at the speed of his father's second marriage after his wife's death, not the reason for it.

'That doesn't mean your father didn't mourn,' she told Rufus gently. 'Sometimes, when you've loved someone very much, to lose them is to lose part of yourself, and to love someone new is the only way you can feel complete again.'

Rufus looked at her closely, shaking his head slightly, as if he was surprised at her astuteness. 'You're very wise for someone so young, Annie—and again, I wasn't talking down to you,' he added quickly. 'My father said something along the same lines when I was old enough to question him on the subject. Unfortunately,' he continued hardily, 'by this time he had realised what a terrible mistake he had made in choosing Celia as his second love!'

It was often the case in rebound love, but in this instance they had produced a child. And the marriage had survived. Although, judging by Rufus's bitterness on his father's behalf towards Celia, not exactly happily.

So Rufus had grown up with a stepmother he disliked, and a half-brother he despised...

For years Annie had wished her own mother hadn't died when she was only a baby, had longed for a family of her own. But if the Diamond family were any example…!

'I did warn you not to take us as a typical family,' Rufus reminded her as he once more seemed to read her thoughts. 'Still want to work with Jessica?'

'Most definitely,' she answered without hesitation. 'And I'm really sorry about her accident. One moment she was in the saddle, the next the two of them were on the ground and Jessica was crying.' She could still remember that awful moment when she'd realised Jessica had really hurt herself.

'The two of them?' He looked puzzled.

'Jessica and the saddle.' She nodded. 'Didn't she tell you it came off with her?'

'No,' he rasped. 'Who the hell saddled the horse for her?'

'James, I presume…' Annie answered slowly, knowing by the darkening of Rufus's expression that the knowledge boded ill for the man in charge of the Diamond stables, which were situated at the back of the large house.

Jessica was very fond of the taciturn old man, and always managed to bring a smile to his weather-lined face—which probably accounted for why Jessica hadn't told her father about the saddle coming off with her when she fell… Oh, dear!

'The strap that goes under the horse came undone. I'm sure there was nothing James could have done about it.' She tried to make amends for her earlier gaffe.

Rufus drew in a deeply controlling breath, his jaw clenched. 'Probably not,' he muttered tightly.

But it was a subject he intended to pursue, the grimness of his expression told her.

Annie looked around for some way of diverting his attention, her sight resting with some relief on the chess-set that stood on a table in the corner of the wood-panelled room. 'I had no idea Jessica could play chess.' She referred to the challenge Rufus had issued to his daughter earlier for a match tomorrow. 'She seems very young to have mastered such a complicated game.'

'She asked me to teach her when she was five.' This was obviously an achievement of his young daughter's that he was proud of. 'She's quite good too,' he added ruefully. 'Although she hasn't managed to beat me yet!'

Annie doubted that many people had bested this man at anything. 'Yet,' she echoed mischievously. 'I know exactly how determined Jessica can be.'

He chuckled softly. 'A trait she inherited from her father, do you think?'

Now it was Annie's turn to give him an innocent look. 'I wouldn't know,' she returned mildly, eyes glowing with fun, a slight curve to her lips as she held back her smile.

His laughter deepened. 'I'll just bet you wouldn't! You—' He looked up sharply as the study door opened behind Annie without warning. 'What the hell do you want?' Rufus barked over Annie's shoulder at the intruder. 'And isn't it usual to knock before entering a room?' he demanded of his brother.

Anthony was completely undaunted, Annie could see, now that she had half turned in her seat to look at the doorway. And as he looked at her accusingly she began to feel guilty about the laughter he must have heard between Rufus and herself as he'd approached the study. Then she rebuked herself for feeling guilty; Rufus was her employer, Anthony was the one engaged to another woman!

'I was passing Jessica's room just now,' Anthony informed them disapprovingly, 'and she said her ankle was too painful for her to sleep. I gave her one of the pills the doctor left for her, but I have a feeling she really just wanted you to go up and see her again.'

Annie had stood up to go to her charge the moment Anthony had said she was in pain, but she hesitated at his last remark, looked uncertainly at Rufus.

He stood up. 'I'll go up to her,' he said decisively. 'It seems our conversation is over anyway.' He shot Anthony an impatient glance.

A gesture Anthony was completely impervious to. He grinned unconcernedly, his bad humour of moments ago seeming to have evaporated. 'Can I help it if your daughter loves you?' He shrugged, obviously having only recently left the dinner table, his hair looking blonder than ever against the dark material of the dinner jacket he still wore.

Rufus strode purposefully across the room, passing close to his brother as he did so, the differences between them at once noticeable, and it wasn't only in their colouring. Anthony's body kept trim and muscular from regular trips to the gym, whereas Rufus's lifestyle seemed to keep him slim and powerful, his slightly scornful expression seeming to say he didn't have time for such niceties as a gym, that the mere battle of life had hardened him physically as well as emotionally.

'It's as well someone does,' he muttered now in reply to Anthony's baiting comment, turning briefly back to Annie before going through the doorway he now stood before. 'Tell me, Annie,' he said. 'Do you play chess?'

She was taken aback at his return to the conversation Anthony had interrupted. But then, most of their discussion had been fragmented! 'Yes,' she answered huskily, not altogether sure why he was asking.

'I thought you might.' He nodded his satisfaction with her answer. 'We'll have a game together one evening. Although I should warn you, I never deliberately let anyone else win!'

She had a feeling that was true of him in most aspects of his life; he was a man who would give no quarter, to himself or anyone else! 'I never for a moment believed you would,' she acknowledged ruefully.

'Good.' He stepped out into the hallway, before once again pausing, turning back to her. 'Oh, and Annie...?'

What now? 'Yes?'

'You do look lovely in that black dress,' he told her throatily, a glitter of triumph in his eyes as he saw the blush on her cheeks before he turned and walked away, a quiet whistle floating in the air behind him.

Annie stared after him in dismay, knowing he had made that last comment to cause mischief; Jessica hadn't said she looked lovely earlier, only older! But she knew, as Anthony's mouth tightened in irritation, that Rufus's jibe had hit the target it was meant for.

She shook her head disbelievingly; these two men were like two little boys trying to score points off each other. For men aged thirty-nine and thirty-six, it was incredibly destructive...!

Anthony looked at her scowlingly. 'You and Rufus seem to be getting on well together.' It was more of an accusation than an observation!

'He seems happy enough that I continue to work with Jessica.' She deliberately didn't rise to the bait, having no intention of becoming yet another bone of contention between these two: they already shared enough ill feeling, without adding her to it! Besides, Rufus had meant to cause mischief...

Anthony cheered up at the statement. 'Well, that's good, isn't it? For us, I mean,' he said happily, moving closer to her. 'It means we'll have more time to get to know each other.'

Annie looked up at him, once again dazzled by his charming good looks, his normally pleasant disposition having returned. 'I suppose so,' she said slowly.

Anthony's arms moved smoothly about the smallness of her waist as he pulled her close against him.

'Someone might see us,' she protested.

'Who cares?' he dismissed. 'Besides, my mother and Davina are deep in discussion about some boring subject or other. I'd much rather be here with you.'

But Davina was his fiancée. This couldn't be right; Annie knew it couldn't. She tried to move gently but firmly out of his arms. 'Anthony—'

'Oh, for goodness' sake!' He thrust her away from him as he felt her struggle against him, a flush to his cheeks as he looked down at her. 'You weren't so damned particular on Sunday when I kissed you.' His eyes narrowed suspiciously. 'Or is it that, having met my older brother, you think he might be a better prospect?'

She gasped at the injustice of that accusation. She hadn't meant for that kiss to happen between them, had been racked with guilt about it ever since, very conscious of his engagement, no matter how disastrous that might appear to be. She certainly had no romantic interest in Rufus Diamond...! That would be pure madness on her part, even more so than her attraction to Anthony.

'I'm sorry, Annie.' Anthony was instantly contrite as he saw the tears sparkling in her eyes, once again holding her close to him. 'I shouldn't take my jealousy out on you.' He shook his head in self-disgust. 'Do you forgive me?' he encouraged softly, his forehead resting lightly on hers as he easily held her gaze.

How could she resist him when he looked exactly like a little boy, no older than some of the children she had looked after?

'Of course I forgive you,' she told him huskily. 'But Rufus is my employer, nothing else.' She pushed firmly from her mind her complete awareness of the older man.

'I'm glad you said that.' Anthony nodded his satisfaction. 'Because I would hate for Rufus to hurt you simply because he has an old score to settle with me.'

Annie looked up at him, troubled. Surely he wasn't referring to his mother's marriage to Rufus's father, and his own birth soon afterwards? No matter what Rufus considered to be the sins of the mother, they wouldn't have been passed on to an innocent child...

'I met Joanna first, you see,' he sighed, grimacing as Annie looked even more confused. 'Rufus's wife,' he explained wistfully. 'We met in London when I was at university there, had something of a—relationship,' he admitted. 'But it all ended when I came back here. At least, as far as I was concerned it did.' He shrugged. 'Unfortunately, Joanna hadn't taken our affair as lightly as I had, and she followed me down here, got a job locally, and once I had convinced her I didn't want our relationship to continue she set her sights on Rufus. Initially, I'm sure, to pique my interest. Which it didn't.' He grimaced again. 'But that just seemed to make Joanna more determined where Rufus was concerned, and before I knew what was happening the two of them were married. As Joanna related to me afterwards, her wedding gift to Rufus was to tell him I had been her lover first!'

Annie gasped at the cruelty of such a thing, no longer surprised at the animosity between the two men. Rufus was a man who would hate knowing his brother had been his wife's lover before their marriage!

'I hadn't mentioned my relationship with Joanna to Rufus because I really didn't think he was serious about her.' Anthony shook his head. 'I don't think he's ever really forgiven me for that.'

But the marriage had survived, and the couple had had Jessica together. Otherwise Annie wouldn't be here at all.

She had wanted to work with a family, had deliberately chosen to do so—but what a complicated family the Diamonds were turning out to be—the first Diamond bride dead, Celia becoming the wicked stepmother, Rufus's own bride tainted in a way he would never have been happy with, and she a Diamond bride who had also died.

Could it possibly have been one of these two women who had committed suicide in that rocky cove below Clifftop House? And, if so, which one...?

CHAPTER FOUR

'I TAKE it your interview last night with my stepson went well?' Celia Diamond queried briskly as she sat forward to pour the coffee that had just been brought in to them in Celia's private sitting-room.

Annie had answered the summons to join the other woman for morning coffee with some trepidation. But Jessica was in her father's study playing the promised game of chess, so she didn't really have a valid excuse not to join Celia.

She chose her words carefully, not really sure in her own mind of the success, or otherwise, of that meeting with Rufus. 'He seemed satisfied with my references,' she replied noncommittally.

Celia narrowed pale blue eyes. 'So you're to stay?'

Annie drew in a deep breath. 'It would seem so,' she said slowly.

'Good.' Celia sighed her satisfaction with this reply, then started sipping her coffee thoughtfully. 'I doubt that Rufus will stay here very long, anyway,' she said after a while. 'He never does!'

Well, Annie sincerely hoped that this time, for Jessica's sake he would. Although she could understand why he didn't usually prolong his visits—the tension in the house, since his arrival yesterday, was so tangible you could almost reach out and touch it!

'And I'm so glad you're to stay,' Celia continued evenly. 'Davina and I were discussing the wedding last night after we all had dinner, and it will be much easier for everyone involved if we don't have the added worry of Jessica's care to think of.'

'Wedding?' Annie echoed numbly. She could think of only one wedding Davina would want to discuss—her own! Was this the 'boring subject' the two women had discussed, that Anthony had referred to when he'd sought Annie out last night? She had a feeling that it was...

'The wedding has been brought forward to Christmas,' Celia explained, seemingly unaware of Annie's distress. 'Which, as it's to take place in London, means a lot of rearranging. The reception will be the problem, of course, because on such short notice we could end up with somewhere ghastly, and— But I'm sure all of this can't be of any interest to you,' she dismissed lightly. 'I merely want to assure myself that you will be here to take care of Jessica.'

Did she? Was that really all Celia wanted to do? Annie wasn't so sure. Or was it simply that she was looking for hidden meanings in everything now? Until yesterday she had taken all the Diamond family at face value; today she seemed to be looking for double meanings in every statement. It was Rufus's doing, of course. There was no way Celia could possibly know of her attraction to Anthony, and his interest in her. Was there...?

She was doing it again! Stop this, she inwardly berated herself, picking up her own cup of coffee and sipping it, grateful for the distraction. Poor Anthony; it seemed he was being pushed into this marriage from all sides!

Her coffee drunk, the conversation concluded to her

satisfaction—whatever that might be!—Celia excused herself, saying that she had some flowers to arrange and they were having guests to dinner this evening.

It was just Annie's luck that as she left the sitting-room immediately after Celia Anthony should be descending the stairs. They had parted in Rufus's study the previous evening, Anthony giving her a brief kiss on the lips before he went back to join his mother and Davina. A mother and a fiancée who had been discussing his forthcoming marriage. To say Annie was confused was putting it mildly!

Anthony gave her a searching look. 'Anything wrong?'

Yes, he was going to be married at Christmas, a matter of months away! And last night he had kissed her—again. Of course there was something wrong! But she was as much at a loss over what to do about it as she had been yesterday, down on the jetty.

'Anthony, I think we need to talk,' she began. 'Your mother has just told me—'

'About the wedding!' His grimaced his own feelings about that subject. 'Don't worry, Annie, it won't happen.'

She looked up at him with dark brown eyes, lashes long and silky. Because of her? She wasn't sure she wanted that responsibility, her own feelings towards him in total confusion. Since Rufus's arrival...

'And when do you intend telling Davina that?' she challenged. 'When the two of you reach the altar?'

Anthony's mouth tightened at the undoubted rebuke. 'I think that's my business, don't you?' he snapped resentfully.

Not because of her, she realised thankfully, noticing

things about him today that hadn't been visible when she'd been blinded by his charm and obvious good looks. With his anger came a slight twist of cruelty to his mouth, a coldness to his eyes, and—

'Hey, stop looking so worried,' he cajoled smilingly, that cruelty and coldness instantly gone, the laughter back in his eyes. 'I'm not really angry with you.' He grasped her arms lightly. 'Just a bit frustrated with the situation. Come on, Annie,' he encouraged softly. 'Smile for me.'

She was still confused, and it wasn't a situation she was comfortable with at all. 'I—'

'Trouble in paradise?' mocked a voice that was becoming increasingly familiar, Annie turning with a start to see Rufus coming down the hallway towards them, a sardonic grin curving those sculptured lips.

He looked taller than ever today, almost predatory in a black silk shirt and black denims, his dark hair long and unruly, even his eyes appearing black.

Annie had seen him only briefly earlier when he'd come to collect Jessica for her game of chess, and she found she was looking at him differently with the knowledge of what his marriage to Joanne must have been like. His arrogance was unmistakably an integral part of his nature, and she could only wonder at the blow his pride must have taken when he'd realised Anthony had been Joanne's lover—first...!

His eyes rested on her as he reached the two of them, one brow raised in silent query. It was a question Annie would never answer, wishing she didn't have knowledge of his wife at all, that Anthony had never told her. It gave Rufus a vulnerability she would never have associated with him otherwise.

Rufus's gaze hardened as he turned to his brother. 'You were born a century out of time, Anthony,' he rasped contemptuously. 'This fascination you have with the female members of the household staff—no offence intended, Annie,' he added mock-apologetically before turning back to Anthony with cold black eyes. 'It would have been more understandable a hundred years ago—although no more acceptable!'

Anthony had released Annie the moment his brother had first spoken, a flush to his cheeks now. 'At least I can appreciate a beautiful woman when I see one!' He returned the insult.

Rufus remained unmoved by the open retaliation in his brother's voice. 'You're engaged to a beautiful woman,' he replied. 'I suggest that in future you stick to her.' He took a firm grip of Annie's arm. 'And leave innocents like Annie alone!'

She felt like a bone argued over by two equally determined dogs! Besides, she didn't like the way Rufus, when it suited him, treated her as being no older than Jessica...

'That's rather a big assumption to have made on my behalf on so short an acquaintance,' she told him pleasantly as she quietly but firmly moved out of his grasp, meeting his gaze squarely.

'Are you saying you aren't an innocent?'

They might have been the only two people standing there, their eyes locked in silent battle.

She wasn't a complete innocent, had had her share of boyfriends in the past, but in the true sense of the word, in the way that Rufus meant—

'Anthony, darling.' Davina Adams strolled down the stairs behind them, a tall, willowy blonde of twenty-eight, and beautiful, as Rufus had already stated. 'My headache is better now.' She smiled at her fiancé, her wide blue eyes seeming to take in the tension surrounding the three at the bottom of the stairway—then dismissing it. 'Shall we go for that drive into town now? We could have some lunch out too,' she continued lightly. 'Rufus. Annie.' She acknowledged them rather belatedly before turning back questioningly to her fiancé.

Annie had met Davina for the first time over the weekend, and she was no nearer getting past that outer façade of charm to the real person beneath than she had been then. Perhaps it wasn't a veneer. But if that was the case, then Davina was a very shallow person, seeming to have no other interests than shopping, and her own appearance. But, nevertheless, she was very beautiful...

'Fine,' Anthony agreed easily. 'If you'll excuse us?' he threw carelessly at Annie and Rufus, Davina clinging to his arm as the two of them left the house.

'When Davina says jump, he jumps,' Rufus drawled into the silence that followed their departure.

Annie looked up at him frowningly. Exactly what did he mean by that remark?

'But she is very beautiful,' Rufus added.

'Yes,' Annie agreed flatly.

'And rich.'

'Yes...'

'It's a fact of life, Annie—' Rufus shrugged '—that my brother has already gone through most of his inheritance, and that he does have expensive tastes. And there's no getting away from the fact that Davina is a very wealthy young woman.'

Annie frowned. 'And I'm obviously not?'

Rufus frowned too now. 'I don't believe we were discussing you, Annie,' he said curtly. 'Were we...?'

This man was an investigative reporter, and it had never been more obvious to her than at this moment how good he was at his job. She had just given him information he hadn't asked for, had confirmed, without actually saying the words, her own interest in Anthony! Albeit an interest she was no longer sure of...

'No,' she responded briskly. 'Shall I go to Jessica now?' She deliberately resumed her role as his employee. 'I'm sure you must have things to do.'

'I do.' He nodded, still looking at her intently. 'Apparently I'm taking you out for lunch. The two of you. At Jessica's request,' he added—as if he sensed the refusal she had been about to make.

Her refusal had been purely instinctive, a wish not to spend any more time in Rufus Diamond's company than she needed to. But his mention of Jessica reminded her of exactly what she was doing here!

'Of course,' she accepted coolly. 'I'll just go up and get Jessica's coat.' She turned to ascend the stairs.

'Annie...?'

She had almost reached the top of the wide staircase—almost escaped what now felt like an emotional battering. Rufus Diamond was not a relaxing man to be around; in fact, he was the opposite. She felt as if she constantly had to be on her guard around him.

She drew in a deep breath, turning slowly. He stood exactly where she had left him, tall and infinitely powerful, despite the obvious grandeur of the surrounding reception area and wide curved staircase. Master of all he surveyed!

'Yes?' Even to her own ears her voice sounded apprehensive!

He grinned at her, that slightly wolfish grin that was so disarmingly charming. 'I'll beard the lioness in her den and tell Celia we're all deserting her for lunch!'

Her breath left her in a relieved sigh at the innocuousness of his comment—the first indication she had had that she was still holding it in! 'Fine.' She nodded dismissively.

'Oh, and Annie...?'

She had reached the top of the stairs now, had thought he had finished with her, turning impatiently as she realised he hadn't. Was he doing this on purpose? The laughter in those deep blue eyes seemed to say he was!

'Yes, Rufus?' she replied ruefully.

The grin widened, those laughter lines appearing now beside his nose and mouth. 'Don't bother to change on my account; you look good in denims too!'

The appreciative look he gave her told her he had been watching her as she'd walked up the stairs, and she was suddenly very conscious of the fit of her jeans as they clung to the curve of her bottom and long, slender legs.

'I wasn't about to,' she told him waspishly, finally making good her escape, but she could hear his laughter following her as she hurried down the hallway to collect coats for Jessica and herself, hot colour in her cheeks as she realised she was the reason for his amusement.

And she now had to spend the next few hours in the man's company! Wonderful! She was already starting to regret her earlier wish that Rufus would stay longer this time; now she hoped he would soon leave again!

Although later she felt really guilty for wanting that

as she watched Jessica's pleasure in having her father's company for a few hours. Jessica obviously adored him, and the affection was more than reciprocated. Whatever might have gone wrong in his marriage, Rufus Diamond loved his daughter very much.

Annie stood slightly outside of the relationship, feeling slightly superfluous as Jessica turned to her father for all her needs.

'You look sad all of a sudden.' Rufus softly interrupted her reverie, another indication Annie had that he had been watching her without her being aware of it. 'Nothing I've said or done, I hope?' He quirked that left brow of his in the disconcerting way he had, looking at her closely.

They had gone for a drive before stopping off at a pub for a light lunch, where Jessica was in her element seated between the two adults, her good humour unmistakable. And Annie had realised, in the last few minutes, that if Rufus ever decided to return home permanently she would no longer be needed. At the same time she knew how selfish her thoughts were, that it would be much better for Jessica to have her father at home with her than to be in the care of a hired nanny.

'No,' she assured him wistfully. He hadn't said or done anything; he just was who he was, and Jessica adored him.

Rufus still looked concernedly at her over the top of his daughter's head. 'Sure?'

'Sure.' She gave him a bright, meaningless smile. He wasn't to blame for the fact that she had become so fond of Jessica, the thought of ever being parted from her was like a physical pain. Not to become too emotionally involved with her charge had been part of her training, and at the kindergarten that hadn't been too difficult to do, but now...

'Has anyone ever told you that you have the most expressive eyes...?' Rufus muttered.

She gave him a startled look, suddenly feeling, as their gazes locked and held, that they were the only two people in the noisy, crowded room.

'The most amazing eyes!' he muttered again, shaking his head, as if he was under a spell he wanted broken.

'I thought you said they were expressive?' Annie murmured huskily.

'Expressive! Beautiful! Amazing...! God damn it—'

'Granny said not to use that word unless in prayer,' Jessica said reprovingly to her father—reminding the two of them that she was there! 'And you weren't praying, Daddy.' She grinned up at him teasingly.

Rufus looked down at his daughter for several stunned seconds, and then he smiled at her, lightly ruffling her hair. 'In a way, that's exactly what I was doing,' he told her softly, his expression enigmatic as he glanced across at Annie.

Annie gazed back just as enigmatically at him—because she didn't understand him at all! One minute they had been discussing the fact that she had gone very quiet, the next— Her eyes...? There seemed to be no connection between the two to Annie.

'I prayed last night too, Daddy.' Jessica continued the conversation, taking it at its face value. 'I prayed you wouldn't go away again for a very long time. What were you praying for?' she added guilelessly, completely unaware of the heart-wrenching effect her words had had on both adults.

Annie now felt even more ashamed of her earlier

thoughts, and as she looked across at Rufus she wondered how he felt at learning just how upsetting his daughter found his long absences.

His face was softened with love as he looked at Jessica. 'I prayed for the same thing, love,' he told her gruffly.

Jessica nodded in that totally adult way she sometimes had. 'Perhaps if we both pray for the same thing it might happen. I prayed for a new mother for a long time, and that didn't happen. But maybe that was because I prayed on my own,' she said consideringly, wrinkling her nose up in thought, again completely unaware of the bombshell she had just dropped into the conversation. 'What do you think, Daddy?' she looked up at him, her brow furrowed.

Annie could have laughed at the totally stunned expression on Rufus's face. He'd obviously had no idea that Jessica had hungered for a new mother—and he had no idea how to respond to her either.

Annie took pity on him. 'I think the two of us should go to the ladies' room and wash our hands after that delicious meal,' she told Jessica quickly. 'It will give you a chance to show off your prowess on your crutches,' she added encouragingly as she saw the slightly rebellious look on the little girl's face.

The crutches had been supplied by the hospital on Sunday, and Jessica took great delight in using them whenever she could, especially when she had an audience, as she did in this crowded pub.

It certainly diverted Jessica's attention from a subject her father obviously found uncomfortable, to say the least; he still looked slightly bewildered as Annie stood up to accompany Jessica across the room.

'Where the hell did that come from?' he said in a low voice before Annie could move out of earshot.

She turned to him with a sympathetic smile. 'It's one of the reasons I like working with children so much; you never quite know what they are going to say next!' It was obvious Rufus certainly hadn't expected this!

'A new mother!' he repeated incredulously.

Annie's smile widened. 'I shouldn't worry about it.' She patted his arm comfortingly. 'She's obviously given up praying for that!'

'Thank God!' He gave a relieved sigh, taking a much needed swallow of his beer.

Annie's smile faded as she turned to follow Jessica. She had forgotten how disastrous his marriage to Joanne had been; no wonder he didn't find the subject of a replacement in the least funny. It obviously wasn't an experience he cared to repeat. And who could blame him...?

He seemed deep in thought on the drive back to the house, manoeuvring the black Mercedes as if on automatic, and Jessica, tired from her trip out, fell asleep in the back of the car.

Annie was glad of the brief respite to be able to think of her earlier conversation with Anthony. He hadn't seemed the same today, certainly hadn't liked her comments about his forthcoming wedding. But what was going to happen about that? Did he intend going through with the marriage? He said not, but—

'He isn't worth it, you know.' Rufus gently interrupted her reflections, the fact that he seemed to know what—whom!—her thoughts were about proving he wasn't as lost in introspection himself as she had thought he was.

Colour warmed her cheeks. 'I don't know what you mean,' she denied awkwardly.

He sighed. 'Yes, you do. I don't know how he does it.' Rufus gave an impatient shake of his head. 'But every woman that comes within twenty feet of Anthony seems to fall for his charm—such as it is! However, no matter what he may have told you, Annie, he is going to marry Davina. Celia will see that he does,' he told her gently.

Celia...? But— 'Why?' Annie was perplexed.

Rufus shrugged. 'For the reasons I've already tried to explain to you.'

Because Davina was wealthy. And Anthony had expensive tastes. It didn't seem a very good basis for a marriage to her. And it really didn't seem any of Celia's business whom her son married. Oh, it would be better for everyone if Celia approved of her son's choice of wife, but surely it was more important that Anthony approved of her!

'I don't understand.'

'You will,' Rufus assured her grimly. 'I'm just trying to make things as painless for you as possible. Or is it too late for that?' He quirked dark brows.

Was it? She didn't know. Yes, she had been charmed by Anthony from the first, flattered by his attention in the preceding weekend visits. But his arrival with Davina this last weekend had totally thrown her. Now she wasn't sure what she felt.

'I hope to God it's not, Annie,' Rufus continued harshly. 'My brother has ruined too many lives already to add you to that number!'

His own marriage was top of that list, Annie felt sure. But surely that hadn't been Anthony's fault— Was it ever...? She didn't know any more, needed time to think, to work things out in her own head.

But there was no time for thinking once they got back to the house. Jessica needed to be seen to; the two of them were to have tea together up in the nursery as there were guests coming to dinner. And thankfully Annie didn't see anything of Anthony; she needed some time to herself before she saw him again.

To her surprise Celia was still in her bedroom suite when the time came for Jessica to say goodnight to her grandmother, the older woman in her dressing-room, trying to decide what she would wear for the evening ahead.

Her hair already styled, make-up expertly applied, only her dress and shoes to be donned, at that moment wearing a peach robe over her ultra-slender body, Celia looked elegantly beautiful. It was surprising really that she hadn't remarried after her husband's death six years ago; she was certainly still an extremely attractive woman.

'Ready for bed?' She turned to greet her granddaughter, Jessica already in her pyjamas and dressing-gown. 'Is it that late already?' She looked slightly flustered at the realisation.

Annie gave the other woman a searching look as she said goodnight to her granddaughter. There were signs of strain beside Celia's eyes and mouth that she had never really noticed before, and she looked tired too, despite the rest she had just taken before dinner. Obviously having Anthony and Davina here, plus the disturbing Rufus, was proving a strain for Celia too! Only Jessica—and possibly the vacuous Davina— seemed to be unaffected by this strange family gathering.

'And what are you going to do this evening, my dear?'

Annie blinked as she realised Celia's question was addressed to her. Once Jessica was in bed, what was she going to do? Her normal routine had been totally upset since the rest of the family had arrived!

'I have some labels to sew into some of Jessica's school uniform,' she ventured. 'And then I might go and choose a book from the library, if that's all right?' She had been enthralled with the Diamond library since the day she'd come to work here. She had always been an avid reader, and after years of a shortage of available books the large room on the ground floor of the Diamond house, which was completely dedicated to their collection of literature, was like an Aladdin's cave to her.

And as her own life seemed more than a little complicated at the moment losing herself in someone else's world seemed a very attractive proposition!

Celia smiled brightly. 'An excellent idea. Feel free to go and choose a book any time you like.'

Annie looked at the older woman more closely. Perhaps it was the strain of having Rufus back, or maybe the other woman was just mellowing on better acquaintance, but Celia had actually sounded warmly friendly just then!

'Thank you,' she accepted slightly dazedly.

'And now I really must finish dressing for dinner.' The older woman stood up smoothly, patting Jessica absently on top of her dark curls. 'I'm sure Davina's mother will be wearing something beautifully elegant; she usually does!' Celia wrinkled her nose irritably as she once again began to look through her own extensive array of clothes.

Davina's mother… It was Davina's parents who were the guests for dinner this evening! No doubt so that they could all discuss wedding plans together…

Annie went mechanically through the motions of putting Jessica to bed, even managed to sew name-tags into Jessica's new winter uniform without really being aware she was performing the tedious task. Then she found herself down in the library without really knowing how she had got there, knew that Davina's parents were close by in the dining-room, having heard their car in the driveway earlier. And wedding plans were definitely on the menu!

Where did that leave Annie? Was Rufus right? Was she to have been just another of those meaningless flings Anthony seemed to have indulged in over the years? Was he just playing with her emotions while intending to marry Davina after all? He certainly hadn't been very pleased earlier when she had questioned him about his marriage to Davina…

What a mess! She had come here to work so happily, enjoyed being with Jessica, and now, because of an involvement with Anthony that should never have begun in the first place, she had put the whole thing in jeopardy. How could she carry on working here when she had made such a fool of herself over Anthony? But she didn't want to leave, had realised that only too clearly this afternoon when she'd thought of Rufus returning for good and Jessica no longer needing her.

Without really being aware that she was doing it, Annie began sobbing quietly, for what or for whom she wasn't quite sure, everything still too muddled in her mind. One thing she did know was that whatever her relationship with Anthony was—and even now she couldn't quite put a label on it!—it would have to end.

End! It had never really begun, except in her own naive head. Rufus was right: emotionally she was young and impressionable—

'I told you he wasn't worth it!'

Annie looked up sharply at the man she had just been thinking of. Rufus was very tall and dark in his black evening suit and snowy white shirt, the expression on his face, as he strode forcefully into the library and shut the door firmly behind him, just as dark and forbidding.

'He certainly isn't worth crying over,' Rufus barked as he crossed the room with long, powerful strides, pulling Annie roughly to her feet to shake her slightly. 'Stop crying, damn it!' he grated harshly, his expression fierce now.

His annoyance just made her realise exactly how stupid she had been, which just made her cry all the harder. She had believed Anthony's interest in her to be genuine, had started to fall in love with him, and now she just felt totally stupid. Young and impressionable!

'Annie!' Rufus shook her again. 'God damn it!' His voice rose at his frustration with her tears.

She did try to stop crying, was trying very hard to stop, but the fact that it was Rufus who was witnessing her humiliation just seemed to make the whole situation worse. He was her employer; what was he going to think of her for having made such an idiot of herself over a man she was rapidly coming to agree with him wasn't worth it? Perhaps Rufus would just decide to dismiss her anyway, because she was proving a damned nuisance!

She drew in several gulping breaths. 'Jessica said you shouldn't use that word unless you're praying,' she reminded him, in an attempt to ease some of the tension of the situation.

It seemed to have no effect on Rufus, his displeasure deepening. 'Damn what Jessica says,' he grated. 'And damn what Anthony has to say too. Damn the lot of them!' His hands were still tight on her arms as he looked down at her. 'Oh, to hell with it,' he growled, before his head lowered and his mouth claimed hers.

Fiercely. Possessively. Completely!

Annie was so taken by surprise that she could do nothing but remain in the hard possession of his arms as that plundering mouth continued its ravishment of hers. She had been kissed before—quite recently!—but never like this.

And then the anger seemed to go out of Rufus, his arms no longer like steel bands but holding her tenderly against him, his mouth sipping and tasting hers, causing her pulse to leap erratically as she slowly began to return his caresses, her arms moving slowly up about his shoulders as she stood on tiptoe to deepen the kiss.

It was an invitation Rufus accepted, curving her body into his now, his mouth moving erotically against hers, his tongue moving lightly over the inner softness of her lips, causing heat to course through her body.

She was tingling all over, alive with desire, never wanting this pleasure to end—

It ended abruptly as Rufus put her away from him, eyes so dark they looked black again. 'You aren't in love with Anthony, Annie,' he bit out coldly. 'You aren't in love with anyone. You wouldn't have kissed me the way you did just now if you were. So stop your damned crying and get back to doing what you're paid to do— looking after Jessica!' He turned sharply on his heel and slammed out of the room as suddenly as he had entered it.

Annie stared after him with bewildered brown eyes, her confusion—and despair—utter and complete...

CHAPTER FIVE

'WHAT the hell is going on between you and Rufus?'

Annie had just come down the stairs from the nursery with a used lunch tray, hadn't seen Anthony since their brief conversation yesterday. In fact, she hadn't seen any member of the Diamond family today except Jessica, didn't know how to face Rufus again after what had happened between them last night.

She gave Anthony a startled look now—surely he didn't know that Rufus had kissed her? And, more importantly, that she had kissed him back!

'What do you mean?' she said guardedly, holding the tray defensively in front of her as Anthony glared at her across its width.

'Put that damned tray down,' he instructed impatiently, not waiting for her to do so but wrenching it out of her hands and depositing it unceremoniously on the table that stood in the centre of the huge hallway, one of the cups falling over in its saucer with a loud clatter, although luckily nothing actually broke. Not that Anthony seemed in the least concerned that it might have, turning to her angrily. 'Rufus has just informed me that you're all off to London for a few days,' he told her accusingly.

She looked startled. 'He has…?'

'He has,' Anthony echoed uncompromisingly. 'So what's going on?'

She would like to know that herself—because it was

the first she had heard of a trip to London! Not that there
was anything unusual about a nanny being expected to
travel with the family; it was just that, in Rufus
Diamond's case, and in view of what had happened between them last night, it was—strange. Well…the timing
of it was strange.

Goodness, she was becoming flustered just at the
thought of it!

'Annie!' Anthony demanded an answer from her.

And she didn't have one. She didn't know why they
were going to London, or for how long; she simply knew
nothing about it. 'Are you sure he said I was to go as
well?'

'Positive,' Anthony confirmed grimly.

And knowing Rufus—even as little as she did—he
had enjoyed telling Anthony too!

'Just what am I supposed to do while you're off in
London with my brother?' Anthony snapped.

Annie's eyes widened incredulously as she looked up
at him. Considering he had spent yesterday evening with
his fiancée, her parents and his mother, discussing their
Christmas wedding plans, he had a damned cheek even
asking her that question!

'I would say,' she said carefully, 'that you'll be doing
exactly what you've been doing the last five days: enjoying your holiday, at your family home, with your fiancée!' Indignation hardened her voice as she delivered
that last comment.

'Oh, I see.' Anthony took a step back from her, a
knowing smile on his lips. 'We're playing those sort of
games, are we?' he derided.

She didn't know what *he* was doing—she had virtually given up trying to work that one out!—but she cer-

tainly wasn't into playing games of any sort. 'I've just told you that Rufus hasn't even spoken to me about this yet, so how can I possibly be playing games—of any kind?' she said exasperatedly.

Anthony studied her assessingly. 'You're angry with me because of the wedding.'

Angry? She didn't think she was at all angry about it. She had been confused, but she didn't think she was any longer, not where this man was concerned. Now, Rufus was a different matter completely…!

'Not at all,' she answered Anthony smoothly. 'I'm sure bringing the wedding forward to Christmas will all work out perfectly. Now, if you'll excuse me…?' She moved to go past him to pick up the tray, only to find he was gripping her arms. 'Anthony, you're hurting me.' And he was, too, his fingers painful on her upper arms. 'You—'

'Annie, my dear.' Celia seemed to have appeared from nowhere, moving gracefully towards them. 'I wanted to have a few words with you about this trip you're taking with Rufus to London.'

Annie had desperately been trying to release herself from Anthony's grasp, but at his mother's mention of Rufus she suddenly found herself completely free as Anthony thrust her away from him. She turned to face Celia, her gaze stubbornly averted from Anthony's accusing one. 'I really don't know anything about it yet, Celia,' she replied. 'Perhaps Rufus only means to take Jessica with him.'

'But of course he doesn't.' The other woman easily cast that idea aside. 'I was speaking to him only a few minutes ago, and he definitely said you were to go as well as Jessica.'

Well, she wished he would stop speaking to everyone else about it and actually tell *her* what was happening! It seemed that everyone else in this household knew what she was doing for the next few days, but she didn't have a clue!

Why were they going to London? Where were they staying? How long was a few days...? Because she shouldn't spend a few days—and a few nights!—anywhere with him. Even if Jessica was there too.

'You'll have a wonderful time, my dear,' Celia encouraged as she saw the reluctance in Annie's expression. 'You may even find the time to visit some of your friends while you're there.' She smiled brightly.

Annie felt, rather than saw, the glowering look Anthony cast in her direction. Obviously the thought of her meeting up with friends—in Anthony's mind, probably male friends—did not please him. Well, she did have a lot of friends in London, and some of them were male, but they weren't those sorts of male friends. And even if they were it was none of Anthony's business; he was engaged to someone else, had no right to approve or disapprove of her seeing any of her friends, male or female.

Whew—that was a change in her attitude towards him from five days ago when he had first kissed her!

But he was engaged. And with the bringing forward of the wedding, the talk last night with Davina's parents—the other woman's father actually being Anthony's boss—it seemed a foregone conclusion that the wedding would go ahead at Christmas. What role was Anthony thinking of offering her in all that? It wasn't too difficult to guess—and neither was the answer she would give him. She had been born because her mother had been involved with a man who refused to leave his wife for her, even when he knew she was expecting his child; Annie had no intention of history repeating itself!

She had been living in cloud-cuckoo-land even thinking it would be any different for her with a man like Anthony Diamond. But thank goodness she had come to her senses now. And if Rufus Diamond believed it would be any different with him then he was in for a shock too! Young and impressionable she might be, stupid she was not!

'Yes, it would be nice,' she answered Celia lightly, ignoring Anthony's scowling expression. 'I'm sure Rufus will talk to me about it eventually.' When he had stopped telling everyone else! 'Now, if you'll both excuse me, I really do have to get this tray back to the kitchen.' She picked it up and turned to leave.

'Annie—'

'Anthony, I would like to talk to you about Davina's birthday next week,' his mother told him smoothly. 'And I'm sure Annie has a lot of other things she should be doing,' she added with hard dismissal.

And obviously talking to her son wasn't one of them!

Annie had half suspected, over the last few days, from her comments and topics of conversation, that Celia had a pretty good idea of what had transpired between her son and Jessica's nanny. She was even more convinced now that Celia knew. And Rufus was right: Celia meant to see Anthony safely married to Davina.

It was just her luck that Davina herself was walking down the hallway as Annie made her way through the large house to the kitchen. Really, she wasn't having much luck today at all!

'Ah, Annie,' Davina drawled in recognition. 'I've been meaning to have a few words with you.'

Another one!

Annie gave a resigned sigh. 'If it's about going to London with Rufus then Celia and Anthony have already told me about it.'

Davina looked mildly surprised, then shook her head. 'I can assure you it has nothing to do with London or Rufus,' she rejoined frigidly. 'I have no interest in either subject.'

Until this moment Annie had thought the girl beautiful but a bit insipid characterwise, but at this moment she sensed a steel in Davina she hadn't known was there. And if she didn't want to talk about this proposed trip to London with Rufus, what did she want to talk about? Annie found herself tensing guardedly.

Davina continued to look at her with those freezing blue eyes. 'It's about Anthony—'

'There you are, Annie,' Rufus calmly interrupted as he strode towards them. 'I've been looking for you everywhere.'

Everyone else in the family seemed to have found her, so why couldn't he?

'Hello, Davina,' he greeted the other woman warmly. 'I didn't see you standing there.'

Considering that Davina was much taller than Annie, with golden hair that gleamed brightly in the autumn sunshine, how could he possibly have missed her?

Annie had been dreading this first meeting with him after they had kissed each other last night, but, in view of the intervening conversations with Celia and Anthony, now she just felt angry with him. It didn't make her feel any less irritable towards him knowing he had probably just saved her from a very uncomfortable conversation with Davina. Because she was sure now that Davina had just been about to launch into a discussion about Anthony's overfriendliness with her. Perhaps it was as well, after all, that she was going away with Rufus and Jessica…!

'Well, you've found me,' she told Rufus ungraciously, aware that she sounded as irritable as she felt, but she couldn't help it; she was feeling emotionally battered by this family.

Rufus quirked his left eyebrow in that enigmatic way that he had. 'So I have,' he murmured speculatively.

Annie blushed at the intended rebuke. 'I'm just on my way to the kitchen to deposit this tray,' she informed him flatly. 'But I'll be more than happy to talk to you as soon as I've got rid of it.' It was starting to annoy her too now that the used plates and cups reminded her of the pleasant lunch she had shared with Jessica such a short time ago; it seemed like hours ago!

Rufus nodded. 'I'll be in the library,' he told her softly.

The library! Annie felt her heart sink at his voice, her hands shaking slightly, rattling the used crockery on the tray. The library, the place where they had kissed each other so passionately, was the last place she wanted to go to speak to him!

Which was probably the very reason why he had chosen it, Annie acknowledged heavily as she finally made her way to the kitchen and passed the tray over to the cook; Rufus was nothing if not damned annoying! He was also irritating, infuriating, a thorn in everyone's side. But especially hers!

And yet she had kissed him last night, kissed him as if she really meant it.

Well, he had kissed her too—and his parting comment about getting on with the job of looking after Jessica showed he hadn't meant it at all!

And that was what was important about last night; Rufus had only kissed her to show her she wasn't seriously emotionally involved with Anthony. That was what she had to remember about it—not that she had responded!

Rufus was seated in one of the winged leather armchairs that sat at either side of the fireplace when Annie entered the room a few minutes later, a book open on his lap, glancing up at her casually as he sensed her presence in the room.

'Dickens.' He snapped the book shut, turning to put it back on the shelf. 'Not one of my favourite authors.'

Or hers, she inwardly acknowledged, not willing, at this moment in time, to outwardly agree with him on anything. But she found Dickens a little too depressing for her taste. Actually, he would probably suit her mood just now!

'You wanted to talk to me?' she prompted abruptly.

Rufus tilted his head to one side, looking at her with amusement. 'Who's rattled your cage?' he taunted.

Her mouth tightened. 'Sorry?'

'Uh-oh.' Rufus grimaced. 'It's me you're angry with, is it?'

She drew in a harsh breath. 'Why on earth should I be angry with you?'

To her chagrin, he grinned. 'I should sit down if I were you, Annie.' He indicated the chair opposite. 'Before the carpet around you explodes into flames!' he said ruefully. 'And to think I initially doubted you were a real redhead! Okay,' he encouraged once she was seated. 'Tell me what I have to apologise for, and let's just get that out of the way. Then we can move on.'

So he was a let's-sort-this-out-and-move-on sort of person. Strange, that wasn't the impression Anthony had given with regard to Rufus's wife… But perhaps that was different; there was certainly a lot of antagonism between the two men.

'Is it last night?' Rufus was watching her closely. 'Do you want me to apologise for kissing you—is that it?'

She had been hoping he wouldn't even mention the subject. But she supposed that had been just too much to hope for!

'Well, I suppose I could apologise,' Rufus said slowly, taking her silence as confirmation. 'But I really can't see the point, when I can't promise it won't happen again.' He grinned that wolfish grin as Annie gave an audible gasp. 'That certainly woke you up!' he said with satisfaction, relaxing back in the chair. 'Is it last night, Annie—?'

'No!' she denied sharply. 'I'm just— Everyone has— We're going to London,' she concluded as she realised she was rambling.

'We are,' he nodded, eyes narrowed. 'Don't you want to go?' he prompted gently.

'Yes. No.' She gave a sigh, annoyed with herself for appearing so flustered. 'Yes, of course I do,' she said.

'You just wish I had mentioned it to you before I told anyone else,' he said knowingly. 'From your mention of "everyone", I presume the rest of the family have taken great pleasure in informing you of my plans before I had a chance to talk to you about them. I only mentioned it casually over lunch, Annie,' he told her. 'I have no idea why they all took it into their heads to tell you about it.'

She did: Anthony because he was furious that she was going away with his brother, albeit as nanny to his daughter, Celia because Annie had a feeling the other woman wanted her as far removed from Anthony as possible in the immediate future, and Davina hadn't wanted to talk to her about the trip to London at all but something much more personal! In retrospect, perhaps this interlude in London was the best thing for her too!

'It doesn't matter,' she returned easily. 'I only—'

'But of course it matters, Annie,' Rufus interrupted. 'Despite what I may have said to you last night, I don't want to hurt or upset you; I think there are probably enough people in this household intent on doing that already, without my joining in!' he went on darkly. 'And for deliberately doing that last night I do apologise.' He looked across at her, his eyes that dark, fathomless blue. 'I shouldn't have made that remark to you about looking after Jessica,' he explained at her questioning look. 'I only have to see the two of you together to know that you care for Jessica very much. And that the feeling is more than reciprocated.'

Annie swallowed hard, her voice husky when she spoke. 'Thank you.'

He grinned. 'Don't mention it.'

He was incorrigible; and how could she possibly stay angry with him when he behaved so disarmingly?

'So...' She spoke firmly, determined to get this conversation back on a businesslike level. Which wasn't easy when he had told her he couldn't promise he wouldn't kiss her again!

He mustn't kiss her again. Because if he did she was

very much afraid she would respond in exactly the same way she had last night. And becoming involved with this man, the father of her charge and a man who was out of the country more than he was in it, would be more ridiculous than her infatuation with Anthony had been!

'When do we leave?' she asked briskly. 'I'll need to get some things together for Jessica and myself.'

'We're leaving later this afternoon. And don't worry about too much for Jess; she already has quite a lot of clothes at my apartment,' Rufus replied.

His apartment! She had assumed they would be staying at a hotel…

Rather a stupid assumption for her to have made when Rufus was obviously based in London for his job. But his apartment…!

'Don't worry, Annie,' he teased at her woebegone expression. 'It has four bedrooms, so I won't be expecting you to share mine!'

God, was she so transparent? Not that she had expected to share his bedroom—he was just being deliberately mischievous now!—but she did find the thought of going to stay in his home, even with Jessica present, more than a little disturbing.

'Jessica's would have been the more obvious choice,' she told him calmly.

His mouth twisted. 'But not half as much fun!'

She gave him a look, not taking him seriously for a moment; he was obviously enjoying toying with her. And it was time it stopped. 'I had better go and get my things together, then.' She stood up to leave.

'Just enough for a few days,' Rufus warned. 'We are coming back.'

'Don't worry, Rufus.' She smiled at the almost panicked expression on his face. 'I brought all my worldly possessions down here in one large suitcase; I really won't pack that much for two or three days!'

He looked relieved to hear it. 'At last, a woman who knows not to pack the kitchen sink, along with everything else in the house!'

She laughed, giving a wry shake of her head as she crossed the room to the door.

'There is one thing, though, Annie.' The tone of Rufus's voice stopped her at the door. 'Do pack the black dress,' he told her gruffly as she slowly turned to face him.

Her eyes widened. 'Will we be going out in the evenings?'

He met her gaze unblinkingly. 'Probably not,' he returned. 'But pack the black dress anyway.'

She gave him a reproving look as she left, no longer sure whether he was serious or still playing with her. He had seemed angry last night when he had kissed her, but a night's sleep seemed to have changed all that—

'Annie!'

She frowned as she turned to see Anthony standing in the doorway of his mother's private sitting-room, that frown deepening as he beckoned to her to join him. God, she hoped Celia and Davina weren't in there too, so that all three of them could tell her how she was wasting her time over Anthony; that was all she needed on top of her puzzlement concerning Rufus. Besides, they could save their breath if that was their intention; she was cured of her infatuation with Anthony!

'Come in here, Annie,' he commanded. 'I want to talk to you.'

There was no one else in the room, she discovered

when she reluctantly entered it. Although that didn't mean Celia wouldn't arrive at any moment—

'My mother is upstairs resting.' Anthony instantly dispelled that thought as he closed the door firmly behind them.

In that case he had chosen the perfect place for them to talk in private; usually no one else but Celia entered this room, not unless she had invited them in. Celia seemed to be resting rather a lot recently... Unless it was just her way of keeping out of Rufus's path!

'What is it, Anthony?' Annie looked at him, feeling unsettled. 'I was on my way upstairs to pack for this trip to London.'

He scowled darkly. 'You're going with Rufus, then.' It was an accusation, not a question.

'I'm accompanying Jessica, yes,' she answered carefully.

'You're going with Rufus,' he repeated.

She bristled at the accusing tone in his voice. 'And you're staying here with Davina,' she reminded him tautly.

He looked at her consideringly. 'That really bothers you, doesn't it?' he said.

Of course it bothered her; he was an engaged man. And he acted as if he owned her, which, apart from being unacceptable, was a very strange experience for someone who had been on her own all her life.

'I think...' she spoke slowly '...that you need to get your life in order, Anthony.'

'In what way?' He was unsure.

'In every way!' she said exasperatedly. 'A few days ago you kissed me, then a couple of days later you made an assignation to meet me down on the jetty. Admittedly you didn't get there,' she continued determinedly as she could see he was about to interrupt her, 'but that was only because your fiancée wanted your time instead. Which she has a perfect right to expect. Now, correct me if I'm wrong,' she went on scathingly, 'but this engagement, which you tell me is such a sham, now seems to have progressed to discussing Christmas wedding arrangements. In view of that, I'm not really sure where you think I fit into all this!' Her eyes flashed deeply brown with her barely contained anger.

'Rufus was right, you know.' Anthony looked at her admiringly. 'You really are rather beautiful when you're angry!'

She gave him an indignant glance, stepping back as he would have moved towards her. 'I believe Rufus merely commented on the fact that I was obviously a true redhead.' She knew exactly what he had said—and the word 'beautiful' had never been used!

'Whatever,' Anthony responded carelessly, his smile full of charm. 'I think you look beautiful when you're angry. Except—' now he did move a step closer, mere inches away from Annie '—I'm not sure I like you being angry with me,' he added tenderly, reaching out to lightly grasp her arms. 'Lighten up, Annie,' he encouraged soothingly as he sensed her resistance. 'We could have a lot of fun together if you would just relax a bit.'

Fun! This hadn't been fun so far; she had been mortified, and then guilt-stricken, that she had kissed—and allowed herself to be kissed by—a man engaged to another woman. And Anthony called this having fun! Well, he could have it without her!

'Until your wedding at Christmas,' she rebutted, pulling away from him.

'And after—if things work out between us. And I can't see any reason why they shouldn't.' His hands tightened painfully on her arms as she again tried to pull away from him.

Annie's eyes widened, her breathing so shallow she was barely breathing at all. 'You can't?' she bit out tautly.

'Not if you lighten up, no,' he chided easily.

Annie was barely resisting the impulse she had to punch him on his aristocratic nose—and he obviously had no idea just how vexed she was as he gave her his most disarming smile. 'If I lighten up?' she echoed slowly, the fury building up inside her.

'Exactly.' He grinned. 'Okay, so I'll have a wife, but I'll still visit here often—and I'll make sure Davina stays in London when I do.'

'You will?' Her emotions were barely contained now. Anthony was digging himself deeper and deeper into a hole that at any moment now she was going to take great pleasure in pushing him into!

'Of course,' Anthony continued unconcernedly.

'I would be your mistress?' Her hands were so tightly clenched at her sides, her nails were digging into her palms.

'It's a bit of an old-fashioned way of putting things,' he acknowledged. 'But yes, I suppose that's exactly what you would be.'

'Well, that's where you're wrong!' Her control finally snapped as she pushed him away from her, and the expression of surprise on his face at her obvious wrath would have been laughable—if she hadn't felt less like laughing than ever before in her life!

And she had thought he cared about her—had imagined the two of them together, falling in love—when all the time he was no better than her own father had been!

'I should stop right there, if I were you, Anthony— unless you have some sort of perverted desire to be the recipient of the punch on the nose I so much want to give you!' She was breathing hard in her agitation, breasts heaving, eyes blazing. 'I don't intend—ever!— being your mistress or any other man's!' And with that last furious comment she turned and slammed out of the room.

She had been right earlier. A mistress! Good God, he had chosen completely the wrong woman to offer that role in his life. She—

'Well, you certainly told him,' remarked an admiring voice.

Annie swung round to face Rufus, anger burning brightly in her cheeks as he stood leaning casually against the wall, his relaxed pose seeming to imply he had been standing there for some time. For how long? Surely he hadn't heard all—

'Sorry about that.' He straightened away from the wall. 'I was just passing, and I happened to hear the word "mistress" being used. I'm afraid I was hooked after that.' He shrugged. 'Although I'm really rather sorry you didn't punch him on the nose as you said you wanted to.' He grinned.

Annie didn't think, didn't want to think, acting instinctively as she reached out and slapped him hard across his cheek, still too angry to cry. Then she simply turned on her heel and walked away.

CHAPTER SIX

HE HADN'T followed her!

Annie hadn't stopped walking until she'd reached her bedroom, but with each step she had expected to feel Rufus's hand roughly on her arm as he turned her to face him and told her she no longer had a job looking after his daughter!

But it hadn't happened.

She had sat on her bed for the next ten minutes, waiting for him to burst into the room.

That hadn't happened either.

Why hadn't it?

She didn't know now. She had smacked Rufus for no other reason than he'd happened to be in the wrong place at the wrong time, had vented on him the anger she actually felt towards Anthony. And towards herself, if she was honest, for being so stupid, so *young and impressionable*!

Perhaps that last was partly the reason why she had hit out at Rufus—because he had been right!

Which was no excuse at all. Rufus couldn't be blamed for knowing his brother better than she did. But he had certainly paid the price for that knowledge. The evidence of it—livid red marks on his cheeks—still showed two hours later!

If Annie turned her head slightly from where she sat next to him in the front of his Mercedes, Jessica comfortably ensconced on the back seat, then she could actually see the imprint her hand had made on the hardness of his cheek.

But she tried hard not to turn her head any more, not even fractionally. In fact, she hadn't been able to do more than mutter a few words as Rufus had put her small overnight bag in the boot of the car at the beginning of their journey. She didn't want to be here at all, didn't want to draw any more attention to herself than was strictly necessary. It was bad enough that—

'I'm sorry, Annie.'

She turned sharply to face Rufus as he drove, swallowing hard as she instantly saw those marks on his cheek. Marks she had made. She had always believed herself incapable of physically hurting another human being, and yet looking at Rufus she could see what she had done to him. And he was apologising to her! What on earth for?

He reached out with one hand and lightly squeezed both her hands as they lay tightly clenched together in her lap. 'Anthony is a bastard,' he said tightly, his eyes focused on the road ahead.

Annie glanced quickly round at Jessica, relieved to see the girl was fast asleep.

'She hates long journeys,' Rufus said, looking at his daughter in the driver's mirror, as Annie faced back to the front once again. He released his hold on her hands. 'Sleep is her way of avoiding them,' he explained indulgently.

Annie wished she could fall asleep too, wished today had never happened! 'I'm sorry I hit you—'

'Hey,' he chided softly. 'I've just been trying to tell you that I deserved it—'

'Not you.' She shook her head firmly.

'Believe me—' he grimaced ruefully '—that isn't the first punch I've taken for Anthony.'

'It will be the last from me.' She shivered with reaction at what she had done.

Rufus ran a hand over his bruised cheek, while his other gripped the steering wheel. 'That's quite a powerful right you have there, Miss Fletcher—'

'Please don't,' she groaned, tears of contrition flooding her eyes now. 'I'm so ashamed. Can't believe I really did that.' She shook her head, the tears wet on her cheeks. 'You must—'

'I mustn't anything, Annie,' he cut in gently. 'You were hurting, and the best way to get rid of some of that hurt was to—'

'Hit you!' She groaned again, burying her face in her hands, crying in earnest now. Which was all she seemed to have done just recently!

'Aw, Annie, don't cry!' Rufus moaned protestingly. 'I can't stand it when you cry. Especially over someone like Anthony.' His voice had hardened. 'Annie, stop it!' he instructed harshly as he gathered her up into his arms.

It was the first indication she had that he had stopped the car, and she raised her head to look around them dazedly, realising as she did so that Rufus had pulled the car over onto the hard shoulder and parked there. Something that was completely illegal, unless it was an emergency—

'This is an emergency, Annie,' he stated, and Annie realised she must have spoken the words out loud.

Then, as his mouth came forcefully down on hers, she wasn't thinking at all, only feeling.

And was she feeling! She had never known anything

like this searing pleasure she found in his arms, never felt this heat in her body, a need for more, for—

'Are we there, Daddy?'

It was as if Rufus and Annie had received an electric shock as they simultaneously registered the sleepy sound of Jessica's voice from the back of the car. They moved quickly apart, Annie more flustered now than she had been a few minutes ago. Every time this man kissed her she responded unrestrainedly. She hardly knew herself!

'Annie—'

'Daddy, are we there?' Jessica's voice rose querulously as she received no response to her first question.

Rufus gave Annie a look before turning in his seat to look at his daughter. 'No, Jess, we aren't there yet—'

'Then why have we stopped?' Jessica persisted, totally disorientated as she looked around her.

Annie returned Rufus's gaze helplessly as he looked back at her for assistance; they could hardly tell the little girl the truth!

'Er—well—Annie had something in her eye!' Rufus finally burst out awkwardly, giving Annie a censorious glare as she tried to hold back her laughter.

Something in her eye, indeed. Mud, probably!

She had allowed Rufus to kiss her again. Last night he had kissed her because he was angry. And she was upset. Today he had kissed her because he felt sorry for her. Because she was upset. The common factor to both incidents seemed to have been her tears. Then she would just have to make sure she didn't cry again! In his presence, anyway...

'Is it better now?' Jessica, thankfully, was still sleepy.

Rufus gave Annie a mocking glance. 'Is it better now?' he teased softly. 'Did I kiss it better?'

She gave him a frowning look before turning to Jessica. 'I'm much better now, thank you. So much better, in fact—'

'Oh, hell!' Rufus muttered with feeling, watching the driving mirror in front of him.

Annie looked at him in alarm. 'What is it?' she prompted in a puzzled voice. 'Rufus?'

He shook his head. 'The trouble you've caused me, woman!' Even as he spoke he was thrusting open the car door next to him. 'I find it difficult to believe I've only known you forty-eight hours!' He swung easily out of the car.

Annie turned just in time to see a policeman approaching the Mercedes, a brightly marked police car parked a short distance behind them. Their having stopped here was, as she had already surmised, illegal. And she very much doubted that the policeman would accept the story of there having been something in the eye of the lady passenger in Rufus's car. Rufus was right: she was nothing but trouble!

Jessica scrambled up into a sitting position, looking out of the back window. 'Has Daddy done something wrong?' Her voice sounded slightly awed. 'Is he going to get told off?'

She hoped not—or she would never hear the end of it!

The two men continued to talk on the roadside for several minutes, and Annie's heart sank with dismay as the young policeman took his notebook out of his pocket and began to take notes. He was booking Rufus! And it was all her fault. Rufus was going to be furious with her this time, no doubt about it.

She inwardly prepared herself for his blistering attack

as he parted from the policeman, a folded piece of paper in his hand as he walked briskly back to the car, his expression grim. There wasn't going to be any kissing better this time—even if she was upset!

She wasn't sure whether she was relieved or sad about that...

And she really didn't have the time to dwell on the subject as Rufus got back into the car beside her.

'Daddy—'

'Not yet, pumpkin,' Rufus told his daughter tautly, glancing in his driving mirror. 'I need to get us back onto the road as soon as possible.' He switched on the engine, put the car into gear, and very neatly manoeuvred the vehicle back into the swift flow of traffic.

Annie didn't know what to say, wasn't sure she should say anything; it might just make matters worse. If that were possible!

'A bit of luck, that.' Rufus was finally the one to break the silence, sitting back more comfortably in his seat now that they were well away from the police car.

'Luck?' Annie echoed incredulously; it was the last description she would have applied to the encounter!

'Mmm.' Rufus gave her a brief grin. 'The policeman recognised my name, and it seems he's a fan of mine. He particularly liked a piece I wrote last year about suburban crime; his brother, another policeman—it seems to run in the family!—was mentioned in it quite favourably. Apparently he meant to keep the article, but his wife unwittingly used that newspaper to light the fire; he asked if I could send him a copy. I've got it on disk somewhere in the flat, so I'll look it out for him when we get there.'

The piece of paper Rufus had been given wasn't a

ticket at all, but the policeman's address. And she had been imagining all sorts of horrors—charges, court appearances...!

'So there are some benefits to being famous,' she said tartly.

Rufus glanced at her again briefly. 'I'm not famous, Annie,' he finally said slowly.

'But your work is,' she challenged, not really sure why she was so angry, only that she was!

'Perhaps.' He shrugged dismissively. 'What the hell? It saved us from a severe reprimand. He just laughed when I told him I'd stopped because you had something in your eye!' Rufus reached out and squeezed her hand again, conspiratorially this time, before replacing his own hand on the wheel.

'Shall I go back to sleep for a while, Daddy?' Jessica spoke again from behind them.

Reminding Annie of exactly what she was doing here! She was here as Jessica's nanny, was here on sufferance, had no right to be angry—about anything.

'If you like, pumpkin.' Rufus answered his daughter absently. 'We'll be a while yet.'

Jessica gave a weary sigh as she settled down again on the back seat, and Annie could have sighed along with her; they hadn't even reached London yet, and she was already wishing she weren't here! How on earth was she supposed to share an apartment with this man for the next few days, even with Jessica present...?

'You've gone very quiet,' Rufus remarked a few minutes later.

She looked across at him. 'Have I?' she said guardedly—because on her guard was how she was going to have to be with this man in the future!

'You know you have,' he bit out impatiently.

Annie let out a breath. 'I don't believe I've ever been a chatterbox.'

'I didn't say that's what you are, you just— Damn it woman,' he snapped irritably. 'I never know whether to kiss you or shake you when you annoy me like this!'

She swallowed hard. 'In future I suggest you stick to shaking me—it's probably safer for everyone!'

Rufus threw her a stunned glance, and then he threw back his head with that now familiar shout of laughter. 'You, young lady, are not good for my ego,' he explained once his amusement had abated.

Her own mouth quirked with laughter in spite of herself, her bad humour of a few minutes ago totally dispelled. 'It wasn't your ego I was thinking of,' she taunted lightly. 'The next policeman may not be a fan of yours!'

'True,' he agreed dryly. 'But the onus is on you not to do anything that will make me want to kiss or shake you!'

She wasn't quite sure, at the moment, how she was supposed to do that; if she spoke she seemed to say the wrong thing, and if she didn't speak that seemed to be wrong too!

The safest thing to do seemed to be to join Jessica—and go to sleep!

She closed her eyes, feigning tiredness, and very soon she wasn't pretending at all, but genuinely asleep...

It was dark by the time they entered London, and, having just woken up, it was a minute or two before Annie realised in which part of the city they were. It wasn't one she was too familiar with, Mayfair being an area she had only passed through in the past. But she wasn't at all surprised when Rufus turned the black Mercedes down into an underground car park situated beneath a prestigious apartment building; he effectively owned Clifftop House and all the land around it, so it stood to reason that his London home would be just as prestigious.

She wasn't surprised by the security of the building, either, a guard situated in the car park itself, another one in the lobby upstairs. Not that the men challenged their progress at all, obviously recognising Rufus as one of the wealthy tenants. The apartment itself didn't actually seem like part of a block, being on the ground floor, with its own high-walled garden at the rear.

It was beautifully furnished, too, with obviously genuine antique furniture, the carpets in muted golds and greens. Elegance was the word that came to mind as Annie looked around. It was a far cry from the minute flat she had shared with three other girls until a short time ago; the huge sitting-room was almost as big as their whole accommodation had been!

'I only rent it, Annie.' Rufus was watching her reaction to her surroundings. 'I don't own it.'

The monthly rent on a place like this would probably amount to almost a year's wages for her!

'God damn it!' Rufus suddenly ground out. 'I've never had to apologise for my choice of home before!'

It wasn't his home that bothered her—given the choice she would probably have gone for somewhere like this herself! No, it was the location and obvious cost of it that overwhelmed her, and emphasised the gulf between her own lifestyle and that of the Diamond family. But she certainly wasn't asking him to apologise for it!

'It's very nice,' she told him stiltedly, swallowing hard as he just looked even more annoyed. And they both knew what happened when he became annoyed!

'It's very tidy,' Jessica put in. 'You obviously haven't been home for a while, Daddy,' she added mischievously.

'Not at all in the last three months,' he acknowledged wearily. 'I submitted my last story when I arrived in England on Wednesday, and came straight down to Clifftop House.'

Annie frowned across at him; he had been in a hurry to get there...

To see Jessica? Or had it been something else that had brought him so quickly to the family home?

He returned her questioning gaze enigmatically, and Annie knew she would find no answers there, not unless Rufus was prepared to give her them. He didn't look as if he was!

'I did, however, have some supplies brought in earlier today,' Rufus continued briskly. 'So it's a cup of tea for Annie and myself, and a juice for you, young lady.' He ruffled Jessica's hair affectionately. 'You show Annie to the bedroom next to yours, Jess, and I'll go and make the drinks.'

Annie was glad of these few minutes' respite, if only to accustom herself to her new surroundings. She should have realised that Rufus's apartment wouldn't be anything like the rooms in the old Victorian house that had been her own home until two months ago. He was a Diamond, came from a very wealthy family. She should have expected this.

It was proof of just how lacking in professionalism their relationship had become that she hadn't expected this. She made Rufus laugh, made him angry, annoyed him, and in the last twenty-four hours he had kissed her, twice. She had almost forgotten they were employer and employee. She mustn't forget again.

'It's a lovely room,' she told Jessica once the young girl had shown her to the bedroom she had been allocated. And it *was* a lovely room, the gold and cream decor making it appear warm and welcoming. But it didn't really matter whether it was a lovely room or not; she would only be occupying it for a short time!

'It's ages since Daddy brought me here,' Jessica told her wistfully.

So the trip to London wasn't a regular occurrence; Annie couldn't help wondering what had prompted it this time...

She smiled at Jessica. 'Perhaps twisting your ankle wasn't such a bad thing, after all,' she teased.

Jessica grinned back at her, a grin that was so like her father's. For the first time Annie found herself wondering what Joanne had looked like. There were no pictures of Jessica's mother at Clifftop House, and she had only noticed a large framed photograph of Jessica in the sitting-room here. One thing Annie was pretty sure of: Joanne wouldn't have been a short redhead!

Now that was a strange thought to have come into her head...

'Let's go and have our drinks,' Jessica prompted. 'Daddy isn't very domesticated,' she confided. 'So the tea will probably be awful!'

They were still laughing together over this as they entered the kitchen a few seconds later.

'Care to share the joke?' Rufus invited indulgently as he stood across the room pouring the tea.

Annie looked at Jessica, Jessica looked at Annie, and they both shook their heads at the same time, causing them to burst into laughter once again. In fact, it felt good to Annie to be able to laugh; there had been so little to laugh at just recently.

'Oh, I see.' Rufus nodded knowingly. 'I'm the brunt of it!' he accepted as he handed Annie her cup of tea.

The sight of the tea set the two of them off into peals of laughter once again, so much so that Annie couldn't take the cup from Rufus for fear of dropping it.

'Oh, I understand—it's the tea that caused the laughter in the first place!' He put the cup down, peering down into it. 'I must admit, it does look pretty awful.' He grimaced.

'That's exactly how I said it would look!' Jessica still giggled. 'Why do you think I always prefer to drink juice when I'm here?'

'You little monkey!' Her father gave her an imaginary cuff about the ear. 'I suppose you think Annie can do better?' he challenged.

Annie's eyes widened. 'I wasn't the one disparaging your tea-making skills!'

'No—but you were laughing at them,' he instantly returned.

Annie took a tentative look into the cup he had been about to give her, her distaste instinctive as she saw the mud-coloured fluid. 'How many teabags did you put in the pot?' she asked incredulously.

'I like strong tea,' he defended dryly.

'So do I,' she replied. 'But—I was always told "one for each person, and one for the pot".' She looked at him questioningly.

'It's a big pot,' he muttered grudgingly.

Annie looked at him knowingly. 'How many teabags did you use?' she persisted.

'Enough,' he muttered again.

'Daddy!' Jessica scolded him lightly. 'You're pre-prevar—'

'Prevaricating,' he finished irritably. 'Okay, six. I put six teabags in the pot!' He glared at them both.

Annie bit her lip to stop herself from laughing again, saying nothing more, and went to empty the teapot and start again. At least he had managed to warm the pot for her! 'Would you care for tea, too, Jessica?' She held a fourth teabag over the pot.

'Don't you dare say yes, just because I haven't made it,' her father warned. 'I'll be in the lounge when you've made the tea.'

Annie watched him leave the room, her mouth still twitching with laughter. 'Do you think we've hurt his feelings?' she murmured to Jessica.

'No.' The little girl made herself comfortable on one of the stools that stood in front of the breakfast-bar. 'He'll probably be glad to have a decent cup of tea himself for a change!'

Annie didn't know whether he was or not when they joined him in the lounge, Rufus taking the cup of tea from her without saying a word. But it wasn't an uncomfortable silence, and on reflection Annie had to admit she had enjoyed the exchange in the kitchen. They might have been a real family—

She pulled her thoughts up sharply. Families were for other people, not her. One day she might have a family of her own, but until then she must guard against becoming too attached to Jessica. And her father...!

Rufus made her laugh. She had never really been able

to do that with a man before. And that laughter was even more heady than his kisses had been. Dangerous territory, she realised that. Because Rufus wasn't the marrying kind. He loved his daughter, that much was obvious, and no doubt there had been women in his life since his wife died, but his choice of career didn't allow for any permanent relationships. And he already knew, from the conversation he had overheard between herself and Anthony, her views on mistresses—

She brought her thoughts up sharp once again. What on earth was she thinking of? The man had kissed her twice, not declared undying love for her. Or anything else, for that matter!

'Very nice.' Rufus put his empty cup down.

'Daddy!' Jessica reproved him once again.

'I said it was nice, didn't I?' he retorted irritably. 'Can you cook too?' He turned to Annie, his expression hopeful.

'Please say you can!' Jessica looked at her imploringly.

She hadn't thought about it before, had become used, over the last couple of months, she realised, to the fact that there was a cook in residence at Clifftop House to prepare the meals for everyone. But this was a bachelor apartment, had none of those niceties…

She nodded. 'Just basic stuff, you understand,' she explained hastily; cordon bleu she was not!

'Daddy can't even boil an egg,' Jessica confided candidly.

'I can so,' he instantly protested, but there was laughter dancing in his eyes.

'No, you can't,' his daughter contradicted him. 'Remember that time you—?'

'Okay, okay.' Rufus held up his hands defensively. 'I can't cook,' he conceded wearily.

'He forgot to put any water in the saucepan,' Jessica told Annie in a whisper deliberately loud enough for her father to hear. 'I don't know if you've ever seen an egg explode, but—'

'No, Jessica, I haven't, although I'm sure it's very— interesting,' Annie cut in swiftly as she could see Rufus was going to be the one to explode if this maligning of his culinary skills went on much longer. 'Now I know the real reason the two of you wanted me along on this trip!' she added with mock indignation. 'You just didn't want to risk your father's cooking—or to starve!'

'She's sussed us out, Jess.' Rufus winked at his daughter conspiratorially.

'It wasn't too difficult,' Annie returned witheringly. 'So what are we having to eat this evening?' She arched questioning brows, sure he had had the food for their evening meal delivered today too.

'Steak and salad,' Rufus answered instantly. 'But Jess and I can do the salad—'

'I'll do it, Daddy,' Jessica cut in firmly, turning to Annie. 'The last time Daddy made the salad I found a slug in my—'

'Okay, I'll leave you two girls to get dinner.' Rufus stood up decisively. 'I have some calls to catch up on, anyway. I'll be in my study—first door on the right out of here—when it's ready.' He strode purposefully out of the room.

Annie turned to Jessica, a smile curving her lips. 'I think we drove him away with our teasing!'

'Don't you believe it; he was glad to escape.' Jessica

shrugged dismissively, starting to help with the preparations for dinner.

It was a happy half-hour, Annie concentrating on seasoning and grilling the steaks she had found so conveniently in the refrigerator, while Jessica hobbled about preparing the salad. They laid the table between the two of them once the steaks were sizzling away, Annie having found a French loaf to accompany the meal too. It all looked very appetising once it was put on the kitchen table, Annie having opted for this casual comfort rather than the formal dining-room she had seen earlier, anxious that Jessica did not put too much strain on her slowly healing ankle.

'Not bad.' Annie nodded her satisfaction with the meal they had put out on the table. 'Even if I do say so myself.'

'I'll go and get Daddy.' Jessica was eager to show him their handiwork.

'I'll go,' Annie told her firmly. 'You've done enough walking on that ankle for one evening.'

'Can I light the candles, then?'' Jessica prompted eagerly.

Annie turned at the door. 'Not until I come back with your father. And if he says yes, then you can.'

The candles had been Jessica's idea, as had the two wineglasses for herself and Rufus; Jessica had assured her that her father would want wine with his meal. Annie wasn't sure whether he would or not, but she was happy to go along with it, although one glass of wine was her own personal limit; any more than that and she was apt to get silly.

She could hear Rufus talking on the telephone as she approached his study, hesitating outside the door as she wondered if she should interrupt him. But she didn't want their meal to ruin either, and—

She became suddenly still, actually about to knock on the door, when she unwittingly heard part of his conversation.

'Please ask Margaret to call me when she gets in.' Rufus spoke firmly. 'I really need to talk to her.'

Margaret…? There was only one Margaret that Annie knew of who had come into the conversation recently, and that was her predecessor.

Rufus was in contact with Margaret. And he really needed to talk to her…

Why? Oh, Annie accepted that the other woman had left without notice, but even so—

'Yes, I received her letter.' Rufus was still talking to the other person on the end of the telephone line. 'But I still need to talk to Margaret herself.'

The other woman had written to him! They were on close terms…?

Was Anthony not the only member of the Diamond family who had a penchant for the servants…?

CHAPTER SEVEN

'YOU were very quiet during dinner,' Rufus remarked. The two of them were in the sitting-room, Jessica safely in bed.

Annie was surprised she had even been able to eat the meal, with each mouthful threatening to choke her! And as for her personal limit of one glass of wine—! She had accepted every refill of the red wine that Rufus had offered her, her thoughts tumbling over each other in their haste to be considered.

Rufus and Margaret...

So many things had fallen into place now. Rufus had seemed very upset at finding the other woman was no longer at Clifftop House, had questioned everyone as to the possible reason for her abrupt departure. And he had wasted no time in coming back to London once he'd realised that was where she must be. Obviously so that he could speak to her in person.

Perhaps the two of them had had a row, or maybe Margaret had just decided the relationship wasn't for her after all. Whatever her reasons, Rufus desperately wanted to see her again.

Annie had got through dinner in miserable silence, hardly able to believe her stupidity. She hadn't fallen for the wrong man once, but twice, and within days of each other! How naive could she be? Anthony, she had quickly realised, had been a terrible mistake on her part, but Rufus—! Rufus was something else entirely... He was tall and strong, honest and dependable—hah, dependable!—or so she had thought until a short time ago.

She had been falling in love with him, she had realised as she'd stood numbly on the other side of his study door.

She had enjoyed being in his company, felt she could relax and be herself with him, while at the same time feeling completely challenged by him. And he made her laugh...

Well, she wasn't laughing now. And she hadn't laughed through dinner, either. It was as if all the friendly banter and teasing that had preceded the meal had never been; dinner had just been something she had to get through.

But she had got through it, had accepted with a bright, meaningless smile the compliments about her cooking, had seen Jessica settled into bed while Rufus cleared away—something Jessica had assured her he *could* do!

Now all Annie wanted to do was escape to her own bedroom and lick her wounds in private. And to her dismay there were wounds, her mistake where Rufus was concerned hurting her deeply.

'Annie?' Rufus prompted in a puzzled voice at her lack of response to his comment.

She stood up abruptly, her hands clasped tightly together to stop their trembling. 'I'm very tired. I think I'll go to bed too, if you don't mind?' To her chagrin, she couldn't even look at him, talking to a spot somewhere over his left shoulder as he sat in one of the armchairs.

'You haven't even touched the brandy I poured for you,' he pointed out mildly.

And rightly so—any more alcohol and she was likely to fall over!

Had he entertained Margaret here too, with or without Jessica present? Had he poured Margaret brandy after dinner and expected her to sit in here and drink it with him? Was that how it had all started? Had the two of them—?

'Annie, you don't look too well.' Rufus stood up, putting his brandy glass down on the table before crossing the room to her side. 'A few seconds ago your face was flushed; now you've gone deathly white.' He looked at her worriedly.

A few seconds ago she had been flushed from the wine she had drunk, and now she had gone white because she was going to be sick!

She turned quickly and ran from the room, just getting to the bathroom before she was violently ill, bringing up all the food she had so painstakingly forced down her throat such a short time ago, her eyes watering from the suddenness of the attack. Rufus came in behind her.

'You really aren't well, are you?' he said soothingly, pressing a damp cloth to her forehead.

His presence in the bathroom only succeeded in making her feel more ill. She should just die right now, just lie down and—

'Come on, I'll help you to your bedroom,' Rufus told her indulgently, still keeping the cloth pressed against her forehead.

Annie straightened, flushing away the evidence of her illness as she did so. 'No!' she said sharply. 'Really. I'm fine.' She pushed the cloth away, relieved to see her hand was shaking only slightly. 'I've never been a good traveller,' she said by way of an excuse. 'It was probably that that made me ill.'

'Motion sickness.' Rufus nodded understandingly.

More like *emotion* sickness! 'Something like that,' she agreed, just wanting the privacy of her bedroom now, sure she must look a sight.

'Horses and cars,' Rufus said dryly. 'You don't have a lot of luck, do you?'

Especially where men were concerned, she inwardly groaned. And they were conducting this conversation in the bathroom, of all places!

'Not a lot,' she acknowledged weakly, sidestepping out of the room.

Rufus followed her out into the hallway. 'Do you remember the way to your bedroom? I didn't know if you had a geographical problem, too,' he added at her puzzled expression.

Annie sensed that he was laughing at her, although she could tell nothing from his expression as he met her gaze with that left brow raised enigmatically. That was enough in itself to tell her he was indeed mocking her.

'No, only horses and cars,' she snapped. 'I'll feel better in the morning.' She would make sure that she did! A severe self-talking-to was what she needed. And it was what she was going to get, too! 'If you'll excuse me...?' She turned in the direction of the bedroom she would be occupying during her stay here.

'Annie?'

She stopped as Rufus softly called her name, turning reluctantly to look at him. 'Yes?' she said warily.

He looked so handsome standing there, still wearing the black shirt and blue denims he had worn for the drive down here—he hadn't had time to change before eating, after concluding his telephone call. To Margaret...

He grinned that heart-stopping grin. 'Goodnight,' he said.

'Goodnight,' she returned abruptly, turning quickly now and making good her escape before he could delay her any further.

She checked on Jessica before going to bed herself. The little girl was fast asleep, curled up into a ball in the bed, a half-smile of contentment on her lips. The sleep of the innocent...

Well, *she*, Annie, was still an innocent too, she decided once she reached the privacy of her bedroom. She should have realised Rufus's concern over Margaret's departure had been too extreme to be about the simple leaving of an employee. Even Anthony, completely self-centred as he was, had questioned Rufus's interest in it.

Rufus and the unknown Margaret...

Oh, she had realised that Rufus would have been involved with other women since his wife died; he was too virile a man for it to be any other way. Especially if, as Anthony had implied, he and Joanne hadn't been particularly happy together. But Annie just hadn't realised Jessica's previous nanny had been one of those women. And from the way Rufus was still pursuing Margaret it was far from over as far as he was concerned!

The laughter, the banter, the kisses that they had shared—all meant nothing. Not to Rufus, anyway...

As far as her own feelings were concerned, the sooner Rufus disappeared on another assignment the better!

If he wasn't around, a constant reminder of the feelings she had for him, then surely, with time, she would get over him?

She certainly hoped so! In fact, she was determined that she would. From tomorrow morning onwards she would make sure their relationship stayed strictly within the boundaries of employer and employee.

That decision made, she fell asleep. Maybe not as innocently and trouble-free as Jessica, but she was so tired that she did sleep.

She had overslept!

The clock face on the bedside radio alarm read nine-fifteen! She couldn't remember the last time she had slept as late as this. What on earth was Rufus going to think of her tardiness? At this rate she was going to be sacked!

She dressed hurriedly in denims and a burnt-orange-coloured jumper, the latter making her hair appear an even deeper red than usual. There was no time for any make-up, and she only ran her brush quickly through her hair before hurrying out to the kitchen. Jessica would be wanting her breakfast, Rufus too, if last night's description of his culinary skills was anything to go by. They would—

The large piece of paper attached by a magnet to the front of the refrigerator door read, 'I've taken Jessica to the park. Help yourself to breakfast. Hope you slept well.' It was signed 'Rufus'.

Annie sat down abruptly at the kitchen table; all her haste had been unnecessary. Jessica wasn't even here to be looked after. Annie wasn't altogether sure that last remark on Rufus's note, about sleeping well, wasn't sarcastic...

She found herself looking down at the piece of paper, which she had taken down from the fridge door. It was the first time she had seen Rufus's handwriting, and she found herself studying it. It was large and strong, the R at the beginning of Rufus written with a flourish. It was rather like the man himself, big and slightly overwhelming, larger than life.

The apartment seemed very empty without him in it. And Jessica too, of course. But it was Rufus she really missed. He had only gone to the park and she missed him. And last night she had decided the sooner he went away the better!

She groaned, burying her face in her hands. She was in love with Rufus!

What she had felt towards Anthony was nothing compared to the emotions surging through her for Rufus. And he was just as out of reach as Anthony had been, also had another woman in his life—

She almost fell off the chair in surprise as the telephone on the kitchen wall began to ring!

She simply looked at it for several seconds; should she answer it or not? It was Rufus's telephone, and the call would obviously be for him. But it could be an emergency. It could even be Rufus himself, telephoning because something had happened to Jessica.

She had to answer it!

'Rufus Diamond's residence.' She spoke stiltedly into the mouthpiece, tightly gripping the receiver to her ear.

There was silence on the other end of the line for several awkward seconds, telling Annie that the caller was as stunned to hear a female voice on the line as Annie had been reluctant to answer the call at all!

'Could I talk to Rufus, please?' The accent was Irish, the voice slightly husky—and definitely female.

Which only increased Annie's nervousness. Surely this wasn't another one? Rufus gave such an impression of being relaxed with himself and confident, but surely he couldn't be that relaxed or confident if there were a number of different women in his life? What if they all decided to turn up at his apartment at the same time? What if, like now, one of those women answered a call from one of the others…?

'Er—not at the moment,' Annie answered evasively, not at all comfortable with this conversation. 'He's taken Jessica to the park.' Surely it was all right to mention Rufus's daughter? Although, from the way he usually lived here alone, a lot of people probably didn't even know he had a daughter. Maybe this woman didn't know—

'How is she?' The woman's voice softened affectionately as she spoke of the little girl.

Not only did this woman know of Jessica, she had obviously met her!

'Very well,' Annie answered sharply—she registered the slightly possessive note in her own voice. But she couldn't help the way she felt, both Jessica and Rufus having become so very important to her.

'That's good,' the woman returned just as briskly. 'And would you be the housekeeper?'

Annie bristled. 'No, I wouldn't be the housekeeper,' she answered quickly, at the same time having no intention of saying who she was. 'Can I take a message?' she offered abruptly.

'If you wouldn't mind,' the woman accepted mildly,

telling Annie her resentment had been felt—and reacted to.

She sighed. 'No, I wouldn't mind.'

'Would you tell Rufus that Margaret called? That I'll be at home for the rest of the day if he would like to call me back when he gets in?'

Annie barely heard the last bit of the message; the name Margaret was the only thing that had really registered. This was Jessica's ex-nanny, the woman Rufus had tried so desperately to talk to the evening before?

She swallowed hard. 'I'll tell him.'

'Thank you,' Margaret returned gratefully. 'And say hello to Jessica for me, and give her my love,' she added before ringing off.

Annie sat down again. She didn't want to give Rufus the message. And she didn't want to pass on Margaret's love to Jessica, either!

Which was ridiculous. If she didn't tell Rufus about the call, so that he couldn't return it, then Margaret was sure to telephone again. And then Annie would look a complete fool for not telling him Margaret had called this morning while he was out! But she wasn't even sure she could say the words, thought they might possibly choke her!

She could always write it down, and just hand the message to Rufus... The piece of paper on which he had written his note to her was still on the kitchen table...

Coward, she admonished herself as she hastily scribbled Margaret's message down. But she couldn't help that; with her own newly recognised feelings for Rufus, to tell him of another woman's telephone call would hurt her deeply.

After writing down the message she busied herself

unstacking the dishwasher, filled with crockery from dinner last night, had almost finished putting the things away in the cupboards when she heard Rufus's key in the door followed by Jessica's happy chatter.

'You're up, Annie.' Rufus seemed surprised to see her in the kitchen.

Her mouth twisted wryly. 'It is after ten o'clock. I'm sorry I overslept.' Even as she made the apology she was helping Jessica off with her coat. 'I don't usually. I can't remember the last time I—'

'I wasn't criticising,' Rufus cut in gently. 'Merely making an observation. We had a great time at the park, didn't we, Tuppence?' He ruffled Jessica's already windblown hair.

Without Annie. She was starting to feel superfluous. And not a little sorry for herself too, she acknowledged painfully. She loved this man, and his daughter, so much, and one day she would have to leave both of them. Sooner rather than later, if Rufus's determination where Margaret was concerned was anything to go by!

'We had fun.' Jessica grinned in agreement, her cheeks flushed with the exercise.

'You're probably both cold.' Annie was aware that she sounded a little stilted, but she couldn't help that, either; she suddenly felt very uncomfortable in Rufus's company. 'Would you like a hot drink? I promise to only put three teabags in the pot,' she added as an attempt at a joke.

Rufus sat on the stool next to Jessica at the breakfast-bar. 'What about the "one for the pot"?' he teased, seeming to be looking at her rather intently.

Which was probably just her imagination; it only felt as if she had the words 'I love Rufus Diamond' emblazoned across her forehead, it wasn't actually a fact! Rufus couldn't possibly know how she felt about him. And it was up to her to make sure he never did.

'I'm not having a cup of tea,' she answered him dismissively. 'I thought I would just tidy the bedrooms while the two of you drank yours,' she explained. She had left her bedroom so hurriedly this morning she hadn't even taken the time to make her bed! Now seemed as good a time as any to go and do that.

Rufus was still watching her, his eyes narrowed darkly. 'The bedrooms can wait,' he said slowly. 'Anyway, Jess and I have already done ours. Sit down and have a cup of tea with us.' He leant over and dropped another teabag into the pot she was in the process of filling with boiling water.

She didn't want to sit down and drink a cup of tea with him! Actually, being in his presence at the moment just made her more jittery than she had been earlier when she'd realised how she felt about him. She needed time alone to pull herself together...

She shook her head. 'I really would like to go and tidy my bedroom.' She couldn't quite meet Rufus's gaze; it might be the undoing of her fragile control if she did! 'The tea is in the pot ready to be poured, and—'

'We don't want twins, do we?' Rufus told her.

She frowned across at him. 'Twins?' she echoed in a puzzled voice.

He nodded. 'I was always told that the person who made the tea should also be the one to pour it, otherwise one of the two people will have twins!' He met her eyes innocently. 'It's an old wives' tale.'

'I think it's just an excuse for Daddy not to have to pour the tea!' Jessica exclaimed knowingly.

'So do I,' Annie agreed. 'And I don't know any old wives, so I've never heard that particular tale, either,' she told Rufus sceptically.

His mouth twisted ruefully. 'Does that mean I get to pour the tea?'

'I think so,' Annie nodded. 'And I wouldn't leave it too much longer before you do it, either, otherwise it will be stewed.' She walked to the door. 'Oh, by the way...' She turned casually back to Rufus—as casually as she was able to on legs that suddenly seemed to be shaking. 'There's a telephone message for you on the table.' She deliberately made her voice light.

'There is?' He frowned, hurriedly moving to pick up the piece of paper, quickly scanning the message Annie had written there—so quickly that Annie hadn't even had time to make good her escape when he looked up again! 'When did she call?' he demanded.

Annie swallowed hard. 'About half an hour ago.'

'Damn!' He crumpled the piece of paper savagely in his hand. 'I have to go out soon, so could you two girls amuse yourselves for a while?' It was a statement rather than a question, his thoughts already elsewhere.

To see Margaret, Annie guessed heavily. Because she had no doubt that was where he was going. He wasn't going to return the other woman's telephone call at all, but was going to see her in person!

'There's plenty of food in the fridge for lunch,' he assured them.

'I'm sure we'll manage,' Annie told him distantly.

Rufus looked up at her sharply, obviously sensing her coolness. 'What, exactly, did she say?' he asked shrewdly.

Annie deliberately kept her face expressionless. 'Once

she realised that you weren't at home, exactly what I've written down there.' She didn't mention, as he hadn't, who 'she' was, sensing that he didn't want to talk of Margaret in front of Jessica. She had no idea why not, unless he just didn't want a lot of questions from his daughter concerning her previous nanny, but it suited Annie not to mention the other woman too. She was starting to hate Margaret even though she had never even met her!

He nodded, his expression distracted once again. 'Off you go to your room and do whatever it is you need to do while Jess and I drink our tea, and then I'll go out.'

He could hardly wait to be gone, Annie acknowledged miserably as she went slowly to her bedroom. Or, at least, he couldn't wait to see Margaret again...

Annie sat down on the bed once she had made it, battling with feelings of jealousy that she had never known before. She hadn't even been jealous of Davina once she'd realised she was Anthony's fiancée, just disappointed that Anthony seemed to be trapped in an engagement he hadn't the courage to get out of. But she had learnt the real truth of that when Anthony had offered her the role of mistress in his life! Now she pitied Davina more than anything else.

Margaret, however, was a different matter. She had actually sounded nice on the telephone, which made disliking her all the more difficult. And yet Annie was so jealous of Rufus's obvious desire to see the other woman again that she was having trouble breathing.

But she certainly couldn't hide out here in her bedroom indefinitely, would have to go back to the kitchen and take care of Jessica while her father went out. To see Margaret...

Oh, God! She buried her face in her hands as she cried; surely loving someone wasn't supposed to be as painful as this? Laughter and pain… She had never thought of the two emotions in the same context before, but Rufus made her laugh, and at the same time the pain of loving him, when he didn't return the emotion, was unbearable!

What was she going to do?

What could she do? She didn't want to leave Jessica. And in all honesty, even though her love wasn't returned, she didn't want to leave Rufus either! But if Margaret came back into Rufus's life, possibly took over the care of Jessica again as well, then Annie might not have any choice in the matter. But until that time—

'Annie?' Rufus knocked on the bedroom door as he called her name.

She stood up, wiping all sign of tears from her cheeks as she moved to open the bedroom door. 'Yes?' she replied. 'Do you want to go now?'

'As soon as I've changed,' he said, studying her closely. 'Are you feeling any better than you did last night? Because, to be honest, you don't look better,' he told her before she could answer him.

'Thanks!' she returned tartly. 'You really know how to make a woman feel good!' She really had to start behaving more naturally around him, and the best way to do that, she decided, was to return his banter. Margaret wasn't back in this life yet, and until she was… All was fair in love and war, wasn't it…?

'I certainly hope so!' He grinned unabashedly and her cheeks reddened as he neatly turned the comment back to her.

Annie's mouth twisted wryly. 'Don't worry about

Jessica and me,' she told him lightly. 'I'm sure we'll be just fine while you're out.'

He sobered and nodded grimly. 'I shouldn't be long.'

On the surface Annie found she *was* fine as she and Jessica decided to bake some cakes to pass the time. It was only inside where she let her thoughts wander to wonder how Rufus was doing with the other woman...

There weren't half the ingredients they needed to make the cakes, and the finished products looked far from appetising, but the two of them had had a lot of fun making them, which was really the whole point of the exercise.

'The real test is in the tasting,' Annie pressed the young girl.

'Go on, then.' Jessica giggled, looking at the flat, slightly burnt cakes. 'I dare you!'

'You're the youngest,' Annie reminded her, also pulling a face at the unappealing cakes.

'All the more reason why I shouldn't be the one to try them,' Jessica asserted. 'I still have all of my life in front of me!'

Annie looked at Jessica, and then to the cakes, and then back to Jessica again. 'I know!' She put the tray of cakes on the side to cool. 'We'll offer one to your father when he gets home.'

'That's mean.' Jessica giggled again, although she didn't reject the idea.

Perhaps it was. But, in all honesty, Annie couldn't say she was feeling very charitable towards Rufus right at this moment. He—

She turned with a puzzled frown as the apartment door slammed shut with a resounding bang. What on earth—? Who on earth...? It couldn't be Rufus—could it?—he had barely left an hour ago.

Rufus stormed into the kitchen, his expression thunderous as he glared across the room at them both. 'Women!' he pronounced disgustedly. 'They're all illogical, of course,' he said to himself, throwing his jacket over one of the kitchen chairs. 'The only time any of you make any sense is when you're asleep!' He glared at Annie and Jessica again. 'And even then you're all damned enigmas!' He turned sharply on his heel. 'I'll be in my study making a telephone call,' was his parting comment.

And I don't want to be disturbed, he could have added, but didn't. Although his wish to be left alone was all too obvious, even to these two 'damned enigmas'.

'I wonder who's upset him?' Jessica murmured in an awestruck voice. 'I've rarely seen Daddy that angry,' she explained.

Indeed, who had rattled his cage? as Rufus had once asked her!

But Annie didn't need to wonder who or what had annoyed him; he had gone out to see Margaret—it was obvious that meeting was what had upset him. It obviously hadn't gone well.

And, for all that it had made Rufus so angry, Annie couldn't help her own elation that it hadn't!

CHAPTER EIGHT

'I SOMEHOW don't think just now is the time to offer him one of our burnt cakes, do you?' Jessica very wisely threw all of them away in the bin. 'I don't think he's in the mood to see the joke.'

Strangely enough, Rufus's obvious bad humour had brought a return of Annie's good one! Whatever had transpired between him and Margaret, it hadn't gone well. Annie couldn't have been more pleased.

Perhaps that was slightly wicked of her, maybe even more than slightly, but she couldn't help the way she felt. She didn't want him reunited with Margaret. She loved Rufus herself; how could she possibly want that?

'Let's start preparing lunch,' she suggested breezily. 'It looks as if your father will be joining us, after all.'

Although whether or not he would actually feel like eating was another matter!

When Rufus didn't appear back in the kitchen by the time twelve-thirty came round, and lunch was ready, Annie decided to go in search of him.

He was still in his study, didn't appear to have moved as he bade Annie to enter after her knock, sitting back in the chair behind the desk, his feet actually up on the desktop.

Annie's brows rose. 'Comfortable?'

'Moderately,' he snapped, his expression as glowering as it had been when he'd arrived back earlier, his elbows resting on the arms of his brown leather chair, his hands linked together under his chin as he looked at Annie over the top of them.

'Lunch is ready,' she told him cordially.

'I'm not particularly hungry,' he returned, still making no effort to move.

Annie didn't move either, remaining exactly where she was. 'Jessica says it's your favourite.'

His mouth contorted. 'Does she? What, exactly, is it?' he asked uninterestedly.

'Bacon omelette with lots of toast.' It didn't exactly sound exciting to her own ears, but Jessica had insisted it definitely was her father's favourite meal.

It was really too bad if it wasn't; there were provisions in the refrigerator, but they weren't exactly extensive. Obviously Rufus lived very simply when he was here.

'It is my favourite meal.' Rufus swung his legs off the desktop, sitting forward in his chair, the dark gloom that had been emanating from him, and filling the room, dispelled as he grinned at her. 'Jessica is going to make some lucky man a good wife some day,' he told Annie as he stood up to follow her back to the kitchen.

Annie turned as she heard him chuckling softly behind her. 'Is something funny?' she said slowly; she certainly couldn't see any joke.

'Your face just now when I made that remark about Jess.' Laughter danced in the darkness of his eyes. 'Go on, tell me what remark you instinctively wanted to make back.'

She gave him a reproving look. 'You said it just to annoy me!'

'And I succeeded.' He still grinned, his bad humour of a few minutes ago apparently forgotten.

'Okay.' She nodded. 'I thought your remark extremely

chauvinistic. And I'm surprised you don't want more for Jessica,' she added challengingly; two could play at his game!

'That's an interesting comment,' Rufus said. 'You don't think a successful marriage is enough for a woman?'

'Is it enough for a man?' she instantly responded.

He paused at the kitchen door. 'I suggest, as Jessica's lunch will spoil, if we don't soon eat, that we continue this conversation some other time. And no, I'm not avoiding an answer,' he stated at her derisive expression. 'It's just too wide a subject to dispense with in two minutes.'

Annie was already regretting the challenge she had thrown out. Oh, not because she didn't mean what she said, because she did; it was just that she realised now that when Rufus had something on his mind he could be deliberately provocative. She didn't for a moment believe *he* had meant what he'd just said; he was just spoiling for an argument! And if he couldn't get anywhere where Margaret was concerned he was going to argue with someone else—namely Annie!

After claiming he wasn't particularly hungry, he certainly did full justice to the omelette and toast, even asking for more of the latter. His bad temper seemed to have disappeared too as he teased and joked with both of them throughout the meal. Not that Annie was fooled by this for a moment, knowing he would return to their earlier conversation once they were on their own again.

'That was excellent.' Rufus sat back, replete after his meal. 'What more could a man ask for than two women pandering to his every whim?' He looked at Annie as she made them all coffee.

He was still baiting her. But she wasn't about to bite, not this time. 'Coffee.' She smiled at him sweetly as she put the steaming mug down next to him.

His mouth twitched as he easily guessed that she was inwardly seething at his taunting. 'Thank you,' he returned just as politely.

'You know something, Rufus...?' Annie continued to smile at him as she gave Jessica her drink before picking up her own mug of coffee and resuming her seat. 'You have a lousy temper!' she told him pleasantly before calmly sipping her coffee.

He continued to look at her for several stunned seconds, and then he began to laugh, that loud shout of laughter that showed he was enjoying himself. And he wasn't laughing at her this time, but with her.

'You're right, Annie.' He finally sobered enough to be able to speak. 'I do have a lousy temper. But for some reason you seem to be able to get me out of it.' He looked at her consideringly. 'I wonder why that is?'

Her bravado of a few minutes ago vanished as he continued to look at her, his gaze warm. After a few seconds of this Annie began to wish he had stayed angry—he was less dangerous that way! To her peace of mind...

'What are we going to do this afternoon?'

It took Annie a couple of seconds to realise Jessica had asked the question, and then, even when she did realise the little girl had addressed the question to her, she was so flustered by the directness of Rufus's stare that she still couldn't answer her!

Rufus was finally the one to turn to his daughter. 'What would you like to do?'

'Well, judging by the little there is left in the fridge

for us to eat, I think we should all go food shopping,' Jessica told him ruefully.

'I think the two of you should go.' Rufus stood up abruptly, taking some money out of his pocket and putting it down on the breakfast-bar. 'I have some work to do. Take a taxi there and back, and don't overstock; we're probably only going to be here another couple of days.' He paused at the door. 'And don't worry about food for this evening; I'm sure Jessica would be very disappointed if we didn't go to her favourite restaurant for pizza.'

'Thank you, Daddy.' Jessica grinned at him, that familiar grin turning to a giggle once her father had left the room. 'Don't worry Annie.' She laughed at Annie's perplexed expression. 'I'm not sure what was going on between you and Daddy during lunch, but I think he wasn't being very kind to you—and I knew if I said we wanted to go shopping he would run away! You're right, Annie.' She shook her head with affection. 'He does have a bad temper!'

For one so young in years, Jessica was very astute. Rufus hadn't exactly been unkind to her earlier, but he had certainly been spoiling for a fight. And as the only other adult within touching distance she was the most likely candidate. Annie had to admit that without Jessica's calming presence she would probably have been only too happy to be his opponent!

Annie laughed softly, her tension instantly easing. 'Let's go and do that shopping.'

Jessica stood up, her ankle hardly troubling her at all now. 'We could get all the ingredients to make a nice hot curry tomorrow; that should steam Daddy's temper out of him!'

'Now, that isn't nice,' Annie reproved her lightly, but she couldn't help but smile at the thought of Rufus with steam coming out of his ears…

Rufus wasn't in that deliberately provocative mood any more when they went out for dinner later that evening; in fact he barely spoke at all, seeming totally distracted. Annie wasn't sure which was worse—a taunting Rufus or an almost silent one!

'Bad-tempered, and now he's very quiet,' Jessica ruminated as she climbed into bed later. 'I've never, ever seen Daddy be quite like this…'

Annie shrugged dismissively, although she had to admit it hadn't been a very comfortable evening for any of them. 'He obviously has something on his mind.' Or someone! The problem of the elusive Margaret was obviously still with him. But she couldn't exactly tell Jessica that!

In fact, it suited her that Rufus didn't want to discuss Margaret in front of his daughter; feeling about him as she did, it would be too painful for her to talk about his preoccupation with another woman!

'I hope he isn't going to leave again,' Jessica said wistfully, sitting up in bed, her arms wrapped about her knees.

Annie felt her stomach lurch at the thought of it. Rufus go away again… He had been gone for three months the last time!

The thought of not seeing him for another three months made her feel sick. She couldn't imagine not having him around, whether he be teasing or deliberately baiting her. How different were her feelings towards him now from when he had first arrived home—was it only three days ago? Then she had believed herself in love with his brother. How weak and insipid were the emotions she had felt towards Anthony compared to what she now felt for Rufus. She could hardly wait to get away from Anthony yesterday, whereas the mere thought of Rufus leaving made her feel physically ill.

'Do you think he is?' She looked anxiously at Jessica, her lips feeling stiff and unmoving as she spoke.

The young girl shrugged. 'It's difficult to tell,' she sighed. 'When he goes, he just goes.'

Which was probably the real reason why he had brought Annie along this weekend—he couldn't just abandon Jessica here on her own if he was called away suddenly. Annie's heart felt even heavier at this realisation.

She smoothed back Jessica's hair as she settled her down onto the pillows. 'Well, I wouldn't worry about it until it happens,' she soothed—she would do enough worrying about it for both of them! 'Just enjoy the time you do have with him.' As she intended to.

Rufus was sitting in the lounge, staring morosely into the glass of whisky he cradled in his hands, when Annie returned from putting Jessica to bed. He didn't look as if he was in the mood to enjoy anything!

'Jessica is worried about you,' Annie told him bluntly as she stood in the open doorway.

She at once had his attention as he looked across at her. 'Jess is?' He looked troubled.

'Mmm.' Annie moved further into the room. 'She thinks you may be going away again.'

'Well, I'm not,' he said flatly.

'I didn't say you were.' Although she couldn't help

but feel relieved that he wasn't. 'Only that Jessica thinks you are.'

He looked irritated. 'And why should she think that?'

Probably because he hadn't really been here all day! 'I have no idea,' she replied. 'You would have to ask Jessica that.'

'Is this your roundabout way of telling me to go up and reassure Jess?' he ventured.

He obviously wasn't a man who liked to feel he had been manoeuvred into anything! 'I don't use roundabout ways, Rufus,' Annie told him evenly. 'I am merely relating to you what Jessica said to me—'

'Okay. Okay!' he bit back impatiently, putting his glass down heavily on the coffee table as he stood up. 'I'm going.' He held up his hands defensively. 'God save me from a woman trying to be reasonable,' he said as he crossed the room to the door. 'It isn't in the nature of the beast,' he added insultingly as he left the room.

He was the one being completely unreasonable. Annie didn't doubt for a moment that she was the recipient of his redirected anger. Rufus was again going out of his way to pick a fight with her, and if this carried on much longer he was going to get one!

'I thought we could have a game of chess.' Annie looked up and smiled at him when he returned a few minutes later.

The chess set was already set up in the corner of the room; she had merely moved the table over so that it stood between the two armchairs.

If Rufus wanted a fight, this was the safest way of having one. Besides, if he was concentrating on the game, then he couldn't sit and brood…

'Unless you have something else to do this evening?'

she added as an afterthought. Although one thing she
was sure of: he wasn't going to see Margaret!

'Nothing that can't wait,' he answered as he sat down
opposite her. 'Are you any good at this?' he rasped, eyes
darkly probing.

'I haven't played for a while.' There hadn't been too
much time in between working and taking care of herself.

'Great!' he responded bad-temperedly. 'You had better go first, then.' He hunched over in his seat.

Annie felt the warmth of angry colour in her cheeks.
'It's customary to toss a coin for it,' she said softly.

He opened his mouth to give her another sharp reply,
but something in her expression seemed to stop him. He
closed his mouth again, sighing deeply. 'I'm being a
moody bast—swine aren't I?' he realised self-
disgustedly.

'Yes,' she replied without hesitation, grateful to him
for changing the word he had been going to use to describe himself.

He chuckled softly, some of the humour returning to
his eyes. 'At least you're honest!' He grinned.

She looked across at him defiantly. 'For a woman?'

'God, I have been an insulting swine today, haven't
I?' He shook his head. 'Will one apology suffice, or shall
I go through each and every one of them?' he cajoled.

Annie couldn't help her lips curving upwards at his
remorseful expression. 'Why don't we play the game of
chess first—and then see if you still feel like apologising?'

His brows rose. 'Are you that good...?'

She gave him an enigmatic smile in reply. Although,
in truth, she was no longer sure how good she was; she

hadn't played for such a long time. She wanted to beat him; she knew that.

She won the toss of the coin, and began the game. And for the next half an hour there was barely a word spoken by either of them as they concentrated on their moves. But Annie could tell they were pretty evenly matched.

'You are good,' Rufus murmured appreciatively as Annie took yet another one of his pawns.

'Thank you.' She accepted the compliment for exactly what it was.

He sat back, looking across at her. 'I really am sorry for the way I've been behaving today. 'I just— Look, Annie, you're a woman— Did I say something funny?' He reacted as she gave a choked laugh.

'Not at all.' Her eyes glowed with repressed humour.

'Considering I've thrown every insult at you today that I could think of concerning women!' he acknowledged knowingly.

'Not every insult, surely?' she teased; there were certainly one or two she could think of that he hadn't mentioned.

'All the ones that are relevant to my particular problem. Tell me, why would a woman agree to talk to you on the telephone, but when you turn up in person instead refuse to see you?' His brow furrowed.

Margaret had refused to see him this morning! And he had been stamping around like a bear with a sore head ever since!

Annie raised her shoulders indifferently. 'Any number of reasons.' She moved one of her pieces on the board.

His eyes were narrowed. 'Such as?' He made an answering move.

She looked across at him consideringly. 'Would you be the person this woman refused to see?' she asked—knowing, of course, that he was...

'What the hell does that have to do—? Yes,' he confirmed impatiently as she arched questioning brows.

'Well, in that case, I can think of a very good reason why I would refuse to see you.'

'Yes?' he prompted curtly.

She moved uncomfortably, wondering if she was going too far. But he had asked, and she could only answer him truthfully. 'You're very— You can be—' She stopped awkwardly.

'What?' he snapped. 'What am I?' he looked at her exasperatedly.

She hesitated again. 'You're my employer, Rufus. And I happen to like my job, and—'

'Forget I'm your employer,' he cut in irritably, 'and just answer the question, damn it!'

She had managed to forget he was her employer on several occasions—that wasn't really the issue. 'But can you forget I'm your employee?' she persisted. 'Perhaps it isn't really fair to ask me this question.' She paused. Honesty had its place, but she wasn't sure whether that was between this employer and this employee!

'Forget fair!' he dismissed arrogantly. 'Just tell me why you would refuse to see me.'

She drew in a ragged breath. 'Basically for the very reason you have just demonstrated,' she said carefully.

'I just—?' His brow cleared. 'I forced you to answer me,' he realised slowly.

'Exactly,' she confirmed with relief; she hadn't had to call him a bully, after all! 'If you tried that approach over the telephone, then I could just put the receiver down on you.' Face to face, this man was much more formidable. 'And so, presumably, could this other woman,' she added gently. He still hadn't mentioned it was Margaret from this morning's call that they were talking about, but she knew that it had to be. And it hurt even to have this conversation, his deep need to talk to Jessica's former nanny was so patently obvious.

'She already did,' he growled.

One of the telephone calls he had made when he'd got back this morning…

'She refused to see me when I went to her home,' he admitted. 'And then, when I telephoned her later, she put the receiver down on me.'

'As you've already said yourself, Rufus—' she moved her piece on the board '—your mood has been a little—aggressive today. Check,' she told him with satisfaction. 'And mate.'

'I've felt aggressive because— Did you say checkmate?' He looked astounded, staring down at the chessboard in disbelief at her claim.

It was the expression on his face that made Annie laugh; he had probably never been beaten at chess in his life before—and he had just been thrashed at the game! 'Don't look so surprised, Rufus; a chess set was something the children's home could afford—and there are a lot of rainy days and evenings in sixteen years.' She said the last without rancour. Her childhood in care hadn't been an unhappy one—a little lacking in love, perhaps, but certainly not an unhappy time.

He looked across at her admiringly before looking down at the board once again. 'Well played, Annie,' he told her with genuine warmth. 'You're a worthy opponent.' He nodded appreciatively.

She didn't want to be his opponent, longed for the light-hearted companion from the drive down here, the man who had kissed her...

'Enough of this.' He stood up, moving the chess table back to the corner of the room. 'You're right, I've been a grouch most of the day. I know that isn't what you said,' he acknowledged dryly as she almost protested. 'But I know it's what I've been. Some break away in London you and Jess have had!' he added with self-rebuke. 'Well, that's about to change. If you could pour us both a brandy, I'll light the fire.'

Brandy and a fire... The brandy she didn't particularly like, and a fire...! It was a little too cosy considering she worked for this man.

'It's a little late in the evening for either,' she said, looking pointedly at her wristwatch. 'Especially as I overslept this morning.'

'As far as I'm aware, you haven't had any time off in the last few days. You're here to enjoy yourself, not just to look after Jess.' He sat back on his heels. 'Perhaps you would rather go out and visit friends for the rest of the evening?' he queried with a penetrating look as the thought seemed to occur to him.

It would probably be safer than being cosily ensconced in this room with Rufus!

But a part of her didn't really want to be safe. She had stayed safe all of her life, never causing waves at the home, being easygoing with her three flatmates, undemanding of the few friends she had had over the years. She didn't want to be safe any more—and she knew that with Rufus she most certainly wasn't!

'I'm really not a night person.' She refused the offer to let her go out. 'I'll pour the brandy.' To make sure that hers was considerably smaller than his. She needed to stay completely sober around this man.

He picked up his brandy glass, dimming the lights before moving to sit next to Annie on the sofa. 'There's nothing like a fire,' he told her contentedly. 'The fireplace was the reason I decided to lease this particular apartment.'

She had to admit the fire was lovely—it was also quite seductive sitting here next to the man she loved, watching the flames dance. The few sips of brandy she had taken had warmed her totally.

Rufus relaxed his own head back on the sofa. 'This is nice,' he murmured softly.

'Nice' wasn't quite the way Annie would have described it. She should have gone to bed. Or gone out. Anything else but be sitting here in this dimly lit room with *this* man. Because at this moment she wanted very much to kiss him!

As if sensing that need, Rufus turned to look at her, his eyes very dark, the firelight dancing in their depths. 'The company is pretty good too,' he said huskily.

She felt the warmth in her cheeks—and it had nothing to do with the heat from the fire!

'I mean that, Annie.' He reached out and clasped the hand that didn't hold her brandy glass. 'You aren't a woman who chatters on about nothing. When you do speak, it's because you have something relevant to say. Otherwise you just stay silent.'

He hadn't released her hand!

She knew she should move her hand away, that this was indeed the danger she had been aware of. But she didn't want to be released. She loved this man. And she might never have the chance to be this close to him again.

She arched dark auburn brows. 'You like that in a woman?' she asked playfully.

He smiled. 'I wasn't having another go at women, Annie. I actually like women. What I was trying to say just now—and not making a very good job of it!—was that I particularly like you.'

Annie drew back slightly, but somehow he didn't seem any further away. In fact, he seemed closer than before!

Because he had moved too! He was no longer sitting on the other side of the sofa. He had gently taken the brandy glass from her unresisting fingers to place it on the coffee table beside his own, his face only inches away from hers now.

'Those eyes,' he murmured wonderingly. 'I could drown in them!'

She couldn't breathe! And as his mouth claimed hers she found she didn't want to. All she could do was feel, drowning herself in the passion that surged through her as his mouth hardened on hers, his arms moulding her to the muscular strength of his body, her arms encircling his neck as she drew him closer to her.

His mouth left hers, but only to travel over her cheeks, kissing each of her closed lids in turn, her temple, the lobes of her ears, gently nibbling there as she quivered in reaction, tasting the perfume of her throat before once again claiming her mouth with his own.

She was on fire as she felt his hand caressing her breast, her nipple instantly responding to his touch, hardening, sensitive to his every caress.

Annie groaned low in her throat, melting against him,

her body like liquid fire, her hands clinging feverishly to his shoulders.

She offered no resistance as he lowered her back onto the sofa, her legs becoming entangled with his as he lay down beside her, her blouse open now, smoothed back to her shoulders, Rufus's eyes dark with desire as he looked down at the peach colour of her satin bra, her skin as smooth and silky as that material.

She watched him through half-closed lids as his hands moved slowly over the pertness of her breasts, enjoyed the pleasure she saw in his face, knowing she was the one giving him that pleasure.

As Rufus was giving her pleasure too, his mouth closing over one hardened nipple against the silky material, his tongue caressing in slow, heat-giving strokes, his other hand seeking and finding its twin, touching, feeling her response.

Annie arched up into his pleasure-giving mouth, her hands entangled in his hair as she held him to her, filled with the strangest mixture of emotions, wanting to cradle him to her protectively while at the same time wanting more than the pleasure he was already giving her.

Then the barriers of her blouse and bra were no longer there, and it was flesh against flesh, Rufus's chest naked too, the dark hair there at once silky to the touch, his skin firm and unyielding to her caressing fingertips.

She ran her hands down his muscled back, her nails lightly scratching the dampness of his skin.

'Oh, yes...!' Now it was Rufus's turn to groan, even as the moistness of his mouth claimed one hardened nipple.

Heat. Fire. A longing that made her thighs ache as she moved restlessly against him, his mouth against her breasts no longer enough for either of them—the pulsing of Rufus's thighs against hers told her that.

'I want you, Rufus,' she told him longingly, eyes so dark brown as she looked up at him that it was impossible to distinguish the pupils from the irises. 'I want you!' she repeated achingly.

He stood up to swing her easily up into his arms, his smile tender as he looked down at her. 'My bed is bigger than yours,' he told her. Picking her up, he strode from the room to his bedroom with her still in his arms.

He carried her as if she weighed very little, gently kicking the bedroom door closed behind them before laying her down on the bed, kneeling on the carpeted floor beside her as he slowly removed the rest of her clothes, folding each item carefully before laying it down on the floor beside him.

Annie felt slightly self-conscious as she lay naked before him, but as he began to slowly kiss and caress each slender curve she could see the beauty of her body in his eyes.

'You too, Rufus,' she encouraged tenderly, longing to touch him in the same way.

And when he finally stood naked before her she wasn't disappointed, as she had known she wouldn't be. Rufus was beautiful, his skin tanned, his body all smoothly muscled planes, his waist slender, thighs firmly muscled, long legs covered with the same dark hair as his chest. Naked, with his dark hair long onto his shoulders, he looked like a warrior of old.

And she wanted to be his captive, completely, wanted to know his full possession, and as Rufus lay down on the bed beside her she could feel the promise of that possession leaping against her thighs.

He began to kiss her again, her lips, her breasts, her thighs, making her cry out in wonder and need.

Then her groans of pleasure became whimpers, crying out as pleasure like she had never known before engulfed her, leaving her mindless, lost in a vortex of such scorching pleasure it reached to her fingertips and toes.

She looked up at Rufus in wonder as he moved to lie beside her once again, gently kissing her flushed face. 'I've never—I— Oh, Rufus...!' Her arms moved about his shoulders as she hugged him to her.

He raised his head slowly, his gaze gentle now. 'Have you never made love, Annie?' he asked gruffly. 'Or just never known the pleasure it could give you?'

'Neither!' she choked a little self-consciously. She was such an innocent, had never guessed, never known...!

Rufus's smile deepened. 'Then I'm glad, and honoured, that I'm the first.' He smoothed back the dampness of her hair from her brow, gently brushing her lips with his own. 'Now I think we should get under the covers, cuddle up, and go to sleep.' He stood up, folding back the duvet invitingly.

Annie blinked up at him. 'But you— We haven't— You haven't—'

He knelt on the bed beside her again, lightly touching her heated cheeks. 'I don't have anything with me, Annie. And I doubt very much, in the circumstances, that you do...?' He raised questioning brows, shrugging helplessly as she shook her head. 'I don't want the consequences of our first time together to be something that you spend the next few weeks worrying about.' He settled her under the duvet before climbing into the bed next to her, his arm about her shoulders as he moulded her into him.

Annie didn't doubt for a moment that he had wanted her as much as she had wanted him—had felt his need. And he was denying himself all that because of her innocence...

Her arms moved about him as she held on tightly to him. She loved this man; she knew that without a doubt as his steady breathing lulled them both into a deep sleep.

CHAPTER NINE

ANNIE was totally disorientated when she woke up the next morning and found herself not in Rufus's bed or his arms but back in her own room, in her own bed, and by herself.

Rufus must have carried her here some time during the night or early morning. As she sat up in bed she saw her neatly folded clothes—even her blouse and bra—laid on the bedroom chair.

Jessica...

Rufus had been aware, even if Annie hadn't, that Jessica shouldn't find them snuggled up in bed together this morning. Or some of Annie's clothing scattered about the sitting-room!

She stretched in the bed, her body feeling different somehow, still very much aware of the aching pleasure given by Rufus's hands and lips. Her only regret was that she hadn't known his full possession. But that might still happen.

What would his behaviour towards her be like this morning? Would he be her employer once again? Or would there be the memory of last night in his eyes too? God, she hoped so. Because she would never forget it! She didn't think she could bear it if Rufus chose to ignore the passion they had shared so completely—

'Tea,' Jessica announced brightly as she entered the bedroom after the briefest of knocks. She put the cup down on the bedside table before sitting on the side of

Annie's bed. 'Don't worry, Daddy didn't make it!' She grinned teasingly. 'He's gone out,' she added a little wistfully.

Annie frowned at the bedside clock. She had overslept again, but it was still only eight-thirty. Who on earth had Rufus gone to see so early on a Sunday morning? He certainly didn't strike her as someone who went to church every Sunday morning, regardless.

She sat up to drink her tea, realising as she did so that she was completely naked beneath the covers, pulling the sheet up with her to hide her nudity from Jessica.

'Where did he go?' She kept her voice casually unconcerned between sipping at her tea.

Jessica didn't know. 'He made a phone call, then said he had to go out. He didn't say where. Or when he would be back.'

Margaret…

Somehow Annie knew the other woman was the person Rufus had telephoned and then gone out to see.

She closed her eyes, hiding the pain she knew must be evident in their depths. Maybe she had been mistaken last night; maybe Rufus hadn't drawn back from making love to her because of her innocence; maybe it was the complete opposite: he had been thinking of someone else entirely!

He had gone to Margaret this morning. She knew it as surely as if he had told her so. Oh…!

'Are you all right, Annie?' Jessica sounded worried. 'I didn't wake you up too suddenly, did I?'

It was as well someone had! She had been lying here daydreaming about Rufus, about last night, about the two of them having a possible future together… How stupid. How totally juvenile. Just because a man made love to you, that didn't mean he wanted to spend the rest of his life with you. She should know; it was usually the opposite! Didn't she have her own mother as an example of that? And hadn't Rufus gone to see Margaret this morning...?

She drew in a deep, controlling breath, opening her eyes to smile brightly at Jessica. The last thing she wanted was to alert the child to her inner distress, because if she did Jessica would only tell Rufus—and he would know exactly why she was so upset.

She had to be adult about this. After all, what had really happened between herself and Rufus? For her, everything. But for Rufus, a man of obvious experience, probably very little. She was a conquest, that was all, a willing woman to share his bed. Because the one that he really wanted no longer would!

But all that might have changed by the time he returned, and Annie certainly didn't want him to think last night had been more important to her than it obviously had to him!

'No, you didn't wake me too suddenly,' she assured Jessica warmly, and the little girl's worried face instantly cleared. 'Would you like some pancakes for breakfast?' She knew they were Jessica's favourite, the answer a foregone conclusion. 'Give me ten minutes,' she requested at Jessica's eager nod, 'and I'll come through to the kitchen and make them.' It would also give her the privacy to get out of bed without Jessica seeing her nudity.

'I'll go and get everything out ready for you,' Jessica told her with enthusiasm, getting up from the bed to skip out of the room.

Annie fell back against the pillows as soon as she was

alone, wishing she had the energy—the happiness!—to skip like that. But with morning had come reality in all its harshness, and last night was starting to seem like a dream.

Maybe it had been? Maybe she hadn't woken in Rufus's bed because she had never been there?

But as she got up out of her own bed she knew none of it had been a dream, her nipples slightly tender from Rufus's ministrations, muscles in her thighs that she had never been aware of before aching slightly, her whole body filled with an unaccustomed lethargy. She might wish it had never happened, but it certainly had.

And when Rufus returned she would have to face him with that knowledge firmly imprinted on her body and mind...!

Jessica had eaten her pancakes, while Annie drank two cups of coffee, by the time they heard the apartment door slam, heralding Rufus's return. Annie stiffened when she heard the sound, her back turned towards the kitchen door as she started on her third coffee; she was hoping it might wake her up and give her some courage too. She knew that it hadn't as she heard the kitchen door swing open. Her stomach seemed to drop to the floor, her hand shaking slightly as she carefully put her cup back in its saucer.

'Daddy!' Jessica cried her own pleasure at seeing her father, hopping up and down excitedly, the injury to her ankle almost forgotten now.

Annie didn't move. But she had to. If she didn't, Rufus would surely realise something was wrong. And she really didn't want him to know what last night had meant to her. She had some pride.

She drew in a deep, calming breath, turning slowly, shrinking back on the stool as she saw Rufus's expression. Last night, in the circumstances, was surely regrettable, but it surely wasn't as bad as all that...? Rufus looked—

'How soon can you and Jessica be ready to leave for Clifftop House?' he barked.

Annie was taken aback, both by the coldness of his voice and the question itself. Yesterday he had told them to stock up on food for another couple of days; now it seemed he intended leaving immediately. What had happened between then and now to cause this sudden change of plan?

Last night had happened...

And from Rufus's arrogantly distant expression it wasn't even a subject he cared to discuss, let alone repeat!

'Clifftop?' Jessica was the one to answer in a woebegone voice. 'But, daddy, you said—'

'I know what I said, Jess,' he bit out. 'But—circumstances have changed. We're going back today.'

He didn't so much as glance at Annie as he mentioned those changed circumstances, but she felt the accusation in the words anyway. Obviously going to bed with his daughter's nanny—the second one!—had not been on his agenda.

Well, it hadn't been on hers either—had been the last thing she'd expected to happen this weekend. In the circumstances, she couldn't wait to leave either, could envisage nothing more painful than spending another couple of days here with the two of them trying to be polite to each other, for Jessica's sake.

'Fifteen minutes.' She stiffly answered his original

question, looking in his general direction but her eyes remaining unfocused, the coldness she had seen in his face earlier enough to deter her from looking at him properly.

'Make it half an hour,' he told her in short reply. 'I need a cup of coffee myself before we make the drive back.'

'I'll go and pack,' Annie agreed, making no effort to offer to make his coffee for him; if she didn't get out of this room soon she was going to make a complete fool of herself by bursting into tears!

'Annie?' Rufus reached out to grasp her arm as she would have walked past him out of the room. 'You're very pale.'

Probably because for her, unlike him, last night had been unique. It had been wonderful, magical—falling asleep in his arms like no other comfort she had ever known. And briefly—very briefly!—she had imagined being able to do that for the rest of her life.

How naive. How stupid she had been. Last night hadn't been about for ever. And, far from being considerate of her innocence, Rufus had probably felt like running a mile from her inexperience. He hadn't been being kind at all, had probably lost interest in making love to her the moment he'd realised she was an inexperienced virgin!

'We need to talk—'

'I don't think so,' she replied, much more calmly than she felt, moving slightly so that his hand dropped away from her arm. 'Unless it has to do with going back to Clifftop House?' she added in a businesslike tone; after all, she did work for this man.

'No.' He looked down at her. 'Believe me, Annie, we

do need to talk, and I'm sorry I wasn't here this morning—'

'You obviously had important business to attend to,' she cut in with a warning look in Jessica's direction. The last thing she wanted was for Jessica to realise Rufus was talking about not being in bed beside her when she woke up. That would just be too awful!

'It wasn't business,' he rasped. 'But it was important. It still is. And until I sort it out, one way or another, it has to take priority over everything else. Is that going to be okay with you?' His gaze was suddenly warmly probing now.

And Annie found she couldn't withstand that warmth, her cheeks no longer pale as she wrenched her own eyes away from his, feeling their heat as she recalled all too vividly how Rufus had looked at her last night, how he had touched and caressed her until she almost shattered in his arms.

'Perfectly okay with me,' she told him coolly. 'I'm just an employee, Rufus; I go where you tell me to go.'

Her chin was wrenched up as Rufus forced her to look at him. His gaze moved searchingly over her face now: the brown eyes that couldn't hide the hurt she felt, the slightly dark shadows beneath their depths from the lack of sleep she had known in his arms, the mouth she could only just stop from trembling, tears very close now.

'I don't believe that for a moment, Annie,' he said huskily. 'God, this is all such a damned mess!' He ran an agitated hand through the dark thickness of his hair. 'Can you try to be patient with me until I've sorted it out?'

Until he had sorted out exactly what his feelings were towards Margaret, he meant! Wasn't it enough that he had gone to the other woman this morning? There really was nothing to sort out as far as Annie was concerned; she had loved—still loved!—and had most definitely lost! There was nothing else to say. Because no amount of talking could change that...

Once again she moved away from him. 'We all make mistakes, Rufus,' she told him evenly. 'Let's mark last night down as one.'

'Is that what it was?' he demanded. 'A mistake?'

'Most definitely!' She shuddered as she remembered how utterly stupid she had been. In her naiveté she had believed that if Rufus made love with her everything would turn out right between them, but now she accepted that a man could make love to one woman and actually be in love with another one. A man's emotions didn't necessarily follow the instincts of his body.

Rufus drew back from her, his expression closed now, totally unreadable. 'Jessica, go and help Annie pack anything you want to take with you.'

Jessica pulled a face. 'Does this mean I go back to school tomorrow?'

His expression softened as he looked at his daughter. 'It most certainly does. The way you've been moving around on that ankle the last few days, I think you could run a four-minute mile if you had to!'

'Oh.' She pulled another face.

'Come on, Jessica,' Annie encouraged. 'Just think, you can tell Lucy all about your week when you see her tomorrow.'

'That's true,' she acknowledged grudgingly as she crossed the room to join Annie at the doorway without even the slightest of limps.

It took Annie less than ten minutes to pack the few

things she had brought with her, but Rufus had said half an hour, and so she took that full half-hour, taking advantage of the spare twenty minutes to apply some make-up to her pale cheeks. The end result was quite pleasing—at least she no longer looked ill, the blusher adding a peachy glow to her cheeks.

The disillusionment in her eyes was something else entirely; she couldn't hide that with any amount of make-up!

The drive back to Clifftop House was made in almost complete silence, Jessica once again choosing to fall asleep in the back of the car, Rufus stony-faced and lost in thought, Annie immersed in her own private misery.

It was the longest journey she had ever undertaken, not in miles, but in terms of emotional trauma. She had never been as happy to see the gothic proportions of Clifftop House as they turned into the long driveway— not even on the day she'd first come to work here!

That seemed such a very long time ago now...

So much had happened in that last two months. She had thought she had fallen in love once, only to realise Anthony wasn't the man she thought he was, and then she had really fallen in love, with a man who was everything she thought he was, and more—he was in love with another woman!

She barely waited for Rufus to stop the car in front of the house before getting out onto the gravelled driveway, opening the back door to help Jessica out too.

'You two go inside; I'll bring the bags in.' Rufus stood on the drive too now.

Annie didn't need any persuading to do exactly that, relieved to at last be away from Rufus. It was going to be difficult staying out of his way for the rest of his visit here, but it was what she intended doing whenever possible. If she didn't see him, perhaps this ache for him inside her would go away.

Celia was crossing the entrance hall as Annie and Jessica entered the house, the raising of her already arched blonde brows the only outward sign she gave that she was surprised to see them. 'You're back,' she stated smoothly. 'I didn't expect you back so soon.'

'Rufus has some business to attend to.' Annie was the one to answer her.

'He is with you, I take it?' There was a slight edge to her voice. 'And not still in London?'

'No, I'm here, Celia,' Rufus told her evenly as he entered the house with the bags.

Celia looked at him coldly. 'And which member of staff do you intend to dismiss while you're here this time?'

Rufus's eyes narrowed. 'I take it you're referring to James?'

'I am,' Celia confirmed abruptly.

'Then I'm afraid you have it all wrong, Celia. I didn't dismiss James; he decided it was time for him to retire.'

'Indeed?' She pursed her lips sceptically. 'Rather sudden, wasn't it?'

Rufus sighed. 'It was his own decision,' he repeated flatly. 'He feels Jess's accident was his fault, and after talking to him I'm inclined to agree with him—'

'I think we should go to my sitting-room and discuss this in private,' Celia put in sharply.

Away from her, the listening servant, Annie inwardly surmised. But if, as Rufus said, James had retired because he felt responsible for Jessica's accident—

'James has gone?' Jessica groaned in dismay, turning to her father. 'Daddy—'

'As I've already told your grandmother—' he gave Celia a censorious look for having discussed this in front of Jessica in the first place '—James feels responsible for your accident. He believes that he didn't check your horse was saddled properly—'

'But I should have checked it too,' Jessica wailed in distress. 'You always told me to. And I—'

'Jessica, I think you and I should take our things upstairs,' Annie encouraged gently, 'and leave your father and grandmother to talk in private.'

'But—'

'Then you can telephone Lucy and tell her you'll be back at school tomorrow,' she added lightly at Jessica's rebellious expression. The little girl could be as stubborn as her father when she chose to be!

'All right,' the young girl conceded grudgingly. 'I'll see you later, Daddy,' she added, almost questioningly, as if she had a feeling he might decide to leave after his conversation with her grandmother.

'You will,' he confirmed easily. 'Annie...?' He stopped her halfway up the wide staircase.

She turned slowly, almost dreading what he was going to say to her. She swallowed hard. 'Yes?' Even to her own ears her voice sounded wary.

He smiled, not that mocking grin, or that knowing smile, but with genuine warmth. 'I'll see you later, too,' he told her huskily.

Annie frowned down at him for several long seconds, and then she assented. 'I'll be with Jessica.'

They ascended the rest of the stairs unhindered, and Annie, for one, was glad when they reached Jessica's bedroom. She could finally breathe normally once again. It seemed as if she hadn't been able to do so for so long. Since she woke up this morning, in fact!

What was she going to do? That was the question she had put off asking herself all day. Even if Rufus went away again soon, he would eventually come back. And then she would have to face him all over again. Still loving him. Because the love she felt for Rufus was like nothing she had ever experienced before. Or, she was sure, would ever feel for anyone again. But Rufus was in love with another woman. A woman who didn't seem to return his love. What a triangle of misplaced emotions.

'Can I go downstairs and telephone Lucy now?'

She looked up at Jessica with unfocusing eyes, hadn't even been aware of the fact that the two of them had unpacked what little Jessica had brought back with her. But they had, and the little girl now wanted to make that promised telephone call. But Annie wasn't sure whether Rufus and Celia would have moved out of the hallway yet—there had been the light of battle in their eyes!

'Use the telephone in my bedroom,' Annie suggested. 'That way you can talk for as long as you like.'

Jessica was more than happy with this arrangement, running off to Annie's room to make the call. Leaving Annie on her own again, which was something she didn't particularly want. She had time to think then. And her thoughts were all of Rufus.

Margaret was still in London, so why, if Rufus was hoping to have the other woman back in his life, had he rushed them all back here? Maybe he had just wanted to get her and Jessica off his hands, and despite what he had said downstairs he would soon be returning to London?

It would make more sense for him to be on his own in the city. Certainly for Annie not to be around. Especially after what had happened between them last night.

Was it really only last night…? It seemed unreal now, almost a dream—or a nightmare! Because that was what all this had now become.

And she couldn't sit here lost in thought in Jessica's bedroom for ever! Everything was once again tidy, and there was nothing in here for her to do. A cup of coffee sounded like a good idea. She could bring a drink back up with her for Jessica, too.

But what if Celia and Rufus were still at the bottom of the stairs?

Of course they weren't; Celia would never have a private conversation with Rufus where one of the servants might overhear them! And, from the angry expressions on both their faces earlier, the conversation between the two Diamonds was going to be very private indeed!

She was right—the area at the bottom of the stairs was empty as she descended, not even the murmur of voices to be heard anywhere in the house—so as least Celia and Rufus weren't actually shouting at each other. They—

'Annie…! Thank God!' An agitated Rufus appeared in the doorway of Celia's private sitting-room. 'Dial Emergency and ask for an ambulance to be sent here as soon as possible!' he told her forcefully, his face pale.

She blinked up at him dazedly. What—? Who—? Surely he and Celia hadn't actually come to blows?

She didn't believe that for a moment; Rufus might be

many things, but she knew without a doubt that he would
never be violent with a woman. So what—?

'Annie, call the damned ambulance!' Rufus repeated
savagely. 'Celia has collapsed. I think it may be a heart
attack!'

CHAPTER TEN

ANNIE didn't need telling again, galvanised into action as she rushed to find the nearest telephone, surprisingly calm as she gave the details of Celia's collapse and exactly where the house was. The operator on the other end of the telephone line assured her an ambulance would be dispatched immediately, and would arrive shortly.

Annie hurried to Celia's sitting-room as soon as the call was ended, finding Rufus bent over her as she lay supine on the sofa, her face looking grey, and suddenly very old, the hauteur all gone, leaving an ageing, vulnerable-looking woman.

'What happened?' Annie prompted softly as she moved to stand beside Rufus.

He didn't look up. 'One minute we were talking— rather heatedly, I admit.' He frowned darkly. 'But then, Celia and I have always talked to each other like that,' he went on harshly. 'But this time she suddenly went that sickly grey colour and collapsed.'

Annie came down on her haunches beside him. 'What were the two of you talking about?'

'Anthony!' Rufus said disgustedly. 'What else?'

She reached out to touch Celia's cheek, finding it clammy, her hands icy cold. 'She loves him very much,' she told Rufus distractedly. 'She's very proud of him.'

'He's a selfish, egotistical, insensitive bastard!' Rufus rasped forcefully.

'He's her son,' Annie reminded him gently. 'And a mother's love forgives most things.'

Rufus straightened abruptly. 'I wouldn't know.'

Annie looked up at him, brown eyes shadowed. 'Neither would I,' she agreed. 'But I'm sure that if I had a child I would be as protective of him as Celia is of Anthony. As you are of Jessica.'

A nerve pulsed in his tightly clenched jaw before he turned away to stand with his back towards her as he stared out of the window.

Annie wondered if he was actually seeing anything out of that window, or if it was just his way of avoiding looking at her and the grey-faced woman on the sofa. The latter, she believed. Whatever anger had possessed Rufus this morning, it was still there. And it was directed towards Anthony...

'The ambulance is here,' Rufus suddenly said, turning back into the room. 'I suggest I go to the hospital with Celia while you stay here with Jessica. And wait for Anthony to return,' he added frostily. 'Apparently he drove Davina back to London early this morning, but will be back later this afternoon.'

His suggestion that he go with Celia made complete sense; Celia was his stepmother, and he was the obvious choice to accompany her. But Annie didn't particularly relish the idea of being the one to wait here for Anthony's return!

But she didn't voice any of her own feelings, standing back as Rufus admitted the paramedics to do their work, feeling rather superfluous as they took over, eventually lifting Celia onto the stretcher and carrying her out to the waiting vehicle, Rufus following closely behind.

And then the ambulance, plus Celia and Rufus, was

gone, and an eerie calm settled over the house. Eerie, because it certainly wasn't restful.

It was left to Annie to break the news to the rest of the household, including Jessica, who, after being buoyant from her chat with Lucy, suddenly became very quiet.

'Is Granny going to die?' Jessica suddenly burst out, her throat moving convulsively as she choked back the tears.

It would be so much easier to say no, she wasn't— and pray that was the truth. But Annie really couldn't do that, had no idea how serious Celia's condition was.

'I don't know, Jessica,' she answered honestly.

'My grandfather died when I was a baby,' Jessica rejoined evenly.

Annie held the little girl's hand tightly. 'I know, darling.'

'My mummy died, too,' Jessica said tightly.

Annie felt her heart contract at the stark truth of Jessica's words; her mother had died and left her. As had Annie's own mother. And Rufus's. Everyone died eventually. That was the one true fact of life that was inevitable.

Her hand tightened around Jessica's. 'Let's hope that Granny will get better.'

Jessica chewed on her bottom lip, still fighting the tears. 'My mummy went out on a boat with Uncle Anthony, and never came back.'

Annie frowned. Joanne and Anthony...? Was this the boating accident Rufus had spoken of the very first afternoon she met him? Joanne—and Anthony?

'That doesn't mean Granny won't come back from the hospital,' she assured Jessica.

'Will I be able to go and see her?' Jessica persisted, suddenly looking very young.

'If your daddy says she's well enough,' Annie answered evasively—because she really didn't know how ill Celia was! 'Let's have a game of chess while we wait to hear from him,' she encouraged as a distraction. 'Your father tells me you play well.'

Jessica gave her a derisive look that reminded Annie so achingly of Rufus. 'Daddy tells me you play even better!'

Annie laughed, relieved to have something to laugh at. 'He wasn't really concentrating last night when we played.' His thoughts had all been with another woman!

'I don't mind losing,' Jessica admitted. 'Daddy says it's good experience.'

'Does he?' Annie returned dryly; she very much doubted Rufus had ever been pleased at the experience of losing!

Jessica giggled at her wry expression. 'I don't think he thought so last night...!' She giggled again. 'I still can't believe you actually beat him.' She shook her head as they set up the chessboard. 'I don't think that's ever happened to him before.'

Annie bent her head over the game as her own smile faded; she didn't think it would ever happen again, either. Because she very much doubted she would spend any more time alone with Rufus...

But she was relieved the suggestion of chess seemed to have taken Jessica's mind off her maudlin thoughts of death. It was sad that Jessica had such tragic memories to carry through life with her. And how awful that her mother had died in such a terrible way. Drowning, fighting for breath and simply taking in water instead of air, was a horrible way for anyone to die.

But at least now she knew Joanne wasn't the one who had committed suicide down in the cove.

Which meant that probably Rufus's mother had...

How awful if two Diamond brides had met their death by drowning.

And now Celia, a third Diamond bride, was seriously ill in hospital—Annie realised she was becoming maudlin herself now, and that wouldn't help anyone!

How quickly she had become caught up in the lives and emotions of this family. But they seemed to be a family dogged by misfortune. Even Anthony was marrying a woman he had no intention of being faithful to. She sincerely hoped Rufus was right, and that this was not a typical example of family life!

She managed to beat Jessica at chess quite easily, although she could see by Jessica's strategy that, as she got older, she would be a force to be reckoned with; no doubt she would have the same determination to win as her father!

'Do you think Daddy will ring us once he knows how Granny is?' Jessica asked once they had cleared the game away.

Obviously Jessica hadn't been distracted by the chess game at all! 'Let's hope so.' She stood up. 'Come on, it's time to go in search of some lunch.' Empty tummies weren't going to help anyone, either.

It was mid-afternoon before the expected call came through from Rufus, and he sounded incredibly weary. 'Celia is awake now,' he said tonelessly. 'It wasn't a heart attack, after all, but she's going to stay on in hospital for a few days anyway. I'm just arranging for a private room for her now,' he told Annie. 'I should be back soon.'

He seemed to be missing a lot out; if it hadn't been a heart attack, why had Celia collapsed in that way? Why were they keeping her in hospital for a few days? Surely twenty-four hours was the normal time for observation?

But Annie was very aware of Jessica hopping from one foot to the other as she stood at Annie's elbow, desperate to know her grandmother wasn't going to die. 'Jessica would like to see Celia,' she told Rufus bluntly, hoping he would realise why Jessica was so anxious to do that; she could hardly explain exactly why, with Jessica standing so close.

'Not today.' Rufus's voice was harsh. 'Maybe tomorrow, when Celia is more—composed.'

He sounded strange, not at all the confident Rufus she was used to. Maybe Celia's collapse had made him realise he did have some affection for his stepmother, after all...

'Could you give Celia Jessica's love?' She smiled as Jessica nodded enthusiastically beside her. 'And my best wishes.'

'I'll do that,' he returned distantly. 'I don't suppose Anthony is back yet?' His voice hardened as he spoke of his brother.

Not yet. And Annie couldn't say she wasn't rather relieved that he wasn't. They hadn't parted on good terms, and she didn't think he would thank her for being the one to pass on the news about his mother, either.

'No,' she answered Rufus evenly.

'Fine,' he rasped. 'I did try telephoning Davina's parents, hoping to catch him there, but apparently he left a couple of hours ago.'

Which meant that Anthony could be back any time now. Annie felt her stomach muscles contract at the thought of seeing him again. The last time they had spoken he had offered her the role of mistress in his life—an offer she had turned down in no uncertain terms.

'Annie?'

She mentally shook herself as she realised Rufus was still talking to her. 'Yes?' she prompted huskily.

'Don't get carried away on a wave of pity for Anthony because his mother isn't well,' Rufus bit out insultingly. 'He's still a first-class bastard. And he always will be.'

Annie bristled resentfully at Rufus's condescending tone. She might have behaved rather stupidly where Anthony was concerned, but she wasn't completely stupid; she now knew exactly what sort of man Anthony was. 'I'll keep your advice in mind,' she told Rufus frostily. 'Was there anything else?'

His answering chuckle was not what she wanted to hear! How dared he laugh at her? Because she had no doubt that was exactly what he was doing. Damn him!

'I'll be back very soon, Annie,' he told her gruffly. 'Keep the bed warm for me!'

Keep the—!

She drew back from the receiver as if it had reached out and struck her, dropping it back into its cradle with a clumsy clatter. How dared he? How could he...? She had been absolutely mortified all day over what had happened between them last night—and he was making a joke out of it!

'Annie? What happened? Why did you ring off so

suddenly?' A stricken-faced Jessica looked up at her worriedly.

She was alarming the little girl with her behaviour, and that would never do. 'Your daddy had to go and sort out a hospital room for your grandmother.' She smiled, smoothing back Jessica's silky fringe from her brow. 'But everything is all right. And your father will be home soon.' Something she now dreaded even more than seeing Anthony again! Rufus was—

'Ah, my two beautiful girls.'

It seemed as if the thought of Anthony had somehow made him appear as he stood tall and handsome in the doorway of the library where Annie and Jessica had settled for the afternoon, his demeanour as charming as ever, appearing to remember nothing of the last, acerbic conversation between himself and Annie as he gave her his most charming smile. He had obviously forgotten that the last thing she had done before going to London with Rufus was threaten to punch him on the nose! Or maybe he was just arrogant enough to think that conversation wasn't important. Or simply foreplay!

'Uncle Anthony!' Jessica stood up to launch herself into his arms. 'I'm so glad you're here.'

'Well, it's nice to know one of you is,' he drawled, giving Annie an enquiring look over Jessica's shoulder as he hugged the little girl.

'Your mother is ill.' She hadn't meant for it to come out quite that bluntly, but somehow it had. 'Rufus is at the hospital with her now, and—'

'Hospital?' Anthony repeated slowly, lowering Jessica to the carpeted floor, his gaze fixed on Annie. 'My mother is in hospital?'

Annie swallowed hard. 'She had a— She collapsed shortly after we returned from London this morning—'

'And exactly where was Rufus when this—collapse occurred?' Anthony interrupted, looking very like his older half-brother at that moment.

'Daddy was talking to Granny—'

'The hell he was!' Anthony exploded angrily, eyes narrowed ominously.

Annie ignored him for the moment, turning to Jessica. 'It's turned a little cold; could you possibly go up to my room and get my jumper off the bed for me?' she encouraged smilingly.

'But—'

'Please, Jessica,' she prompted firmly.

A reluctant but obedient Jessica went off in search of the unwanted cardigan, Annie waiting until the little girl was safely out of earshot before turning back to Anthony. 'Rufus and your mother were talking when she became unwell,' she confirmed evenly. 'Rufus has just rung from the hospital—'

'Which hospital?' Anthony interjected his face taut with tension.

Annie looked confused. 'I have no idea…' she realised dazedly; she simply hadn't thought to ask. 'But your mother is okay; it wasn't a heart attack or anything like that. They're keeping her in for observation for a while—for a few days,' she continued lamely. Rufus had irritated her so much over the telephone that she really hadn't managed to find out any firm facts about Celia's condition. 'Rufus will be back soon…' she finished unhelpfully. A few minutes ago she had been dreading Rufus's return; now she just wished he were already here.

'It would be better for everyone if he never came back here,' Anthony ground out, hands clenched at his sides. 'Every time he comes back he causes trouble. Surely you can see what a trouble-making swine he really is?'

'Jessica is coming back,' Annie warned as she heard the young girl coming down the stairs. 'Please try and remember that he's her father.'

Anthony gave a contemptuous snort. 'Is he?' he jeered. 'Can you be sure of that? Can *he*?' he added sneeringly.

Annie became very still, a look of dawning horror on her features as she realised exactly what he was implying. Anthony and Joanne's affair in London—had it ever stopped, even after the other woman was married to Rufus? Anthony had been the one out on the boat with Joanne when the accident happened. Anthony and Joanne...

She turned to Jessica as she came into the room, taking in the dark, tumbling curls, the deep blue eyes, the face that was so like Rufus's. 'Oh, yes,' she breathed softly in answer to Anthony's scorn. 'He can be sure. And so can I,' she stated with controlled anger. 'I don't think he's the trouble-maker, Anthony; I think you manage that quite well on your own! Now, I suggest you go and telephone the local hospitals and check on your mother's condition for yourself,' she told him firmly, the anger in her eyes that glittered towards him not in the least beautiful, she was sure, before she turned to take her cardigan from Jessica with an appreciative smile.

'I intend to,' Anthony replied crisply, looking at her with assessing eyes. 'Have a good weekend, did you?'

The insult intended in his question was obvious from his tone, and Annie looked at him dispassionately; how had she ever thought this man was attractive? He was like a spoilt child, hitting out without conscience or thought for anyone else's feelings.

'Very good, thank you,' she answered briskly. 'Your mother,' she prompted pointedly as he made no effort to move.

'I'm going,' he assured her. 'But if I were you I wouldn't put too much trust in what happened over the weekend. Much as he may hate it, Rufus and I are more alike than he cares to admit!' And with that last taunting comment he left the room to make his telephone calls.

Annie didn't need that final remark of his explained, knew exactly what Anthony was referring to. Rufus had been involved with Margaret. Was probably still involved with her. But it hadn't stopped him almost making love to her last night.

She closed her eyes to stop the tears from falling. She would survive this. She had survived so many let-downs in her life already, she would survive loving Rufus too.

She had to!

CHAPTER ELEVEN

THE first indication Annie had that Rufus had returned was when she heard the sound of raised voices echoing through the house!

Jessica was in the kitchen helping Mrs Wilson bake a cake, and so Annie had taken advantage of this free hour to sit quietly in the library and read a book, losing herself in a tale of pirates and plunder, transporting herself into the life she was reading about, needing that escapism at this moment.

Until she heard Rufus and Anthony shouting at each other somewhere in the house...

Anthony hadn't even left for the hospital yet, and it seemed unfortunate, for all concerned, that Rufus should have returned before the other man had gone; their argument, as far as Annie could tell, had been going on all their lives, and could surely have waited another few hours!

'And I'm telling you it *is* my business, damn you!' Rufus spoke savagely.

Annie shrank down into the high-backed armchair as she realised the two men had brought their argument into the library where she sat, the slamming of the door indicating they had actually come in here for privacy. And she was sitting in this large armchair that faced away from them, unnoticed by both of them!

What should she do? She couldn't just sit here and listen to the two of them. But if she made them aware of her presence it was highly likely they would both turn on her—that had happened more than once!

'Did you already know?' Rufus's voice was dangerously low now. 'Did Celia know too?' he added almost incredulously.

'It's private family business, Rufus—'

'And I'm the head of this family!' Rufus thundered furiously.

'When you choose to be,' Anthony acknowledged scornfully. 'Which isn't that often!'

'I asked you a question, Anthony.' Rufus's voice was icy cold. 'Did you know Margaret was expecting your child when she left here?'

Annie couldn't hold back her sharp intake of breath, unable to breathe out again in her shock, hands shaking as she desperately tried to hang onto the book she had been reading, knowing that if she hadn't already been sitting down she would probably have fallen down!

Margaret was expecting Anthony's child...!

'Of course I knew,' Anthony answered baldly.

'And Celia,' Rufus persisted softly. 'Did she know too?'

'Yes. Yes, yes, *yes*!' Anthony confirmed impatiently. 'Why do you think she's in such a hurry to bring the wedding forward to Christmas?' he scorned. 'She doesn't want anything to stop my marriage to Davina.'

'And another woman expecting your child would definitely do that,' the other man rasped harshly.

'Margaret is expecting that child because of her own stupidity,' Anthony dismissed uncaringly. 'She didn't tell me that because of her religion she wasn't using contraceptives. And she won't get rid of the child for the same reason,' he added disgustedly. 'The stupid little fool, was—Aagh!' Anthony's scornful tirade was cut short as the sound of flesh making contact with flesh was heard, quickly followed by the sound of furniture crashing to the floor.

Rufus had hit him! Annie couldn't see what had happened exactly, but she knew anyway. She would have done the same thing herself if she were Rufus; in fact her hands were clenched into fists ready to do so! Margaret was expecting Anthony's child, and to him it was just an inconvenience, something to be got rid of—

'You've knocked one of my teeth out, you bastard!' Anthony said disbelievingly, obviously struggling to get back onto his feet.

'Think yourself lucky it's only one of your teeth!' Rufus ground out savagely. 'What I really want to do is take you apart and then throw away the pieces! You're a disgrace to the Diamond name, and I want you out of this house—'

'You can't do that, Rufus,' the younger man told him with gloating assurance. 'Our father stated quite clearly in his will that, although this house is yours, my mother has the right to live here until she dies—'

'She's dying now, Anthony,' Rufus cut in evenly.

There was complete silence after this announcement, and Annie could only imagine Anthony's shock. She was shocked herself!

'Wh-what did you say?' Anthony sounded as if Rufus had punched him again, but emotionally this time, not physically.

'Celia is dying, Anthony,' Rufus told him gruffly. 'She has terminal cancer. She's known for some time. And that's the reason she's trying to rush your wedding. She wants to see you safely married before she dies.'

'But—I— You— I don't believe you, Rufus,' Anthony denied, but there was an edge of uncertainty to his voice.

'You don't have to believe me,' Rufus told him wearily. 'Celia intends telling you herself when you get to the hospital.'

There was silence after that last heavy statement, and Annie could only guess at Anthony's bewilderment. He was almost completely selfish; his mother was probably the only other person he had any genuine affection for.

Celia was dying... No wonder Anthony was having trouble accepting it as fact; Annie had trouble believing it herself. In fact, there was a lot about the conversation she had overheard that seemed totally unreal. Although it also answered a lot of unasked questions...

'It's the truth, Anthony,' Rufus said quietly.

'I have to go to her,' Anthony muttered distractedly.

'She's expecting you,' Rufus agreed.

There was the sound of the other man walking to the door, but he paused before opening it. 'I'm not sure how you found out about Margaret and the baby,' Anthony bit out angrily. 'But it's still none of your damned business!'

'Someone will have to support her while she brings up your child,' Rufus told him bluntly. 'And I meant what I said earlier, Anthony; you can continue to visit your mother here until she dies—and after that I don't ever want to see you again.'

'Once I'm married to Davina, and to all the Adamses' money, I won't need to come here again!' Anthony announced triumphantly, closing the door behind him as he left.

Annie sat very still in the chair, torn between a need to go and comfort Rufus and a fear of incurring his displeasure at knowing she had overheard this very private conversation between the two brothers.

Anthony was everything she had come to believe him to be—and worse. He didn't give a damn about the fact that his relationship with Margaret was to produce a child. And how Rufus must be hurting to know that Margaret, too, had betrayed him with Anthony! No wonder he—

'You can come out now,' Rufus said softly.

Annie froze. Not that she had moved since the two men had first come into the room, but with Anthony's departure Rufus had to be talking to her. He knew she was sitting in this wing-backed armchair! How long had he known...?

'Since we first came into the room, Annie,' Rufus told her dryly, easily able to guess at her panicked thoughts as she still made no attempt to show herself. 'I would know that perfume of yours anywhere. Besides, I saw your hair over the top of the chair before you sank down into it!' he teased, although he sounded incredibly weary too.

He had known she was here from the first! And she couldn't even begin to work out why he hadn't exposed her...

She straightened, standing up slowly, putting the book down carefully on the table before turning to face Rufus, her eyes widening in shock as she saw how haggard he looked, how utterly exhausted as he sat in one of the armchairs. Not at all like the arrogantly confident man she had come to expect. Although, in the circumstances, that wasn't surprising!

'It's been a tough day,' he acknowledged as he ran a

hand through the already rumpled darkness of his hair. 'What did you make of all that?' he prompted.

She smoothed her hands self-consciously down her denim-clad thighs, taking her time answering him. 'I— It's a bit of a mess, isn't it?' she finally stated ruefully.

Rufus continued to look at her for several long seconds, then his mouth began to twitch, until finally he gave one of those shouts of laughter Annie had grown to love. She was glad she could make him laugh, even unintentionally; he certainly had little to laugh at at the moment.

'"A bit of a mess",' he finally repeated with an agreeing nod, his mouth still smiling, although his eyes were once again grave.

Annie crossed the room to sit on the carpet at his feet. 'But not an insurmountable one.' She laid a comforting hand on his knee. 'Margaret may be having a baby, but think how much worse off she would be if Anthony had actually offered to marry her—and she had said yes!' She looked up at Rufus anxiously, knowing how much he must be hurting inside.

'God, yes!' He ran his hand over tired eyes. 'The poor girl may have made a mistake, but she doesn't deserve that fate!'

Annie tried to smile at his attempt at humour, but her smile didn't quite work either. She loved this man—and she was trying to help comfort him over his love for another woman. God, it hurt!

'There's usually a silver lining to every situation,' she told him shakily.

He dropped his head, frowning down at her. 'And what's yours?' he prompted huskily.

She swallowed hard, unable to think of one at the

moment. She loved someone who didn't love her, and whether he stayed or left she was going to continue loving him for a very long time.

Rufus reached out to gently touch the hair at her temple. 'I'm sorry you had to hear about Margaret in the way that you did, but in all honesty I don't know if I would ever have been able to tell you any other way. I couldn't have hurt you with that knowledge.'

She blinked back the sudden tears, swallowing hard again. 'It isn't your fault, Rufus,' she said tremulously, his very gentleness almost her undoing. 'Besides, I already knew about Margaret.'

'You knew she was pregnant?'

'Oh, no, not that.' She firmly shook her head. 'But I knew how you felt about her.'

'How I—?' He sat forward in his chair, grasping the tops of her arms as he did so. 'Annie, what are you talking about?'

She pulled away, getting to her feet, unable to be that close to him without totally giving herself away. After all, she had some pride. Not a lot, she admitted, because she had still almost made love with Rufus knowing how he felt about the other woman. But she had hoped—had wanted—

'It's very sad about Celia,' she told him evasively.

So much made sense about the other woman's behaviour now—the extra rest she had seemed to be taking, the fact that she was even thinner now than when Annie had come here two months ago, and this driving need she had to see Anthony married to Davina. The latter probably wasn't just because of Margaret and the baby, was also partly because she had known Rufus and

Anthony would probably end up killing each other if they lived here together once she was gone!

'It is sad about Celia,' Rufus agreed slowly. 'It wasn't until the doctor told me this afternoon what was going on that I realised I actually have feelings for the woman, that the thought of her dying is actually painful for me.' He looked sad at the knowledge.

'I'm glad,' Annie said with feeling.

'So am I,' he admitted throatily. 'I've spent so long blaming her for taking my mother's place that I actually didn't realise I cared for her I—I told her that today,' he added gruffly.

'I'm glad about that too,' Annie told him warmly. Celia might have her faults, but she did genuinely care about the Diamond family; of that Annie had no doubts.

'Mmm,' Rufus concurred. 'We talked today as we probably never have before. She—she told me something I never knew.' His voice was so husky now, it was barely audible. 'My mother suffered severe post-natal depression after I was born. They don't really know how to deal with that now, but thirty-nine years ago there was no help for her! I— It was during one of these bouts of depression that she went down to the cove and killed herself.' He shook his head. 'I never knew any of that,' he groaned. 'My father never told me. And I have to admit that—all these years, I've been drawing my own conclusions.'

Probably that his father had been involved with Celia before his wife died; Rufus had been so bitter about Celia's marriage to his father, and the birth of Anthony, that it was a natural assumption for him to have made. Even if it was wrong.

And it was Rufus's mother who had committed suicide in the cove…

'I'm sure your father tried to protect you, didn't want you, an innocent child, to feel in the least responsible for what happened to your mother,' Annie reasoned. 'Post-natal depression can happen to anyone, and it certainly isn't the baby's fault.'

Rufus looked at her with pained eyes. 'You're very wise for someone so young,' he said achingly. 'He and Celia discussed it, apparently, and that's exactly what they decided. And, to give Celia her due, she's kept that secret all these years. It would have been better, for everyone probably, if she hadn't.' He looked pained at all the time he had spent hating a woman who had actually tried to protect him in the only way she could.

It was a tragedy, Annie agreed with that, but there was still time for Rufus and Celia to come to some sort of understanding. In fact, she was sure they were already well on the way to doing exactly that…

'Now—' Rufus straightened '—I want to know what you've been thinking about my—now, what was it you said?—my feelings for Margaret.'

She should have known he wouldn't dismiss that subject as easily as he had seemed to. But couldn't he see how much this was hurting her? Obviously not, because he just looked totally baffled.

She began to pace in front of the unlit fireplace. 'You were upset when you came back here and found she had gone—'

'I already knew she had gone,' Rufus interjected. 'There was a letter from her waiting for me at the newspaper offices when I got back last week.'

Annie shot him an irritated look before resuming her

pacing. 'You were desperate to know why she had left—'

'I wasn't desperate, just interested.' Once again Rufus cut in.

'You were very *interested* in why Margaret had left here so suddenly,' Annie corrected forcefully. 'You took Jessica and me to London with you this weekend because—'

'Why, Annie?' he said slowly. 'Why do you think I took the two of you with me?'

'Because you didn't want to leave Jessica here—'

'It was partly that,' he acknowledged fiercely. 'God, when I came back this time and found out that she had been involved in an accident it took me back five years, to when Joanne died. She was out on a boat with Anthony that day; did you know that?' He looked at her intensely.

She nodded. 'Jessica told me.' But she had no intention of telling him what Anthony had implied. The woman was dead; raking up old grievances couldn't help anyone now.

Rufus gave a regretful smile. 'Anthony doesn't behave too well as a lover scorned. Although if you've heard Anthony's version of what happened I'm sure it doesn't show him in that light?' He sighed as Annie shook her head. 'He and Joanne were involved before our marriage, and it was a relationship Anthony tried to revive once she was married to me. Our marriage was never the love of the century, but Joanne drew the line at having an affair with my brother. Anthony was furious,' he recalled grimly. 'I've never been a hundred per cent sure her accidental death was exactly that, and then when Jess had her fall...!'

Annie stared at him in horror. He couldn't think—didn't believe Anthony—

'I've given him the benefit of the doubt all these years, but Joanne was an excellent swimmer, and Anthony hated water, has done since we were children, which was why his story about not being able to save Joanne when she fell overboard was always believed.' He raised his shoulders fatalistically. 'And for years I've accepted that as the truth. But I have to admit I was shaken when you told me Jessica had fallen from her horse; she's as good a horsewoman as her mother was a swimmer.'

'You thought Anthony had tried to harm her...' Annie realised the horrifying truth of why he had been so shaken by Jessica's accident.

'Only for a short time,' Rufus acknowledged. 'James feels it was his fault. He's started forgetting things lately, and he admitted to me that he really couldn't remember even putting Jessica's saddle on her horse, let alone whether or not it was fastened properly. I know Jessica is upset that he's gone, but it really was his own decision.'

A wise one, in the circumstances. And Jessica would understand that when it was explained to her properly.

As Annie now understood that Anthony's story about his relationship with Joanne was all a figment of Anthony's vindictive mind. She didn't doubt for a moment that Rufus's side of things was the truth, remembered how Anthony had turned on her when he'd sensed she was becoming attracted to his brother...! She agreed with Rufus: the further Anthony stayed from this family in future the better.

'Now,' Rufus said firmly, 'I want to know exactly

why you think I'm in love with Margaret. You do think that, don't you?' He searched her face with his eyes.

Annie couldn't meet his gaze. 'She was the woman you talked about, the one who would speak to you on the telephone but wouldn't meet you.'

'She was,' he concurred. 'And I finally realised one very good reason why she wouldn't actually meet me.'

'Because of her relationship with Anthony?' Annie realised.

'Yes!' he rasped. 'Indirectly.'

'Indirectly?' Annie echoed in a puzzled voice. 'I don't understand.' And she didn't. Surely it was perfectly straightforward; in Rufus's absence Margaret had begun an affair with his brother.

Rufus stood up too now. 'I have a feeling you aren't going to like it once you do understand,' he admitted grudgingly.

She didn't like this conversation at all, hated discussing his feelings for another woman. And Rufus seemed aware of that now. Did he also realise it was because she was in love with him? It would be too humiliating if he did.

'You may as well tell me,' she sighed.

He drew in a deep breath. 'Last night, when we were making love—'

'Do you have to bring that into this?' she burst in tremulously, her cheeks red and burning. Was she to be left no pride?

'I told you you wouldn't like it,' Rufus reminded her.

'Is it necessary?' she said agitatedly.

'If you want to know about Margaret, and why she wouldn't see me, then I'm afraid it is, yes.'

'Oh, very well,' Annie agreed uncomfortably. 'If you must.'

Rufus reached out to put his hand beneath her chin, lifting her face up so that he could look into her eyes again. 'Do you wish last night had never happened?'

'Yes! No. No...!' she admitted with a self-conscious groan. Last night might be all she ever had with the man she loved.

'I'm glad about that,' Rufus said with relief.

Annie looked up at him with wide brown eyes. 'You are?' she said uncertainly.

'Oh, Annie, of course I am.' He reached out and folded her into his arms. 'Haven't you realised yet that I love every infuriating, tantalising inch of you, that the main reason I took you and Jess to London with me was because I didn't want to be away from you, not even for a few days?' he added indulgently.

She was hearing things. She had to be. Rufus couldn't really have just told her that he loved her. He just couldn't have done. Could he...?

CHAPTER TWELVE

'ANNIE?' Rufus raised her chin once more with gentle fingers, but this time she wasn't able to look at him. 'I love you, Annie Fletcher,' he whispered. 'And it's been a long time since I said that to anyone other than Jess.'

Annie stared at him. She couldn't seem to do anything else. He had said it again! 'But—I—Margaret...!' she groaned desperately.

Rufus shook his head, smiling. 'After what you've just said to me, I have a fair idea of the thoughts that have been running around in your beautiful head, although for the life of me I can't imagine where you got them from. Margaret was Jess's nanny to me, nothing more.'

'But—'

'Nothing else, Annie. Ever,' he insisted firmly. 'I'm not saying I've been celibate during the five years since Joanne died, but there haven't been that many women either, and Margaret certainly wasn't one of them. No, I've been waiting for a little red-haired witch who makes me laugh and want her all at the same time.' He smiled at her in a way he never had before, the love he talked about shining in the dark depths of his eyes. 'I love you, Annie. I want to marry you, have children with you. I'm sorry I don't have a better family to offer you.' He grimaced with feeling. 'But they're the only family I have. And eventually we'll have children of our own, and then—'

180

'You want to marry me?' She couldn't believe he was saying these things to her.

'I insist on it,' he told her sternly. 'After all, you've compromised my reputation by sharing my bed.'

'Compromised your—!' Annie broke off, chuckling at the ridiculousness of what he was saying.

'It won't be so bad, Annie.' His arms tightened about her once again. 'I intend staying around in future. It's time I stopped all the travelling. And, in truth the only reason I've done it for so long is because I couldn't stand being in this house. But if you're going to be here I don't want to go away. I'm going to write a book, Annie. It's been floating around in my head for years now, but the thought of staying in one place long enough to write it has never appealed before. Now it does.' He drew back slightly to look down at her. 'But you aren't saying anything now,' he said uncertainly. 'Tell me if I'm going too fast, or assuming too much. Don't let me carry on like a drivelling idiot if this isn't what you want too, if it's Anthony you love after all.'

To be married to Rufus. To be with him and Jessica always. To have children of their own...!

'Oh, Rufus...!' She sank weakly against him. 'I don't love Anthony—I never did,' she said with certainty. 'I would very much like to marry you. I love you, too. And I can't imagine anything more wonderful than being with you for ever.' She clung to him so strongly now, it made her arms ache.

His breath left him in a deep sigh of relief. 'Thank God for that!' he groaned. 'You had me worried for a moment. But I couldn't imagine your having let last night happen at all if you didn't love me.'

'I wouldn't have,' she agreed.

Rufus bent his head to kiss her, and it was some time later, with Annie sitting on his knee in one of the arm-chairs, that they resumed their conversation about Margaret.

'Do you remember why we didn't completely make love last night?' Rufus looked at her with teasing eyes as she blushed. 'I'm glad we didn't, Annie. Our first night together will be our wedding night. The way it should be. The way you deserve it to be.'

'Margaret,' she prompted pointedly, before they became side-tracked once again.

'It was the conversation we had last night that made me realise a very good reason why Margaret wouldn't actually meet me in person. She's five months pregnant, Annie,' he said flatly. 'And it shows.'

Rufus didn't love the other woman, he never had; he had just wanted to know, especially after she had written to him telling him she had left, exactly why she had done so.

'We'll have to help her, Rufus,' Annie told him. 'That child is your niece or nephew.'

'We'll help her, Annie,' he assured her.

And she knew that they would. She also knew that they would care for Celia until she didn't need caring for any longer.

As the years passed the two of them would grow closer, and Rufus would be able to talk to her about his childhood, his father, the mother he couldn't even remember, and his never-the-love-of-the-century marriage. And she would be able to tell him about her loneliness as a child, the children's home, the feeling of never belonging.

Because she belonged now. Belonged with and to Rufus.

How different her life was going to be. She would be a dearly loved, and loving, Diamond bride.

'It's bad luck, you know,' Annie scolded affectionately.

Rufus lifted his head from the soft cushion of her satin-covered breasts, grinning down at her. 'Another one of those old wives' tales? The one concerning twins didn't come true!'

'Not yet,' Annie warned. 'But that's probably because we haven't fully made love yet,' she reminded him with a self-conscious blush.

'But we will. Very soon,' he promised, resting on his elbows as he looked down at her. 'The thought of you having even one of my children does the nicest things to my body,' he murmured, moving closer to her as he began to kiss her.

Annie could feel exactly what nice things it did to his body, groaning low in her throat with the same longing.

The last three months had been the happiest Annie had ever known, loving and being loved by Rufus.

Jessica couldn't have been more pleased when told that Annie was going to be her new mother, eyes agog at this very satisfactory answer to her prayer!

It had been a time of talking, laughing, sharing, discovering—their love for each other deepening as each day passed.

And today was their wedding day...

And Rufus, after flatly refusing Celia's suggestion that he spend the night at a hotel, had brought Annie a cup of coffee up to her bedroom half an hour ago—and hadn't left again!

His eyes were almost black now as he raised his head to look at her. 'Annie, I—' He broke off as a knock sounded gently on the bedroom door.

'Annie, are you awake?' Celia called softly. 'It's time to start getting ready.'

'Oh, hell,' Rufus said to himself and he sprang up from the bed, his unbuttoned shirt slightly crumpled, his hair ruffled from Annie's caressing fingers. 'Celia is sure to know the same old wives' tale!' He scowled at the lecture he was probably about to receive.

'Rufus?' Celia prompted suspiciously. 'Rufus, are you in there?' she added sharply.

Annie lay back on the pillows, laughing softly at Rufus's hunted expression. 'Come in, Celia,' she invited lightly, receiving a glare from Rufus for her pains.

'I thought I heard your voice,' Celia scolded Rufus once she was inside the bedroom. 'Don't you know that it's unlucky to see the bride before the church service on your wedding day?' She looked disapprovingly across at him.

'You see.' Rufus turned to Annie. 'I told you she would know that one, too!' He shook his head. 'It's a lot of nonsense. The Diamond brides aren't known for their luck anyway.' He frowned. 'I almost didn't ask Annie to marry me for that very reason.'

'Now that is a lot of nonsense,' Celia told him briskly, coming further into the bedroom, still extremely fragile to look at, although at the moment her condition seemed not to have deteriorated any further. 'I've already explained to you about your mother's death, and Joanne's death was just an unfortunate accident. Besides, Rufus, I was a Diamond bride, and, despite what you may have

thought to the contrary, David and I had thirty happy
years together!'

Annie had watched with pleasure, over the last three
months, as these two stubborn Diamonds had become
quite good friends. And Celia certainly couldn't have
been more helpful concerning the wedding arrangements, helping Annie shop for her dress and Jessica's
bridesmaid's dress, the little girl absolutely thrilled at
being asked to be her only attendant.

Anthony and Davina's wedding had taken place almost a month ago, Anthony continuing to visit his
mother here, albeit keeping well away from Rufus and
Annie. Anthony's plans to make those visits alone were
neatly foiled by Davina, as she continued to accompany
him every time he came. In fact, Davina's helpless-little-
girl act—and the breathless voice, much to Rufus's
amusement—seemed to have vanished overnight, and in
her place was a woman even more domineering than
Celia had been. Anthony had met his match where he'd
least expected it!

And Anthony's ceremony neatly out of the way, his
future very definitely decided, Celia had turned all her
attention to Rufus and Annie's wedding. In all honesty,
Annie had been grateful for her help, had come to realise, over the last few months, that a lot of Celia's imperious manner was, in fact, a barrier put up to protect
herself from being hurt. The past having finally been put
to rest, that barrier was no longer necessary, and as a
surrogate mother to Rufus, and indeed Annie, Celia had
proved more than capable. They were all going to miss
her when the time came for them to say goodbye.

'I'm sure you did.' Rufus gently squeezed Celia's
shoulder. 'Just as I'm sure Annie and I are going to have

many happy years together.' He turned to her, his love for her blazing in the dark blue of his eyes.

Annie was sure they were too, the last three months spent with Rufus more than enough to reassure her of their future happiness together.

She couldn't possibly have guessed how it would turn out when she'd decided to work as part of a family— but she really was part of a family now. She and Rufus were their own family, with Jessica and Celia drawn into that loving fold.

The Diamond bride was to become the Diamond wife and mother.

Utter and complete happiness.

For ever.

THE DIAMOND DAD

LUCY GORDON

Lucy Gordon cut her writing teeth on magazine journalism, interviewing many of the world's most interesting men, including Warren Beatty, Charlton Heston and Sir Roger Moore. She also camped out with lions in Africa and had many other unusual experiences, which have often provided the background for her books. Several years ago, while staying Venice, she met a Venetian who proposed in two days. They have been married ever since. Naturally this has affected her writing, where romantic Italian men tend to feature strongly.

Two of her books have won a Romance Writers of America RITA® Award. You can visit her website at www.lucy-gordon.com.

CHAPTER ONE

'*YOU!*' Garth Clayton said in a stunned voice. 'What are you doing here?'

Faye, his estranged wife, faced him with her head up. Inwardly she was thinking, Two years, and he still hasn't forgiven me! Will that make it easier, or harder, to do what I have to?

'Aren't you going to invite me in?' she asked.

He didn't move. 'When you left this house you swore that you'd never come back.'

'We both said a lot of angry things on that night, but we didn't mean them.'

'I meant every word,' he said, unyielding.

He seemed older than his thirty-five years, she thought. There was a new darkness in his brown eyes and fine lines at the corners that hadn't been there before. He looked as though he lived on his nerves, neither eating nor sleeping enough. But he would always be a tall, handsome man, whose sensual, mobile mouth had once thrilled her, even though that mouth now had a look of strain and bitterness.

Faye knew that she, too, had altered. The gauche teenager of their wedding day had become a mother of two children with a mind of her own and enough strength to stand up to her husband's forceful personality. These days she had a poise and confidence that was reflected in the strong colours she wore, replacing the delicate hues of a few years ago.

'I've come to talk,' she said.

5

He stood back to let her pass. She could feel his eyes on her, taking in the new short crop of her light brown hair. She wasn't expensively dressed, but she had a tall, slender figure that made everything look good. Her russet suit with its gilt buttons looked stylish, suggesting a woman who was at ease with herself.

He indicated the living room and Faye was a little surprised to find it just as she remembered. Garth had been so angry when she left that she'd pictured him wiping out all traces of her, but everything was the same. This was where they'd had their final quarrel, when she'd tried vainly to make him understand why she had to escape him.

'A drink?' he asked.

'No thank you. I'm driving.'

His eyebrows raised a little. 'You've learned to drive?'

'Yes, I found it quite easy.'

'When you had an instructor who could keep calm,' he finished wryly.

'That helped,' she admitted.

Their very first vehicle had been a shabby third-hand truck to get Garth started as a builder. Later, when the money had flowed freely, he'd bought her an expensive car and had tried to teach her to drive, but it had been a disaster. She'd lacked the confidence to try again, and when she fled she'd left the car behind.

Disturbing feelings began to play back. Perhaps she shouldn't have come to this luxurious house, which he'd built 'for her' but which reflected his own tastes. Here, she'd shared a bed with Garth but nothing else, and she'd always disliked the place. Yet she'd smothered her true feelings, as so often in her marriage, and pretended delight to please her husband.

That, however, was in the past. Their marriage was over in all but name. She was her own woman now.

Once her heart had beat with eager anticipation at the thought of seeing Garth Clayton. With his dark hair, vivid looks and lithe grace, he'd seemed almost godlike to the eighteen-year-old Faye. He'd worked on a building site that she'd passed every day on her way to work in a dress shop. Sometimes she would stop and regard him from a distance, admiring the way he leaped over the scaffolding, never afraid of the drop, or lifted heavy weights as though they were nothing.

She was so innocent that she hardly recognized her admiration for his splendid body as the flickering of desire. She only knew that she *had* to make him notice her. When at last he winked at her, she blushed deeply and scurried away to the shop. For the rest of the day she was nearly useless, having to be recalled from a trance when someone spoke to her, and giving customers the wrong change. Her boss spoke sharply, but Faye barely heard. She was in seventh heaven.

He was waiting for her at the wire next morning. 'Didn't mean to upset you yesterday,' he said gruffly.

'You didn't. I was just—surprised.'

'Surprised? A pretty girl like you?'

Bliss! He'd called her pretty.

They went to the cinema but to her disappointment he didn't kiss her, only brushed her hand against his cheek. She was wretched, sure that he found her boring. But he asked her out again, and on the third date he kissed her. She thought there couldn't be more happiness than that in the world.

But there was. The memory of their first lovemaking could still bring tears to her eyes. The young Garth had vigour rather than subtlety but he was kind and gentle, treating her as something precious.

'Don't go yet,' he begged as she got dressed.

'I have to. I'll miss my last bus.'

'I'll come home with you. I don't want to say good-bye.'

'But there's no bus back,' she said, loving him for not wanting to say goodbye.

In the end he came to the stop with her and held her close until the bus appeared. She sat at the back so that she could watch him standing in the road with his hands stretched up to the glass. And when the bus moved off he stayed there, his eyes fixed on her until she turned the corner.

When they weren't making love, they talked. He told her how he dreamed of being his own boss, a builder with a little business that would grow. For him, the sky was the limit. Faye couldn't remember discussing what she wanted from life. But then, all she wanted was him.

When she told him she was pregnant he said, 'I've got a week free between jobs next month. We'll use that for our honeymoon.'

'Honeymoon?' she echoed joyfully. 'You mean—get married?'

'Of *course* we're going to get married!'

She was too happy to care that he told her, not asked her. She wanted to be his wife more than anything in the world. They were married in a register office and spent a week by the sea in a borrowed caravan that had seen better days. With almost no money, there was little to do except walk hand in hand on the beach, eat whatever was cheap, and love, and love, and love. It was a time of unspoiled bliss and she was sure that their marriage would be a success.

But that was when she was an innocent who believed love was for ever, before the discovery of Garth's true character and the gradual destruction of all that gave her happiness. Now they'd reached the end of the road, and she'd come driving through the darkness to Elm Ridge to confront him.

He followed her into the living room and stood waiting for her to begin. The air was alive with tension and she knew this was going to be harder than she'd thought. To give herself a moment she slipped off her jacket, revealing a sleeveless olive-green shirt, adorned by a chain.

Garth studied that chain. Solid gold if he was any judge. Simple, yet very costly. Not something she would have bought for herself, nor one of his own gifts, most of which she'd left behind.

Her perfume was elusive, like woodsmoke drifting on the breeze. It had a subtlety that told him more clearly than anything else that he no longer knew this woman.

'You sure picked your moment to come calling,' he said. 'I was about to go to bed.'

'I left it late to give you time to get home from work. I hope I haven't interrupted you when you have company.'

'A woman? No, that was one accusation even you were never able to throw at me, although apparently I was every other kind of villain.'

'I never said that, Garth. It was just that I couldn't live with you any more.'

'So you claimed. I never quite understood why.'

'I tried to explain—'

'I gather that my crime was to work day and night to give you a comfortable life, with every luxury you could want. For this I was punished by the loss of my wife and both my children.' A touch of iron in his voice made it clear that he was as unyielding as ever.

'Perhaps I'd better go away and return another time...'

'No! You must have come here for some reason. You've kept well clear of me, Faye. Even when the children visit me, you never come with them. When I collect them from your house, you speak to me as little as possible.'

'I don't want to upset them with fighting.'

'How are they? It seems a long time since I saw them.'

'You could have seen them last week if you'd come to Cindy's school play, as you promised. She had the lead. She was longing for you to be there and be proud of her.'

'I meant to, but at the last minute something came up.'

Faye sighed. 'Something always did come up, Garth. A business deal was always more important than your children.'

'That's not true. I was there for Adrian's birthday.'

'Only for two hours. And you didn't come to see him playing football, did you? He really minded about that. And Cindy was heartbroken when you missed her birthday last year. She loves you so much, and you let her down all the time. It's her birthday again next week. She'll be eight. Oh please, Garth, try to be there, just this once.'

'Saturday? Hell, I don't think I can make it. I've got a client—' He saw her looking at him with resignation and said, 'Was this what you came for?'

'No, I came to say I want a divorce.'

He took a sharp breath. 'That's a bit sudden, isn't it?'

'We've been separated for two years. You've always known I wanted a divorce.'

'I thought you'd have seen sense by now.'

'You mean, return to you?' She gave a brief, wry laugh. 'I remember that your version of seeing sense was always people doing what suited you.'

'Because I was the reasonable one! Look at how you behaved after you left. It was always crazy for you to live in that poky little house while I was alone in this huge place. You could have a beautiful home but you prefer a rabbit hutch. You wouldn't even let me give you enough money for a decent place.'

'You pay to support the children—'

'But you won't accept a penny for yourself,' he said bitterly. 'Do you know how that makes me feel?'

'I'm sorry, Garth, but I don't want to depend on you. That puzzles you, doesn't it? Your life is dedicated to squeezing the last penny out of every deal. You don't understand someone who doesn't want money from you, but I don't. I never did. I wanted—' She checked herself.

'What, Faye? What did you want? Because I swear I never found out what it was.'

'Didn't you? And yet at one time you gave it to me,' she said with a touch of wistfulness. 'When we were first married, everything I needed came from you. On our wedding day I was the happiest woman on earth. I had your love; I was expecting our baby—'

'We rented a two-roomed flat with no hot water,' he recalled.

'I didn't care. All I cared about was loving you, and having you love me.'

'Did I ever stop?' he demanded. 'Was there one day of our marriage when I wasn't trying to give you the best of everything? I did it all to please you, and you tossed it back at me like so much garbage.'

'I already had the best of everything. But you took it away.'

'I didn't stop loving you,' he said almost angrily.

'But you stopped having time for me.'

He would have answered, but the phone began to ring. He snatched up the receiver. 'I'll get rid of whoever it is. Hello— Look, I can't talk now, I'm tied up— Oh, hell! Can't he call back later?— I know I've been trying to get him, but— All right! Put him through.'

'I see your technique for getting rid of people hasn't improved,' Faye said lightly.

He scowled. 'Five minutes. That's all. I'll take it in the study.'

'Can I make myself some tea?'

'This is your home. Go where you like!' He vanished into the study.

The big, glamorous kitchen had all the latest gadgetry cunningly concealed beneath oak and copper pots. That and the dark red tiles on the floor gave it an air of warmth, but Faye had never found it warm. Garth had told her to select whatever decor she liked, but then promoted his own preference so insistently that she'd yielded. It seemed to have been chosen not for herself, but for someone called Garth Clayton's wife. Was it then she'd started to feel that she didn't fit the role? No, much earlier.

How eagerly he'd first shown her the house! It was set in its own grounds on a slight incline, surrounded by elm trees. 'Here you are, darling,' he'd said. 'Welcome to Elm Ridge. Your new home, like you always wanted.' His pride had been touching, and she'd lacked the heart to say that it wasn't the home she'd wanted. Nothing like it.

Her dream home had been 'a little place all our own', as he'd once promised. And two years after their marriage they'd had a small house, for Garth was a man born to succeed. She'd been completely happy. But four years later he'd swept her away into this big, unfriendly mansion. She'd even had a housekeeper, a bustling, kindly soul called Nancy. Faye made friends with her and enjoyed many a chat in the kitchen, for she felt more at home with Nancy than with any of her husband's new, moneyed friends.

When the tea was made she wandered back to the study door, behind which she could hear him arguing with someone. Long experience made her murmur, 'Half an hour at the least.'

Wherever she looked she could see few changes. The pictures on the stair walls were the ones she'd chosen. She'd taken one of them with her, and its place was still blank.

Here she'd once been unhappy and stifled. Garth had been generous, giving her everything that money could buy, but he'd also arranged her life and their children's lives, from on high. The little builder's yard he'd managed to scrape together had nearly gone under in the first year. He'd saved it by the skin of his teeth, but Faye had known nothing about this until she'd learned by accident three years later. The discovery that she'd been excluded from his inner counsels had been like a blow over the heart.

He'd failed to see that she was no longer the blindly adoring girl he'd married. She'd matured into a woman with a mind of her own, who still loved him, but now knew that he wasn't perfect.

They argued about the children. Garth was pleased with his son yet hardly seemed to notice his daughter. But Cindy adored her father and Faye often saw a wistful look in the child's eyes at his neglect.

Adrian, too, suffered a kind of neglect. Garth would buy him anything, but he wouldn't take time off to watch Adrian play in the school football team. He was determined to rear the boy to be 'successful' as he understood the word, but Adrian wanted to be a footballer. Garth dismissed this with a shrug. 'He'll grow out of it,' he told Faye. 'Just don't encourage him.'

She yielded in their disputes, telling herself that to be with him was enough. But her children were another matter. She stood up for them with a strength that surprised Garth. Arguments became quarrels. When she could stand it no longer, she left him, taking the children.

The last thing he said to her was 'Don't fool yourself that it's over, Faye. It never will be.'

She continued upstairs, to what had been Adrian's room, but the door was locked. So was Cindy's, and the one that led into the bedroom she'd shared with Garth. Frowning, she returned downstairs.

Here the doors were open and next to the study Faye found Garth's new bedroom, little more than a monkish cupboard, with a plain bed and a set of mahogany furniture. The walls were white; the carpet biscuit-coloured. Everything was of excellent quality but the total effect was bleak, as though the man who owned it carried bleakness within himself.

The sole ornament was a photograph beside the bed, showing a young boy of about nine, with a bright, eager face. Faye smiled, recognizing Adrian, but her smile changed to a frown as she saw there was no picture of Cindy.

She waited in the hall until he emerged from the study.

'What's the matter?' he asked, seeing her face.

'I'd like to see your study. There's something I have to know.'

The study told her the same story. There on the desk were two photographs of Adrian, but none of Cindy.

'How dare you?' she said, turning on him. 'You had no right to censor your own child out of existence. Cindy's still your daughter, and she loves you.'

'I don't know what you—'

'Where's her picture? You've got Adrian's. Where's Cindy's?'

'Look, I'm sorry. I didn't do it on purpose. I just didn't notice—'

'You never noticed her, and you broke her heart. The only one you cared for was Adrian, and then only when you could see yourself in him. But he isn't like you. He's gentle and sensitive.'

'There's nothing gentle about him when he's kicking a ball around a pitch.'

'How would you know? You've hardly ever seen him. Yes, he plays a tough game but he's a nice person. He looks after Cindy; he cares about people.'

'Everything I'm not, apparently,' he said in a tight voice.

'Yes. He doesn't like the things you like, and I won't have him forced to be someone he isn't. That's one of the reasons I left: to protect them from you.'

'That's a dreadful thing to say,' he told her, his face very pale.

'It's a dreadful thing to be true. Garth, I came here tonight because I'm tired of living in limbo. I really want that divorce.'

'I'll never give you one. I told you that when you left.'

'Yes, you said you'd take the children if I went for a divorce. That scared me at the time. You even used it to make me give up my job—'

'You didn't need to work. I offered you a large allowance—'

'But I wanted to be independent.'

He didn't understand that. He never had. He'd thought it madness when she'd struggled to get a diploma in bookkeeping through a correspondence course. She'd been thrilled to get work with Kendall Haines, a local environmentalist, but Garth's bitter anger had made her leave the job.

Refusing to be defeated, she'd approached the problem in a different way. She had a real flair for bookkeeping and began taking in freelance work from several small, local businesses. She'd used a computer that had been very basic even when she'd bought it second-hand, and which now looked as if it had come out of the Ark. The budget wouldn't run to the modern machine she longed for, yet still she was content. She'd won her independence in the face of Garth's hostility.

But his high-handed action still rankled. 'I was happy in that job until you forced me to leave it to stop you claiming Cindy and Adrian,' she told him now. 'I couldn't see it then, but that threat was nonsense. No court would have given you the children, and if it had you wouldn't have known what to do with them. It's just that you can't bear to let go of what was once yours. But we're not property, and it's time to let go.'

'What makes you think I've changed my mind?'

'It doesn't matter. Time has passed. Sooner or later we'll divorce, and I'd like it to be sooner. Our tenth wedding anniversary is coming up, and I don't want to be legally your wife on that day. Can't you see that it would be a mockery?'

'You were still my wife on our ninth anniversary. What difference does it make now?'

'The tenth is special,' she argued. 'It's the first of the big ones: ten, twenty, twenty-five, fifty. Ten is like a milestone. It says that your marriage has lasted. But ours hasn't.'

He looked at her closely. 'Is that the only reason?'

Under his keen gaze, she coloured. 'No, I—I want to get married again.'

She waited for his anger at this offence to his pride, but it didn't come and this disconcerted her. 'Tell me about him,' he said mildly.

'He's a kind man and I love him.'

'And you think he can fill my place with my children?'

'He already does and he's doing a terrific job. He's *there* for them.'

'He has no right to be. I'm still their father, just as I'm still your husband.'

'And what you have, you hold. I might have known.'

He touched the gold chain about her neck. 'Did he give you this?'

'Yes.'

'I wouldn't have thought Kendall Haines could have afforded that. He's obviously more successful than I realized. But he still isn't the right man for you.'

'I never told you his name. How did you—?' She gasped in outrage. *'You've had me spied on!'*

'I always keep up-to-date information about my investments,' he said coolly. 'I knew when you went to work for him, and the first time you dated him.'

She drew a sharp breath. 'That was why you made me leave that job,' she said angrily. 'Because I was falling in love with him. You're even trying to control me now.'

'This man isn't right for you.'

'I think he is and I'm going to marry him. I can't be browbeaten any more, Garth—'

He took a quick breath. 'Browbeaten? Is that how you think of a marriage in which I gave you everything—?'

'Except yourself. Once you got your own business you were never there when I needed you. You handed your gifts down from on high and expected me to defer to you, and when I started answering back you didn't like it. I had to escape—'

'You'll never escape me,' he said harshly. 'I won't allow it.'

'You think you're going to turn the full might of the law onto me—?'

'No, it's much simpler than that,' he said softly, and pulled her into his arms.

He was too quick for her to avoid him and before she knew it his lips were on hers, caressing her with the same fierce purpose as in the past. In the beginning it had delighted her. Now, she was filled with outrage at his arrogance. Once, their sexual rapport had been perfect. Even when they had quarrelled it had still been there, giving them an illusion of a marriage. Now he thought he had only to remind her of that to overcome her will.

She fought to remain still and inwardly resist him. It should be easy with her anger to help her. Besides, she was strong now. If she waited, he would soon see that it was no use.

But his lips were full of persuasion, coaxing her to

relive hot, brilliant moments, when the world had been full of love and beauty. If he'd been possessive, so had she, caressing and cherishing his body, rejoicing that he had chosen her for this magic gift. He had been young and his frame had been at its magnificent best; long legs and arms, a smooth brown chest, and hips whose power could make her cry out with ecstasy.

In the lonely, sobbing nights after their separation, she'd fought to deaden those memories and believed she'd succeeded. But he was here now, the living, breathing man, determined to make her remember what had united them, and forget what had driven them apart.

'You'll never escape me,' he murmured against her mouth, 'as long as we have *this*.'

His lips moved insistently against hers. This. One little word to sum up a dazzling, glorious and finally bitter experience: passion and grief intermingled. Love, pain, disillusion. All these things were there the moment he touched her, indestructible after all this time.

'I never forgot you,' he said hoarsely. 'Not for a moment. You were always with me—just as I was always with you—'

She tried to deny it but the treacherous warmth was already filling her body, weakening her will, making her want things she had no right to want. She'd sworn this wouldn't happen, but the memory of his passion still lived in her flesh, recalling her to life. She had once loved him so much, and though love might be finished, she was what that love had made her, and the past could never be destroyed completely.

For a few treacherous moments her body moulded itself to his, burning with remembered desire and need. She'd belonged to him completely, but that was a long time ago—although it seemed only yesterday—this very moment—for ever—

'It's not so easy, is it, Faye?' he whispered. 'It's not so easy to forget the truth...'

But the arrogant words shouted in her brain like a warning. Faye shuddered as she saw how close she'd come to weakening. Garth was a clever man and this was no more than a cynical mockery of love. She took a deep breath and forced her head to clear.

'The truth is that everything is over between us,' she said emphatically. 'Can't you understand that?'

'Why should I?' he growled. 'You don't kiss me as though it was all over.'

'I'm in love with another man...'

'Little liar!'

'And I'm going to marry him. You can't stop me.' Putting out all her strength, she broke free of him. 'You thought it was going to be easy, didn't you, Garth? When I arrived tonight you were sure I was going to drop into your hands. But I'm not like that any more. I've made my own life and there's no room in it for you.'

Garth was very pale. 'We'll see about that.'

But he was talking to empty air. Faye had fled the house.

CHAPTER TWO

'FAYE, you shouldn't have been alone with this man. He's a monster.'

Faye smiled at Kendall Haines, the man she planned to marry as soon as she was free. 'Garth isn't a monster,' she protested. 'He just steamrollers over people.'

'All the more reason for you to stay away from him.'

It was the day after Faye's visit, and she and Kendall were spending the afternoon together at her home. It was as small and modest as Elm Ridge was rich and grand, but it was her very own and she loved it. The furniture was mostly second-hand, and it showed the wear and tear of two boisterous children. The house looked what it was, a place where a family lived, a real home.

Faye was dressed to fit in with the furniture, in a worn pair of jeans, topped off by a flowered shirt.

Kendall's voice became firm. 'You must promise never to do such a thing again. I can't bear to think that you're still legally his wife.'

'Not for much longer.'

Faye plumped up the cushions as she spoke so as not to let him see her face. There were things about her meeting with Garth she couldn't speak of. She was still shocked at the treacherous way her body had responded to him at the very moment she was rejecting him.

'Do you mean that he's actually agreed to a divorce?' Kendall demanded.

'Not exactly…'

'Then he's still fighting you.'

'It doesn't matter,' Faye said with a conviction she was far from feeling. 'When we broke up he threatened to claim custody of the children if I insisted on a divorce, so I didn't. But after all this time, he hasn't any cards to play.'

'It's time I went to see him,' Kendall mused.

'Ken, no. Don't even think of it.'

'But you're not handling him very well, and perhaps some straight talking would do the trick.'

Kendall believed in straight talking. He was a vet and a minor celebrity in the ecological world. Occasionally he was invited onto television panels, where his forthright manner went down well.

'Straight talking is the worst thing with Garth,' Faye protested. 'He can talk back even straighter.'

'You think I can't handle him?' he asked, raising his eyebrows in amusement.

She could understand his confidence. There was a massiveness about Kendall, both in his physique and his personality. He was six foot two, broad-shouldered, with copper hair that touched his collar, and a beard. He sometimes resembled a lion.

But if Kendall was a lion, Faye thought, Garth was a panther, ready to spring and demolish unwary prey.

'Ken, please, forget this idea,' she begged. 'It would only make things worse.'

His mouth tightened slightly in displeasure. Then he shrugged, good humour restored, and drew her close for a kiss. But they jumped apart almost at once as the front door banged and there came the sound of children's voices. Faye sat up hastily, straightening her hair just in time.

Two attractive children, both dressed in jeans and trainers, bounced into the room and greeted Kendall.

Cindy, almost eight, had the dark hair and intense eyes of her father. Nine-year-old Adrian had his mother's fairness, her fine features, and her sensitivity. He and Kendall grinned at each other. Cindy regarded her mother's friend with more reserve but still offered him a toffee, which he accepted at once for he had a very sweet tooth.

'Tea will be ready in ten minutes,' Faye said, hugging her. 'Go and have some sort of wash.'

Both children made ritual groaning noises, but headed for the door. Adrian turned back to Kendall. 'You will play football with me before you go, won't you?'

'Promise.'

Adrian vanished, satisfied.

'Do we have to jump apart like a pair of canoodling teenagers?' Kendall asked plaintively. 'The kids know about us. They even like me.'

'Adrian especially,' Faye agreed. 'But Cindy still adores Garth. That's why we have his picture over there. It's part of her make-believe that one day things will come right. I get so angry that he doesn't treasure her picture in the same way.'

'Don't let him get to you,' Kendall said with a shrug.

'You're right. He's the past.' She put her arms about him. 'Once I've got this divorce, everything will be fine for us.'

For three days Faye waited to hear from Garth, but there wasn't a word. Reluctantly she decided that she would have to contact him again, but just now she was snowed under with work.

She was settling down to it one afternoon when a sound outside drew her attention, and she was surprised to see a luxurious black car drawing up outside. The next moment Garth stepped out and headed purposefully towards the house.

Faye pulled open the door. 'I wasn't expecting you,' she said.

'I only decided this morning. May I come in?' The question was a formality, as he'd already taken her shoulders and moved her gently but firmly out of his way.

She concealed her annoyance at his high-handedness, thinking that perhaps he'd come about the divorce.

'You left this behind,' he said, handing her a parcel. Inside, she found the jacket that she had left behind in her hurry to escape from Elm Ridge. It startled her slightly to realize that she hadn't even thought about it.

'Thank you,' she said awkwardly. 'It was good of you to bring it yourself—'

'I wanted to talk to you. We can't leave things as they are. Are the kids here?'

'No, they're out with Kendall.'

'He's really taken over, hasn't he?'

'He's my future husband. Of course he's getting to know them. They like him a lot. Please, don't let's have a fight about him.'

'All right. I haven't come to fight. Do I get offered a cup of coffee?'

Reluctantly Faye went into the kitchen but she was very aware of him studying the house, the inside of which he'd never seen before. When he'd collected his children for a visit he'd waited outside, or even sent the car with only his chauffeur.

She came into the front room with the tray, to find him studying her computer and the papers strewn on the table.

'What's this?' he asked critically.

'It's my job.'

'You're still working?'

'Didn't your spies tell you? You drove me out of Kendall's job, but you couldn't stop me doing freelance work.' She was struck by a horrid thought and hastily shut down the file she was working on.

'Don't worry, I'm not going to twist anyone's arm to make them fire you,' he said with a wry smile.

'I wouldn't put it past you.'

'Forget it. That's not what I'm here for.'

'What *are* you here for?'

'Because I'm tired of waiting. It's over, Faye. All this living in limbo has gone on long enough. It's time to make final decisions.'

'That's what I was trying to tell you the other night.'

'But we got distracted, didn't we?' he reminded her with a wicked grin.

To her own annoyance Faye found herself blushing. 'That won't happen again. I've made my decision, and in future I think we should talk through lawyers.'

'Faye, if you've become as strong and independent as you claim, why don't you deal with your problems, instead of running away from them?'

'What do you mean by that?' she demanded angrily.

'If I'm a problem, deal with me. Here I am. Confront me. Make me back down.'

'You'd love me to try, so that you could make a show of strength, wouldn't you? You fight your way; I'll fight mine. I don't need to confront you to make you back down over this divorce. I think you should go now. Please tell your driver to— Where is he? Your car's gone.'

'I told him not to stay.'

'When is he coming back for you?'

'Tomorrow morning.'

'You don't think you're going to spend the night here?'

'And tomorrow night, and the night after. I'm moving in, Faye.'

'Over my dead body!' she said explosively.

'It's time I studied the influences my children are receiving.'

While she stared at him, speechless, he opened the front door and began carrying in his bags that were piled up just outside.

'No!' she cried. 'This is my home. I won't have you walking in here without a by-your-leave.'

'We need to be under the same roof for a while. If you don't want me here, come back to Elm Ridge.'

'That's out of the question!'

'Then it'll have to be here.'

'There's no room for you. We only have three bedrooms. One for Adrian, one for Cindy and one for me.'

'We can work something out.'

She was distracted by the sight of Kendall's car drawing up outside. The last thing she wanted was for the two men to meet now. Luckily Kendall was in a hurry. Having watched until the children reached the house, he waved and drove off.

Adrian came in first. 'Cindy's gone round the back,' he told Faye. 'She's got dirty shoes.' His eager look faded as he saw his father, and he edged closer to Faye.

Watching their faces, Faye followed both their reactions easily. She saw Garth wait for his son's whoop of delight, then grow tense when it didn't come. Adrian seemed uncertain. In Kendall he'd found a fellow-footballer, who sympathized with him as Garth never had. Yet he loved and admired his father, and she could see that he was torn between the two loyalties.

'Hello, Daddy,' he said at last. 'What are you—? I mean— Has something happened?'

'I've come to stay for a while,' Garth said, pretending not to notice his son's awkwardness.

'Oh. That's nice.'

'Is that all you've got to say to me, son?' Garth asked, with determined cheerfulness. 'Doesn't your old man get a hug?'

Adrian hugged him obediently. Faye came to the child's rescue. 'Go and change those dirty clothes,' she said with a smile.

He turned to her with relief. 'We had ever such a good time, Mummy. I found a frog.'

'Yuk! You didn't bring it home, I hope.'

'No, I wanted to, but Ken said it would be happier where it was.'

'Thank goodness one of you's got some sense. Off now.'

When the boy had gone Faye saw the condemnation in Garth's eyes. 'I thought he at least would be pleased to see me,' he said bitterly. 'Your boyfriend's done his best to distance my son from me, hasn't he?'

'No, you did that. Ken's simply given him all the attention you never did. He's taken trouble to know who Adrian really is.'

'Evidently I'm here not a moment too soon.'

'Garth, about your staying—'

She stopped at the sound of feet pattering in from the kitchen. Next moment her little daughter was standing in the doorway, a look of ecstasy dawning on her face. Cindy drew a deep, thrilled breath, shrieked, *'Daddy!'* and hurled herself into his arms.

Garth reeled under the impact, then lifted her high off the ground so that she could hug him properly. Two strong young arms tightened around his neck so firmly that he was almost strangled, but he clung on to the one person who was pleased to see him.

'Daddy, Daddy, Daddy...' Cindy squealed in delight.

'Steady, pet,' he said in a choked voice. 'I can't breathe.' He set her down and knelt to meet her eyes. 'Let me look at you. It's been a long ti— That is—er— let me have a good look at you.' He was struggling for the right words. What did you say to a little girl whom you hardly knew? But she made it easy for him, bouncing up and down, hugging and kissing him.

'You came back,' she bubbled. 'You remembered my birthday. You did, you did, you did!'

With a shock Garth's eyes met Faye's. He hadn't remembered Cindy's birthday, and even now he couldn't recall the exact date.

'Mummy said not to be disappointed if you forgot,' Cindy said. 'But I *knew* you wouldn't.'

He had the grace to be conscience-stricken. 'Of course I didn't forget,' he improvised. Frantically his eyes meet Faye's, asking her help.

'Daddy knows it's your birthday on Saturday,' she said. 'In fact he came over to tell us that he'll be spending the whole day with us.'

Cindy squealed again with delight. Garth ground his teeth at the way Faye had backed him into a corner. Saturday was fully booked with important meetings. Faye's eyes were still on him, understanding everything, daring him to refuse.

He thought faster than he'd ever done in his life. 'That's right,' he said. 'We'll all be going out together. You, me, Mummy and Adrian.'

'Adrian's got a football match that afternoon,' Cindy said. 'Can we all go and watch it?'

'Of course we will,' Garth responded at once. 'Actually, I thought of inviting myself to stay with you for a while. Only if you want me, of course.' He was throwing the challenge back at Faye.

'Of *course* we want you,' Cindy declared, shocked. 'We do, don't we, Mummy? We want Daddy ever and *ever* so much.'

'Well, it's not quite that simple,' Garth said, as if giving the matter serious thought. 'You see, this house has only three bedrooms, so there isn't anywhere for me.'

'But it's easy,' Cindy said. 'I'll move in with Mummy and you can have my room.'

'Can I, darling? That's very nice of you.' He looked at Faye. 'You see? It's easy.'

Cindy danced off to find her brother, singing, 'Daddy's home! Daddy's home!' The other two regarded each other.

'I think you're the most unscrupulous man I've ever known,' Faye seethed. 'How dare you use a child's love in that cynical way?'

'But perhaps I'm not being cynical, Faye. You told me I should pay them more attention, especially Cindy. That's what I'm doing. Don't you think I've made her happy?'

'For your own ends, the way everything is for your own ends.'

'She's *happy*. Does it matter why?'

'It *will* matter, when you decide to change tactics and drop her. It's bad enough that you've neglected her until now, but when she finds that this sudden interest is only a way of using her, she'll stop trusting you. I don't want her to lose faith in the world so soon.'

'Would I do that to my own child?'

'You wouldn't even know you were doing it,' she said despairingly. 'But you mustn't do this. Go away, Garth. Leave us alone. We were happy without you—'

'Was Cindy?'

'All right, we weren't happy, but we survived.'

'And you don't think you could be happy with me around?'

'I don't think anyone could be happy with you around,' she said desperately. 'You don't bring happiness, or know how to create it. You only know *things*. Getting them, winning them, and buying them. Go back to that. You're good at it. But with people, you only destroy...'

Her voice choked off, and she turned sharply away.

'What is it?' Garth asked, coming after her.

'Nothing!'

'You're not crying, are you?'

'No, I'm not crying,' she insisted, quickly brushing her eyes. For a moment she'd been shaken by the thought of Garth here, ruining her hard-won peace. But she definitely wasn't crying.

'Here, let me look at you,' he said, turning her to face him. He pulled a clean handkerchief from his pocket and dabbed her eyes. 'There's no need to get upset about this.' His voice softened. 'I'm not really so bad, Faye.'

'Yes, you are,' she said huskily, almost hating him for that gentle note. She could cope with him angry, but gentleness recalled too many sweet memories that she had to block out to survive.

'Then teach me to be better. While I'm here you can show me how to get closer to the children, the way you've always said I should.'

'You're not going to stay here,' she insisted, desperately trying to hold her position against his clever tactics. 'The house is too small.'

'Then you know the answer. Move back to Elm Ridge, which is big enough for all of us.'

'Never. It's all over. You've got to accept that.'

'And suppose I don't choose to?' His voice was quiet, but the undertone of stubborn determination still throbbed through it.

'Doesn't anyone else get a say? What about how your family feels?'

'I think I'm doing the best thing for my family.'

She stood silent, wishing he would release her. His closeness, the feel of his hands on her arms, was recalling her reaction to his kiss only a few days ago. She'd thought herself safe until the devastating discovery that he could still play on her senses. Ten years ago, on their first date, he'd touched her carefully, as though fearing to break something precious. She could stand anything but that memory. If only he would let her go...

'Faye...' he said in an almost wondering tone.

'Garth, please...'

'Mummy, Mummy, I've done it.'

The shock made them break apart, staring at each other with startled eyes. Cindy erupted into the room.

'I've done it, Mummy. I've put my things into your room, and I've put everything tidy so that you won't have a mess to clear up. Honestly I have.' She grabbed Garth's hand. 'And I've taken one of your bags up to my room.'

'They're too heavy for you, pet.'

'It was just a little one. We could take the others up and I'll help you unpack. Let's do it now. *Please.*'

Faye met Garth's eyes, expecting to see in them a look of triumph. But instead there was something that might almost have been a plea. For a moment, father and daughter were almost comically alike, their faces both registering an urgent need to have their own way. Against her will, Faye's lips twitched.

'What's funny?' he asked quickly.

'Nothing that you'd understand,' she said with a smile.

'*Mummy!*' said Cindy insistently.

'All right. Help your father unpack.'

Cindy let out a yell of delight. '*Hooray, hooray, hooray! Daddy's home today*! Hooray, hooray…' She repeated the couplet over and over, dancing a little jig of happiness, while Garth stared at her. It was the first time Faye could ever remember seeing him nonplussed.

Adrian appeared and came halfway down the stairs.

'Daddy's back, Daddy's back,' Cindy told him unnecessarily.

'Yes, I know—' Adrian looked awkward. 'Is it really true?'

'Just for a while,' Faye said quickly. 'None of us knows what's going to happen, but we'll try to make his visit nice.'

'Daddy,' Cindy called anxiously over the staircase.

'Coming,' Garth called, and went obediently up the stairs.

Faye had warned Garth that he was Cindy's idol but now, for the first time, he understood that this was the literal truth. Her joy at his arrival had confused him. He'd found himself instinctively clinging to the little girl as his only friend in hostile territory. Her adoration touched his heart and her relief that he'd returned for her birthday, as she thought, gave him a rare twinge of guilt.

It charmed him to discover that everything about her

was emphatic. Neither her actions nor her feelings was moderate. Her enthusiasms filled the horizon, and whatever pleased her was the very best in the whole world. He knew how she felt, for he'd been the same as a child, and his adult single-mindedness had played a large part in his success.

Later that evening he sought her out where she was sitting on the steps of the French windows surveying the tiny garden, and sat down beside her. At that moment he had no other motive than to repay her love by being a good father.

'It's about time we planned your birthday present,' he suggested. 'Why don't you give me a list of what you want and I'll arrange everything?'

Cindy regarded her father in a way that Faye could have warned him meant she had a secret agenda. 'Anything?' she asked.

'Anything.'

'Anything at all?'

'Absolutely anything in the whole wide world,' Garth promised incautiously. 'Tell me what it is.'

'A dog.'

He felt almost ludicrously disappointed. A dog was too easy. It gave him no chance to show Faye that she was wrong about him.

'Of course. I'll get in touch with a good breeder tomorrow,' he said, 'and I'll bring you the best puppy there is.' Then he recalled Faye's accusation that he settled everything without reference to others and, with a feeling of conscious virtue, he amended, 'No, you'll want to choose it yourself. You get the puppy and—I mean, we'll go and pick one out together.' He was learning fast.

Cindy nodded vigorously, beaming. A growing understanding of his daughter made Garth add, 'I expect you already know where to go.'

'That's right. Spare Paws.'

'Pardon?'

'Spare Paws. It's a home for abandoned dogs. I pass it every day on my way to school.'

'Darling, what do you want an abandoned dog for? Do you think I can't afford to buy you one?'

Cindy frowned, not understanding his argument. 'Nobody wants them,' she explained. 'They keep hoping and *hoping* that someone will give them a home.'

Just as she didn't understand his language, so he didn't understand hers. 'I can get you a pedigree puppy,' he protested, 'with a good bloodline—'

'But Daddy, people always give homes to pedigree puppies. I want a dog that nobody else wants.'

Garth ran a hand through his hair. 'But you won't know anything about this animal,' he argued. 'It might be full of diseases or fleas—'

'No, Spare Paws always gets its dogs clean and healthy before it lets them go,' Cindy contradicted him gently but firmly.

'Do they also make sure the dogs are friendly? Suppose this creature is vicious? No, darling, it's too chancy. You can choose a puppy from a breeder—'

'I don't *want* to,' Cindy said, sticking her bottom lip out. 'I want a dog that nobody else wants, one who's old and ugly, and blind in one eye, with a leg missing, and—and lots and lots and lots of fleas. And if I can't have that I don't want one at all.' She got up and ran away before Garth could reply.

A choke of laughter from behind made him look up to find Faye regarding him. 'If you'll pardon the pun, you made a real dog's breakfast of that,' she told him.

'Thank you,' he said, chagrined.

'Cindy doesn't care about bloodlines. She wants a dog who needs her love.'

'Isn't that true of any dog?'

'Yes, but it's more true if they're abandoned. And that matters to her.'

'The whole idea is impractical. I'm sorry. She can have a dog, but not like this.'

'We'll see.'

'I'm not going to change my mind.'

Faye took a deep breath. 'Well, it doesn't matter whether you do or not, because you don't make the decisions in this house,' she said calmly.

He scowled but she met his eyes.

'You're trying to make me sound unreasonable when I'm just being sensible,' he argued. 'That's very unfair tactics.'

'Well, if we're going to talk about unfair tactics, what about you barging in here?' she said indignantly.

To her surprise his manner held a touch of sheepishness.

'I used any method that would work,' he admitted.

'Anything that would get your own way,' she said lightly.

He grinned, and for a moment there was a touch of the old, boyish charm. 'It's what I'm good at.'

'Not as good as your daughter. I can't think who she gets it from, but she could give you lessons. Go and do your arguing with Cindy. My money's on her.'

CHAPTER THREE

CINDY was far too generous to exult over her victory but when they set off to Spare Paws, on the day before her birthday, there was a skip in her step.

They were met by Kelly, a pleasant woman in her late thirties, who greeted Cindy as an old friend.

'Cindy often helps us raise funds,' she explained. 'We're a charity, and we only exist through people's kindness.'

'Then perhaps this will help,' Garth said, scribbling a cheque.

Kelly's eyes widened at the sum. 'That's very generous, Mr Clayton.'

Cindy squeezed her father's hand gratefully. 'Can we buy some dog biscuits?' she begged, indicating a table where small bags of biscuits were on sale for a nominal price.

'It's hard to stop people feeding the dogs,' Kelly explained, 'so we provide these. Then we know what they're getting.'

Garth stocked up on biscuits. A very young kennel maid called Jane came to fetch Kelly to the phone, and take over her job of conducting the visitors.

'It's my first week here,' she confided to the children. 'I love them all so much that I'd like to take every one home with me.'

The place was overflowing with dogs, in cages that stretched in all directions. Smiling kennel maids passed down the lines with bowls of food. A tall woman in jeans and sweater appeared with six leads in her hand, calling, 'Who's next for walkies?'

'Some of them are never going to leave us,' Jane said with a sigh. 'They're too old, or there's something wrong with them. So we try to make this a home for them.'

The atmosphere was cheerful. Every dog was an individual to be called by name with a friendly pat and a smile. But they were unwanted by the world. Most still had the desperate eagerness of those who clung to hope, and they barked and bounced to attract attention. Others sat in the resigned silence of creatures who'd been passed over too often.

'I want them all,' Cindy said plaintively.

'I know,' Faye sighed. 'It's heartbreaking, isn't it? But we can only have one, darling.'

Jane took several dogs out of their cages to be properly introduced. Cindy hugged them, but none seemed to be exactly what she was looking for.

'I'll know when I find it,' she said in answer to Garth's query.

'How?' he persisted.

'I'll just *know*.'

'I remember hearing you say that in exactly the same tone,' Faye reminded him. 'You'd just got your first builder's yard and you were choosing a foreman. You picked the strangest looking man because you just *knew* he was ideal.'

'And I was right, wasn't I?'

'Oh yes,' she said with a smile. 'Your instinct was always right.' She spoke amiably because the sun and the pleasant atmosphere were affecting her mood. Garth was behaving well, holding Cindy's hand and attending to her. Whatever his motives, Cindy was so happy at this moment that Faye would have forgiven him much.

He'd done something else, too, that had put him in her good books. Seeing her come downstairs in her buttercup-yellow shirt and fawn trousers he'd observed, 'You've lost weight. About twenty pounds I'd say.'

'Only fourteen,' she said regretfully. 'But I'm fighting for another seven.'

'Go for it! You look terrific.'

Since she'd struggled and fought for her weight loss, she appreciated this more than she would have admitted. Kendall's reaction, 'But you were fine as you were', though kindly meant, had been lacking something. Now she knew what it was.

'Oh, Daddy, look!' the little girl said suddenly. 'Poor doggy! He's so sad.'

The biggest St Bernard Faye had ever seen was regarding them soulfully. His great jowls hung from his face, and his eyes were those of one who carried weighty burdens with dignity. When Cindy called to him, he came eagerly to the wire of his cage.

'I want to hug him,' she told Jane earnestly.

'Is that wise?' Faye asked as Jane unlocked the cage. 'He's ten times her size.'

'Don't worry, he's the gentlest dog we've got,' Jane assured her.

'St Bernards are always gentle,' Adrian said. 'They're docile and obedient, and very intelligent. That's why they're used for mountain rescue.'

'Where did you get that?' Garth asked, for it was clear the boy was quoting.

'From Ken,' Adrian said. 'He knows a lot about them.'

Garth's face clouded but he said no more. Cindy was

hugging the huge dog, who received her caresses eagerly. Benevolence beamed from his eyes, and he uttered a bark of approval that almost deafened everyone.

'His name's Barker,' Jane said, uncovering her ears, 'because that's what he is.'

As if in confirmation Barker promptly boomed again.

'His owner died six months ago,' Jane told them. 'He didn't have any family, and it's hard to find him a new home, because he's so big.'

'He's lovely,' Cindy enthused, burying her face in the thick, brown and white fur.

'Yes, he is,' Adrian said, stroking the huge head gently.

'Hey, kids, come on,' Faye said in alarm. 'He's too big for us, as well. We can't have him in our little house.'

'Why not?' Garth demanded. 'There are fields at the back where you can take him for exercise. He looks a terrific dog to me.'

Barker offered a paw, which both the children solemnly shook.

'Daddy, he wants to shake hands with you,' Cindy said.

Under Faye's incredulous eye, Garth took the huge powder puff offered to him. 'Pleased to meet you, sir,' he declared.

This was obviously the right response for both children, who beamed. Garth ran his hands over Barker's vast frame and offered him a biscuit, which vanished with the speed of light. Another went the same way. The next moment Barker's head was resting in Garth's hands, his eyes suggesting that this was his first food for a month.

'He likes you, Daddy,' Cindy said, delighted.

'Yes, I think he does. Hey, you're a splendid fellow, aren't you?'

Barker agreed, his eyes fixed on the biscuits.

Faye was growing more nervous. 'Don't encourage them,' she told Garth. 'It's out of the question.'

'Why is it, if they want him?'

'In that little house?'

He glanced up and her suspicions were confirmed. 'I know what you're up to and it won't work,' she told him in an undervoice. 'Garth, I'm not going to be manipulated like this.'

He moved aside with her, out of the children's hearing. 'Why must you always think the worst of me?'

'Eight years of marriage.'

'Ten,' he said at once.

'Only eight that counted.'

His eyes gleamed sharply, but he didn't retort.

'I know what you're doing,' she persisted, 'and you've got to stop.'

But Cindy was pulling on her hand, pleading, 'Mummy, Daddy, I want Barker.'

'Darling, he's far too big,' Faye said urgently.

'No, he isn't, he's just right,' Cindy said. 'I love him, and he loves me, and he *wants* to come with us.'

'Of course he does,' Garth said, refusing to meet his wife's eyes. 'You can't disappoint him now.'

She was speechless at his sheer lack of scruple. Under the guise of being kind to his daughter, Garth was arranging matters his own way, as always.

But when they reached Kelly's office it seemed he was due for a setback. While the children played outside with their new friend, Kelly said, 'You shouldn't really have met Barker, but Jane's still new here. He's a permanent resident.'

'But why?' Garth demanded. 'He looks fine to me.'

'He's a lovely dog, but also a very old one. Generally the larger the dog, the shorter the life. Barker's ten, and many St Bernards die at ten. It would be better to choose a younger animal. It's not too late.'

But it *was* too late, as the children's glowing faces confirmed. Through the window they could be seen climbing over Barker, who cheerfully accepted their attentions. Faye made a last attempt to change their minds, but their response was to tighten their arms around their new friend and look mulish.

Kelly made a start on the paperwork. 'He doesn't actually become yours for another month,' she said. 'First I must visit you and see how he is. If your home doesn't seem suitable, then I'm afraid I have to take him back.'

'Don't worry. He'll have the best of everything,' Garth assured her.

While Kelly left them a moment, Faye said angrily, 'That's the worst thing I've ever seen you do. He isn't going to live long. But you don't care if they're hurt so long as you get your way.'

'Faye, Cindy's *happy*.'

'Because she thinks this means her father loves her.'

'Are you saying I don't love my children?'

'Maybe you love Adrian, because he's your son. But Cindy's always been an afterthought to you. How is she going to feel when Barker dies?'

'I'll get her another dog.'

'Another one won't be the same.'

'I'll get one who looks just like him.'

She looked at him in pity. 'You don't understand a thing, do you?'

Kelly returned before he had to answer. The formalities were completed, and they were free to take Barker home.

Garth's big car suddenly looked much smaller when it had to accommodate a hundred and twenty pounds of dog. He took up most of the back seat, with Cindy and Adrian squeezing into whatever was left. When he woofed, Garth and Faye had to rub their ears.

It was Cindy's birthday next day. Faye's gift was a dressing-table set, and a new pair of jeans suitable for a little girl who enjoyed muddy pursuits. Adrian had bought her a video of her favourite television programme. And because Faye had done some inspired last-minute shopping, there was even a new T-shirt bearing a picture of a St Bernard, and a tag that said, 'To Cindy, with love from Barker.'

Garth's present was Barker himself, but Faye knew he wouldn't feel he'd done the job properly unless he'd spent money. She'd wondered wryly how he would rise to the challenge of buying something for a little girl he knew nothing about, but she'd underestimated him. He had an excellent, motherly secretary, who spent the lunch hour shopping and returned with a small coral necklace and matching bracelet. They were exquisite, and Cindy was thrilled.

When she'd opened her cards and presents, she willingly turned the spotlight onto Adrian.

'He's got a very important football match this afternoon,' she explained to Barker. 'And we're going along to cheer. I'll tell you all about it when we come back.'

Promptly at eleven o'clock Adrian was collected by the father of a team-mate, ferrying five players to the match site ten miles away. The rest of the family would follow an hour later.

Cindy was ready well before time, bouncing up and

down with excitement. 'Come *on*, Daddy,' she pleaded.
But when he appeared, her expression changed to one
of horror. 'Daddy, you *can't* go like that.'

'What's wrong with it?' Garth asked, looking down
at his neat, conservative suit.

'Nobody dresses like that,' Cindy said urgently.

'I do.'

'*Nobody does.*'

'Faye, do you know what this child is talking about?'

'You're overdressed,' she said. 'You should be in
jeans and sweater like the rest of us.'

'Does it really matter?'

'Garth, if you turn up dressed for a board meeting,
your children will be so embarrassed that they'll pretend
not to know you.'

Garth was about to say that his faithful little defender
would never deny him, when he caught a look on
Cindy's face, and thought better of it. 'I don't have any
jeans,' said the man who'd once lived in them, morning,
noon and night.

'Something casual, then.'

Between them Faye and Cindy went through his
clothes and found garments that Cindy said, 'wouldn't
be too cringe-making'. Much chastened, Garth donned
trousers and a casual shirt, and they were ready to leave.

'Goodbye, Barker,' Cindy said, hugging him fiercely.
'Be good while we're gone.'

But it seemed that the faithful hound had no intention
of staying behind. He followed her to the door, slipped
out and went to sit beside the car. When Garth seized
his collar and tried to command him back inside, Barker
took root in the ground and looked hurt.

'He's afraid to be on his own,' Cindy explained, 'in
case we don't come back.'

'He's a dog, not a person,' Garth protested.

But it seemed that Cindy was right. Having lost one owner, Barker was determined not to lose another. As soon as the car door was opened he dashed inside. Cindy followed him and they sat together, determination written on both faces.

'You might as well give in now,' Faye said, stifling a laugh.

'Do you know what that dog's doing to my upholstery? I've just had it cleaned from bringing him home yesterday.'

'I think it's going to need cleaning again,' she observed with apparent sympathy. 'The trouble is that he's so big. But, as I recall, you wanted a big dog.'

'You're enjoying this, aren't you?'

'Who, me?' she asked innocently. In fact, there was a certain satisfaction in the sight of Garth hoist with his own petard.

He started the car, but immediately flinched away, rubbing his ear. 'Cindy, if you don't stop that animal licking me I'll leave you both behind.'

'Barker,' Cindy reproved him, 'you're a very naughty boy.'

Barker barked. Garth winced. Faye dissolved in laughter.

At the match site there was more of an audience than Garth had expected for a schoolboys' game.

'It's the inter-schools trophy,' Cindy explained to him. 'This is the quarter finals, and this year we've got a real chance of winning. Adrian's terribly good. Ken says so.'

'Ken?'

'He's Mummy's friend,' Cindy said innocently, 'and he coaches the football team.'

'He probably won't be here today,' Faye said quickly.

'He's not really the coach, he just fills in sometimes for the fun of it because the real coach has been poorly. But he's well now, so I doubt if Ken—oh, dear.'

Garth followed her eyes to where Adrian's team had appeared, accompanied by a large, bearded man.

'That, I take it, is Kendall Haines?'

'Yes, but I truly thought he wouldn't be here. He was rushing to finish a book before the deadline.'

Garth hardly heard her. He was watching his son claim Kendall's attention with a question that seemed urgent. Kendall answered at length, with gestures towards the field, while Adrian nodded and seemed happier for what he'd heard. He was completely absorbed, and only when the teams ran onto the pitch did he look at the sidelines for his family.

Faye and Cindy led the cheering from the start, yelling loudest whenever their team did well. When Adrian scored in the first half-hour they crowed with delight. So did Barker. Garth tried to catch his son's eye and finally managed it, giving him a thumb's-up sign that Adrian acknowledged with a grin. But it was Kendall's cry of 'Well done, Adrian,' that really delighted him.

Garth thought of where he ought to be right now, the meetings he'd had to cancel, the lame excuses he'd made. And for what? To be forced to watch a demonstration of his son's allegiance to another man.

Then he felt Cindy's tight grip on his hand and looked down at her with a smile. She was his protector, he thought, astonished. Faye was reserved, except when she was laughing at him, and Adrian still maintained a slight distance. It was Cindy who secured his place in the family.

He felt a rare pang of guilt. He was working skilfully to stay in his daughter's good books, because he needed her. And that meant Faye was right, he realized. He was giving Cindy a raw deal. And not for the first time. Her eyes, shining up at him, were uncritical and full of trust and for an instant he had to look away. How could any man meet that honest gaze without a touch of shame?

'Is anything wrong, Daddy?' she asked.

'No. I was just thinking how pretty you are.'

She beamed and clasped her second hand over his with a sigh of contentment. After a moment he bent down and kissed the top of her head.

In the end, Adrian's goal was the only one and his victorious team carried him from the field. His family walked over to where he was being pummelled joyfully.

'Well done, son,' Garth told him.

Adrian turned shining eyes on him. 'Did you really see my goal?' he asked.

'Every moment of it.'

'I thought you weren't going to be here,' Faye said quietly to Kendall. 'You said you had a book to finish.'

'I got it done last night.' He glanced at Garth. 'Is that—?'

'Yes, that's Garth.'

Kendall made a wry face. 'I wish he wasn't quite so good-looking.'

'Don't say things like that,' she urged. 'He means nothing to me now.'

Garth turned his head at that moment and she wondered how much he'd heard. She made the introductions, and to her relief her husband reacted civilly. So did Kendall but she could see the two men sizing each other up, and the knowledge was there between them.

Garth congratulated Kendall politely on his team's success, but this proved unfortunate as it gave Adrian the chance to say, 'Ken's the best coach we've ever had. He knows everything about soccer.'

'Nonsense, you did it all yourself,' Kendall said, aiming a playful punch at him. 'Golden feet, that's what you've got.'

'Am I really going to be good enough to play professionally?' Adrian asked, his face shining.

The sight hurt Garth and prompted his demon to say, 'It's a bit soon to be asking that, isn't it? After all, this isn't the only thing in life.'

He regretted the words instantly, because a light went out of Adrian's face. But he brightened again when Kendall said, 'Keep up the hard work, and you can do anything you want.'

Barker, evidently feeling that he'd taken a back seat long enough, gave his noisiest woof.

'Barker thinks so too,' Cindy confirmed.

'Is he yours?' Kendall asked.

'Daddy gave him to me for my birthday.'

'He's a fine fellow.' Kendall ran his hands knowledgeably over Barker's frame and tried to look into his mouth, but Barker wriggled free in order to sniff one of Kendall's pockets. 'All right,' Kendall said hastily. 'Don't tear me to pieces. I know what you're after. Here!' He produced something which he tossed to the dog, who swallowed it in one gulp.

'What was that?' Faye asked.

'Aniseed. Dogs love it, and I always keep some aniseed sweets in my pocket for my own dogs.'

'Just for the dogs?' Adrian asked cheekily.

'Meaning that I swipe some for myself?' Kendall asked, all innocence. 'Me?'

'Of course not,' Cindy assured him with a carefully

bland face. 'We know you wouldn't *ever* eat aniseed when there was a starving dog who just loved it.'

Kendall grinned and tossed the 'starving dog' another sweet. 'Shame on you, you terrible brats!'

Both children giggled, evidently finding this form of address acceptable. Garth's hands balled into fists inside his pockets.

'Is Barker all right?' Cindy asked.

'He's fine, but don't let him eat too many sweets,' Kendall said, straight-faced. 'He mustn't put on weight.'

'The voice of the expert,' Garth said in a tone that was apparently friendly, but had a slight edge.

'I don't call myself an expert,' Kendall said. 'Not next to my friend, James Wakeham. He's made a special study of St Bernards and he's one of the finest veterinary surgeons in the world. We were at vet school together; used to pinch each other's girlfriends. He was always in trouble. In fact, he owes me a favour for keeping quiet about— Well, never mind. He could have been thrown out for it.' He was talking for the sake of talking, saying anything to lighten the atmosphere. Garth responded with a mechanical smile.

While Cindy asked more questions about Barker's care, Garth found something else to look at.

'This is Ken's subject,' Faye urged him in an undervoice. 'If he needed advice about business, he'd have to come to you.'

'But he never would need advice about business, would he?' Garth growled. 'I know his kind. He floats loftily above money as though the rest of us were beneath contempt. For pity's sake, I gave her the damned dog!'

'Then why don't *you* tell her how to look after him?'

'What time have I got to study dogs?'

'You're the man who believes in keeping track of your investments,' she reminded him. 'And this sudden rush of concern for Cindy is just that—an investment.'

'You're determined to think the worst of me, aren't you?'

'You make it easy,' she said after a moment, and turned away from him.

They were both relieved when the awkward meeting was over. Adrian parted reluctantly from Kendall, promising fervently to be at the next practice.

'As long as you don't neglect your schoolwork,' Garth said. 'You've got a career to think of.'

Adrian became absorbed in Barker, and didn't reply. It was Kendall who said quietly, 'Surely he's a bit young to be deciding his career! If he wants to be a sportsman why not let him dream his dreams and believe he can do anything?'

'Because the world is a tough place, and a man has no time for dreams in case he falls behind,' Garth snapped. 'And I'll thank you not to interfere in my son's upbringing.'

'Hey, come on! I was only—'

'I know damned well what you were *only* doing. And you'll do it over my dead body.'

Luckily Faye had gone ahead and didn't hear this exchange. Garth was able to conceal his unsettled state of mind on the journey home. They'd meant to go to a restaurant but, since Barker refused to be left behind, this was abandoned in favour of a Chinese takeaway.

Later that night, when Garth had gone in to say goodnight to Cindy, she heaved a sigh of delight. 'Oh, Daddy, wasn't Adrian simply *super*?'

'He was pretty good,' Garth agreed.

'He was more than good,' Cindy said fervently. 'He

was the very, *very* best. I wish I could do something as well as that.'

Garth brushed her cheek with a finger. 'Don't put yourself down. There must be things you do well.'

'Not as good as Adrian. I'm going to clean the boots he played in this afternoon,' she added in tones of ecstasy. 'He says I can.'

Neither his best friends nor his worst enemies would have called Garth a New Man, but this moved him to protest. 'Let him clean his own boots. You're not his skivvy.'

'But I want to.'

Garth gave up. His daughter's eyes were shining with hero-worship. He wasn't deeply perceptive where feelings were concerned, but he guessed that the need to idolize was a part of her character.

That was dangerous, he thought. A girl who worshipped blindly was vulnerable to the wrong man. She would have to be protected...

Another pair of adoring eyes came into his mind. That was how Faye had looked at him once. She'd loved keeping house for him, ironing his shirts with the same pride as Cindy showed at cleaning her brother's boots. He remembered how her single-minded, vulnerable adoration had been there on her face for all to see. When had she changed into the stranger who kept her thoughts aloof from him?

'Go to sleep, now,' he said abruptly.

'Goodnight, Daddy. Thank you for the best birthday ever.' Her arms were tight around his neck.

'Was it really the best birthday ever?' he asked with rare humility.

'Oh, yes, because you came back for it.'

'Of course I did,' he said, hoping she couldn't see his

sudden awkwardness. 'I'm still your Daddy. Nothing can ever change that.'

'No,' she said happily. 'Nothing, ever.'

'Goodnight, darling.' He kissed the top of her head and went out, thoughtful.

As soon as he arrived at his office on Monday, he instructed his secretary to get him a book on dog care, with special reference to St Bernards. She provided an impressive-looking volume by lunchtime, and over a quick sandwich he flicked through it.

By the end of the day Garth was feeling hard-pressed and out of sorts. A supplier had let him down on delivery dates, one client had backed out of negotiations at the last minute, and another one was trying to wriggle out of payment on a flimsy excuse.

But none of this had annoyed him half so much as discovering that the dog book contained a chapter by Kendall Haines.

CHAPTER FOUR

GRADUALLY they settled into an uneasy truce. Faye couldn't live at such close quarters and not be aware of Garth. The sheer animal force that had made him supreme in his world was reflected in every move he made. About the house she tried to avoid all physical contact, knowing that it wouldn't be safe.

One evening he asked casually, 'Do anything interesting today?'

'Yes, I went to see Kendall.'

'Was that really necessary?'

'Why shouldn't I visit my fiancé, Garth?'

His lips tightened but he said no more, and Faye didn't offer any further explanation.

In fact, her visit to Kendall hadn't been the comfort she'd hoped. She'd poured out her worries, hoping to find understanding, but Kendall had frowned and said lightly, 'Must you spoil our few moments together by talking about your husband all the time?'

'I'm sorry,' she'd said stiffly. 'I didn't mean to be a bore.'

He'd apologized nicely, but the fact remained Kendall liked her whole attention, and was irked because he no longer had it. Was that what had made him suggest that she move back to Elm Ridge, as Garth wanted?

'It might help get him out of your system again,' he'd pointed out, adding in an undervoice, 'something needs to.'

'That's not fair. It's all over between Garth and me.'

'Well, I certainly hope so, because I'm beginning to find him a very boring third in our relationship. I think a spell in your old home might remind you of what made you leave him.' He grinned. 'Then maybe you'd have eyes for me again.'

'Kendall, I love you. You know I do.'

'Do you?' he asked coolly. 'Or are you just running away from Garth? I want all or nothing from you, Faye. Being your refuge from Garth Clayton just isn't good enough.'

'But you're not. I do love you,' she protested.

'Then we have nothing to fear.'

But she knew there was something to fear, even though, on the surface, she and Garth were managing to get by well enough. She was glad to see that he made an effort to be with Cindy and Adrian. Even so, he often spent Saturday in his office and arrived home with a briefcase full of work. Faye and the children would take Barker for a romp in the fields behind the house and get back to find Garth there, poring over his computer.

She had been briefly afraid that he would try to take over her own computer, but after one glance at it he'd roared with laughter. She understood why when she saw his machine, a sleek, state-of-the-art beauty that made her green with envy.

Kendall's assumption that there was nothing to fear troubled her. Despite their mutual hostility, Garth still affected her dangerously. That might seem an argument for going to Elm Ridge, where there was more room, but she knew such a move would be even less safe. Garth would assume he'd won the battle to get her back, and she would never let him think that.

In the end it was Barker who settled the matter in an unexpected way. His idea of fun was to chase madly through the little house, pursued by Adrian, Cindy and herself. Garth never joined in these games, preferring to enjoy the spectacle from the sidelines.

One Saturday afternoon Barker varied the game by raiding the laundry basket. Seeing him trailing clothes, Faye launched herself onto him in a frantic rugby tackle. The children tumbled after her, and the four of them rolled on the floor. It was at this point that Kelly arrived for her check-up visit.

'When I let you have Barker I hadn't realized just how small this place was,' she said worriedly, over a cup of tea. 'A dog his size needs far more room. Your garden is like a pocket handkerchief.'

'But we do take him for walks in the fields at the back,' Faye said.

'Every day?'

'Well, not for the last week,' Faye amended awkwardly. This wasn't the moment to mention the mayhem Barker had caused by chasing squirrels, all of whom had evaded him easily.

Kelly sighed. 'I did say, when I handed him over, that if I wasn't satisfied with his conditions it might be a case for taking him back.'

Cindy and Adrian set up such an outcry that Kelly winced. 'I know it seems hard,' she said, 'but it really isn't kind to Barker to keep him here.'

'But we love him,' Cindy said desperately. 'And he loves us. You can't take him. Daddy, don't let her take Barker.'

'He can't live in this tiny space,' Kelly repeated.

Garth's eyes, full of a message, met Faye's. She drew a deep breath, knowing how she was being propelled into a decision she'd sworn not to make, yet unable to do anything about it. The children were looking at her frantically as they realized they might actually lose their beloved friend.

'We do have the chance of larger premises, with a huge garden,' Garth said, 'but there are a few problems.'

'There are no problems,' Faye said briskly, realizing that she'd been backed into a corner. 'Elm Ridge is standing empty and we can move in tomorrow. Kelly, why don't you come and see us there next week?'

The children jumped around carolling loudly, while Barker added his voice to the proceedings.

When Kelly had gone, Faye took the tea things into the kitchen. Washing them up would give her thoughts time to calm down. Garth had outmanoeuvred her, but that only increased her determination not to yield any more ground. He came in after a moment.

'I'm glad we got that settled,' he said.

'Garth, don't read too much into this,' Faye warned. 'Nothing has really changed.'

'If you're coming home, I'd say a lot had changed.'

'I'm not "coming home". I'm changing premises, but only for a while. I still want that divorce, and when I've got it I'm going to marry Kendall.'

'Don't you think living with me will make a divorce rather difficult?'

'Can't you understand? I won't be living with you. We'll be under the same roof but not living as man and wife. We'll have separate rooms and live separate lives.'

His expression hardened. 'And what exactly does "separate lives" mean?'

'It means I'm still engaged to Kendall, and I'll see him when I like.'

'And suppose your husband has other ideas?'

'It won't make any difference.'

'So my wishes count for nothing?'

'That's right. You've won a small victory by getting us there, but that's all. I'm not your wife, and I'll do as I please.'

'My God! It's like beating my head against marble,' he said angrily. 'You were never like this before.'

'I've changed, Garth.'

'You sure as hell have!'

'But so have you. You're not the loving man I married, any more than I'm the docile girl you married.' Her lips curved in a faint, elusive smile. 'Watching you taught me a lot about standing on my own feet, and I've learned the lessons well. Just regard me as a housekeeper.'

'I already have one, in Nancy.'

'Well, now you've got two. And, like any housekeeper, I'll live my own life, and my employer won't ask questions.'

'Oh, won't he?'

'Not unless he wants to receive some dusty answers.' Mischievously she echoed his own words, 'I'm glad we got that settled.'

'I haven't—'

'It's settled, Garth. Believe me, it's settled.'

They returned to Elm Ridge to a huge welcome from Nancy, overjoyed, 'to have some life in the place again', as she said to Faye over a coffee in the kitchen.

'He's been like a bear with a sore head since you all left. Not that he was ever exactly sweetness and light.'

'He was, once,' Faye mused, then stopped. She'd promised herself not to start looking back, no matter how much the house affected her.

But he *had* been different: not sweetness and light, but generous and passionately loving to her. So many nights of physical rapture in the perfect union of their bodies. So many days of sadness as their minds and hearts grew further apart.

Adrian and Cindy eagerly took possession of their old rooms, then introduced Barker to the huge garden, which he tore around as madly as a puppy. This resulted in his first meeting with Fred, who came in two afternoons a week to keep the grounds in order. Fred was a grumpy individual who had his own views on dogs who trampled across his freshly weeded flower beds, and he expressed them loudly. But by then Barker was out of earshot.

Faye was touched to see that Garth had had her room redecorated in her favourite autumnal colours. On the dressing table lay a gift box, containing a set of emerald earrings.

'They're a welcome present,' he said from the doorway. He seemed almost nervous. 'I can show my gratitude, can't I?'

'Garth, they're really beautiful, and it was sweet of you to think of it, but—'

'Just try them on.'

'You don't have anything to be grateful for. You know why I'm here. I don't think I can accept these.' She extended her hand, with the box.

'Look,' he said with almost a touch of desperation, 'it's your birthday next week. Call it an early birthday present. The children will notice if I don't give you something.'

'You can give me something small. I can't take these.'

He was pale. 'Just as you wish.'

For a moment her resolution faltered. There was a look on his face that took her by surprise. Years ago he'd gone without lunch for a week to buy her a special gift, which had broken as soon as it was opened. His expression then had been the same as now, the look of a hurt boy. He controlled it so quickly that Faye wasn't sure she'd seen it, but she spoke her next words gently. 'Garth, I did tell you—'

'Yes, you made your position very plain. I just hadn't expected you to be so—so unyielding.'

'Maybe I was too yielding in the past.'

'Well, you're sure making up for it now,' he said, going to the door. 'And don't worry. I'm still sleeping in the room downstairs.'

Barker might be a daft mutt, as Faye often complained, but he had a sense of self-preservation that made him spend the first week wooing Nancy. In a few days she'd progressed from 'Get your muddy paws out of my kitchen,' to 'Poor doggie, don't they ever feed you?'

During that week Faye saw little of Garth. She was left in peace to settle herself into her old home, and after the first day she found she could cope. She was grateful for Garth's reticence. On the odd occasions when he was around, he gave all his attention to the children and maintained a civil distance from herself.

Cindy and Adrian were so happy, especially with the huge garden, that Faye knew a twinge of guilt. Had she been selfish in taking them away from this lovely setting? But then she thought of Kendall's spacious premises and his collection of rescued animals. The children loved his home. They would be just as happy there when the time came.

Two days before her birthday Garth gave her his present early. It was a computer, identical to his own, that would be a boon for her book-keeping work. But Faye's reaction was divided between pleasure at the gleaming monster and a suspicion that Garth was muscling in on her territory.

'It's another takeover bid, isn't it?' she demanded.

'What was that?'

'It's a show of power. You're saying that I can't even manage my trivial little job without your guiding hand.'

'Well, I'll be—!' he exclaimed angrily. 'Your tortuous mind is something I'll never figure out. You bend my ear about your independence, and how I'm holding you back. Well, I'll tell you what's holding you back: that steam-age machine you're using! You need a better one. *I was trying to be nice, for Pete's sake!*'

He stormed out, slamming the door. Shocked, Faye realized that he was genuinely upset. She stood for a moment, undecided, before following him into his study.

'I'm sorry,' she said at once. 'I shouldn't have said what I did.'

'You really have got me down as a villain, haven't you?'

'It was unforgivable of me,' she said contritely.

His mouth twisted. 'I never found anything you did unforgivable. But I will if you refuse it.'

She smiled. 'I'm not going to refuse it. I'm going to ask you to show me how to work it.'

'Now you're talking.'

The children were fascinated by the machine, but scandalized to discover what it was for.

'Daddies don't give mummies computers for their birthdays,' Cindy protested.

'You think I should give her something more personal?' Garth mused. 'I'll bear it in mind.'

The next morning Faye was deep in work when the phone rang in Garth's study. Nancy was out shopping

and Faye was alone in the house. She hurried in and
snatched the receiver up so quickly that she dropped it.
The weight pulled the whole machine off the desk, forcing her to scrabble on the floor. By the time she'd retrieved everything the woman on the other end was already talking.

'Couldn't think where you'd got to.' She gave a husky
laugh. She sounded young, and there was a note of intimacy in her voice. 'You're usually so punctual that we
could set the clock by you.'

'Excuse me?' Faye said.

After a brief pause the woman said, 'I thought I was
talking to Mr Clayton. Evidently not.'

'No, I'm—'

'I've called to find out if anything's happened to him.
He's usually at work by now.'

'He left at the usual time this morning,' Faye said.
'Perhaps he got stuck in some traffic. By the way, my
name's—'

'He's got a client due in a few minutes,' the young
woman cut across her. 'It's not like him to miss an appointment.'

'Then I'm sure he'll be there,' Faye replied in a voice
that held an edge of annoyance at the woman's rudeness.
'Are you his secretary?'

'Don't be ridiculous,' the young woman said frostily.
'Of course I'm not a secretary. I am Lysandra Bates, the
Director of Publicity for Clayton Properties. I can't
waste time talking. If Garth calls, I want you to give him
a message from me.'

'I'm afraid I'm not a secretary either,' Faye said, feeling bolshie.

'All right, all right, so you're the housekeeper, cleaning woman, whatever,' Lysandra snapped. 'And I sug-

gest you keep a civil tongue in your head, whoever you are. Write this down, and don't waste any more of my time.'

'Actually, I'm Garth's wife,' Faye said, goaded into one of her rare tempers.

She had the satisfaction of knowing that she'd silenced the other woman. After a moment Lysandra Bates said tensely, 'I had no idea— That is, I understood— *Mr Clayton, I've been worried about you.*' She turned back to the phone. 'He's just arrived. Crisis over.'

'I'm so glad,' Faye said politely.

'Good day to you.'

'And good day to *you*,' Faye murmured, regarding the phone, which had gone dead before she could reply.

Nancy put her head around the door. 'I'm back. Want a coffee?'

'Yes please, and make it strong. I need something after that. Have you come across Lysandra Bates, Nancy?'

'Oh, her,' Nancy said in a voice of deep significance.

'I didn't like her either,' Faye said, following Nancy into the kitchen. 'She thought I was the housekeeper.'

'And she talked as if she had a bad smell under her nose,' Nancy supplied.

'Exactly. She's obviously called before. So how come she didn't realize that I wasn't you? Our voices are quite different.'

'She wouldn't notice that, although goodness knows, she's telephoned often enough. To Miss Bates all underlings are beneath her notice.'

'You say she telephones often?'

'Every time she can find an excuse. Once, she turned up with some papers she *said* Mr Clayton needed. I thought he looked a bit surprised myself. Oh, she'd like to make herself at home here. But of course,' she added hastily, 'it's all on her side.'

'It's all right, Nancy,' Faye said, amused. 'You know this situation isn't permanent.' She'd taken Nancy into her confidence days ago.

'But he wants you back,' Nancy said, scandalized. 'You know he does.'

'Hmm. Just the same, I wouldn't put it past him to have my replacement lined up to massage his ego, just in case. I don't mind if they get together. I just didn't like her being rude to me, that's all.'

'There's nothing in it,' Nancy said firmly. 'Just because she's got an eye for the boss, it doesn't mean that he's got an eye for her.'

'I've told you, I don't care if he is interested in another woman,' Faye said, a tad more sharply than she'd intended.

Nancy gave her an appraising glance, but had the tact to let the subject drop.

When Garth returned that night Faye told him about the call, not mentioning Lysandra's rudeness but only his mysterious lateness for work. To her surprise he reddened, mumbled something and quickly changed the subject.

'I wanted to talk about your birthday,' he said. 'I'd like us to have a family evening out, rather than have you spend it with Haines.'

'That's fine,' she said. 'I was planning to stay with the children anyway.'

He hesitated. 'And you don't mind if I tag along?'

'The kids will never forgive you if you don't.'

The following day he offered Faye a tiny gold watch, delicate, restrained, and impossible to refuse.

'That's why I was late for work yesterday morning,'

he admitted. 'I had to go to three shops to find the right one.' Then, seeing her astonished face, he added hastily, 'But it's just a trifle. Nothing that you can't accept.'

Three shops, she mused. Late for work. *Garth?*

She wore the watch to the restaurant, where the whole family went to celebrate that night. It was a pleasant time, with Garth at his best, talking to Faye in a general way that didn't create any awkwardness, and listening attentively to his children.

'Are you getting excited about Cornwall?' he asked, and both youngsters grinned with delight at the prospect of the school camping trip to come.

But then Cindy said worriedly, 'Will Barker be all right without us?'

'Don't worry, you can leave everything to me,' Garth said easily. He saw Faye's lips twitching and said defensively, 'I can be good at things if I set my mind to it.'

'I know you can,' she admitted.

The meal went slowly, because at every course Cindy insisted on a doggy bag to take some home to Barker.

'What happens if *we* want to eat something?' Garth enquired in a spirit of curiosity. 'This is supposed to be your mother's birthday treat.'

'But Daddy, poor Barker's all alone at home,' Cindy pointed out.

'Well, at least he didn't try to get into the car with us this time,' Garth said with a grin.

'Yes, it was strange how quiet he was,' Faye mused.

'I think this is the best mummy's birthday ever,' Cindy said blissfully. 'And mine was the best *me* birthday ever.'

'What about that time I gave you a bike?' Garth asked. 'You were pretty pleased with that.'

'Oh, yes, it was a lovely bike,' Cindy said politely.

Too late he realized he'd put his foot in it. That had been her last birthday before the split, and he'd spent it the other side of the world. Faye had presented the bike. He sought back for a better birthday memory, and was shocked that he couldn't find one. Surely he couldn't have failed her every time?

'All right,' he said, remembering something with relief. 'How about that birthday when we all went to a burger bar. We had a great time, and I got stomachache from eating burgers and ice cream.'

Cindy crowed with laughter. 'Oh, Daddy, you were so funny that night.'

They'd all made silly jokes and laughed madly. It had been a great night out.

'There you are then. Wasn't that your best birthday?'

But Cindy shook her head. 'That was Adrian's birthday,' she said, not complaining but simply stating the fact.

'Oh, yes,' he said awkwardly, 'so it was.'

He had not seen Faye making frantic signals to him. His heart sank. When had he ever been there for Cindy? He hadn't even bothered to keep her photograph, although he had Adrian's, and Faye's too, hidden away in a drawer where nobody could discover it.

Now he remembered the one time he'd had an attack of conscience, buying her some pretty gift in town, only to discover that it was something she already had, without his even knowing. Faye had told him that. Cindy hadn't mentioned it, only rejoiced over her present like someone offered water in the desert.

Under the table he squeezed her hand, and was rewarded by a look of glowing happiness. For her, the past was forgotten, all swept away by the pleasure of his presence now. What must it be like to be able to forgive so easily?

To cover his confusion he raised his glass and said, 'Happy birthday to Mummy!'

Everyone chorused, 'Happy birthday!' and the moment passed.

The rest of the evening went merrily. When it was time to go, the children solemnly took possession of three doggy bags, treasuring them like gold, and carried them out to the car.

'Not on my freshly cleaned upholstery, *please*,' Garth said faintly.

Nancy had gone to visit her sister. When they drove past the railway station Faye spotted her coming out and they stopped to collect her. As they neared Elm Ridge they were astonished to see two police cars and four men.

'My name's Hallam,' a policeman said as Garth jumped out of the car. 'Your burglar alarm went off in the station. Someone's broken into your house. We're going to investigate.'

Faye and Garth insisted on coming too, leaving the children in Nancy's care. The house was in darkness and looked as always except that the French windows, which opened inward, stood gaping wide.

Quietly they slipped into the dark house and moved up the stairs. A muffled noise came from Cindy's bedroom. 'In there,' Hallam whispered. He took a deep breath and charged into the bedroom. *'OK! Nobody move! You're nicked.'*

The silence that followed had a stunned quality. Following quietly, Garth and Faye were aghast to see Barker stretched out on Cindy's bed, regarding them with sleepy surprise.

Hallam spoke through gritted teeth. *'You left your dog out, sir!'*

Faye crept tactfully away, pausing in the hall to call Nancy on the car phone, and telling her to bring the children in. She made coffee, which slightly mollified the police. But before they departed, Hallam paused in the doorway to say stiffly, 'Perhaps you'd like to consider having your burglar alarm disconnected from the station, sir? *Soon!*'

'Who left that wretched animal out?' Garth demanded when they were alone.

'It was you, Mummy,' Cindy claimed reproachfully. 'You called up the stairs, "Barker's in."'

Faye groaned. 'No, I said, "*Check* that Barker's in." I thought you were going to do it.'

'So nobody did it,' Garth said. 'When he found himself locked out, he simply charged the French windows until they burst open.'

He regarded the miscreant who'd eaten the contents of the doggy bags, and was now making a start on the bags themselves. 'Call yourself a guard dog!' he said accusingly. 'You're supposed to scare intruders away, not open the doors and invite them in.'

'Daddy, are you cross with Barker?' Cindy asked.

'Whatever for?' Garth demanded wildly. 'He's only broken into the house, made a mockery of my alarm system, and turned me into the butt of the local police.' He saw her looking worried and took her into the circle of his arm. 'It's all right, pet. He's forgiven.'

His reward was an eager hug. Even Adrian made a small concession, squeezing his father's shoulder as he went past. Faye followed them upstairs, where Nancy had just finished changing Cindy's bed linen.

'I'm sorry Barker gave you that extra work,' Faye said.

'It's no matter,' Nancy said, casting a benevolent eye on the culprit, who'd trotted up after Cindy. 'The poor dog was lonely.' She scratched Barker's head and he responded with a sigh in which fidelity, forgiveness and noble endurance were perfectly mixed. 'You come with Nancy, darling, and she'll find you a special titbit, to make up for all you've been through.'

CHAPTER FIVE

WHEN Faye had seen the children tucked up she returned downstairs, where Garth was on the sofa drinking brandy. He handed her a glass of sherry that he'd poured for her.

'I thought you might need something to recover,' he said.

'Shall I check that everything's locked up?'

'No, I've just done it. Though it seems a wasted effort,' he observed wryly, 'since we have a dog that's keeping open house. What's so funny?' Faye had given a choke of laughter.

'I'm sorry,' she said. 'I was just trying to recall who said that once we were at Elm Ridge Barker couldn't cause any more trouble.'

Garth grinned. 'He was a short-sighted fool, whoever he was.'

'Oh, dear! That policeman's face!'

He gave a shout of laughter.

'Hush, you'll rouse the house,' she said, but her own mirth was bubbling up. She met his eye and suddenly the joke became hilarious. She leaned back against the sofa and laughed until she nearly cried. To her delight Garth was afflicted the same way. He gripped her hand, and she clasped him back, sharing the moment.

When the attack passed they sat together, giving vent to the occasional chuckle. His glance fell on her hand, still held in his. He grew quite still, then he raised it and brushed it against his cheek.

'What happened?' he asked quietly. 'Once, we were always laughing like that. Where did we lose it?'

At first she couldn't answer. His gesture had taken her breath away.

'It disappeared bit by bit,' she said slowly. 'We grew in different directions.'

'But did we have to? Couldn't we have stopped it?'

'I don't know,' she sighed. 'Perhaps we couldn't. We wanted such different things.'

'I never knew that,' he said after a while. 'I thought we wanted the same.'

'I tried to. When I couldn't see things your way, I pretended I did. But the pretence became too much. Something had to give. I know now that I was never the wife for you.'

'I don't believe that,' he said simply.

He raised her hand again, brushing his lips over the back of it. It was a tender, rather than a lover-like gesture. Garth seemed lost in some private dream, only half-knowing what he did. But Faye was intensely aware of his touch, of the sudden beating of her heart, and of a feeling of danger. For a moment she wanted nothing so much as to throw herself into his arms. But she backed away from the feeling.

'It was a lovely evening, wasn't it?' he said.

'It was wonderful,' she told him sincerely.

He looked down at the hand still clasped in his. It was her left, and a band encircled her wedding finger. 'That's not my ring. Did he give it to you?'

'No. I bought it from a market stall.'

'You don't really belong to either of us, huh?'

'Just myself, for a while. I think I should go to bed now. Thank you for a lovely evening, Garth.'

With an almost inaudible sigh her released her. 'Goodnight, Faye.'

She slipped away hurriedly and didn't stop until she'd closed the door of her bedroom behind her. In a few short moments Garth had approached the very heart that she'd shielded against him. She hadn't meant to let it happen, but his gentle, almost wistful, tenderness had taken her by surprise.

The feelings coursing through her were devastating: an irrational sense of happiness, hope, expectancy. Like a giddy teenager, she thought, when the idol first glanced her way. Like herself, ten years ago. Was that why she had the shocking feeling that she'd betrayed Kendall?

But the children needed their parents to be friendly, she reminded herself. When the divorce finally came, they would be happier, knowing that they didn't have to divide their loyalties.

So that was all right, she thought, with relief. She was only doing what was best for Cindy and Adrian and there was no need to feel guilty.

The end of the school term was in sight. The children had started marking off the days and chanting, 'Twelve more days to the holidays. Eleven more days to the holidays. Ten more days...'

'Mummy, have you signed our forms?' Adrian asked one morning as they were leaving the breakfast table. Garth had already departed.

'Forms?' Faye asked blankly.

'The forms about the end of term party,' Adrian explained. 'You're supposed to sign them to say it's all right for us to be home late that day. We have to take them back this morning.'

'Oh, yes, let me find them.'

'I've just put them in front of you,' Adrian said patiently.

'Sorry. Yes. Fine.' Faye hastily signed, aware that her children were giving her puzzled looks.

'Are you all right, Mummy?' Adrian asked.

'Of course I am, darling.'

'It's just that you've been funny lately,' Cindy said. 'You keep going all vague.'

'Nonsense,' Faye said, shaken by her daughter's perception.

'You do, Mummy,' Adrian insisted. 'We say things, and you don't answer.'

'I've got a lot on my mind. Now come on, you kids. I'm going out to warm the engine. You have ten seconds to explain to Barker that you aren't abandoning him for ever. And Cindy, please try to get it through to him this time, because I don't want any more scratch marks on my car.'

She escaped with relief, but she couldn't relax until she'd delivered them to school and could be alone. It was true that she'd been in a strange mood recently. Since the night of her birthday her mind had been troubled, and so had her heart.

Garth had argued and fought her for weeks and she'd held him off. But that night he'd spoken to her quietly and with a touch of wistfulness. For a few minutes she could almost have believed that the man she'd loved still lived somewhere deep in his shell. When he'd brushed her hand against his cheek in unconscious echo of their first date, her confusion had been so great she'd almost snatched her hand away.

She was in more danger now than she'd been since she confronted him two months ago. Suddenly her heart was dreaming impossible dreams, the kind she'd thought she'd put away for ever. Her head was protesting, telling her to see reason, but the voice of common sense was alarmingly faint.

She ought to visit Kendall and let him reassure her. But suddenly she felt unable to look Kendall in the face.

When she reached home she went, as if by instinct, into the room where she and Garth had sat together that night. There was the sofa on which he'd taken her hand...

Her eyes fell on a folder of papers. She'd seen Garth bring it out of his study that very morning, ready to take to work. And he'd left it behind.

Faye snatched up the phone and dialled his office. She was put through to Mary, Garth's secretary, a pleasant, middle-aged woman whom Faye had met several times and liked.

'Mr Clayton is in a meeting and said he wasn't to be disturbed,' she said. 'Can I help?'

Faye was about to tell her about the papers when she was stopped by the memory of a similar incident, years ago. Garth had been annoyed that she'd innocently revealed to one of his staff that he'd made a mistake. It was part of his creed never to show weakness to employees.

'I really do need to speak to him,' she persisted. 'It's very important.'

'Just one moment.'

Mary's voice became fainter, as though she'd turned away. 'It's Mrs Clayton. What shall I do? He said no interruptions.'

From far back in the room Faye could hear another voice that she recognized as Lysandra Bates. 'Go carefully. She's got to be kept sweet. The anniversary range is really important to Garth. I'd better talk to her myself.'

There was a scuffling sound as the phone changed hands, then the woman spoke again in a tone of professional amiability.

'Good afternoon, Mrs Clayton. I'm Lysandra Bates.'

'Yes, we've talked before,' Faye said pleasantly.

'Oh, that hardly counts, does it?' Lysandra said with a small laugh. 'I've been looking forward to meeting you properly, so that we can talk about the arrangements.'

'Arrangements?' Faye asked.

'The publicity arrangements for the anniversary range. It's so delightful that your tenth wedding anniversary coincides with our new range of family houses. I expect Garth has told you that they're going to be marketed with an emphasis on the stability of family life, and a couple who've been married for ten years just epitomizes stability, don't you think?'

Nobody could have guessed from her tone that only recently she'd been shocked to discover that Faye had returned to her husband's home.

'I'm not quite sure,' Faye said very slowly. She was controlling her words, because the thought that was forming in her head was surely too monstrous to be true.

'Well, I expect you find it hard to visualize,' Lysandra Bates conceded in her sweet, icy voice. 'It'll be easier for you when you see everything laid out. The gist of it is that these are houses where couples will want to raise their families, and no one knows that better than the man who built them, and who's celebrating his own tenth wedding anniversary. And, of course, the children. I am right about that, aren't I? You have two adorable children.'

'I do have two children, but I don't want them made a part of any publicity campaign.'

'Well, we can discuss that later,' Lysandra said dismissively. 'I thought you and I might have lunch one day, to discuss how your anniversary should be presented. My diary's a bit full, but what would you say to the week after next?'

'I'm afraid not.'

'Well, I suppose it's a little far ahead. Perhaps I could squeeze you in—'

'Please don't trouble yourself,' Faye said firmly. 'I'm sure you're much too busy. Good day.'

She hung up and sat there, stunned, thinking how easily she'd been taken in! What a blind fool, to imagine that Garth had changed! She'd known what he was like, yet still she'd let him delude her with a few clever words and a show of attention to Cindy and Adrian.

But underneath he was as bad as ever. No, worse! To exploit his neglected children and his mockery of a marriage, showing the world a false picture of harmony, so that he could make money; even she had never thought he could do anything so monstrous. She could have wept to think of the feelings that had lit up the world for her recently. And it had all been a wicked mockery.

Garth was late home that night and Faye waited until he'd said goodnight to the children before she spoke to him.

'You're very quiet,' he observed.

'That's because I've been doing a lot of thinking.'

'About us?'

'About you. There is no "us", and there never will be.'

Something in her voice made him look at her sharply. 'What's up?'

'I've discovered the nasty little game you're playing.'

'Faye, what are you talking about? What "game"? I'm not playing games.'

'Oh, no, the making of money is deadly serious to you, isn't it? How stupid of me to forget it!'

'What's happened?' he asked quietly.

'I called you at work today. You left your papers behind on the sofa. But you were in a meeting and couldn't be disturbed.'

He made a sound of annoyance. 'I'm sorry about that. They should have put you through. Next time—'

'Garth, it's not about that. It's about the anniversary range—or should I say, the *tenth* anniversary range?'

He drew in a sharp breath. 'Damn!'

'Miss Bates naturally assumed I knew, since I'm part of the publicity. I'd have to be, wouldn't I, since you're featuring your happy, united family?'

'Faye, will you just hear me out? I was going to tell you at the proper time, in the proper way.'

'And what would have been the proper time and way to tell your wife that you've been going through the motions of wanting her back so that you could exploit her, and your children? It's all been a wicked pretence; the charming husband, the attentive father—anything to get us back under this roof in time for the press campaign. No wonder you pulled every trick! How could you have sold yourself as the perfect family man while we were living apart?'

'Will you let me speak? It's not the way you think—'

'Garth, you don't know what I think because if you did, you'd shrivel up inside.'

'That's why I didn't tell you before. I knew you'd misunderstand. This isn't a deep laid plot. Actually, it was you who put the idea into my head.'

'Oh, please—'

'It's true. When you came here that first night, every-thing you said about the tenth anniversary—I'd been searching for an angle for this range and suddenly it all fell into place.'

'And of course you had to make use of it.'

'Yes, I did. You know what I'm like. If a good idea comes to me I'll go for it. You solved a problem I'd been racking my brains over. It was almost like Providence, as though you'd been sent.'

'If that's how you think, I don't wonder you see me only as an adjunct to your business. I came here to talk about the end of a relationship that once meant some-thing to both of us, and you thought Providence had sent me to solve your marketing problems. What were you doing when you kissed me? Conducting a feasibility test?'

'How dare you say that?' he snapped. 'That kiss was real. You knew that at the time; we both did.'

'Nonsense! You were faking. *And so was I.*'

Garth grew very pale and there was a look in his eyes that she'd never seen before. 'Would you like to prove that, right now?'

'Not now or ever. I'll never kiss you again, Garth. It's over. Finished. If there was any hope we could get back together, this kills it. I'm going to have that divorce, any way I can.'

'All right,' he said unexpectedly. 'I'll give you one.'

'What?'

'I'm offering you a deal. Stay here just a few weeks longer. Help me out with this publicity. Play my "game" if you're so sure that's what it is. Then you can have a divorce on any terms you like.'

'I don't believe you,' Faye said slowly. 'This is an-other trick.'

'I swear it isn't. An easy divorce. Your terms. The only condition I make is that afterwards I see my kids as often as I want—as often as *they* want. And I'll want to see them plenty.'

'You'd better. If you let them down I'll never forgive you.'

'I won't let them down, Faye. Things have changed. You think it's all been an act, but it hasn't. I've learned to appreciate them now and I'm grateful to you for helping me do that. But I need your help again, one last time. Cooperate over the tenth anniversary, and I'll never ask you for anything else again.'

'What exactly do you want me to do?'

'Stay here. Let the world think we're a happy family. And don't see Kendall Haines.'

Faye gave a bitter laugh to cover the pain. 'I see. This is nothing but an excuse to stop me seeing my fiancé.'

'Don't call him that,' Garth snapped.

'It's what he is. Oh, Garth, you're so transparent! You really thought I'd be daft enough to fall for this one? Kendall is the man I'm going to marry and you're not going to separate me from him. And if that spoils your publicity, why don't you hire someone from Central Casting? She'd probably make a better job of pretending to be your wife than I would.'

'You don't give an inch, do you?' Garth said bitterly.

'I feel safer that way.'

She left the room before he could answer and slipped away into the grounds, where she could lose herself among the bushes. At last she sat down on a tree stump and stared out at the stars. It was all so beautiful and peaceful, but there was no peace in her heart.

She covered her eyes, trying to fight back the tears.

She knew that only strength would help her now, but she didn't seem to have any left.

She felt a freezing shock against her fingers, as though an ice cube had touched them. It turned out to be Barker's nose. He'd followed her.

'It's all right,' she said, drying her eyes. 'Everything's fine.'

He pushed his head under her hand and looked at her out of beautiful eyes. He didn't believe her.

'You're a lovely old boy, aren't you?' Faye said, putting her arms around him. It was a relief to hug the sturdy body and hide her face in his thick coat. Barker's tail thumped the ground. He was doing what he did best.

As a child, Faye had confided her small tragedies to an all-wise teddy bear. Now there was Barker, warm and responsive, who would listen without judgement and break no confidences.

'I've been so stupid,' she told him sadly. 'I thought I was strong enough to cope with Garth, but I was kidding myself. I wanted him to be like he was before: wonderful. And that was really silly of me, wasn't it?'

His eyes were so full of understanding that it was almost as if he'd spoken. *Anyone had the right to be silly.*

'Yes, but I was worse than silly, because I know what he's like, yet I still let myself— Well, anyway it's over between us.'

A small crease appeared between Barker's eyes. *Sure about that?*

'It was over two years ago,' she said, fondling his soft ears. 'I love Kendall now.'

At the sound of Kendall's name, Barker gave the soft, yearning woof of a dog who'd discovered aniseed and never forgotten his benefactor.

'You're perfectly right,' Faye said, brightening. 'Kendall's the one I need to talk to.' She rubbed Barker's head gratefully. 'Why didn't I think of that myself?'

He sighed. *Because you're not crazy about aniseed.*

She knew Garth was watching as she drove away. He would guess, of course, where she was going but she was too angry to care.

Kendall received her news thoughtfully. 'And this way we'd be sure of getting the divorce?' he asked.

'So he says. How do I know he'd stick to that?'

'Oddly enough, I believe he would. I don't like your husband, but I think he's a man of his word.'

'You're right,' Faye said slowly. 'But still—it would mean we wouldn't be able to see each other for weeks.'

'We might sneak the occasional meeting.'

'No,' she said regretfully. 'I can't expect Garth to keep his word if I don't keep mine. We must stay apart, to make sure we can be together afterwards.'

'As long as it doesn't go on too long,' he said. 'You know this is a risk. If you don't love me as much as you say—'

'But I do,' she said firmly. 'You know that.'

'Yes, of course I do.'

Barker greeted her as soon as she returned home, eagerly sniffing her hands and pockets. When he found no aniseed he gave her the indignant look of a dog who'd been thoroughly conned. Faye pushed him aside with difficulty and went to Garth's study, firmly shutting the door.

Despite the late hour he was still up, working. He pushed the work away and regarded her tensely. He looked tired and he'd torn open the front of his shirt, as though he needed to breathe more easily.

'I've been to see Ken,' she told him. 'We've talked it over and he thinks I should do this. So you've got your deal.'

Instead of pleasing Garth, this seemed to annoy him. 'I don't need that man's permission for anything I want to do,' he growled.

'Not his permission, his blessing,' she retorted. 'I wouldn't do it without that. You said yourself I don't belong to either of you. But if I did it would be Ken, not you.'

'You'll never belong to any other man,' Garth said with a sudden flash of temper. 'As long as I want you, *you belong to me*.'

'As long as you want me,' Faye echoed. 'But you didn't want me very long, did you, Garth? Not really want *me*. A mother to your children, yes. But when I grew up you were either hostile or indifferent. A divorce will be as good for you as for me. Then you can marry a doll who'll never answer back.'

'You know nothing about me if you can say a damned fool thing like that.'

'Well, perhaps I never did really know you,' she agreed. 'Or you me. It's better this way. I'll stay with you until the marketing campaign is launched, but only to get the divorce. And I have conditions too.'

'Which are?'

'We leave the children out of it. They're not going to be involved in the publicity. And I won't stop them seeing Ken.'

'I'd rather they didn't.'

'I'm sorry, those are my terms. They like him. Cindy calls him for advice about Barker and Adrian is involved with one of Ken's countryside campaigns. I don't want you worrying them with our private quarrels.'

'And the other condition?' he asked.

'You stay right away from me, or the deal's off.'

'I suppose Haines thought of that one?'

'No, it's all my own idea. I want your solemn promise.'

He sighed. 'Very well. You have my word.'

'So that's settled.' She waited, wondering if he would say something more, but he only shrugged. Once Garth had concluded a deal on the best terms he could get, it wasn't his way to waste time on a post-mortem.

'I hope this means that we won't argue so much, Garth.'

'I've never liked arguing with you.'

'No, you just prefer me to give in without a fight,' she said lightly. 'But this is a business arrangement. Nothing more.'

'Nothing more,' he murmured.

'I'll keep my side and I expect you to keep yours.'

Garth leaned back and regarded her with a wry grin. 'You've become a tough negotiator. You know what you want, and you won't settle for less.'

'You should offer me a job with your firm. I seem to have all the qualifications.'

'Well, maybe I— What the devil is the matter with that dog? He's been trying to scratch the door down ever since you came in here.'

'I'll see to him, then I'm going to bed.'

'Won't you join me in a drink, to celebrate our deal?'

She hesitated. 'No, but I'll shake hands with you, if you will.'

He looked at her little hand, firmly outstretched to him. After a while he took it gently in his own. 'To business,' he said.

'To business. Goodnight, Garth.' She left the room

without looking back, so she didn't see him staring after her.

She had a curious sensation of light-headedness. It felt good to have made a stand, and actually stopped the Garth Clayton juggernaut in its tracks.

She wasn't left to muse for long. Barker, bent on sorting out the misunderstanding, followed her upstairs and waited determinedly in the hall while she kissed her sleeping children.

When she emerged he planted himself firmly in her path. But this, too, failed. Faye hugged him and called him loving names, but there was no aniseed. At last he accepted the perfidy of humans, and retired to his basket in a huff.

CHAPTER SIX

IT WAS halfway through Saturday morning when Garth received a phone call from Bill, his second in command and the one person who knew all his business secrets.

'Garth, sorry to call you at home on a Saturday.'

'That's all right. You know I'm never really off duty.'

'I tried the office first. It felt strange not to find you there.'

'Yes, I've been spending a little more time at home recently,' Garth said, hoping his edginess couldn't be heard in his voice. He'd made a special effort to be at home today, meaning to spend some time with his son, only to find that Adrian had other plans. Even Cindy wasn't there to support him, having taken Barker to spend the day with Jenny Patterson, her best friend.

An hour later Kendall had collected the boy in his old van. Garth had longed for Adrian to tell him where they were going and why, but when he didn't Garth shrugged and refused to show how much he minded.

'What's it all about?' he asked now.

'It's the Outland,' Bill said, naming a patch of land about twenty miles away on which Garth intended to build. 'We may have more of a problem than we thought.'

'We've had problems since the day I offered for the place, but nothing that can't be overcome. First they claimed it was a famous beauty spot, though no one I spoke to had ever heard of it. Then they wanted to have the trees protected. Last week they burst into the council meeting and tried to stop me getting planning permission. But I got it anyway.'

'With some restrictions,' Bill pointed out. 'They may not look much, but they're going to cramp your style.'

'Not if I get them lifted, and I will. Trust me. I know the people to work on. So what is it this time?'

'Butterflies. The Outland is supposed to be the habitat of a rare breed.'

Garth groaned, muttering, 'Give me patience,' under his breath. Aloud he said, 'Stop worrying, Bill. If I wasn't put off by that bearded yob jabbing a placard in my eye and calling me a destroyer of creation, I think I can cope with a few butterflies.'

'I thought you should know that there's going to be a protest march at the Outland this afternoon. I tried to get the police to ban it, but no luck.'

'I wouldn't have done that, myself. It makes them look as if we're afraid of them.'

'Yes, but the television cameras will be there. It'll be on the news tonight.'

'Pity! But it can't do us any real harm. Thanks for letting me know, anyway.'

Later that afternoon Faye brought him a coffee and found him engrossed in the television screen.

'You always said watching the box in the afternoon was a dangerous habit,' she reminded him. 'According to you, it led to self-indulgence and time-wasting.'

'There's a news item that I need to see. I've taken an option on a strip of land and apparently a set of long-haired clowns are tramping over it, predicting the end of the world if I'm allowed to build there. There it is!'

The screen was occupied by a board, bearing the name Melkham Construction, set in an expanse of countryside.

Beside it stood an earnest young man addressing the camera.

'The protesters say that if this land falls victim to developers' frenzy it will be the destruction of a unique butterfly habitat—'

'Developers' frenzy,' Garth repeated angrily. 'I build houses for people to live in; people like that sanctimonious crowd. Where would they live if no one had built *their* homes? With the butterflies, I suppose! *GOOD GRIEF*!'

Startled, Faye followed his gaze and saw what had appalled him. The screen was filled with placards whose owners were hoisting them aloft, trying to catch the cameraman's eye. With an inward groan Faye saw that one of them was Kendall and right beside him, his face shining with enthusiasm, was Adrian. His placard bore the uncompromising words, GREED OUT, NATURE IN.

Garth turned accusing eyes on Faye. 'Did you know about this?'

'Of course I didn't. I knew Ken was going to some sort of ecology protest and Adrian begged to go with him. I think they mentioned the name Melkham, but I didn't connect it with you. You're Clayton Properties.'

'Melkham is a subsidiary. I acquired it last year.'

'Well, I didn't know that. Nor did Adrian.'

'I'll bet Kendall Haines knew, though. He must have loved getting my son to demonstrate against me in public.'

'Not everybody's mind is as tortuous as yours,' Faye said indignantly. 'Kendall is a decent, straightforward man. He'd never pull a stunt like that.'

'I wonder.'

'Garth, you're being impossible. Kendall fights for

what he believes in and so does Adrian. You should be proud of your son. He's one of life's dragon slayers. How was he to know that you were the dragon? He'd be interested to find out.'

'And if I don't tell him, I'm sure you will.'

'Goodness, no! I won't say a word. You must deal with this in your own way. But go carefully. Your son is no fool.'

At the end of the afternoon she drove to the Pattersons' to collect Cindy and Barker. Cindy chattered non-stop about her day but, as soon as she was home, she ran to her father to say it all again. Garth hugged her and Faye was relieved to see that his mood had improved. Barker had vanished to the kitchen, to be lovingly scolded for his muddy paws and fed some of his favourite buttered scones.

'Can we go out and play ball with Barker?' Cindy begged when she was sure she hadn't deprived Daddy of a single detail.

'I thought he'd been chasing around a garden all day.'

'Yes, but it's a very posh garden with lots of potted plants—'

'Oh, heavens!' Faye groaned.

'It wasn't Barker's fault. He didn't mean to knock it over, and he didn't know it was a prize bush.'

'No wonder Mr Patterson looked a bit tense when he said goodbye.'

'It's his own fault,' Garth observed. 'He should have known better than to leave his prize bush around when Barker was there.'

Cindy flung him a grateful look. 'Anyway, Barker wants to run and run in his own garden.'

'Can't you play with him?'

'You can throw the ball further than me. I'll go and get it.' She scampered off.

'Better get two,' Garth called. 'You know he always loses one.'

'Thanks, Daddy.' Her voice faded down the hall.

'I've got a pile of bookkeeping work to do,' Faye protested to thin air.

'Mummy!' came Cindy's imperious voice before Faye could answer. 'Barker wants to *play*.'

Garth grinned wickedly. 'Go on,' he told her. 'You've got your orders. That dog wants to play, and his social secretary is going to make sure everyone jumps to attention.'

'*Mummy—*'

'Coming, coming!'

Faye obediently headed for the garden and threw the ball for half an hour. Although she was annoyed with Garth, she had to admit he was spot on about Cindy. Nothing mattered to the little girl except giving her four-pawed darling whatever he wanted. She smiled with pleasure at the sight of child and dog romping together in perfect understanding.

Then her smile faded into a frown at something she thought she'd seen. She watched Barker carefully and wondered if his back legs really were a little stiff, or was she imagining it? Then he went bounding down the garden after a ball, charging through a tall heap of twigs Fred had just finished gathering up. Fred's little dance of rage and the terrible threats he hurled at Barker's retreating form made her double up with laughter, and the matter passed from her mind.

Adrian arrived home two hours later, full of delight over his day but, to Faye's relief, minus the placard. As she'd promised Garth, she kept quiet about what she knew.

Garth seemed to have forgotten his annoyance. He asked Adrian about his afternoon and listened attentively to his replies. Faye watched a flush of pleasure come to the boy's face. To have his father showing interest in his concerns was an unexpected delight.

'It was great, Dad. We were on telly.'

'I know. I saw you. In fact, I taped it for you to see.'

Adrian beamed. 'Great! Can we see it now?'

Garth put the video tape in and they watched it together.

'That placard is good,' Garth said. 'Greed out. Nature in. Who thought of it?'

'It was Kendall's idea. He's really brilliant at that sort of thing. He says firms like Melkham are nothing but selfish, greedy predators, and they have to be fought in any way you can.'

'Has he got any good ideas about fighting them?'

'Yes, 'cos he knows something they don't.'

'What's that?'

'That bit of land is covered by a special planning act. If anyone wants to build on it they have to comply with special conditions, and they have to do it by a certain date. If they don't, they lose the chance.'

'And that date's coming up?' Garth asked in a neutral voice.

'Next Wednesday. Then Ken's going to court to say they can't do it, because the date's past.'

'That's really clever of him. But suppose Melkham knows about it?'

'Kendall says they can't do, because they'd have done something by now. He says we're going to take them completely by surprise.'

'But shouldn't Melkham's point of view be considered?' Garth asked seriously. 'After all, people need somewhere to live, as well as butterflies.'

'Kendall says it doesn't have to be there,' Adrian explained earnestly. 'Besides, it's not just houses. Melkham is going to build a shopping complex and an office block, because that's where the real money is.'

Garth became acutely aware that his wife was watching him from the doorway and at this pronouncement her eyebrows gave a cynical lift.

'How do you know that?' Garth demanded after a moment.

'Because Kendall says so.'

'But no plans have been pub— That is—he can't be certain what Melkham intends unless he's seen plans.'

'Kendall says he doesn't have to see them. He says he knows shops and offices have got to be there, because it won't be fi—' Adrian hesitated and spoke the next words slowly, 'financially viable without them. And he says the man behind it all never does anything except for money.'

'But perhaps he's got that wrong,' Garth suggested, a slight edge on his voice.

'I don't think so,' Adrian said, frowning. 'Kendall knows everything. He says—'

'Yes, fine,' Garth interrupted him restively. He felt he might do something desperate if he had to hear any more of what 'Kendall said'.

Cindy bounded in, full of delight over her brother's television appearance, and the two of them went away together to tell Barker all about it. Faye remained in the doorway, watching her husband's brooding face. At last he looked up and their eyes met.

'Shops and offices, huh?' she echoed mockingly. 'Fancy that!'

'You know nothing about how these things are done,' he growled.

'But Kendall does, doesn't he? That's why you really hate him, because he's the one person you can't fool.'

'Rubbish! It's because he's stealing my son. He's going to be very sorry about that. Adrian's having a foot in both camps can work for me, as well as against me.'

'Garth, if you make use of what that child has just told you, he'll never speak to you again,' Faye said in alarm.

'Sentimental nonsense! The sooner he learns about the real world the better.'

'And what do you think he'll do? The moment he knows what you're up to, he'll warn Kendall.'

'Don't you understand? It doesn't make any difference. Let Kendall know that I've found out. He can't stop me.'

'All right,' Faye said quietly. 'Go ahead. Use what you learned today to defeat Kendall. Let Adrian find out that you tricked him into betraying his friend. Then get yourself another son, because you'll have lost this one for ever.'

'I'm not that much of a fool. I won't alienate Adrian, but I can't just let it go at this. I've got too much money tied up in that site.'

'Then why didn't you check the legal position before you bought it?'

'I have lawyers whose job it is to do just that and, believe me, heads will roll.' He rose from the sofa. 'I'm going to make some phone calls in the study.'

Faye returned to work at her computer, trying to shrug mentally and tell herself that if Garth wanted to make his son totally disillusioned with him, it wasn't her fault. Perhaps Adrian really did need to discover how low his father could sink.

But the thought of the little boy's pain kept intruding and made it impossible to concentrate. His unhappy face was there before her inner eye, but it kept getting mixed up with Garth's face. Her husband was heading for disaster and he couldn't see it. But when it was too late and Adrian wanted nothing more to do with him, then his suffering would begin.

It was his own fault, her reasonable mind argued. He'd put their marriage on the basis of a business deal. It was time he learned the true cost of business.

If only her heart could be reasonable! It ached for her child's pain, and somehow Garth's pain was in there too, complicating everything.

She worked late, forcing herself to concentrate on figures that meant nothing beside her inner turmoil. At last she got up and went downstairs. She must make at least one more effort to help Garth see what he was doing.

But the study was in darkness. Faye could hear movement coming from his little monastic bedroom, but she stopped with her hand on the knob. Garth slept naked and, however much they'd quarrelled in the past, the sight of his head on the pillow, tousled and vulnerable-looking, had always been able to melt her heart. She couldn't bring herself to go in there.

Guiltily she realized that she'd been too preoccupied to notice the passage of time and she hadn't said goodnight to the children. She looked in on Adrian, kissed him in his sleep and crept out. But she could hear a soft murmuring from Cindy's room, as though the child was talking to someone.

'I thought so,' she said, looking around the door.

Barker was sprawled on the bed, contending with Cindy for the available space. 'Out, dog!' she commanded. 'No sleeping in here!'

Barker eyed her, and stayed where he was.

'Off!' Faye insisted, pointing to the door.

'Oh, please let him stay, Mummy,' Cindy begged.

'Not a chance. Apart from the fact that it's unhygienic, where would you sleep? You're clinging on to the edge as it is.'

'I don't mind clinging on to the edge—'

'Cindy, I'm not arguing about this. Barker has to go. Come along, make him get off.'

Cindy slid her toes beneath Barker and wriggled them, which was usually enough to make him jump down. Not this time. Cindy wriggled her toes again, but he only regarded her reproachfully. She wriggled harder, and he merely settled down more deeply.

'He doesn't want to,' Cindy said unarguably. 'It took him ages to get up. He walked around and around the bed as if he wasn't sure he could do it.'

'Oh, you are an awkward animal!' Faye sighed, putting her arms around him and heaving. Barker tried to take root, but the bedspread was slippery and he slid helplessly off onto the floor. He landed heavily and let out a squeal of pain.

'Mummy, Mummy, you hurt him!' Cindy said, jumping out of bed and throwing her arms about Barker's neck. 'You hurt him, you hurt him,' she repeated in tears.

'Darling, I didn't mean to,' Faye protested, almost as distressed as the child, for Barker was now making a pitiful wailing noise. 'Oh, you poor old boy! What did I do? I'm so sorry.'

Garth and Adrian came in, alerted by the noise.

Adrian tried to entice the dog to his feet with a titbit, but Barker seemed unable to move, even for food. That was when they knew something was really wrong.

'Mummy!' Cindy cried hysterically.

'All right, I know who can help,' Faye assured her.

Garth followed her into her bedroom, but when she reached for the telephone he stopped her. 'Who are you calling?'

'Kendall. He's a vet.'

'Barker is registered with an excellent animal hospital.'

'But it's late at night. He's in pain. He can't wait until morning.'

'He won't have to. They have a night service. I'll call them.'

'And take the poor animal there in the car, when he's like this? Oh, no! If I call Ken he'll come and see him here.'

He seized her wrist, his eyes blazing. 'Faye, that man is my enemy and hell will freeze over before I ask him for help, let alone have him in this house. I'll call the vet and get someone out here.'

He made the call at once and after a few moments handed Faye the phone. 'You'd better explain,' he said.

Faye described what had happened and the night duty vet, a pleasant-sounding woman called Miss McGeorge, said, 'That sounds familiar. If I'm right it's not serious, but I'll know more when I've seen him. Expect me in ten minutes.'

'She's coming,' Faye said as she hung up.

'So there's no need for your friend.'

'As it happens, no!' She eyed him accusingly. 'Would you really have let that poor dog suffer till morning rather than ask Kendall?'

'You obviously think I would.'

'Hell will freeze over—' she reminded him.

'Look, I don't know what I'd have done.'

'Even for Cindy?'

'I told you, I don't know,' he snapped.

Miss McGeorge arrived soon, listened to the story, then gently coaxed Barker to his feet.

'His back legs seemed a little stiff this afternoon,' Faye said self-reproachfully. 'I wish I'd called you then, but I wasn't quite sure.'

Miss McGeorge took hold of one of Barker's back legs and waggled it slightly. From under the thick fur came the sound of a sharp crack.

'Just as I thought,' she said. 'He's got a touch of arthritis. It tends to happen to elderly dogs.'

'Can you make it go away?' Cindy asked anxiously.

'I can make his pain go away,' Miss McGeorge promised. 'I can't cure the arthritis, but I'll give him an injection that will make it stop hurting for tonight. Bring him to the surgery on Monday and I'll decide what pills he needs.'

Her cheerful manner had its effect and soon after she'd given the injection and departed, Barker was visibly better. The children coaxed him back to his basket, settled him for the night and were finally persuaded to return to bed.

Faye slept for an hour, then instinct prompted her to rise and go quietly downstairs to the place where Barker's basket was kept.

'And what are you two doing down here?' she asked unnecessarily.

Two small faces looked up guiltily, then quickly assumed innocent expressions.

'We were checking that he's all right, Mummy,' Adrian said, adding cheekily, 'Just like you.'

Cindy tactfully smothered her giggle and Faye said, 'All right, funny man, how is he?'

'He's just been out into the garden,' Cindy said. 'I think he's all right.'

'What's going on?' Garth asked sleepily, appearing in his dressing gown.

They all explained and he knelt down to scratch the invalid's head. Cindy and Adrian offered biscuits, which were accepted, and Garth observed, 'He's going to make the most of this.'

'Daddy,' Cindy reproached him. 'That's not kind.'

'It's a plain statement of fact. Now his pain's gone he's loving the attention.'

'But you will take him back to the vet for his pills?' she asked worriedly.

'Of course I will.'

'He means that *I* will,' Faye said lightly. 'Daddy has to be at work.'

Garth shrugged. 'If we can set off first thing, I don't mind being an hour late.'

The children looked gratified and Adrian said, 'Thanks for calling the vet, Daddy. Is it very expensive if they come out late?'

'Never mind that.'

'But I can help, from my pocket money.'

'So can I,' Cindy volunteered eagerly.

Garth ruffled her hair. 'You've already had next week's in advance, both of you. You're too young to start getting into debt. Let me take care of Barker.'

Adrian grinned. 'Thanks, Dad.'

Garth grinned back and suddenly they looked uncannily alike, although they didn't share a single feature.

For one brief moment there was understanding between them. Then it passed and they both became self-conscious.

'Off to bed, now,' Garth said.

Faye tried to catch his eye and send him the silent message, 'See how much you've gained. Don't risk losing it.' But then she realized that he was determined not to look at her and she turned away, heavy-hearted.

He was as good as his word, going to work late on Monday morning in order to chauffeur Barker to the vet. But that night he returned home later than ever and Faye guessed that it was the legal challenge over the Outland that took up so much time.

She even considered calling Kendall herself to warn him what was in the wind. But, as Garth had said, it was already too late, and it would have felt uneasily like conspiring with Kendall against the man who was still her husband.

All Tuesday she was braced for a call from Kendall, angry because Garth had met the deadline. But Tuesday passed into Wednesday and Kendall didn't telephone either herself or Adrian. She couldn't raise the subject with Garth, as he'd stayed at his office over Tuesday night.

On Wednesday afternoon she returned from school with the children to find a message from Kendall on her answer machine, telling them to watch the local news. There was no more information and it was hard to tell from his voice whether he was pleased or disappointed.

The very first item on the news was about the Outland and there was Kendall, smiling and talking about a significant victory.

'Now that the deadline has passed we have no more

to fear from Melkham Construction,' he said. 'This is a great day for the countryside.'

An announcer appeared on the screen. 'Melkham, of course, is no more than a wholly owned subsidiary of Clayton Properties, the fast growing empire of Garth Clayton. We tried to contact Mr Clayton to ask how he felt about being beaten to the post, but he wasn't available for comment...'

Adrian turned slowly and stared at Faye. 'He means Daddy, doesn't he?'

'That's right,' Faye said. She sat very still, knowing that she was the only one who'd heard Garth's arrival. She was aware of him crossing the hall to stand just outside the open door, listening to every word.

'But— I told him—' Adrian stammered. 'I gave the whole game away— He could have—' He paled as he realized the full implications.

'Yes, he could have made use of what you said,' Faye agreed. 'But that would have been dishonourable, and your father wouldn't do it.'

''Course he wouldn't,' Cindy said scornfully to her brother. 'Daddy would never do anything mean or dis— dishorrible!'

Adrian was deep in thought. 'Mummy,' he said at last, 'Uncle Ken is one of the good guys, isn't he?'

'Definitely.'

'And Daddy's quite different to Uncle Ken. But Daddy's one of the good guys too.' His forehead creased. 'Isn't he?'

'There's more than one kind of good guy,' Faye explained. 'There's Uncle Ken's kind, and Daddy's kind. But they're both good.'

Out of the corner of her eye she saw Garth back away into the shadows. She longed to talk to him, to tell him how happy she was that he'd put his son's feelings before his profits. But that must wait.

A moment later the front door opened and closed noisily and Garth's cheerful call of 'Where is everyone?' made Cindy and Adrian rush into the hall. Cindy threw herself joyously into his arms. Adrian held off a little, studying his father with a puzzled frown. But at last he, too, snuggled against him.

Nobody mentioned the matter until the children were going to bed. Then Adrian looked Garth full in the face and said quietly, 'Thanks, Dad.'

'You can always trust me,' Garth said, returning his son's gaze.

Adrian nodded before mounting the stairs with Cindy. He didn't speak but, as he turned away, Faye just glimpsed his smile.

'Thank you from me, too,' she said, laying a hand on Garth's arm.

He looked elated, as he'd sometimes looked before when he'd found the key to a tricky situation.

'It should be me thanking you,' he said. 'I was about to make the biggest blunder of all time and you stopped me. I'm grateful, and for the things you said to them about me. I appreciate fair dealing.'

There was something not quite right in his voice, a hint of calculation that troubled her. But she tried again.

'I hate you and Kendall being enemies—'

'In the circumstances, we could hardly be anything else.'

'But couldn't we say that the battle's finally over?'

His air of elation was undimmed. 'Of course it's not over. It's just moved into a new phase. I know my enemy now. He's a subtle man and I was blundering about. But not any more. Now I've learned subtlety too.'

'And just what does that mean?'

'You can hardly expect me to tell you when you have one foot in the enemy camp.'

'Meaning you don't trust me?' she asked, letting her hand fall away from him. 'Despite our differences, I think I've earned better than that from you, Garth.'

'I told you, I appreciate your coming to my defence just now. You're a decent person, Faye, I know that. It's just that I never entirely trust my business partners. Now, I have a lot of work to do. Unless you want me for something?'

'Not a thing,' she assured him in a toneless voice.

CHAPTER SEVEN

'DADDY, you will look after poor Barker, won't you?'

'I've already promised I will.'

'Yes, but *really*?'

'Really. My word on it.'

It was time for Cindy and Adrian to go to the school camp in Cornwall but, on the morning of departure, Cindy had qualms about leaving her friend.

'He's not very well,' she explained for the tenth time. 'He was limping last night and I think his legs are hurting again.'

'Then I'll take him to the vet,' Garth assured her.

'This morning?'

'This morning.'

'You won't make him wait?'

'Cindy, get into the car!'

'But you won't make him wait, will you?'

'I won't make him wait.'

'You're sure?'

'I'm sure.'

'*Sure* sure?'

'Cindy, I'll take him to the vet.' Garth was beginning to sound frazzled.

'Promise?'

'Get into the car.'

'*Promise?*'

Garth tore his hair. 'I promise, I promise. Now, *get into the car*, both of you, or we'll be late and they'll go without you.'

But she couldn't depart without reassuring Barker that he would be all right because Daddy had promised.

'Cindy, I'm leaving in exactly one minute,' Garth said, at the end of his tether. 'With you or without you.'

Both children kissed Faye and scrambled into the car. As they drove away Faye was sure she could hear Cindy's voice faintly, saying, 'Daddy, you're sure you won't forget...?'

She enjoyed a private chuckle. As Garth had said, he was handling his task with subtlety. He'd even gone to watch Adrian playing football. His team had made it to the final of the inter-schools trophy and the whole family had been there for Adrian's big day.

Everyone had enjoyed it enormously, and when Cindy had kissed her father goodnight at the foot of the stairs she'd whispered, 'Thank you for coming, Daddy. You made it really special.'

'Hey, what about Mummy?' he'd queried. 'She was there too.'

'That's different. Mummy's always there.'

Faye had overheard this exchange from the kitchen and had come out, smiling quizzically at Garth.

'Don't take that the wrong way,' he'd said hastily.

'How should I take it?'

'She didn't mean to put you down.' Through his awkwardness she had detected the attempt at kindness.

'I didn't take it that way. Garth, Cindy has just said the nicest thing about me that any child can say about a parent. I promise you, I don't feel put down.'

'The nicest thing—?' She'd watched as comprehension dawned on his face. 'She said you're always there. Yes—yes, I see.' He'd sounded heavy, and she'd felt a stirring of pity for him. He was trying so hard, but something constantly eluded him.

Now it was the great day of departure for Cornwall. Garth returned from dropping off Cindy and Adrian, looking weary. 'I watched the coach go and Cindy was at the window, mouthing ''Barker'' at me,' he said.

'Don't worry, I've called the vet. His appointment is in an hour.'

'Faye — actually —'

'I'll take him,' she said, smiling.

'Thanks. And by the way, before I go, will you make a date in your diary for next Monday, at noon? I'm having a press function for the anniversary range and I need you there.'

'You mean I've got to meet journalists and talk to them?'

'It's no big deal. It's not the proper launch. That will be on the exact date of our anniversary. This is a kind of teaser, to let the property press get a hint of what's in store. We'll have models of the houses on display. I'll give you some booklets about them in advance, so that you can discuss them knowledgeably.'

'I'm just kind of shy about being on show,' she demurred.

'But you promised to help me out,' he reminded her, 'and this is the sort of thing I need you to do.'

'Of course it is,' she said, pulling herself together. 'Don't worry, I'll turn up and do my stuff.'

'Great. And buy a new outfit. The best of everything.'

'So that when they look at me they'll say, ''Boy, must he be doing well if she can afford to dress like that!'''

He grinned. 'You're developing a real talent for this.

Miss McGeorge examined Barker thoroughly and said his painkillers weren't quite strong enough. She prescribed some different pills and gave him the first one immediately. By that afternoon he was moving more easily and by early evening he was as mischievous as ever.

'I see he's back to normal,' Garth observed when he returned. 'Down, boy! This suit's just been cleaned.'

'The vet gave him stronger pills,' Faye said. 'I think they're doing the trick.'

'Good.'

'But it'll be a few days before we're certain. I've made another appointment—'

'You're doing a great job, Faye. Now, I've got a pile of work to get on with—'

'But you need to know all this. *You're* supposed to be caring for Barker.'

'Of course, and I promise you I'm taking it very seriously. But you can brief me later. Tell Nancy to bring me a snack in the study, will you?'

'But Cindy will—'

'By the way, I brought this home for you.' He handed her a thick folder. 'It'll tell you everything about the anniversary range.' He vanished.

Faye glared at his study door, then sighed. When she'd spoken to Nancy she returned to studying a list of traditional anniversary gifts.

'Paper after the first year,' she mused. 'He gave me a book that I'd been longing for. It was terribly expensive, and he starved himself to pay for it. The next year it was cotton and he gave me that lovely summer house-coat. The third year, leather—that was a shoulder bag—'

How his eyes had shone as he offered his gifts to her! How happy he'd been when she was pleased! She drew a breath and firmly dismissed the memory.

At last came the call from the children to say they'd arrived safely. Adrian told her all about the journey, before saying, 'Cindy's here and she—' His voice faded, there was a slight scuffle and Adrian hissed, 'Let me finish, you little brat.'

Then Cindy's voice. 'Hello, Mummy.'

'Hello, darling. Is it nice in camp?'

'It's super. Mummy, how's Barker? Did Daddy take him to the vet? What happened? Is he any better?'

'Just a minute.' Faye pressed a switch to connect the call to Garth's study, and walked in.

'Pick up the phone,' she said. 'Cindy wants to talk to you.'

She stayed there while he answered. She could tell that the little girl must have launched straight into her favourite topic. Garth became slightly defensive, while trying to sound in control.

'Yes, darling, of course I took— That is, Barker's been to the vet and he's much better— Well, because the vet gave him stronger pills,' he finished, repeating Faye's words. From his frown it was clear that he was trying to recall the rest.

'They seem to be working,' he continued gamely, 'but it'll take a few days to be sure— Well, on his next appointment— That's right, he's booked in for—'

He signalled wildly to Faye, who mouthed, 'Next week.'

'Next week,' he repeated into the phone. 'The exact day? I forget—' He appealed silently to Faye, but she shook her head and backed out.

Listening from the hall, she had to admit that he improvised pretty well for a man who didn't know what he was talking about. But the way he slammed the phone down made his feelings clear.

'I suppose you've been standing out here, enjoying yourself,' he grunted, emerging from the study.

'Don't blame me,' she said impishly. 'I tried to give you a full briefing earlier, but you were too busy to listen.'

'So you landed me in it.'

'You landed yourself in it. After all, you know the saying.'

'No, I don't, but I'm sure you're going to have fun telling me.'

'If you can't do the time, don't do the crime.'

'What?'

'If you can't keep the promise, don't make it. If you want to take the credit, you've got to put in the work. Cindy asked you to care for Barker, not me, because it matters to her that *you* should do it.' She smiled at him cheekily. 'So do it.'

'Thanks! Thanks a lot!'

He would have died sooner than let her suspect that she'd startled him, not only with her challenge but in what she'd learned about tough dealing. As a tough dealer himself he respected that. He wondered where his wife had learned all these disconcerting lessons.

Faye finally bought herself a matching blue silk coat and dress. It cost a fortune and looked it, which she knew would satisfy her husband. On the whole she was pleasantly surprised by her own appearance.

She rejected his offer to send his chauffeur-driven car for her and drove herself there. A parking space had been reserved for her. Doors opened at her approach and she was instantly conducted to the top floor, where Garth reigned.

She was interested to see his new London premises, which he'd acquired since their parting. She found them much as she'd expected, quietly luxurious and efficient.

Money had been spent, but not on frills. Garth got value from every penny.

As she stepped out of the lift an overpoweringly gracious young woman was waiting for her. Faye knew at once that this could only be Lysandra. Everything about her fitted the superior voice she'd heard on the telephone. Lysandra was tall and slender, dressed in an elegant charcoal business suit. With her shoulder-length red hair and gold accessories, she looked stunning. Faye had felt stylish until that moment, but next to the super-chic Lysandra she could sense herself retreating into dowdiness.

'Good morning, Mrs Clayton,' she said, advancing with her hand outstretched. 'I'm Lysandra Bates, Mr Clayton's Director of Publicity. We've all been looking forward so much to meeting you.'

'We?' Faye asked, surprised.

'Everyone in the Publicity Department. It's such a coup for us to have you part of the campaign.' Her tone implied that Faye had no other existence.

'Mr Clayton said you were a little hesitant at first, but I was sure you'd be glad you agreed when you knew how much this mattered to us,' Lysandra continued. She led the way into a room that was luxuriously furnished with pale grey leather armchairs, offering her tea, coffee. Nothing could have been more gracious or deferential than her manner, yet Faye detected a faint hint of contempt. This smooth, beautiful young woman had sized her up and found her wanting.

Garth appeared and greeted Faye with a polite smile and a kiss on the cheek. She responded in the same way. They were like two actors performing their roles perfectly on cue.

'Lysandra will show you the models and explain

everything,' he said. 'The press will start to arrive in about an hour.'

'Everything is quite ready,' Lysandra told him. 'Press packs, free samples—'

Faye attempted a mild joke. 'You give free samples of houses?'

Lysandra's laughter managed to combine weary courtesy, exaggerated patience and restrained derision in equal measure. 'Naturally not. But there are many smaller items, which the construction press appreciate. It's part of my job to know them all personally and to select free gifts to suit the individual.'

'I'm sure you've covered every detail admirably,' Garth told her. 'You never let me down.'

Unlike his wife, Faye thought.

'I try not to,' Lysandra told him with a smile that excluded Faye. 'I'll fetch you when they're all assembled.'

'Come into my office as soon as it's over,' Garth said. 'We have a lot to discuss.'

Faye was about to say that she preferred to leave at once when she realized he was talking to his beautiful assistant. When he did address her it was to say, 'Lysandra will look after you. Leave everything in her splendid hands.'

He disappeared.

'It's this way,' Lysandra said, pointing across the corridor. Faye followed her and found herself in a huge corner room with windows on two sides. Six other people, power-dressed women and men in business suits, were already there, crowding around something in the centre. Lysandra introduced them as members of the Publicity Department, and showed Faye what they were looking at. On a large display plinth stood six models

of houses, each one about two feet wide by eighteen
inches high.

'These are our very newest designs, and top secret at
the moment,' Lysandra explained. She flashed Faye a
beaming smile, revealing small, perfectly white teeth.
'Not secret from you, of course.' Everyone laughed at
this witticism. Faye smiled.

'There are two for those with more modest incomes,
two for the executive class, and these two are de luxe,'
she continued smoothly. 'And you'll be delighted to
know that we've finally managed to find the right name
for them.'

'How thrilling!' Faye said.

'Yes, isn't it? It's going to be called the Diamond
Range. We all had to put our thinking caps on but, with
it being your tenth anniversary, of course the name had
been staring us in the face all the time.'

Any minute now she's going to pat me on the head,
Faye thought. Aloud, she said, 'I'm afraid I don't see
the connection with my wedding anniversary.'

'Your *tenth* wedding anniversary,' Lysandra corrected
gently. 'The time when husbands give their wives diamond jewellery. That's why we've called this the
Diamond Range.' She said the last words slowly, as if
to an idiot.

'But there's some mistake,' Faye said. 'The tenth anniversary gift is tin or aluminium. Diamonds are for the
sixtieth.'

Lysandra's perfect smile barely wavered. 'I think not,'
she said sweetly. 'I have the list here.'

Faye studied it with bewilderment, unable to recognize anything. Instead of the traditional paper, cotton,
leather of the first three years, she read clocks, china,
and crystal.

'Fourth—appliances?' she said. 'The fourth was always fruit and flowers. And the fifth was wood, but here it says silverware.'

'I see what's happened,' Lysandra said with a forgiving smile. 'You're thinking of the old list, but we work from the one that came in about fifteen years ago. The tenth anniversary is diamond jewellery. Naturally Mr Clayton will be giving you diamonds. In fact, we've already selected some pieces for your approval.'

'We?' Faye asked.

'Mr Clayton relies on me for everything,' Lysandra said coolly. 'I was able to suggest some diamond pieces that might be suitable, since you were—er—unavailable for consultation. Perhaps you'd care to inspect them now.'

Too dazed to protest, Faye looked on as Lysandra produced several black velvet trays on which sparkled earrings, necklaces, rings and bracelets. They were beautiful, but she felt no pleasure. They seemed like the very essence of everything that had gone wrong between herself and Garth.

'They're lovely, aren't they?' Lysandra cooed. 'So much better than tin, so I'm sure you'll feel you've gained by the exchange.'

'But I don't,' Faye said defiantly. 'I just think it's sad to throw away the old traditions.'

'Old traditions are so sweet,' Lysandra said, 'but not very functional.'

'And your list is very functional, isn't it?'

'Oh, it's been an immense help to people like us in the construction industry.'

People like us. She was talking about herself and Garth.

'But it's so false,' Faye said helplessly.

'False?'

'Artificial. This isn't the real anniversary list. It's just a way of selling more washing machines.'

'The modern customer demands appliances already installed in a new house—'

'Fine, then do that. But don't pretend it has anything to do with wedding anniversaries. I'm sorry, this just isn't what I agreed to help with.'

For the first time Lysandra was nonplussed. 'Well, if you'll—excuse me.' She hurried away, and returned a moment later with Garth.

'It had better be something important for you to have dragged me away from that meeting,' he said and, although he was speaking to Lysandra, Faye felt the words were directed at herself.

'We've got a problem,' she said, speaking pleasantly. 'I'm afraid I misunderstood why you wanted me. My fault, I dare say.'

'Well, I'm sure we can sort it out,' he said, also speaking with determined pleasantness.

'To me the tenth wedding anniversary means a gift of tin or aluminium, not diamonds. I didn't even know there was another list.'

'Well, surely you don't mind having diamonds?' he asked, frowning, and she knew he didn't really understand.

She shouldn't have started this, she thought. Why not just keep quiet and play her part? But some core of her, which had kept quiet too often in the past, insisted on standing firm.

'I do mind. If we're going to tie your new range in with our tenth wedding anniversary, then I think we should do it properly.'

'You're surely not suggesting that I give you tin?'

'It's what you're supposed to give,' she said stubbornly.

'Only from a sentimental point of view, surely?' Lysandra said. 'But this is a business decision. Mr Clayton and I have explored the matter from every angle and this decision offered optimum results.'

'Tin is the right thing,' Faye persisted. She met her husband's eyes, silently pleading with him, *Don't take her side against me. Say at least that you understand my point of view.*

But she knew Garth didn't understand a thing when she saw the anger flare in his eyes. He took her arm and drew her away from Lysandra, speaking in a soft, furious undervoice. 'If we'd still been living in a two-room flat it would be the right thing. But we've moved beyond that, in case you hadn't noticed. I'm a successful man, marketing a range of luxury houses for successful people. I can't celebrate that range with a tin plate. It would make me a laughing stock.'

'I'm sorry you feel that my standards make you a laughing stock, Garth, but that's the way I feel. I think you should do this without me.'

'You're a vital part of this promotion—'

'So why didn't you explain it to me properly?'

'I explained everything I thought needed explaining. I didn't know you were going to go off on this sentimental flight of fancy.'

'Thank you very much.'

He gritted his teeth. 'We'll talk about this tonight.'

'Tonight will be too late. I'd like to talk about it now.'

'Faye, don't do this to me, please. I've got a million things on my mind—'

'If I'm such a vital part of this, perhaps one of those things should be me.'

· 'All right, all right! I handled it clumsily. I'm sorry. Now can we just get on with this?'

'Without me.'

He was pale. 'You're not serious.'

'Garth, it never was a very good idea to put me in the press show. You and Miss Bates will handle everything perfectly together.'

Without another word she turned and walked out. Her head was up and she seemed calm, but inwardly she was seething with anger. As she reached the lift she heard a pattering of footsteps and turned to see Lysandra. When the lift doors opened Lysandra followed her in.

'What an unfortunate misunderstanding,' she said, smiling brightly. 'But I can assure you, Mrs Clayton, Garth didn't mean to upset you in any way.'

'I beg your pardon!' Faye said in frosty outrage.

'He doesn't always understand things the way we women do. Men aren't sentimental, are they? I promise you, Garth would be devastated to think—'

'How dare you?' Faye interrupted her fiercely. 'How dare you presume to explain my husband to me?'

'I assure you, I'm only—'

'You know nothing about him. *Nothing!*'

The lift had stopped. Faye stormed out and immediately pressed the button to make the doors close again. Her last view was of Lysandra gaping with astonishment.

Her fury sustained her all the way home but once there it began to seep away, to be replaced with weariness. The expensive silk clothes felt like an actor's costume for a role that was all wrong for her and she hurried to change them for dark green trousers and a pale yellow shirt. It was a lovely day and, with a linen jacket about her shoulders and flat shoes on her feet, she was ready for a stroll in the grounds.

'Come on,' she said to Barker. 'You're missing the children, aren't you?'

He padded amiably after her as she wandered into the trees. Faye threw the ball and was cheered to see him bound after it, obviously not in pain. But neither did he move with the vitality of a young dog and it brought home to her again how old he was. It was another reason for being angry with Garth.

'We're the same, you and me,' she said, sitting by the stream and fishing in her coat pocket for a biscuit. 'He's making use of us both to get what he wants. Underneath all his clever talk, that's the bottom line.' She stroked his ears. 'How's that for a mixed metaphor? What am I talking about? You wouldn't know a mixed metaphor if it jumped on you, not unless it was offering titbits.'

As if by a signal Barker began to sniff her coat. 'All right, here's a biscuit. Leave my fingers behind! What an idiot I was to make an issue of it! What else did I expect? We made a business deal and that's the only reason I'm here. Who cares what list he chose? It's all over between us, anyway.'

She settled herself more comfortably on the grass and stroked the furry head that was resting on her leg.

'You know who I was really mad at, don't you?' she mused. 'That woman. She acted as though she owned him. And she actually dared to explain him to me. To *me*! To his wife. I know him better than anyone. Oh, what does it matter? I'm not really his wife any more.'

She gave a sudden chuckle. 'But you should have heard me getting on my high horse with Lysandra. I've never done that before. Didn't know I could. That showed her. If you ask me, she sees herself as the next

Mrs Clayton.' Barker woofed agreement and eyed her coat significantly.

'OK, one more! But don't you dare suggest I'm jealous! She's welcome to him. It was just her being so rude that bothered me. Hey, I said *one*!'

They lingered together, enjoying the beautiful afternoon, until the sun began to set.

'Time to go in,' she said reluctantly. 'I'll bet he'll be home early tonight, and he'll have plenty to say to me.'

She was right. Garth arrived half an hour later and came looking for her. 'Can we talk?' he asked in an edgy voice.

'Yes. I'm sorry. It shouldn't have happened.'

'Whatever got into you to leave me with egg on my face like that? Everyone was expecting my wife to be there. I had to say you'd been taken ill. Are you going to do that on the big night?'

'No, of course not. The whole thing took me by surprise. I'd never heard of this other list. Why didn't you warn me?'

'I left everything to Lysandra. Besides, what difference does it make which list we use?'

She shrugged. 'None at all, I suppose.'

'You made a fool of me and I can't stand that. We had a bargain and you're not keeping it.'

'Garth, I'm sorry. What I did was—unprofessional, and I regret it.'

'Why, for heaven's sake? Why?'

'I told you, I was caught on the wrong foot. And that new list is horrible. You're only dragging me in because you think you'll sell more houses if you can make people feel warm and good. But there's nothing warm about washing machines. It's all so cynical.'

'I think I know best about marketing my own product.'

'You don't know much about families and these are supposed to be family homes—sorry, "product", since you have a problem with the idea of homes. You want to sell them to couples with children, people who love each other. Well, most wives and mothers would rather have a piece of tin given with love than all the diamonds in the world in this calculating way.'

'Tin! For Pete's sake!'

'I can remember when you didn't despise tin.'

'I can't.'

'Then it's your loss. When we were first married we ate off tin plates that we bought at a second-hand camping store. In fact, we didn't even buy them. You mended that man's boiler for free, and he gave us some things for the flat.'

'Oh, yes, and I felt ashamed because I'd started our marriage by failing you. I wanted to give you the moon and we ended up with stuff that nobody else wanted.'

'But I didn't care,' she said wildly. If only she could make him understand, even now. 'I was happy just to be with you. I thought you felt the same.'

'I was never happy until I could give you the nice things you deserved. I worked like a Trojan until I had enough for my own little builder's yard, and then a big yard. And then the sky was the limit. I did it for you and all you can do is hark back to the days when I had nothing to give you, because I was nobody.'

'You were somebody to me,' she cried. 'And to the children. But that wasn't enough for you. You've turned into such a different man.'

'Thank goodness!' he said abruptly.

'I'll never say that. I'll never stop mourning the man

I lost. He was all the world to me, but he went away and never came back.' She could see by his face that he didn't understand. They were strangers shouting in the dark, and a sudden burst of anguish made her cry, 'Oh, Garth, don't you remember?'

He was silent awhile before answering. 'Maybe my memories are different to yours,' he said at last, seeming to speak with difficulty. 'We obviously didn't find the same things important.'

'We thought we were together,' she said with a sigh. 'And we were travelling separate paths all along. And now here we are, in sight of the end.'

'Don't,' he said sombrely. 'Don't look back, Faye. We both know that's a mistake. We've each chosen our lives.'

There was a sadness in his face that she hadn't seen before. Suddenly she leaned over and kissed him. It was an impulse. She wasn't even sure what she wanted to come of it, except perhaps to evoke the old Garth, even if only fleetingly.

For a moment she thought it was happening. After a brief surprise he kissed her back, with a kind of yearning ache. She could feel him trembling, though whether with passion or emotion she wasn't sure. She tightened her arms, seeking to reach the part of him that lived behind the proud barrier. Her strong resolutions vanished. If only she could still touch his heart...

'Garth,' she whispered in a pleading voice, 'try to remember...' He lifted his head to search her face. She could see his eyes and read their trouble and confusion. Then he tensed and broke free from her.

'This isn't a good idea, Faye. You were right all along about it being over.'

'Yes,' she stammered. 'Yes I was…'

'There's nothing for us now but to see this through to the end and say goodbye.' A shudder went through him. 'So, for pity's sake, let's get it over with quickly.'

CHAPTER EIGHT

WITH a clash of cymbals the orchestra brought the symphony to an end. The conductor turned to receive the well-earned applause. Faye came out of her happy trance. The music had been magnificent and she was reluctant to return to reality with all its problems and confusions.

It was late in the evening, but while the children were at camp she needn't rush home. For their sakes Garth had often managed to return early, but during their absence he'd reverted to staying late at the office. It was as though he and Faye were holding their breaths in this delicate situation.

Daydreaming, she left the concert hall without looking where she was going, and collided with someone. 'I'm terribly sorry, I— *Kendall!*'

'Hello, darling.' He kissed her cheek.

'Where did you appear from?' she asked, smiling.

'I was at the concert. Come and have a drink with me.'

It was a fine evening and they found a pub with tables outside in the garden, and coloured lights hanging from the trees. Kendall bought cider for himself, orange juice for Faye and hot dogs for both of them.

'Fancy you going to a classical concert,' Faye said. 'Where were you sitting?'

After an awkward pause Kendall said, 'All right, I didn't actually go to the concert. I knew you'd be there because I was with you when you bought the ticket, ages ago. I waited outside.'

It was nice to know that he was so eager to see her, but the little lie troubled her. Then she determinedly pushed it out of her head.

'I've missed you,' Kendall said.

'And I you.'

'Well, there's always the television,' he said, speaking apparently lightly but with a significant edge.

'Television?'

'Last night. What did you think?'

With a gasp of dismay she remembered that Kendall had been on a talk show, due to be broadcast the previous evening.

'It's all right,' he said, reading her face. 'I don't suppose you could watch it with him around.'

She wasn't fooled by his easy tone. Kendall had a touch of vanity about his media appearances. Faye had always found this slightly endearing and had fondly made much of him, while he basked in her admiration. She knew she ought to make amends now by inventing a convincing excuse, but suddenly she was too tired for white lies and the truth came out before she could think properly.

'Kendall, I'm sorry, Garth wasn't even in last night. But I've got so much on my mind just now—'

'That you didn't give me a thought. Fair enough.' He spoke with a kind of determined brightness that set her at a distance.

'Kendall, please—'

'Forget it. I'm sure you're having a very difficult time. Is your husband making life hard?'

'Not really. He's behaving well to the children. It's lovely to see him with Cindy. She just basks in his attention. And he's doing better with Adrian, too. But I worry that he's just using them.'

'I suppose he might have honestly seen the light. Perhaps he's afraid of a lonely old age.' Kendall shrugged. 'I should think he's certainly heading for one.'

'Garth's not afraid of anything. He's got too much self-confidence. He's— Oh, I don't how how to say it—'

It was useless trying to define Garth. The more she tried, the more he slipped through her fingers. She could describe his manner and his infuriating behaviour. But there were no words for his sudden grin, full of devilment and charm, or the wild wonderment of his dreams. Once he'd shared those dreams with her and it had been like watching shooting stars. But that was a long time ago.

She gave up, remembering that it irked Kendall to hear too much about Garth. 'Tell me how things are with you,' she said.

'There's not a lot going on in my life at the moment,' he said. 'I work, and I think of you.'

'Have you finished your book yet?'

'I told you I had, at the football match.'

'Oh, yes, you did. Sorry, I forgot. Are you happy with it?'

'I'm never happy with my writing, you know that.'

'Yes, you were always changing things until the last minute.'

She persevered with the theme of his writing, conscientiously asking all the right questions, until the subject was exhausted. She searched for another one then realized, with dismay, what she was doing. She and Kendall had always found plenty to talk about. Yet tonight something was wrong. The air didn't vibrate with excitement as it did when Garth was around.

But she wasn't her usual self at the moment, she remembered with relief. When things returned to normal everything would be well between them again. But try as she might, she couldn't find the elusive spark that would bring her alive in Kendall's company.

'It's very late,' she said at last. 'I should be getting home now.'

'I'll walk you to your car.'

She tucked her hand in his arm and everything was comfortable between them, as it had always been. But it was no longer enough. When they reached the car she said, almost desperately, 'Kiss me goodnight.'

Kendall's embrace was the same as always but his kiss didn't thrill her, and now she wondered if it ever really had.

'Faye…' Kendall said tensely.

'Kiss me again,' she pleaded.

'Better not. Your thoughts were wandering. Like I told you, it has to be all or nothing with me. Goodnight, Faye.'

As she went through the front door Faye could hear Garth's voice from behind his study door, sounding as though he was on the phone. She was glad, as she couldn't bear to talk. She went up the stairs, straight to her own room.

A shower made her feel better. Wrapping a soft towelling dressing gown about her she returned to the bedroom and switched off all the lights except a soft lamp by her dressing table. Her mind was in turmoil.

Something had been different tonight and Kendall had recognized it too. It was all because of Garth. He'd kissed her that first night and her body had responded out of sheer surprise. If she'd been more prepared she might have stilled those treacherous impulses. But she hadn't stilled them and the memories had remained. They had prompted her to reach out to him on the evening after the disastrous press show. But he hadn't wanted her. They'd grown too far apart. There was an ache of desolation in her heart.

She remembered the lithe firmness of Garth's body and how good it felt to hold it. He'd been a generous as well as a skilful lover, warm and tender and eager for her pleasure as well as his own.

She knew it was dangerous to dwell on these memories, but they were part of the happiest time of her life. The fulfilment hadn't just been physical. Garth's love had filled the world, making her feel valued and totally a woman. Without her even knowing it, a smile touched her lips. Then it faded into a sigh.

She was so absorbed in her reverie that she didn't see the door open and Garth enter quietly. He stood watching her, his eyes darkening with anger at the look of tender introspection on her face. She thought she was alone, so it wasn't teasing that made her lips curl in that sweet smile as if she was thinking of something—or someone—who made her blissfully happy.

Suddenly she seemed to become aware of him and turned her head. 'You shouldn't be here,' she said.

'I wanted to talk to you.' He looked like a man under terrible strain, and his eyes were haggard.

'Garth, you can't just walk into my room. We had an agreement—'

'It's not me that's breaking it, Faye. You gave your word that there'd be no dates with Haines—'

'I didn't make a date with him—'

'*Don't lie to me!* You were with him tonight. I saw you as I drove home.'

'I said I didn't make a date with him, not that I didn't see him. I bumped into Kendall as I came out of the concert and had a drink with him. That's all.'

'Not quite all. You were kissing him.'

'You really studied us, didn't you? Or are you just protecting your investment?'

'I don't like people who don't keep their word.'

'It was an accident.'

'Was kissing him an accident?'

'No, I did that because I wanted to,' she said defiantly.

'And to hell with me?'

'I never gave you a thought,' she said, meeting his eyes. 'What's this all about, Garth? You said yourself there's nothing for us now but to see this through to the end and say goodbye.'

'Perhaps I've changed my mind,' he said, reaching for her determinedly.

'Oh, no!' She put up a hand. 'Our agreement—'

'You broke it, Faye. Now it's my turn. I don't like being overlooked and I'm not going to be any longer.' Before she could protest he covered her mouth with his own, kissing her with fierce, angry intent.

As soon as their lips touched Faye knew what had been missing from Kendall's kiss. The opposition of her mind meant nothing while Garth could still cause vibrations of pleasure to go through her at his lightest touch. Anger at the way he simply took what he wanted warred with a pleasure that her body had once known, and for which it still yearned.

She couldn't cope with her feelings because they reminded her how totally he could possess her. Worse still, they brought back the hot, sweet nights of their early love. With that love gone, it was cruel that her flesh still responded to him.

'Let me go, Garth,' she told him, eyes blazing.

'Why should I? This was what you wanted the other night.'

'Like you, I've changed my mind. Let me go now.'

'Am I trespassing on Kendall Haines's property? Do you think I care?'

'I'm not his property, and I'm not yours.'

'You were mine once, because that was how you wanted it. You gave yourself to me completely, with trust and love. Do you remember that, Faye?'

'Don't,' she whispered.

'Why not? Do you think I'm going to let you wipe our past away as though it never existed? It did exist. It *lived*, and it's part of us both, however much you wish it wasn't.'

She struggled to speak firmly. She wouldn't let him win. 'I don't remember anything, Garth. The past is dead.'

'Damn you,' he said softly.

He took possession of her mouth, and the pleasure was so poignant that she gasped. The hand she put up was meant to push him away but somehow it ended by caressing him instead, fingers in his hair, turning and twisting, enjoying the springy feel.

He tugged at the belt of her bathrobe until it came loose and he could pull the robe from her shoulders and embrace her totally. Half knowing what she did, Faye began to open the buttons of his shirt. She wanted everything about him: his agility and strength, his skill and tenderness, all the things that had once been hers. So much had gone for ever but there was still the pleasure of clinging to him, feeling his hands wandering over her, making her come alive.

Garth held her against him, looking down into her flushed, dreamy face.

'You remember,' he said arrogantly. 'You pretend not to, but you do. You remember everything, how much I want you, how much you want me—'

'It's not true,' she gasped.

'I can make it true. I'm still there, aren't I, Faye? Deny it as much as you like, *I'm still there*.'

'Yes,' she said in a helpless whisper. 'But, Garth, please—this isn't the answer.'

'What is the answer?' he demanded between kisses. 'Cosy little chats to relive every detail of our mistakes? Who needs words when we can talk like this?'

He smothered her mouth with his own, silencing all further argument. Faye could feel the last of her reason slipping away in the tide of passion that flowed over her.

She felt the silk of the counterpane beneath her back, the slight sinking of the mattress as Garth lay down beside her. His eyes seemed to feast on her, like a starving man presented with a banquet, and he ran a hand appreciatively over her slim frame.

'You managed the other seven pounds, I see,' he murmured admiringly. 'I had a feeling you'd do what you set your mind to. Looks great.'

He didn't wait for her to speak, but kissed her again. Longing flooded her. It was useless to protest to herself. She wanted Garth as much as he wanted her, and now she could only yield with a deep sigh of fulfilment.

He groaned as he pulled her against him, enfolding her in his arms and running his hands over her beautiful form. Their hearts and minds might have parted, but on this level nothing had changed. Ten years ago their physical harmony had been immediate and ecstatic. It was the same now. He knew how to please her, and he used his knowledge to the full.

Although it was their physical need that drove them, he was still the considerate lover that she remembered. He knew how to wait, to give her time to feel easy with him again. Looking up, she met his eyes and found them brooding over her like a miser with recovered treasure.

'You're still mine,' he murmured. 'You always were mine, and you always will be.'

She knew she should dispute this, but the delight flooding through her left no room for argument. Whatever the future held, she was his at this moment and her heart knew it.

The time they'd spent apart had brought its changes and as lovers they were strangers again. But they'd been strangers the first time they made love and it had been wonderful. Now Faye felt almost as she had then, breathless with eagerness, not sure what to expect of him but hoping for everything.

She thought she surprised a moment of hesitancy in his face, as though he, too, were moving cautiously as he reclaimed unfamiliar ground. She knew that look. It meant he wanted to be reassured. So she did so, touching his face gently, one of their old signals, and the result was all she'd hoped. His embrace grew stronger, more confident and possessive. Just as it had been that first time.

And something else was the same, the beauty and wonder of becoming one with him. Once she'd been sure that life could hold no more happiness than this. Now she knew for certain that it was true. The years without him had been a lonely ache of desolation, and secretly she'd always been waiting to come home.

There was a new edge to their passion. Now she, too,

had confidence. She knew herself as a woman who could drive this attractive man wild. What was happening had always been bound to happen.

She murmured his name and he looked at her quickly. 'Faye?' he said. 'Faye?' It was a question, as though he thought she might vanish from his arms.

She held him close, demanding more and more, and he gave freely and bountifully. Their climax was a burst of dazzling light, a flowering of the world that left her exhausted, trembling and utterly satiated.

She could see that it was the same with him. He was gasping slightly from the lengths to which she'd driven him and his face registered pure amazement. Faye wondered if her own face revealed her feeling of triumph.

She looked at him out of eyes that were hazy with fulfilment. Her whole body was relaxed as it hadn't been for two years. The world was a good place after all.

'I didn't mean that to happen,' he said slowly, watching her.

'Didn't you?' she asked softly. 'I thought you'd meant it to happen from the start.'

'I made you a promise—'

Oh, yes, she thought vaguely. The promise.

'It's too late to worry about that,' she murmured, wondering why he was making a fuss about it. Unconsciously, her lips curved into a blissful smile.

'Don't smile at me like that,' he said hoarsely. 'Not unless you want to drive me mad. *Faye!*'

He took hold of her shoulders to give her a little shake, but he didn't let go. He couldn't. The moment he touched her they both knew their desire was far from exhausted. And this time it was even more irresistible, because of what they'd both discovered.

He said her name once more, before his lips descended on her mouth. Faye gave a sigh of anticipation, and it all began again.

Garth was already downstairs when Faye descended next morning. She waited for him to look up, for the consciousness that would be between them. Perhaps he would smile.

But there was only trouble in his eyes when he raised his head. 'I owe you an apology,' he said in a low voice.

'An—?'

'Look, I know what you're going to say. I broke my word. You told me to stay away from you or the deal would be off. Please—' He raised his hand when she tried to speak.

Faye's voice faded at once. She couldn't have forced the words out through the stone that was encasing her heart.

'Just hear me out,' Garth insisted. 'I swear that nothing like it will ever happen again. I was in a bad state last night, business worries, nothing serious, but I wasn't myself. I'm sure you're angry, Faye, but there's no need to be. It's over, finished. I'll draw a line under it, if you will.'

'By all means, let's draw a line under it,' she said. 'Nothing could suit me better.'

CHAPTER NINE

AT LAST it was time for the children to return from Cornwall. After that first delight, Faye was relieved to have their laughter filling the house. The cheerful sound covered the spaces between herself and Garth.

Their passionate lovemaking, so intense and shattering at the time, seemed to have slipped past without leaving any impression on him. Instead of growing closer to her, he'd seemed determined to keep his distance.

The morning afterwards he had been able to speak only of his broken promise. But he'd mentioned that while they had lain together and she'd put his mind at rest. She couldn't recall her own words exactly, but she knew she'd said that she wasn't angry about the promise. His obsession with it next day had made no sense, unless he had been using it as an excuse.

As the days went by she realized that this was the answer. There was a constraint in Garth's manner that hadn't been there before, and he was seldom at home. When they spoke it was usually to discuss the anniversary celebrations that were nearly on them.

One evening he said, 'I'm going to Newcastle tomorrow and I have to leave at seven in the morning. There's no need for you to get up then.'

'All right,' she said quietly. It was obvious that he didn't want her. 'How long will you be away?'

'I might stay overnight. Word's already getting around about the Diamond Range and I'm meeting a consortium that may put in a big order. It'll be a great coup if I bring it off before the range is even launched.'

'That's wonderful,' she said politely. 'Will you be going in the plane?'

'No, someone's driving me up. I can make calls in the back of the car without being disturbed.'

She was awake before Garth left next morning and lay listening to him moving about downstairs, until the front door closed and she heard him drive away.

Sunk in her own thoughts she barely heard the children chattering over breakfast, but at last the word 'zoo' reached her.

'What, darling?' she asked Cindy.

'Daddy said he's taking us to the zoo on Saturday. He will be back by then, won't he, Mummy?'

'I'm sure he will, pet. He's due back tomorrow.'

But she wondered if Garth had remembered the zoo. He'd mentioned staying over for one night, but that might stretch to a second. It would be wise to send him a reminder. Mary, his secretary, would be in Newcastle with him, but she had an office junior whom Faye could telephone.

But when she called his headquarters, she found herself talking to Mary herself. She was friendly, and one of the few people in the office whom Faye found congenial.

'I thought you'd have gone away with Garth,' Faye said.

'I was supposed to but I've got family problems at the moment,' Mary told her. 'I'd rather not be away overnight. Luckily Lysandra came to my rescue.'

'You mean—Lysandra has gone with him?'

'Yes, wasn't that kind of her?'

'Very kind,' Faye murmured.

She gave her message, which Mary promised to deliver, and hung up, trying to silence the disquiet in her breast. She'd settled with herself that she wasn't jealous of Lysandra, so what did it matter? After the divorce, Garth could marry anyone he liked.

'Oh, no, he can't!' she said suddenly, aloud. 'I'm not having that woman become stepmother to my children.'

It was a relief to know the reason for her disturbance.

It was good to have the children home and she was determined to make the most of their company. A shopping trip in town turned into a spending spree and they returned with new trainers and sweaters with zoo animals printed on them. They immediately put them on and headed for the garden.

'Hey, save those sweaters for the zoo,' Faye called. 'You'll get them dirty out there.'

'We won't, Mummy, honestly,' Adrian called, but even as he spoke he was tussling with Barker for the ball. He finally got it out of the dog's mouth, and rubbed his hand over the elephant's head on his chest.

'Never mind,' Faye grinned. 'I can always wash them before Saturday.'

Barker was like a child himself, bouncing and rolling about, chasing after every ball and uttering deafening barks of delight. The trust and understanding between the three of them was lovely to see.

'Tea in fifteen minutes,' Faye called, and went into the kitchen. She reached up for Barker's dry biscuits, for she knew he couldn't bear to be left out of a meal. He was especially fond of the red ones, so she took two red ones apart. Always afterwards it was imprinted in her memory how she'd smiled as she'd set the biscuits by the kettle in the last split second before the world was turned upside down.

At first she hardly registered that Barker had suddenly made a different sound. But then it was followed by a dreadful scream from Cindy and the little girl came flying into the kitchen.

'Mummy, Mummy! *Come quickly!*'

Barker was lying on his side, heaving, his eyes full of pain. 'He was running and he just stopped and fell over,' Adrian cried.

'I'll call the vet,' Faye said urgently and raced back to the house. Adrian came with her but Cindy stayed with Barker, holding his head in her arms and murmuring comfort.

'They're sending an ambulance for him,' she told Adrian. 'It'll be here any moment. They'll make him better.'

She tried to sound convinced, but she knew what had happened, and how it would probably end. But she would protect her children until the last moment.

Then Adrian said, 'Someone at school saw his grandfather have a heart attack and he told us what happened.'

Their eyes met and she saw how grown up her son was. 'Yes,' she said. 'I think Barker's had a heart attack. He's quite old.'

Adrian's eyes were wet and he closed them for a moment while his hand groped for Faye's. When he opened them he said, 'We mustn't tell Cindy yet. She's just a child.'

'The vet's very good,' Faye said. 'Barker might come through it.'

The ambulance arrived and two attendants moved the dog gently onto a stretcher. Cindy walked beside him, stroking his head and fighting back her tears in case he should see them and be dismayed. She never doubted that he understood human reactions.

'I'm going with him,' she said, preparing to climb into the ambulance.

'No, darling, they've got things to do for him in there,' Faye said. 'We'll follow right behind in the car.'

On the journey Cindy's tears flowed unrestrained. Faye saw Adrian put his arms around her. His own face was pale and set.

'You did this!' Faye said to Garth in her mind. 'You broke their hearts and I'll never forgive you for it.'

At the hospital the intensive care room was all ready for them. Miss McGeorge examined Barker carefully, listening to his chest, pulling back the lids of his eyes, which had closed.

'X-ray his chest,' she told Andy, her assistant. 'As soon as that's done give him an injection of painkiller, and put him on a drip.'

'Is he going to be all right?' Adrian asked tensely.

Miss McGeorge hesitated. 'He's old,' she said, 'and I think it's bad. We'll do our best, but...'

It seemed an age while they waited for the results of Barker's X-rays. The children were unusually quiet, but their tight grip on their mother's hand revealed their distress and their need of her.

At last Miss McGeorge emerged and her heavy face told the whole story. 'I'm afraid it was a massive heart attack,' she said. 'There's really no chance for him. It might be kinder to put him to sleep now.'

'No!' Cindy's cry of agony was like a sword cutting through the words. 'He's got to stay alive. *He's got to*.'

'Darling—' Faye put her arms about the child '—he's suffering now—'

'But he wouldn't if they made him well,' she sobbed. 'I love him, Mummy. He can't die, not if I love him. Make them save him.'

'I don't know how,' she said helplessly.

'But Daddy will.' The tears were still rolling down Cindy's face, but suddenly it was illuminated by hope. 'Daddy will know what to do, because he gave me Barker. Please, Mummy, call him.'

'Cindy—' Adrian put his arms protectively around his sister '—Daddy isn't a vet. He can't make Barker well.'

'He can!' Cindy shouted. 'Daddy can do anything in the whole world. He can, he *can!*'

'Try to keep Barker alive,' Faye told Miss McGeorge. She pulled out her mobile and dialled Garth's mobile. But it had been switched off. Desperately she dialled the office where he'd said he would be. The operator put her through to Lysandra.

'I need to speak to my husband urgently.'

'I'm afraid Mr Clayton is out at the moment.' Lysandra's tone was sweet with satisfaction at being able to refuse Faye.

'Please ask him to call me on my mobile the moment he returns. Tell him we're all at the vet; Barker is very ill and Cindy is relying on him.'

She stressed the urgency again and hung up. 'Daddy's going to call back soon,' she promised.

An hour passed. Still the phone didn't ring.

'He's not going to call, is he?' Adrian asked in a toneless voice.

'He is,' Cindy told him fiercely. 'He's going to call any moment now.'

'He might not have come back yet,' Faye said. Inwardly she was filled with dread. Garth had been elated at the thought of pulling off this coup. To get it, he would do anything. But would that mean reverting to his old ways, and putting his daughter last?

'There's a drinks machine just down the corridor,' she said. 'I'm going to get us something.'

When Faye had gone, Cindy's attention became riveted on the bag she'd left on the floor. Adrian frowned as he saw his sister reach inside and pull out the mobile phone.

'What are you doing?' he asked.

'I'm going to call Daddy.'

'But you don't know his number.'

'It was the last thing Mummy dialled,' Cindy said, triumphantly pressing the redial button.

While Adrian regarded her with a kind of awe, she listened to the ringing tone from the other end.

'Blow your nose,' Adrian advised, holding out his own, clean handkerchief. 'You don't want them to think you're just a little kid.'

She gave him a look of gratitude and did so, just before someone answered.

'My name is Cindy Clayton,' she said with dignity. 'And I want to talk to Daddy.'

'Just one moment.' The operator sounded confused.

A moment later Cindy heard another voice on the line. It was softly implacable and she hated it on instinct. 'I'm afraid Mr Clayton is too busy to talk now.'

'But it's Cindy. I know he'll talk to me.'

'I'm sorry, he has some very important men to see. I've given him your message and he says he's sure you'll understand why he can't talk to you now.'

Cindy began to tremble. 'But it's Barker,' she said in a stammering voice.

'I'm sure it is, and he'll call you just as soon as he's free. But he really can't spare the time just now.'

Faye returned from the machine with her hands full to find Cindy staring ahead, her face a ghastly colour.

'It's Daddy,' Adrian said in a hard voice. 'She called him. He wouldn't even talk to her.'

Cindy's tears had dried now. The father in whom she'd pinned her faith had simply brushed her aside. There were no tears for such a devastating betrayal. Only silent despair.

'He said—' she choked at last '—that—he was sure—I'd understand wh-why he couldn't talk to me.'

'Oh, did he?' Faye said ominously. 'Well, I *don't* understand and I'm going to tell him so.'

She called again, hoping against hope that she might be answered by someone other than Lysandra. But the fates were against her.

'I wish to be put through to my husband, *at once*,' she said firmly.

Lysandra's voice was equally firm. 'I'm very sorry, but Mr Clayton's orders were explicit. He's engaged in serious negotiations and must not be disturbed.'

'Tell him it's an emergency and I *have* to speak to him. Do it right now.'

'Mrs Clayton, I'm sorry but you force me to be blunt. I take my orders from Garth, not from you.' The phone went dead.

The children were watching her anxiously, but their faces had changed. Instead of the blind trust that had been there only a short time ago, now they looked ready to endure even more disappointment. How much more of this could they take? she wondered.

'All right,' she said with sudden determination. 'Time to take the gloves off.'

They watched her, puzzled, as she called Mary. 'I need to get to Newcastle as fast as possible, and that means by plane. How can I reach Garth's pilot?'

She heard the little gasp before Mary assumed her

well-trained voice. 'Bill should be at home. Garth gave him a few days off.'

'I'd like his number, please.'

'You're going to ask him to fly you there? But Bill only takes orders from Garth himself. Wouldn't it be better if I called Garth—?'

'Fine! If you can get through to him, get him to call me,' Faye said, suddenly hopeful.

But in two minutes Mary was back on the line, seething.

'That woman,' she said in tones of deep loathing. 'She said she'd get him to call me back, "when he could spare a moment". Garth's never refused to talk to me before. OK. Here's Bill's mobile number. And good luck.'

'Thanks. I'm going to need it.'

Bill was a good-natured, lazy young man who preferred sleeping to any other activity except flying. Faye roused him from a nap, but when he heard what she wanted he was fully alert.

'I can't take the plane out unless Garth orders me,' he said aghast.

Faye took a deep breath and crossed her fingers before saying, 'But he has ordered you. I'm acting with his blessing. He wants you to fly me there at once. I can't tell you details, but it's a real emergency. Believe me, if Garth misses out on this, and then finds it was because you disobeyed his orders to help me, well—I just don't know what he'll do.'

It was barefaced blackmail, the sort of action that once she would never have dared, and her heart was beating hard at her own temerity. But all that mattered now was that Garth should put Cindy and Adrian first. If he couldn't save Barker, at least he could save his children's faith in him.

Bill was nervous. 'Couldn't you get Garth to confirm—?'

'No, I couldn't,' she said firmly. 'This is a matter of life and death and I've no time to waste.'

'All right, Mrs Clayton, but you won't mind if I call him first—'

'You won't get through. He's not talking to anyone. Besides,' she added with a casualness she was far from feeling, 'I just wish I could be a fly on the wall if you manage to haul him out of a big meeting to ask him if his wife's a liar.' She even managed a laugh. 'Still, it's your head on the block.'

'Yes, it is,' he said thoughtfully. 'Oh, well, I suppose if you tell me it's all right—'

'I do. The responsibility is all mine. I'll be there in half an hour. Please have the engine running.' She hung up and leaned against the wall, drained and shaking from tension. That had been *her* speaking, gauche, shy Faye who'd once looked out at the world from under Garth's shadow. Now that seemed a very long time ago.

A suggestion that the children should go home was instantly vetoed. Neither of them would leave their friend. Faye called Nancy and told her to come to the surgery.

'It's not Daddy's fault,' she told the children. 'There's been a misunderstanding and I'm going up there to sort it out.'

She only wished she felt as confident as she sounded.

She left the moment Nancy arrived and began the drive to the airport. Her stomach was churning with nerves. She had no idea what was waiting for her in Newcastle. Garth had tried to block out his family again, and when she gatecrashed his meeting he would be furious. If only she didn't fail! If only she could keep her nerve long enough to confront him!

An efficient machine took over as soon as she arrived. Someone took her car to park it. Someone else told her Bill was ready to leave at once. The engine was running just as she'd said, and in a few minutes they were airborne.

'There'll be a car waiting the moment we land,' Bill said.

'Thank you, Bill. You're very efficient.'

'That's what Mr Clayton says,' Bill said gloomily. 'What he'll say to me after today I don't like to think.'

'But I told you this was with his blessing.'

'That's right, you did,' he said in a voice of deep gloom.

'You just stick to it that you believed me. I'll take the flak.'

As he'd promised, the car was there and in a few moments she was delivered at the headquarters of Garth's clients. A man on the front desk politely enquired her business.

'I have to see Mr Clayton. I'm his wife, and it's extremely urgent.'

The confident way she spoke had its effect. The man showed her the lift and said, 'Top floor, madam.'

One hurdle over.

On the top floor there was a young woman at a reception desk who rose and tried to block her way.

'I'm sorry, but my instructions are to let nobody through,' she said, smiling but implacable.

Faye also smiled. 'If you don't let me through I shall scream the place down,' she said.

'Then I should have to call Security,' the receptionist said.

'Do so,' Faye said almost amiably. She felt cool and in control. To call anyone, the receptionist would have to move out of her way.

Too late the young woman realized this and for a split second she hesitated between the desk and Faye. That instant was enough. Faye moved her aside and swept on. Over her shoulder she could hear the receptionist telephoning someone and hurried lest security guards should appear.

But it was Lysandra who came out and stood in her path. She was holding a file across her chest, as though in defence, and she looked very much in command. But then Faye's heightened senses made her acutely aware of the other woman's pallor and unease. Suddenly Lysandra wasn't confident any more. Her knuckles were white where they grasped the file and she was angry and afraid.

'Let me pass,' Faye told her quietly.

'Absolutely not! Garth says he doesn't want to be bothered by disturbances now—'

'Well he's going to be whether he wants to or not. Now, I'll tell you for the last time, *get out of my way.*'

Lysandra seemed to take root in the ground and for a moment Faye's new-found courage almost failed. Then she remembered Cindy's frantic sobs and Adrian's white-faced tension and knew that nothing was going to stop her.

Moving so fast that she almost couldn't follow it herself, she seized the file Lysandra was holding and sent it whirling across the floor. Lysandra gasped with outrage, made a small lunge then thought better of it. But it was too late. Faye took hold of her shoulders, swung her around and marched on.

A set of double doors loomed before her. Faye took a deep breath and was through them before she had time to think. She found herself in a large room, dominated by a long table, around which sat a dozen men. At the far end, deep in paperwork, sat Garth, so engrossed that he knew nothing until a silence fell. The other men stared, nonplussed, as the pale, distraught-looking woman strode into the room and walked to the head of the table.

At last Garth looked up, astonishment on his face as he saw his wife. 'Faye? What are you doing here?'

'Are you really surprised to see me, after the message you sent?'

'What message?'

'Don't pretend not to know what I mean,' she said angrily. 'I came to talk to you, and that's what I'm going to do.'

'Then we'll go next door,' he said calmly. 'Excuse me a moment, gentlemen.'

He took her arm and drew her through a side door into a little room. When they were alone his urbane manner fell away and she could see that he was coldly angry.

'Now, perhaps you'll tell me what you mean by bursting in and speaking to me like that in front of my colleagues,' he said in a tight voice.

'I wouldn't have needed to if you'd deigned to speak to me on the phone,' Faye said fiercely. 'Why don't *you* tell me what you mean by sending your daughter a message by Lysandra Bates that you were too busy to talk to her.'

'What the devil are you talking about?'

'Oh, please, Garth! Don't pretend ignorance. It's all

been an act, hasn't it? Letting Cindy think she meant something to you, then brushing her aside when she needs you most. You've broken her heart, but why should you care as long as business isn't disturbed?'

'What do you mean?' he interrupted. 'Why does she need me? What's happened?'

'Barker's had a massive heart attack. He's dying!'

He closed his eyes. 'Oh, dear God! No!'

'I told you he was very ill when I called.'

'When did you call? This is the first I've heard of it. Who did you speak to?'

'Lysandra. She said you were out and I left a message for you, saying Barker was ill and please call me back urgently, but you never did. So Cindy called, and that woman said she was sure Cindy'd understand why you couldn't talk to her. But she *doesn't*. She was sure you could cure him. She thought you could do anything in the world—always assuming she can get in touch to ask you.'

'Faye, I'm telling you I knew nothing of this. Lysandra never passed any message on to me and I'm damned well going to find out why.'

He wrenched open the door. Lysandra was just outside, a nervous smile on her face. Now Faye understood why the other woman had been so alarmed at her appearance.

'What's this about a message from my wife that never reached me?' Garth demanded.

'I knew you didn't want to be interrupted,' Lysandra said smoothly.

'I never gave you authority to block out my wife,' he snapped.

'I'm sorry if I misunderstood your instructions, Mr Clayton. I thought I was acting for the best.'

'Were you acting for the best when you told Cindy that her father wouldn't speak to her?' Faye demanded. 'That wasn't a misunderstanding. It was a lie.'

'I agree,' Garth said, regarding Lysandra coldly. 'I gather that my eight-year-old daughter telephoned, herself, and you actually refused to put her on to me. How *dared* you do such a thing?'

Under the black look he was giving her, even the super-cool Lysandra quailed.

'I'm—I'm sorry,' she stammered. 'I assure you such a thing will never happen again.'

'It certainly won't, because you don't work for me any more,' Garth said flatly. 'Don't even set foot in the office again. I'll have your things sent on to you.'

Lysandra gasped. 'Garth—you can't mean that.'

'I can and I do. Get out of my sight.'

She placed a hand on his arm. 'Please, can we discuss this—alone?' She glanced significantly at Faye.

He shook her off. 'We have nothing to discuss alone. We never did, but I couldn't make you realize that. You were efficient at your job. That was my sole interest in you.'

Lysandra's face became distorted. 'You'll regret this,' she spat. 'How are you going to manage that meeting in there without my support?'

Garth eyed her narrowly. 'Don't ever fool yourself that I can't do without you, Lysandra. *Nobody* is indispensable to me. Anyway, that meeting is closing down because I'm leaving.'

'You can't,' Lysandra gasped. 'They'll never give you the contract—'

'Then they can give it to someone else. Now get out of my sight. I don't want to see you again.'

The look Lysandra gave Faye might have struck her

down if she hadn't had more important things to think of. As it was, she barely noticed.

'I'll send for the car,' Garth said when Lysandra had gone, 'and we'll drive back together.'

'No need. I came in your plane.'

'You—?' He stared at her for a moment, then seemed to pull himself together. 'Wait here.'

He marched back into the conference room and she could hear him explaining that a family tragedy had unfortunately made it necessary for him to leave.

A male voice expressed polite sympathy, but then said, 'You know we're behind schedule already. I hope we can continue this discussion tomorrow.'

'My time will be taken up for a week at the very least,' Garth replied. 'It might even be longer.'

There was a murmur. When the voice spoke again it had a slight edge. 'It must be a very close relative.'

'My daughter's dog is ill,' Garth said flatly and the murmur became a hum of disapproval.

'A dog? We're expected to put our plans on hold for a dog?'

'Not at all, gentlemen. I'll understand if you want to find another firm. I apologize for having wasted your time.'

Next moment he appeared in the side room where Faye was waiting, and said, 'Come on.' He took her arm and they went out to the lift together.

As they drove to the airport, Garth called Bill's mobile and spoke for a few minutes. When he hung up he was frowning. 'He's there at Newcastle Airport, waiting for us,' he said. 'You really did take the plane.'

'You thought I was making it up?'

'No, but—Bill answers only to me. How did you get him to do it?'

'I told him I had your authority.'

'You did *what*?'

'It was the only way.'

'And no doubt you also persuaded him not to call me and check?'

'Of course. I told him I'd like to be a fly on the wall when he asked you if your wife was a liar.'

Garth stared at her, something like fascination in his eyes. '*You* did *that*?'

'I had to. Don't get mad with Bill. It wasn't his fault.'

'I'm only too aware of that. I'm not mad, I'm just astounded at you doing all this. It's the sort of thing I'd have done, but—you?'

'Maybe we're more alike than you know.'

'I'm beginning to think we are.' He was still regarding her as if he were seeing her for the first time.

CHAPTER TEN

WHEN they reached the airport Bill was waiting apprehensively, but Garth eased his fears by remarking, 'Thanks for getting her here, Bill. Good work.'

On the flight home Faye told him all the details of Barker's attack. 'The vet says that at his age he hasn't much chance,' she said, and Garth groaned.

'Don't rub it in,' he said morosely.

'I'm not. I was just trying to make you see what a job you've got. Cindy's sure you can solve the problem.'

'I can certainly get the best specialist there is,' he said, becoming the Garth she knew.

His arrival at the animal hospital was greeted by a frenzy of delight and relief. 'I knew you'd come, I knew it,' Cindy squealed. 'Now Barker will be all right.'

'I'll do my best, darling,' he promised her, concealing his apprehension.

He tried to talk to Miss McGeorge in private, but the children refused to be excluded and the whole family gathered in the room where Barker was lying.

The vet laid it on the line. 'He's still alive,' she said, 'but there's no strength left in his heart. He'll have another attack in days. I ought to put him to sleep now.'

'No,' Garth said at once. 'There must be something that we can do. What about when people have heart attacks? You don't put them to sleep, do you? You give them operations to save them.'

'If you're talking about a bypass operation, there's only one man I know of who could tackle this.'

'Then get him.'

'He's abroad and not due back for days,' Miss McGeorge explained. 'It would cost you a fortune—'

'Do you think that matters?'

'And it isn't worth it. The animal is half dead now.'

'He's not "the animal", he's Barker,' Garth said firmly. 'And anything is worth it if it gives him a chance. What is this man's name?'

'James Wakeham.'

'Can you call him right now?'

Miss McGeorge sighed. 'Very well, I'll try.'

'Tell him he can have anything.'

James Wakeham was attending a conference in Belgium and it took a few nail-biting minutes to locate him. Cindy stayed by Barker, stroking his inert head and whispering words of love into his floppy ears.

At last Wakeham was located. Miss McGeorge explained the situation and then went into a detailed clinical description of Barker's state.

'Yes, I see,' she said at last. 'No, of course not— Well, that's what I said— I'll explain—I'm sure they'll understand. Hey!' She spluttered indignantly as Garth removed the phone from her hand.

'Mr Wakeham, I'm Garth Clayton, and Barker is my children's dog. I want him kept alive at all costs, and I'm told you're the only person who can do it.'

The voice that reached him was thin and cool. 'I understand that, of course, but from what I hear of his description there would be no point in attempting an operation.'

'You don't know there's no point if you don't try it,' Garth protested desperately. 'When you get here you may find it looks more hopeful. I'll pay all your expenses and any fee you like. Just name it.'

'Mr Clayton, I appreciate your feelings, but I have a meeting at any moment and I'm afraid I can't break into it for a hopeless case. Will you please put me back to Miss McGeorge?'

'No, I damned well won't,' Garth said furiously. 'Barker may be just a hopeless case to you, but to my children he's a friend that they love. What's so important about a damned meeting that you can't leave it for a sick dog?'

'I'm preparing a very important paper—'

'The paper can wait. My dog can't. You're his last chance.'

'Your dog has *no* chance. An operation would be a total waste of time and I don't have the time to waste.' The phone went dead.

It took a long time for Garth to replace the receiver, because he was trying to come to terms with the fact that his money and power, the talismans he relied on, were useless. He was almost in a state of shock.

The room seemed to have developed an echoing quality, and details stood out with alarming sharpness. Cindy had climbed onto a chair next to Barker and was lying against him, her arms as far around him as they would go, her face buried in his thick fur. She was sobbing frantically, having understood that her father had failed.

Adrian's face was pale and set, as though he were clenching his teeth. Faye was standing beside Cindy, stroking her head and murmuring useless words of comfort. She looked up and her expression was the hardest thing of all to bear. She hated him. She'd warned him of this on the day they'd found Barker and he'd brushed her aside for his own selfish convenience. Now his children were paying the price in anguish and Faye would never forgive him. Nor did he deserve to be forgiven.

The echo vanished as he controlled his shock. The room became normal again. But his daughter was still crying her heart out and something agonizing was happening to his own heart, as if it were being torn out of him.

'What did he say?' Miss McGeorge asked.

'He won't come,' Garth said bleakly. 'It's more important to go to some meeting.'

'Mr Wakeham is a brilliant surgeon, but I'm afraid he's ruled by vanity. He wouldn't take on a case as far advanced as this. A failure would spoil his record.'

Faye stepped back as Garth approached Cindy and touched her head. 'Darling,' he said tentatively.

She looked up at him with a flash of hope that he might have thought of something at the last minute.

'I'm sorry,' he said heavily. 'There's nothing I can do.'

'There *is*,' she insisted. 'There must be. You can't just give up.'

'That man was our last chance and he won't come.'

'But you could *make* him come.'

'I can't force him.'

'You could if you really wanted to.'

'Cindy, I do really want to—'

'No, you don't. You don't care if Barker dies.' She was heaving with sobs as she fought to get the words out. 'I thought—when—you came—everything would be all right—'cos you can do anything—but you don't want to—'

'Darling, please believe me—'

Garth reached for her but she fought off his embrace wildly, screaming, 'You don't! You don't care! You don't care about anyone! I hate you, *I hate you, I HATE*

YOU!' She flung herself into Faye's arms, sobbing violently.

Garth backed out of the room, his horrified eyes fixed on his daughter.

By now it was late. The animal hospital had spacious grounds. Garth didn't know how long he walked through them, pursued by his own thoughts like avenging furies.

This was the day Faye had warned him would come; the day when his sins would come home to him. And they were terrible sins. Wandering wretchedly under the trees, Garth accused himself of the worst kind of selfishness, neglecting his little daughter then using her love to get his own way.

He remembered her joy when he'd appeared at Faye's house. It was completely irrational that she should have still loved him when he'd given her so little. He knew he deserved no praise for having kept her love. It was to the child's credit, not his own. Uncritical devotion was a part of Cindy's character, as it was with her mother. With both of them he'd taken it as a right. And he'd betrayed both of them.

His only saving grace was that Cindy's adoration had touched his heart and he'd opened his arms to her with true warmth. Now their mutual love was genuine. But that was no credit to him either, for who could help loving Cindy?

And there was Adrian, who'd been rightly suspicious of his father at first. He'd regarded that as a challenge and set out to overcome it. With the Outland incident he hadn't even seen the pit that yawned at his feet. But for Faye, he would have fallen in. He'd meant to use what Adrian had told him, but in the very act of signing the documents something had held him back. He'd torn them up and even tossed away the pen, as though it was contaminated. He'd lost the land, but he'd gained his son. Thanks to Faye's timely warning.

In the darkness he experienced the most terrible depths of self-disgust. His beloved children were enduring heartbreak and it was his fault. His wife had abandoned him as a lost cause and he knew now that she'd been right. He blighted everything he touched and nothing could live near him. Cindy's hate was a dreadful punishment, but infinitely worse was the knowledge that he deserved it.

He sat down on a bench and buried his head in his hands. He'd always been the man in control, but now that it mattered as never before he was totally helpless.

He felt a light touch on his head, and looked up to find his daughter regarding him. He almost flinched away from her, but there was no judgement in her small, tear-stained face.

'I'm sorry, darling,' he said huskily. 'I did my best. Truly I did. But I don't know what else to do...'

'It's not your fault, Daddy,' she said gently. 'I'm sorry for what I said.'

Her generosity brought tears to his eyes. For a moment he couldn't speak. When he tried to say something the words came out haltingly.

'It *is* my fault— He was always too old— I should have insisted on another dog—'

She shook her head decidedly. 'Then it wouldn't have been Barker.'

'But you'd have had him for a lot longer—'

'It wouldn't have been the same,' Cindy said simply. 'Barker is—*Barker*. Even if we didn't have him for long, we did have him.'

'A few short weeks,' he murmured, unwilling to let himself off the hook.

'But we had those weeks, that's what counts.'

There was an ache in his throat that made it hard to speak. 'I wanted—to save him for you, darling, but—but—'

Overwhelmed, he put his arms about her and held her close, his shoulders shaking. She hugged him back. 'It's all right, Daddy,' she whispered. 'Truly, it's all right.'

He looked up at her, and she stroked his face in wonder. 'Are you crying?'

'No, of course not,' he said hastily. 'Daddies don't cry.'

'Don't they really? Mummies do.'

He tensed. 'Does your mother cry?'

'She cried a lot when we went away two years ago. I didn't understand. Why did she leave you if it made her so unhappy?'

'Perhaps it made her even more unhappy to stay,' he said slowly. 'Does she cry now?'

'I don't know. Sometimes I think, but she doesn't let on.'

They held each other in silence. Several times he thought she was about to speak, but she always hesitated. 'Daddy,' she said at last.

'Yes, darling?'

'I think—we ought to—stop trying to keep Barker alive.'

He looked closely into her face. 'Do you really mean that?'

'It's not kind to let him suffer.' Suddenly the tears were pouring down her cheeks. 'Oh, Daddy, I love him so much—but if you love someone—you've got to let them go—if it's best for them.' She clung to him, not sobbing as before, but weeping softly with resignation.

'Cindy, are you sure you mean that?'

'Yes, yes—*I mean it, I mean it*—'

Garth hugged her tightly, wondering at his child's courage, so much greater than his own. He saw his son standing quietly in the shadows. 'We should ask Adrian what he thinks,' he said, desperately playing for time.

Adrian was very pale. 'I've been listening. Cindy's right.'

Garth held out an arm and his son went into its circle. The three of them clung together. Faye, watching unobserved, silently backed away. Something painful was happening in her heart. Tonight Garth had become again the warm, emotional man she'd fallen in love with, and what she'd feared most had happened. Her feelings for him flowed freely again, and it hurt.

He joined her a few minutes later. His self-reproach was painful to see. 'I'm useless,' he said desperately. 'There's not a thing I can do—not a thing—' His voice trailed away. He was staring into the middle distance.

'What is it?' Faye asked.

'I'd forgotten—' he said slowly. 'I should have remembered before— There *is* something I can do.' He began to walk urgently around the building to where the car was parked.

'Garth,' she said, following him. 'What is it?'

'I'd forgotten what he said—but it may not be too late. Tell Miss McGeorge to keep Barker alive tonight at all costs. And call Bill. Tell him to take off as soon as possible for Brussels Airport to collect James Wakeham.'

Faye heard the car door slam and the vehicle pull away fast.

*   *   *

The door was opened by a pretty young woman with long, auburn hair, no make-up and an intense expression.

'I'm looking for Kendall Haines,' Garth said, puzzled. 'Does he live here?'

'Yes, come in.' Garth gave her his name and she stood back and called into the house, 'There's a Mr Clayton for you, love.'

Kendall appeared. It seemed to Garth that he was smoothing down his hair, but he was too preoccupied with his errand to observe much. 'I have to talk to you urgently,' he said without preamble.

Kendall showed him into the front room and said, 'Coffee please, Jane.'

'Yes, Ken.' She spoke eagerly and rushed into the kitchen as if he'd offered her a treat.

'I need your help,' Garth said. 'My children's dog is dying. His one chance is an operation, but the best man for that is James Wakeham and he's abroad. He says it's not worth returning. But I remember your telling me that he's a friend of yours.'

'You've spoken to Wakeham?'

'Yes. I told him to name his own price, but I can't budge him. He kept talking about his conference, the important people he had to see. You're his friend. Can't you make him understand that none of those things matter if it means hurting a child?'

'We're not precisely friends,' Kendall said slowly.

'But he owes you a favour—'

'Possibly.' Kendall stood for a moment, sunk in thought.

'Haines, for God's sake!' Garth said desperately. 'If you want me to plead, I will. I'll do anything, but you must get that man back here, because otherwise—' he paused and a shudder went through him '—otherwise I've done something unforgivably selfish and cruel.'

'But even if I do convince him, he may not get a seat on the plane at such short notice.'

'No problem. My own plane has already taken off to collect him.'

'You're a man of great self-confidence, I see.'

'No,' Garth said heavily. 'None at all.'

'Do you have his number?' Garth gave it to him and Kendall dialled. From the conversation that followed Garth deduced that Wakeham wasn't immediately available, but would call back soon.

Jane entered with a tray of fresh coffee and poured for them both. She handed Kendall his cup as he was putting the phone down.

'Can I do anything else for you?' she asked eagerly.

'Yes, finish those papers we were working on in the study.'

'Nothing here?' she asked, sounding disappointed.

'Just leave us alone, there's a dear,' Kendall said kindly.

'If you want me, you'll be sure to call me?'

'I promise.'

'My secretary,' Kendall said when the door had closed behind Jane. 'We were working late.'

'At this hour? She must be very obliging,' Garth said with a slight edge on his voice.

'I know what you're getting at, but who's fault is it? I was happy when Faye worked for me, but you wrecked that. Jane's good at her job and she's always there when I need her.'

'You mean, unlike Faye?'

'It was Faye's own choice to drift away. She returned to you.'

A strange confusion of feelings warred within Garth. He should be glad that this man was getting out of his way, but his dominant feeling was one of anger. How dare this jerk dump Faye!

'I'd hardly say that she returned to me,' he said cautiously.

'But you're determined to get her back, aren't you? If you want to impress her, it was a shrewd move, coming here. Maybe that's why you came yourself instead of asking her to approach me.'

Garth stared, shocked into speechlessness. It simply hadn't occurred to him to send Faye.

The phone rang and Kendall answered. 'James,' he said heartily. 'Long time, no see. I'm here begging a favour—well, to call one in actually, since you still owe me for keeping quiet about that little matter— All right, you old dog, I was only joking. Actually, this is serious. You spoke to a friend of mine earlier— That's right, Garth Clayton—'

Garth had never doubted his own courage before, but suddenly he couldn't bear to listen. Everything in the world hung on this conversation. He left the room and stood in the hallway, nerves stretched to breaking point, until Kendall looked out.

'He's agreed,' he said, and Garth had to clutch the wall against the dizzying surge of relief. 'You'd better tell him about the plane yourself.'

The conversation was short and curt. Wakeham had been convinced, but was thoroughly displeased with everyone involved, himself included.

'I'll meet you this end,' Garth concluded.

When he'd hung up he allowed himself a few seconds' indulgence picturing Cindy's face when he told her. But it would take him fifteen minutes to get back to the surgery, and fifteen minutes could be a long time. He dialled at once and gave the news to Miss McGeorge, then to Faye.

'Tell the kids their old man pulled the rabbit out of the hat,' he said.

Her voice was husky. 'I knew you would. I just knew it.'

'Tell them quickly. Don't delay for a single moment. I'm on my way to the airport to fetch him.'

'Garth—'

'Yes?'

'Nothing. Just—take care.'

'I will. Tell Barker to hang in there.'

Kendall Haines was watching him with a calculating expression on his face. Garth tried to thank him, but Kendall shrugged him away.

'Before I go, there's one question I'd like to ask,' Garth said. 'Did you know that I owned Melkham Construction when you took my son on that demonstration?'

Kendall grinned. 'Of course I knew.'

'You were playing a damned devious game.'

'Don't give me moral outrage. You've played a few devious games in your time.'

'Not by making use of children.'

'All's fair in love and war,' Kendall said with a shrug.

'And you're in love with my wife?'

There was a small pause before Kendall said, 'I'm still engaged to her—as of now.'

'That's not an answer.'

'It's the only one you'll get.'

'Is she in love with you?'

'Ask her.'

'I have.'

'Then you already know the answer.'

In Kendall's position Garth knew he would demand to know what Faye had said. The other man's refusal to ask implied great self-restraint, or maybe something cooler. Garth recalled Jane and her worshipful expression. He saw Kendall looking at him wryly, bid him goodnight, and left quickly.

James Wakeham looked exactly as his voice had sounded, prissy and self-righteous. He gave Garth a nod to indicate that he forgave nothing, and got into the back seat of the car.

But his curtness fell away from him when he saw Barker and a cloak of authority descended like a mantle as he went through the readings on the machines.

'Stabilized? Good. Let's get to work then.'

The children were beyond words but their shining eyes, as they hugged their father, said everything. Cindy whispered, 'I knew you could do it.' She seemed convinced that Barker was certain to survive now and Garth lacked the heart to tell her any different.

Nancy, who'd gone home earlier, now reappeared with sandwiches and a flask of tea. Darkness had fallen, and the hospital was empty but for themselves and the two vets with Barker's life in their hands.

'The children ought to be home in bed,' Faye said ruefully. 'But I don't think they'll budge. Anyway, if Mr Wakeham can't save him, they'll want to be near Barker at the end.'

'Yes,' Garth said heavily. After his brief triumph it was salutary to be reminded that he might have achieved nothing at all.

'How did you get him to come over, after he refused?' Faye asked.

'Oh—I manoeuvred a bit.' He couldn't bring himself to tell her everything, in case it might seem like asking for praise.

'You mean you offered him more money?'

'Money!' he growled.

'Garth, I'm not criticizing, honestly. You were right to do anything that worked.'

Anything that worked. His own philosophy of life, but he'd meant money and power. It occurred to him that he'd always been thinking about these things. But this time it had been about something genuine and true. How strange, then, that he couldn't bring himself to speak of it!

Cindy and Adrian came and hugged him.

'Thanks, Dad,' Adrian said gruffly.

'Thank you, Daddy,' Cindy whispered.

'We're not out of the woods yet,' he warned them.

'But you did it,' Cindy insisted. 'You can do anything.'

He kissed her, but didn't say any more. Only he and his enemy knew the real sacrifice he'd made.

CHAPTER ELEVEN

THE operation lasted two hours.

'I did my best, but I can't work miracles,' James Wakeham said, emerging from the theatre and speaking brusquely. 'He's still alive, but it's too soon to be hopeful. You'll know by the morning.'

He resisted Garth's offer of hospitality. 'I'd like to go straight to the airport,' he said in his precise voice. 'No, don't drive me. I prefer a taxi. I expect your pilot to be waiting for me.'

'He will be,' Garth assured him.

'Not a charming character,' Miss McGeorge said when Wakeham had gone. 'But he's a genius at his job. You gave Barker the best possible chance.'

'But it's not a good chance, is it?' Garth asked.

'I'm afraid not. His age is still against him.'

Before being taken home the children begged to be allowed to say goodnight to Barker. Faye was reluctant, but Garth took their side.

'I'm afraid they'll be upset if they see him attached to a lot of machinery,' she protested.

'Not as upset as they'll be if he dies without them seeing him,' Garth said. And she realized he was right.

Like shadows they crept into the dimly lit room where he lay. As Faye had feared he was attached to drips and monitors, but both children simply ignored the machinery. They came close to Barker lying on the table, completely motionless except for the rise and fall of his breathing, and took it in turns to lift one of his floppy ears and whisper.

'I told him I loved him, so he's got to get well,' Cindy confided to her parents. 'But you must tell him too, so that he'll know we all need him.'

Faye murmured something loving into Barker's ear. But the really astonishing sight was Garth leaning down to say, 'Hang in there, boy. I've got a bone waiting for you at home like you wouldn't believe!'

'He heard you,' Cindy breathed. 'His nose twitched when you said "bone".'

'Darling, he's deeply unconscious,' Faye said.

'His nose twitched,' Garth said firmly. 'We saw it, didn't we?' He appealed to Adrian, who nodded.

They all crept out, pausing in the doorway for one more look at their friend who lay so silent and still.

By now it was long after midnight and the children could hardly keep their eyes open. Faye and Garth settled them gently in the back of the car and drove home. Nancy had gone ahead and was waiting to help put Cindy and Adrian to bed.

Faye went into the kitchen to make some tea. But as she reached out to the kettle she saw Barker's biscuits lying there, where she'd left them in the last moment before the nightmare began. The two red ones were still set apart, so that he could have them first. Perhaps he would never want them now. Suddenly unable to bear the sight, she rushed out of the kitchen and upstairs.

In her own room she was free to give way to her emotions. She left the light off and went to stand at the window, overlooking the spot where Barker had collapsed. She couldn't tear her eyes away from it and barely heard the click as Garth entered. He came close and touched her uncertainly on the shoulder.

'Faye,' he said quietly. 'Please—'

'It was down there,' she said huskily. 'They were playing ball and suddenly he made a different sound. Cindy called me and when I ran out he was lying stretched out on the ground—right there.'

'Hush!' he said, taking her into his arms. But she couldn't stop. The fear and grief of the day had caught up and overwhelmed her.

'He lay so still,' she choked. 'He's always been so full of life—into everything, and—and suddenly—he just didn't move—'

'Come away,' he said, drawing her away from the window.

'Suppose he never moves again—'

'Don't,' he begged her. 'You can't blame me more than I blame myself.'

'No, no, I didn't mean that— It's just that—he's one of the family and—I love him so much.'

'I know,' he said wryly. 'So do I.' He pressed her gently down on a small sofa and sat beside her. 'Take this,' he said, putting a glass into her hand. 'It's brandy. I brought it up because we both need one.'

She sipped it, and blew her nose. 'It's such a short time we've had Barker,' she said. 'Yet I can't imagine doing without him.'

'Perhaps we won't have to.' Garth drank some brandy and tried to steady himself. He'd skipped breakfast to make some final notes for his meeting and since then the only thing he'd had was Kendall's coffee. Now tension and an empty stomach were making him light-headed. It was hardly possible that he could be sitting here with Faye, talking like this in the darkness. At the same time, it seemed perfectly natural.

Faye was in no better state. Unlike Garth, she'd had

breakfast, and later a sandwich at the surgery. But she was exhausted and glad of the brandy.

'Dry your eyes,' he commanded, dabbing her face with his clean handkerchief. 'We've got to be positive about this. We've won so far and we're going to win in the end.'

'Are you sure?' He sounded so confident that she began to relax.

'Completely sure,' he said firmly. 'Barker's a fighter. He never gives up. Have you ever known him give up when there was something he wanted? Titbits, the best chair, making you stop work to throw his ball? Anything?'

'No,' she conceded. The authority in Garth's voice was almost hypnotic. He'd achieved so much today and it was suddenly easy to believe that he could order everything just as he wanted.

'You're right, he won't give up.' She managed a wonky smile. 'Stupid mutt. Always in the way—'

'Greedy, noisy, clumsy,' Garth supplied. 'Greedy.'

'You said greedy before,' she reminded him.

'However many times I said it, it would still be true. And dirty. Paws like plates, always covered in mud. Unscrupulous.' He hunted for something else. 'Greedy.'

'Scheming,' she supplied. 'Devious. He'd sell his grandmother for a titbit.'

'Dimwitted. Awkward.'

'And greedy.'

'Unreliable.'

'Not unreliable,' Faye protested. 'You could always rely on him to do the wrong thing.'

'That's true. Offend your neighbours, burgle your house, scratch your car—'

Faye broke down again. 'Oh, Garth, he will be all right, won't he? He's got to be.'

He put his arms around her and held her tightly, murmuring, 'It's all going to be fine. We couldn't go through all this for nothing.'

'You were wonderful getting Wakeham to come over.'

'Mr Fixit! That's me!'

'No, I'm serious. It meant so much to the children that you pulled out all the stops.'

'Only to the children?'

'Well, to me too, of course.'

'Yes, of course,' he said with a faint sigh. 'But I got it all the wrong way around, didn't I? If I'd listened to you in the first place—'

'Don't brood about that for ever. I heard what Cindy said to you tonight. She was right. They had him, even if just for a little while. Cindy's a very wise little person.'

'She's wonderful, isn't she? Just recently I've realized how like you she is. All heart. It worries me, because it makes her so vulnerable—mostly to me, at the moment.'

'Yes, she is. But at least you know. You can protect her.'

'Maybe I'm not so good at that. When you were—'

'What?' she asked, for he'd stopped, as if reluctant to say more.

'When we met—you were such a little thing, so delicate and young. You knew nothing about the world. I wanted to protect you from every wind that blew.'

'But I grew up,' she reminded him. 'And then you didn't know what to say to me any more.'

'Maybe I didn't want you to grow up,' he agreed. 'We were so happy then. I didn't want to let any part of it go. Besides, I thought you wanted me to be the strong one, and look after you. You said something once—'

'What did I say?'

'It was the week before Adrian was born and I'd just lost my job. Things looked about as black as they could be. I felt such a failure. Do you remember what you said?'

'Not the exact words, but I know I tried to tell you that I had confidence in you.'

'You said, "Don't worry. I know you'll make everything right." For a moment I was so scared at the trust you were putting in me. Then I knew I had to justify that trust, never trouble you with the burdens, but just make everything right for you—as you wanted me too.'

'But Garth,' she whispered in dismay. 'I was only trying to say that I believed in you, not that you should bear everything alone. I wanted to share all your troubles, but you started hiding them from me.'

'That's why.'

Light dawned on her. 'That time you nearly lost the builder's yard and you only just managed to save it—I didn't know about that until years later.'

'You weren't supposed to find out, ever. I was trying to make everything perfect for you, as a sort of thank-you.'

'Thank-you—for what?'

'For marrying me. I was so grateful. On our wedding day—' He stopped with an awkward laugh.

'Tell me,' she said eagerly. 'Don't stop now.'

'You were five minutes late at the church and I nearly went crazy. I thought you'd taken fright and weren't coming.'

'Why should I take fright?'

'Well, you didn't really want to marry me, did you?'

he said heavily. 'It was only because I made you pregnant.'

'But Garth—'

'I always knew, you see. You were so young. You wanted to laugh and have fun like other girls, and you had every right to. And because of me you ended up tied down, surrounded by a flat full of nappies. Oh, you never complained. You were very sweet about it. But it was always there between us, that I'd stolen your youth. I tried to give you everything to make up for it, but it was no good. I never really got it right, did I?'

Faye stared at him. 'You—*wanted* to marry me?'

'But you knew that. I did everything to get that ring on your finger.'

'Garth, I swear I didn't know. I thought I'd trapped you into marriage.'

'I never said you had.'

'No, but—you never mentioned marriage until then.'

'I didn't dare in case I frightened you off. When you told me about the baby I was thrilled because it was an excuse to make you marry me. I know I practically bullied you into it—telling you instead of asking you. But I was scared to ask in case you said no.' He gave an awkward laugh. 'You know what I'm like when I want something. I tend to grab. I grabbed you before you slipped through my fingers. I thought I'd won but I paid for it, because I was never certain of you afterwards.'

They stared at each other, with the truth between them for the first time.

'I never knew,' she whispered.

'Nor did I. Oh, Faye, what fools we were! All those years— Why did we throw them away?'

She shook her head, dumb with sadness.

'We might have had so much,' he said, 'and we missed our chance.'

'But we still had more happiness than many people have. Things went wrong, but at the start—'

'Yes,' he said heavily, 'we'll always have those memories. And we'll always know that it might have been better still if I hadn't been blind.' He sank his head on his hands.

Faye put her arms about him, overwhelmed by tenderness. 'It wasn't all your fault,' she murmured. 'We lost each other because we both made mistakes.'

He raised his face to her and she took it between her hands to kiss it gently. At first he did nothing, keeping perfectly still and letting her kisses fall on him like sweet balm. As he felt their loving message, the pain and tension seemed to fall away from him and he clung to her.

She wrapped her arms about him, finding again the vulnerable boy she'd fallen in love with. When she laid her lips softly on his, she felt his instant response.

'We might have had everything,' he whispered.

'Hush.' She kissed him to silence. 'We can still have everything, just for tonight.'

The last time they'd lain together in her bed it had been a union of bodies. Now it was a union of hearts. It was she who led the way, drawing him on at every step. Nothing mattered but consoling his pain.

He clung to her in need as well as passion, savouring the warmth of her skin against his, losing himself in her bounty. Sometimes he seemed hesitant, but she offered him all of herself with a loving tenderness that enfolded him and he felt a man again, because this woman loved him.

She'd promised him everything, and she gave him everything. It might, as she'd said, be only for this one night, but they would have this memory in the years to come. Perhaps they would be lonely years, but the moment when their hearts and souls were one again would never entirely leave them.

In the darkness, his face pressed to her sweet-smelling body, it was easy for Garth to see that she, and she only, had given the world a meaning. He'd thrown it all away but she gave it back to him out of a generous spirit. He was more than making love to her. He was seeking refuge in her. And now he understood that this was how it had always been.

As the first light came through the curtains Garth rose from Faye's bed. He stood looking down at her, sleeping as peacefully as a child, then turned away as though the sight smote him. He was hearing Cindy's voice the night before, knowing that her words were wise and generous yet not wanting to face it.

He bent and kissed his sleeping wife, softly, not to disturb her. His heart was heavy as he slipped quietly out of the room.

His children were up before him, standing watching the hall telephone.

'Can we ring the vet and ask now?' Adrian demanded.

'It's too early. They'll still be checking him. But if Barker— If anything had gone wrong in the night, they'd have called us by now.'

'Perhaps they haven't got our number?' Cindy suggested.

'They've got it, I promise.'

They drifted out into the garden. Cindy found the ball Barker had dropped, scrubbed it with her hanky and put it back in exactly the same place on the grass. Garth wondered if it would ever be needed again. He watched

Cindy with anxious eyes, struck by her strength and self-control; surely too much for a child?

Faye came down and he greeted her with a distant smile, but didn't go to her. The resolution he'd made in the early hours hung heavily on him and he was sorely tempted to abandon it. But he stopped himself. It had taken him too long to decide on the right thing. But he knew now what it was and there would be no weakening.

'Why don't you just call the vet?' Faye asked Garth softly.

'They'll call us when they're ready.'

She stared. Garth had never been afraid to barge in and demand answers. And then she understood. He was scared. Everything hung on what they would learn this morning. Tenderly she squeezed his hand.

The phone rang.

Everyone jumped. Nobody moved. Then Garth forced himself to answer. The silence seemed to last a long time, before he said, 'Thank you for telling me.'

He laid down the receiver very carefully, as though delaying the moment when he must speak. Then he grinned at his family and said, 'Barker's eating a hearty breakfast.'

Barker was home in a week. He still needed care, but nobody could have done the job more thoroughly than his family. Cindy appointed herself head nurse, with Adrian to assist her. Nancy deputized while they were at school, with Faye and Garth permitted to visit the invalid with appropriate gifts, all of which were consumed in seconds.

Cindy was fast growing up, becoming more firmly in charge and more like her father. When she decided the patient was gorging himself and not getting enough exercise, she read him a stern lecture and forbade all further titbits. Barker began to look harassed.

'Don't worry, old fellow,' Garth reassured him after three weeks of this. 'I've got a special present for you tomorrow; one you're going to love, and ''Matron'' won't be able to lock it away.'

He was home early the next evening, looking as though he was concealing a secret.

'Where are the kids?' he asked Faye quietly.

'Playing with Barker in the garden.'

'Good. I've brought someone home with me and I want you to be the first to meet her.'

'Her?'

'Wait here,' he said, with a touch of mischief.

When he returned a moment later, Faye's eyes widened at the sight of his companion.

'Her name is Peaches,' Garth said.

Peaches was a really lovely St Bernard with liquid eyes and a melting expression.

'She's a year old,' Garth explained, 'and her owner had to rehome her because she's a bit of a handful. But she's—er—' he paused, seeking for words '—just ready to become a bride,' he finished delicately. 'I thought Barker would like her.'

From outside came a squeal and the sound of thundering paws. Barker appeared, followed by the children, and stopped dead in the doorway, his gaze riveted by the vision of beauty before him. Peaches gazed back. Their eyes met across a crowded room. Cindy and Adrian regarded the scene with awe.

'He just suddenly dropped the ball and dashed inside,' Cindy said. 'It was like he knew...'

'I think he did,' Garth agreed. 'Meet Peaches. She's come to keep Barker company while you're at school.'

The children made a fuss of Peaches, who responded amiably, but her languishing gaze constantly travelled towards Barker, whose virile form had clearly made a deep impression.

'All they needed was a swelling orchestra,' Garth said with a grin when he was alone with Faye later.

'What made you do it?' she asked.

'Barker's still an old dog and he's getting older. We can't put the sad day off for ever. But this way, we'll never really lose him. Why are you surprised? I told you I'd do something.'

'But I thought you were simply going to get another dog.'

'And I have. But just any dog wouldn't do. It's Barker who matters. With Peaches's help, he'll leave something of himself behind.'

CHAPTER TWELVE

To THE amusement of the whole family, Barker's passion for Peaches developed into slavish infatuation. She was a domestic tyrant, blowing hot and cold; one day allowing him to smooch her lovingly, the next, growling him away. But nothing could cool Barker's chivalrous devotion and in the presence of his beloved he was reduced to a state of doting idiocy.

'Poor Barker,' Cindy consoled him. 'You're a henpecked husband.'

'And when his pups are born he'll be a henpecked father,' Garth had observed, tweaking her hair. 'Like me.'

Four weeks after their first meeting, Miss McGeorge had confirmed that Peaches was pregnant. Barker strutted about, every inch the proud father, and Cindy and Adrian began to squabble about names for the pups.

The tenth anniversary was growing closer. Faye had relented about letting the children take part, because she was grateful to Garth for putting them before business, even at the cost of the Newcastle contract. He never complained, nor even mentioned the matter, and Faye only knew for sure that he'd lost it when Mary told her. It was like the old days, when he hadn't confided in her.

There was something else he'd kept to himself, which hurt far more. Kendall had telephoned to ask how she was and she'd told him about Barker's crisis. That was how she learned that Garth had sought his help in getting James Wakeham. At first she was delighted. This was exactly the kind of generous act she'd dreamed of seeing him make. But joy was succeeded by sadness at the way he'd excluded her. He'd done it for Cindy and although he could have won his wife's approval, it seemed that he hadn't bothered.

Then Kendall said something else that astonished her.

'It's nice that you're still speaking to me.'

'Why shouldn't I be?'

'I imagine Garth told you all about Jane.'

'She's your new secretary, isn't she? Why should Garth have mentioned her?'

'You mean he didn't? That's amazing. I thought he'd have made the most of it.'

'Kendall, I don't know what you're talking about.'

'Jane works late for me sometimes, and we have a meal together, and—and so on. She was here the night Garth came. Look, I was just a bit lonely for you. It doesn't have to mean anything if we don't let it.'

As Faye understood what he was really saying she waited for the surge of pain it should have brought her. But there was nothing. Kendall had found someone else to flatter his vanity. He was a kindly enough man in his way, but he liked being the centre of attention. What had followed was inevitable and perhaps she had always secretly guessed it.

'Tell me, Kendall,' she said, 'does Jane ever forget to watch you on television?'

'Well—no,' he admitted sheepishly.

'Then you should marry her without delay. And I'll dance at your wedding. Goodbye, my dear.'

She hung up, her thoughts in turmoil. It was ironic to remember now how she'd once said about Garth, 'I wouldn't put it past him to have my replacement lined up to massage his ego, just in case.' But it was Kendall who'd done exactly that and Garth who had remained true.

But no longer, it seemed. He'd known that Kendall had found someone else, yet he hadn't tried to make any use of it.

If he'd truly wanted me, she thought despondently, he'd have told me about this, hoping to turn me against Kendall.

But he'd preferred to leave Kendall's image untarnished. There was surely only one explanation. When the anniversary gala was over, he would be finished with her.

Cindy was looking forward to the banquet, and was thrilled with her new party frock. Adrian eyed his formal clothes askance and muttered, 'Do I have to, Mum?'

She'd bought the kind of glamorous dress Garth wanted, a black, figure-hugging creation that would be a good background for diamonds. The children were loud in their admiration, and Faye was agreeably surprised by her own appearance.

Garth, too, approved. At least, he nodded and said, 'Good. You'll look just right.'

She'd smiled to cover her disappointment that he showed so little warmth. But what had she expected? Since the night of their loving she'd hoped for so much and been granted so little. She'd had a glimpse of Garth as he'd once been, as she longed for him to be again. But he'd retired behind a barrier from which he emerged only for his children.

Since Kendall's revelation, she knew that Garth was simply biding his time until their final break-up. And, with terrible irony, this happened just as she faced the fact that she'd never really stopped loving her husband.

But he'd reclaimed her only out of pride, and lost

interest when she was his for the asking. Sometimes she would surprise him with a strange look in his eyes, as though he was planning the next move. Perhaps he would offer her money to move out and let him keep the children?

She flinched at the thought of leaving them, but wouldn't it be kinder to let them stay here, with the father they adored?

Only a little while ago she'd seemed to have almost everything. Now she was on the verge of losing every-thing. And worst of all was the thought that Garth might have planned this from the start.

On the evening of the banquet Faye let Cindy help her on with the black velvet evening cloak, with its white satin lining.

'You look gorgeous, Mummy,' the little girl breathed.

'Thank you, darling.'

'Doesn't she?' Cindy demanded of her brother.

But he was covered in nine-year-old male confusion and could only mumble, 'Yeah.'

Cindy ran off to inform her father that Mummy looked simply *gorgeous*. Adrian regarded his mother awkwardly for a moment, before pecking her cheek and offering her his arm.

'Thank you, kind sir,' she teased.

Garth's eyes never left her as she made her entrance down the staircase. He looked satisfied. There was some-thing else in his expression, too, but she couldn't read him any more.

'You look gorgeous,' he said as she reached the bot-tom. 'I've been instructed that that's the right word,' he added with a teasing glance at Cindy, who was watching him severely. The little girl smiled and relaxed, evidently feeling that he was doing the proper thing. Faye couldn't help smiling too, at the perfect understanding between father and child. She put her head up and assumed a dazzling smile as she offered Garth her hand and let him lead her to the waiting car.

The reception was being held at the Ritz. They travelled there in a stretch limo, with the children sitting up ahead, which gave the two adults the illusion of privacy. Faye had a curious feeling that Garth was nervous, yet his words sounded confident.

'The place will be packed tonight. We didn't get a single refusal.'

'I shouldn't think they dared,' she quipped. 'Not once you'd made your wishes known. Another huge success for Garth Clayton. Isn't that how it goes?'

'Some successes matter more than others,' he observed in a strange voice. But he was looking out of the window, not at her.

As he'd predicted, every seat was taken. When the family walked in, the crowd rose in applause. The lights were too brilliant for her to discern much but she'd been through a rehearsal and knew that models of the houses were placed around the great ballroom, and everywhere there was silver glitter the colour of diamonds.

Afterwards she couldn't remember details. There was a perfectly prepared and served meal, with excellent wines. Speeches followed. Faye heard none of them, until Garth rose to his feet.

She was on edge in case he spoke about their marriage, twisting the facts into a publicity presentation. But to her relief he began talking about the start of his business.

'It was a builder's yard with a door that didn't lock properly. Not that it mattered much, because there was nothing in there worth stealing,' he announced, to laughter. 'You never saw a shabbier place, but I called it Clayton Properties.

'My wife and I had two tin plates to eat off, and we were so poor that I used to take one to work for lunch, to save buying a third. Once I forgot to take it home at night, so we shared hers.'

Yes, it had happened like that, she thought. They'd squabbled over that plate, each wanting the other to have it first. In the end, they'd eaten together and Garth had marked the occasion by scratching two entwined hearts in the centre. She'd wanted to keep the plate, but Garth had taken it to the yard, and lost it.

'Since then, Clayton Properties has grown and grown again,' he said. 'But I still fondly remember that first little yard, how proud I was of it—and how proud my wife was of me. She never saw it as a dump. She thought that now I'd entered the market the rest of them might as well give up.' There was friendly laughter and a smattering of applause, then he went on. 'And because she believed that, I began to believe it. I went on because I had to justify her faith in me. And I found I could take giant strides I'd never dreamed of.

'I did things I was scared to do, because I couldn't risk Faye finding out that I had feet of clay. Of course, she knew that all the time, but she didn't let on because she didn't want *me* to find out.'

This time the laughter was loud, with a warm, friendly tone. Everyone knew that this was an excellent speech, striking just the right note for the occasion.

But Faye never thought of it like that. She was listening intently to the man she loved, breathless with hope.

'Clayton Properties has been as much her creation as

mine. And that's why it's right that I should honour her tonight, on our tenth wedding anniversary.'

He took her hand to raise her up, and opened the black box in front of him. A rivière of diamonds glittered inside. The crowd rose in thunderous applause as he fitted the lavish jewels about her neck. Faye hardly heard them. She was looking into Garth's smiling eyes, feeling the warm touch of his hands on her neck. Everything was coming right at last. He'd only been waiting for tonight.

In her joy she was able to pose for the photographs with a truly radiant smile. It was going to be all right. Tonight, when the children had gone to bed, he would tell her what was in his heart and they would find each other again. She could have sung with happiness.

It seemed an eternity until the party broke up, but at last they were all moving towards the door. Her hand was tucked in Garth's arm. She could see the car waiting for them through the great entrance. In a few minutes they would be inside it, perhaps in each other's arms. Cindy and Adrian would giggle, but they were welcome.

Suddenly Garth tensed and stopped. He seemed awkward. 'Faye, I should have told you this before. Something came up this afternoon.'

She stared at him in disbelief. Oh, this couldn't be happening again!

'I was going to France in a few days, but I've had a call to say they need me earlier. I've got to leave for the airport straight away.'

'You're not even coming home with us?' she gasped.

'When you get there you'll understand. Please believe me— This is best.'

Cindy and Adrian came beside them, looking up with silent questions as they sensed the changed atmosphere.

'Daddy has to go to France on urgent business,' Faye said, hardly knowing what she was saying.

'You mean you're not coming home with us?' Adrian asked.

'Not just for the— Cindy, what have you got there? It's not a doggy bag, is it?'

Cindy guiltily produced not one bag but two.

'There's Peaches as well,' she explained, 'and she's eating for three or four or five or—'

Something strange seemed to happen to Garth. He closed his eyes and for a moment Faye could have sworn that his lips were shaking, as though he was on the verge of tears. But that didn't make sense.

'I just hope you've got enough for her,' he said at last. He dropped to one knee and put an arm around each child, hugging them tightly. ''Bye kids,' he said huskily. 'Be good.'

There was a mysterious undercurrent in his voice. Faye stared at him, trying desperately to understand.

'I'll take you to the car,' he said.

'Garth—' she cried. She was suddenly scared.

'Faye.' He said her name so softly that she barely heard. He reached out and touched her cheek and there was something in his eyes that broke her heart. Abruptly he seized her and pulled her hard against him, burying his face in her hair. Then, just as quickly, he thrust her from him.

'Goodbye, Faye,' he said hoarsely, and turned back inside.

It was all over, she thought, as she was borne home. The distance he'd set between them recently had been a warning. Tonight he'd played his part so beautifully that she had been taken in.

In her heart she knew what she would find when she

reached home. There would be a letter announcing that everything was over between them. He'd had all he needed of her.

Nancy was waiting up to put the children to bed. She didn't comment on Garth's absence. Nor did she look at Faye as she said, 'There's something in your room. He told me to put it there when you'd all left.'

The envelope was lying on her pillow, her name written in Garth's bold hand. With trembling hands she opened it, and read:

My darling Faye,

This is the hardest letter I've ever had to write, because it's a goodbye, and that's a word I swore I'd never say to you. I love you so much. I never stopped loving you for a moment, but I killed your love and couldn't get it back.

Once it seemed easy. I thought I had the power to force you back to me. I managed it in one way, but the more we were together, the more I realized that your heart had slipped away. Perhaps I was never the man for you. I only seem to make you unhappy.

There's something you must know. When Barker was dying I went to Kendall Haines and begged him to use his influence to get James Wakeham. I meant to tell you next day, when things were calmer. But I never did, because that night something happened that changed everything.

Earlier Cindy had asked me to have Barker put to sleep. She said, 'If you love someone, you've got to let them go, if it's best for them.'

I didn't see the implications for us at first, but then you loved me with such sweetness and warmth that I knew only the best was good enough for you. And the best is to escape from me. You once said that nobody could be happy with me. And you were right.

So I never told you about approaching Haines, because it might have made it harder for you to leave me. I didn't want you staying because I'd 'earned' it, but only because you loved me. And you're safer not loving me.

I learned something about Haines too, that night. He's not the man you think he is. He co-opted his secretary to fill your place without much loss of time. I wasn't sure whether to tell you, or whether it would be interfering in your life. You might not even have believed me. But now I won't be here, you must know the truth. Don't marry him, my darling. Wait for someone else who's better than both of us.

It's taken me too long to learn wisdom from my daughter, but I know now that the truest way I can show my love is by letting you go.

I won't be returning to Elm Ridge. I want you and Cindy and Adrian to stay there. After the divorce I'd like to see the children often, but I promise never to trouble you.

It's the tenth anniversary of our wedding, and I've showered you with diamonds, as the firm expected me to. But my real anniversary gift is something else. You'll find it in a parcel next to this letter. I wonder if you'll recognize it. If so, I like to think it will still mean something to you.

Goodbye, my dearest. I love you so very much.

                                        Garth.

She had to read the letter twice. There was a blank look in her eyes as the incredible truth came home to her, and she let out her breath in a long sigh.

'You fool,' she murmured. 'How could you be so blind?'

But did she mean him, or herself? She honestly couldn't have said.

The little parcel lay on the bed. It was plainly wrapped in brown paper and carried no tag. She was almost afraid as she opened it.

Inside she found the tin plate Garth had mentioned in his speech, with the two entwined hearts scratched in the centre. Tears began to roll down her cheeks. She'd thought he'd tossed those early days aside contemptuously, but he'd remembered as vividly as herself. Despite his brash exterior, he'd secretly treasured this memento all these years. Now it had a slightly forlorn, abandoned look.

Her happiness was almost too great to be borne, but her tears still flowed. They were for him, going away, believing that she didn't love him. How could it end this way? How could two people who loved each other so much manage to lose each other?

Then her head went up. She wasn't going to give in without a fight. With trembling fingers she dialled the airport number and was put through to Bill's little cubby hole.

'Bill, it's Faye. Is Garth there yet?'

'No, but he's due at any moment. Our take-off slot is in half an hour.'

'He mustn't go. Bill, you've got to stop him.'

'Stop him?' Bill sounded aghast. 'You mean you want me to give him a message from you?'

'No, there's no message.' Garth could be stubborn when he'd made a decision. If he knew she was following him, he would leave all the faster.

'Then I can't delay him,' Bill protested.

'You simply must. Develop a mechanical breakdown, chuck a spanner in the engine. *Anything*. But stop him leaving.'

Bill's voice became plaintive. 'Mrs Clayton, have you any idea what's it's like being caught between the two of you? You're as bad as each other.'

'I'm sure you can manage to think of something, Bill.' She found Nancy. 'I've got to go out.'

'At this hour? Where are you going?'

'To save my marriage,' Faye said and hurried outside.

She was a careful driver, who disliked driving at night. But when she saw the road clear ahead she put down her foot. She was relying on Bill to hold Garth up, but how long could he manage it?

Half an hour kept throbbing through her brain. Half an hour and it might all be too late. It was no use to argue that she could contact him later. The moment was now and if she missed it, it would have gone forever.

'Wait for me, Garth,' she murmured as she drove. 'Don't take off. Listen to me calling you. Listen to my love, and turn back to me.'

At last she could see the lights in the distance which told her she was nearing the airport. Luckily the security guard recognized her.

'Has my husband taken off yet?' she asked in terrible fear.

'Just about to.'

'No,' she cried frantically.

As the hangar came into sight she could just make out two figures walking towards the plane. One of them was Bill, who seemed to be arguing frantically. The other was Garth. With the wind in her direction Faye could hear him say, 'That's enough, Bill. Now let's get on, I'm in a hurry.'

'Garth!' she called. *'Garth!'*

But the wind whipped her words away and she knew he hadn't heard her. She'd reached the steel barrier, beyond which she couldn't take the car. Wildly she jumped out, pushed through a small gap in the barrier and began to run as if her life depended on it.

'Garth!' she screamed.

At last he heard her. She saw him stop, but he didn't turn. It was as if he feared an hallucination so sweet that it must be resisted.

She called his name again and this time he looked round, his face torn between hope and despair as he saw her.

'I love you,' she called. 'We all love you. Don't leave us.'

He began to run back to her, but at the last moment something stopped him. 'Faye, did you get my letter?' he called.

'Yes, I read it, and you've got everything wrong. We love you. Don't you understand? We love you.'

'We?'

'*I* love you. I always have. It broke my heart to leave you two years ago, but I thought you didn't love me.' She drew nearer to him. 'After the night we came together I was sure everything would be all right, but then you pushed me away.'

'I was afraid. I thought I'd taken advantage of you— You were so unhappy— The brandy— Maybe you didn't know what you were doing—'

'One glass! What do you think I am? Some brainless little girl who needs her hand held? Maybe I *was* when I married you, but not now. Garth, how dare you make this decision without consulting me. I knew exactly what

I was doing that night. I was loving you, and that's what I meant to do.'

'*Faye—*'

'And I'm going to go on doing it. I'm sure about that too. You're not going to France tonight.'

'Aren't I?'

'No, because this time I'm making the decision. And my decision is that you're coming home with me, and we're going to awaken our children and tell them that our marriage is on again, and this time it's for ever.'

He came close and searched her face. 'Is that what we're going to do?' he asked breathlessly.

'That's exactly what we're going to do. Any arguments?'

He seized her in his arms.

'Not from me,' he said joyfully. 'Let's go and do it right now.'

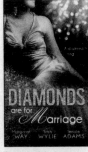

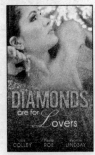

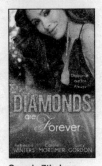

The World of Mills & Boon®

There's a Mills & Boon® series that's perfect for you. We publish ten series and, with new titles every month, you never have to wait long for your favourite to come along.

Blaze.
Scorching hot, sexy reads
4 new stories every month

By Request
Relive the romance with the best of the best
9 new stories every month

Cherish
Romance to melt the heart every time
12 new stories every month

Desire
Passionate and dramatic love stories
8 new stories every month